THE FLAWED DESIGN

THE FAR HORIZONS
BOOK 2

A.R. KNIGHT

ONE

UNWANTED PACKAGE

What to do with freedom?

One choice stood across our conquered territory, leaning against a friendly, emerald-lit exit. She crossed one ankle over the other, and at her toes planted a jagged silver-black metal bar. Her eyes looked outside the Nursery into the Conduit's blue-tinged misty middle.

Delta guarded our little sanctuary, several large square rooms holding human lives by the thousands. Those lives, squeezed into small frozen tubes, waited for a coming resurrection, one it was my duty to provide. It hadn't always been so, but the machines watching over these static souls had been corrupted by time, poor programming, and zero supervision.

I had my left hand on one now, a nursing mech with wheels for feet, several soft hands for carrying newborns, and a cheery smile etched onto her cream-colored metal skin. My right hand, fingers coalesced into a connection port, lanced into the accepting slot in the mech's side.

Kaydee, a friend both dead and alive, spun her code through my connection. We'd been rewriting algorithms for a day already, twenty-four hours weeding through ifs and thens, functions and variables to clean out faults left to rot by the mech's original programmers.

They'd designed the Nursery to produce top notch children, to preserve genetic excellence and exile any embryos that wouldn't lead to the brightest minds, the strongest muscles, the fastest legs. A flawed goal, particularly when dealing with flawed specimens.

In my left eye I saw the recording, a memory of sorts, play out again: the embryo deposited on the conveyor belt, a long thing resting on my right. The child-to-be started out as nothing. It endured a light, chemical, and physical onslaught to stimulate growth. Every meter the vial crawled along the conveyor belt brought it closer to crawling without the belt at all. By the time the child reached the track's end, a fully formed human infant sat waiting to issue its first wailing cry.

In the memory—the recording—the child never had the chance to speak its mind. Scans I didn't understand washed over the child, cameras and sensors cloaking the small figure only to spit out suboptimal values. Not bad by any measure I could find, but not perfect.

The system didn't approve. The child vanished down a hole we could not follow.

But we could prevent further losses and so we did. Delta and I, together, defeated both our own programming and the Nursery's ruling machine. In doing so we fulfilled our goal. In doing so, we created a target.

The disappearing child created a mission.

Volt, a firebrand mech managing Starship's power, told us the child might yet survive. Told us he'd seen growing usage deep in Starship's lower aft area. Almost to the engines and well back from the Nursery. Volt investigated the pull and found a missing link.

Alpha, myself, and Delta were alive and found. Beta had vanished, woken up by the same guiding remnants that'd brought me up from my programmed slumber only to disappear.

Volt found her watching over the children the Nursery discarded. The question Volt couldn't answer, the one he wanted us to investigate, was why.

"Are you done yet?" Delta asked without turning our way.

She already knew the answer. This was the third time she'd repeated the question.

"When this one moves like the others you'll know," I replied.

"Two ought to be enough," Delta said. Her voice had amber's solid character, color. Rich not so much with emotion as with reason. "They aren't waking up yet."

The two nurse mechs Kaydee and I had already fixed were busy in the nursery's back, cleaning up all the damage we'd caused in our raucous battle with the area's former owner. The caretakers sucked up shrapnel, patched together toys broken in the little playroom, and checked the baby food and milk stores. The latter had enough to carry a thousand newborns through three years, meant to offer humanity a chance to establish itself before taking on a new population.

"We don't know how much longer it will be," I said, eyeing the jack again. Kaydee was taking longer with this one. "The Voices hinted that we're close."

"They hinted at many things," Delta said. "The only way to know for certain is to get back to the bridge."

"Which we'll do *after* we find Beta."

"An unnecessary delay." Delta stepped away from the entry, lifted that jagged blade and swooshed it through the air.

The movements weren't random but precise, calibrated to test her range. She'd been damaged a little in the fight and, unlike humans, we vessels had to have our parts stitched back together.

I'd done the best I could. You couldn't see the slits, but, if you paid close attention, the slightest hitches revealed themselves as Delta looped the blade back and forth. Milliseconds added to a record time.

A problem?

That depended on what remained to fight on Starship. With the Nursery returned to us, we'd pushed against the Voices. I had to hope the ruling, digital council made up of long-dead humans wouldn't throw what forces they had against us. Wouldn't risk all those unborn lives.

But they weren't the only enemies.

"You're concerned about Alpha?" I asked.

Delta didn't nod but her fingers, tightening their grip on the blade's hilt, served as an answer.

"Alvie's watching him," I continued. The mech dog had an unshakeable loyalty to me, programmed in when I'd brought the thing to its metal life. "If Alpha moves, Alvie's going to tear him apart."

"I would trust the dog for an hour," Delta said, "not a day. We should have killed him."

My argument—there were only four of us vessels, killing shouldn't be the first response—died when the jack connecting me to the nurse mech popped free. The nurse mech jerked forward, wheeling around and glaring my way, caring eyes a hot, angry red.

"Sorry," Kaydee said, appearing off to the right with her head shaking. "This one didn't want to play along like the others."

I back-pedaled as the nurse mech advanced. We matched in size and I didn't lack for strength, but I did lack for a weapon. Straight up grappling might get me injured, not something I wanted before embarking on another journey.

"So you made her angry?" I asked Kaydee.

"Threat response algorithm," Kaydee replied, not sounding quite as apologetic as I'd expect. "Try to tamper with a nurse mech and you get an all-out defense."

My back hit a tall rack stuffed with frozen human cells. The mech approached, arms reaching for my neck. I protested, told it I didn't mean any harm.

The mech did as much with them as an angry beast might. She reached towards me and I blocked her, my two hands meeting its match and holding it even. The mech had strength, but my synthetic muscles had flexibility. I pushed the nurse mech's arms aside, drained their leverage.

"Please," I said. "We can still use you."

The etched smile, the red eyes, pressed on silently.

Until Delta's blade appeared, jutting through the nurse mech and nearly poking my own face. Sparks rained on me, little burning twinges wherever they caught my bare skin. The nurse mech's red eyes flickered and faded, its hands dropped, and as Delta withdrew the blade, the mech collapsed onto the floor.

"She failed," Delta said, stamping the blade through the fallen mech's middle to confirm the kill.

"It happens," I replied, brushing off shards.

"Yeah," Kaydee echoed, though Delta couldn't hear her. Kaydee's existence as a program, albeit a complex one, limited her impact to my world. She stuck her tongue out towards Delta, flipped the vessel a middle finger, then sighed. "Some of them are more corrupted, Gamma. This one had her code already scrambled."

We'd witnessed that elsewhere: mechs with their inner functions, ones designed to keep them to strict orders, stricter routines, broken down into aggressive variants. If, say, a mech had been tasked with keeping an apartment clean, the corrupted version would interpret any person entering as bringing dirt inside, and thus act with extreme prejudice to remove the visitor permanently.

Kaydee blamed Alpha, but I wasn't so sure.

So much around Starship seemed to be reaching the long end of centuries spent spiraling. Alpha might have problems, but I didn't believe he'd done so much to ruin the ship. Rather, without regular maintenance, I figured human coding and its flaws bore more responsibility.

"So?" Delta asked. "Are we done here?"

Behind us, I could hear the two successful nurse mechs continuing their work. They'd eventually find this one and trash it, dump it down the Conduit's vast middle to the junkyards below. Then they'd get back to babysitting.

Which left us free to walk away.

"You think those two can keep all these people safe?" Kaydee asked, popping in beside me, staring at the cells stacked in vial upon vial, locked into the freezer rack in its glass-black intensity. "Two nurse mechs against what we've seen already?"

"Who's going to be coming after them?" I replied, Delta shaking her head as I spoke to a person she couldn't hear, see. "The Voices?"

"Maybe."

"Then I have a different idea."

Together, Delta and I left the Nursery for the Conduit. The massive corridor, spanning Starship's length and most of its height, cut through like a hazy blue gash. Not all that long ago, when I'd first walked its length, there'd been chaos. Mechs had been fighting each other, their berserk programming causing the machines to go for violence. Fires, ripping metal, and mechs simply ramming into things turned the Conduit into a horrifying look at robotics gone wrong.

That had been farther up the Conduit, closer to Starship's Bridge and on the Garden's other side. Back here, where Starship's middle class had dominated, the mechs weren't so prolific nor so corrupted. That, and Delta had slaughtered so many already.

Hard to have a riot if everyone's already dead.

"Seal it," I said to Delta as I stepped away from the Nursery entrance's panel.

The little black screen looked for an ID to scan or, failing that, the screen would give you a chance to enter in a code that'd turn the red-glowing gem in the Nursery's door green.

"You won't be able to get back in," Delta replied.

"We'll just cut a new hole," I answered.

Delta didn't wait for further explanation, stabbing forward with the blade. The sword struck the screen, cut right through that glass and the processor behind it. The Nursery's door stayed red, and now it wouldn't be changing.

I took a big breath. Unnecessary from a survival standpoint, but useful to parse the air, pick out its components. Right now, the Conduit came through clean, albeit with the tiniest moldy undercurrent. Starship didn't have too many biological pieces left, but with few things caring for them, the slow rot lingered.

Delta turned bridge-ward, swinging the blade up and over to rest on her shoulder, "Coming?"

"That's the wrong way, Delta," I said.

"For you," Delta replied. "I have unfinished business."

An incoming noise rose from the Conduit's depths, a rippling hum we both knew well enough. Delta put both her hands on her blade and I stepped up to the Conduit's railing, looking towards the noise.

"And here it comes," Kaydee said, snapping her fingers to send virtual fireworks spitting out over the abyss.

"Here comes what?"

"The twist."

The noise resolved itself into what looked like a bottle coated with arms. The courier's fatter end spewed out a white-gold thrust, sending the bottle mech towards us. What lay in its arms was more concerning, a package the mech let fly free as it swerved near us. The bundle bounced off the Nursery's outer wall, coming to rest on the ground near my feet.

The flying mech completed its loop, turned and jetted back up the Conduit without a word.

Bending over the package, I ran my hands over the metal, the limbs all packed in tight together. The dead eyes and the note etched into Alvie's back. My faithful mech, constructed in Starship's depths from scrap. Tasked to watch Alpha and now here, broken.

"We should have left sooner," Delta said, watching me as I unbound Alvie's limbs.

Vines ripped from the Garden's walls served as rope, though I doubted they'd have held Alvie if the dog still ran. I tore them off, searched for the port that'd give me access to Alvie's insides, a chance to see if anything worked. When I found the port, I found more torn up metal. Alpha had shredded the connection.

Alvie would need to be repaired before I could even see if the dog's mind remained.

"Gamma," Delta said. "Leave it. Alpha's free. We have to get after him."

I shook my head, "We don't know where he is. He could be anywhere, waiting to trap us, trick us. No. The right call is back. With Beta."

"Hey," Kaydee said. "You reading this?"

She pointed to Alvie's back, where Alpha had etched his message. Short, condescending.

"Saving Starship from tyranny?" Kaydee continued as I turned the dog over. "Not blaming you for being weak and following your programming? This guy."

Delta knelt next to me, nodded as she read the message, "We must stop him."

"We'll have a better chance of doing that with friends," I replied, lifting Alvie in my arms. "It's not far and I think it's the best chance we've got."

"Seconded," Kaydee echoed to no one. "Alpha's a scary dude. Better to get overwhelming firepower."

Delta took another long look up the Conduit. I wondered if she was really going to ignore me, dart off on a solo strike, odds be damned. Instead, she shivered once, then turned back my way.

"My programming requires fulfilling a promise, Gamma," Delta said. "I cannot leave Alpha alive any longer."

Holding Alvie, dead and dark in my hands, my equation changed. I couldn't go it alone, and I couldn't let Delta throw herself into danger solo.

Beta and the children would wait.

TWO

CHOOSING JUNK

For all our determination, we didn't make it far down the Conduit before our first stop. The Nursery sat along the central level, a line running through the Conduit's middle. Above us tended to be more residential spaces, apartments with circular red-gemmed doors shut to our interests. Below lived industry, everything from restaurants to factories, all left to idle in a post-human existence. Every so often a lift carved into the sides would offer an opportunity to shift levels, one we ignored.

Eventually this central line would lead us to Starship's Bridge. Delta and I agreed that's where Alpha would likely be, given his whole delusion about controlling Starship's future and everything in it. Getting there would mean crossing through Starship's Hospital, now a mech graveyard after Delta had sliced and diced the institution's malfunctioning robots. After that would be the Garden and its dying beauty.

And then we'd be passing by our home.

"Your home?" Kaydee asked, walking by me. "That's how you think of it?"

"Nothing else comes close," I replied. "It's where I awoke. Was born, in your words."

"You know you were made way up front, right?" Kaydee said. "Leo built a fabrication line for you and the other vessels."

"Then maybe when I see that, I'll call it home instead."

I earned some strong side-eye, but I'd become used to that by now. Kaydee seemed to think everything I did was odd in some form or fashion. At first, not being a human had bugged me, itched like some programming failure. Now, after seeing so much human folly?

I took it as a source of pride.

I cradled Alvie in my arms. Delta stayed ahead several meters, her blade back on her shoulders. Her head constantly turned back and forth, scanning up and down and all around for potential threats.

"That looks exhausting," Kaydee said, pointing at Delta. "How long's she going to keep doing that?"

"As long as she lets the routine run," I replied.

"That'd drive me crazy."

"I assure you, she attaches no emotion to it whatsoever."

"Mechs are so weird."

"But you love us anyway," I said, then slowed down as a particular opening began to our right.

Starship's vast energies needed shepherding, and the tender of this particular power flock resided here. Like too much of the ship, the entry, marked with a big, lightning-bolt display, bore scratches, burn marks, blown off chunks. Battle remnants left to linger. Apparently Volt had higher priorities than appearance.

"You're stopping?" Delta said, somehow picking up my faltering steps without looking.

"I can't fix Alvie alone," I replied. "Volt's the best mechanic I know."

Delta frowned, "Another delay."

"Another ally," I countered. "You know Alvie's good to have in a fight."

"Not good enough," Delta said, then read my narrowed eyes, my resolute stance as I stopped before Volt's home. Swinging her blade down, letting its point rest on the walkway, she waved me in. "Fine. If he's quick about it, we can stop."

Volt, a mech that'd been running for centuries, didn't operate on Delta's timetable. We found him back in his space, hunched over a spider-like mech I stayed well away from. Last time I'd seen that mech, it'd been close to roasting me with a high-energy beam. Actually, it had roasted me. I broke it in the same desperate instance. Volt put me back together, and now he'd turned to the mess I'd made.

Through the entrance sat a wide lobby, a space cleared out but that seemed designed to hold desks. Offices or reception-style setups for the folks coming through looking for Starship's power distribution. Last time we were here, Delta had thrashed more mechs than I could count. Like the Hospital, it'd become a parts graveyard, one Volt had set about to looting.

The black and yellow mech played with his tools as we approached. Volt had more than a few arms, a bug-like head connected to a barrel body, and two stiff legs ending in flat pads for feet. Not particularly flexible, but considering his main function was to tap away on big screens showing Starship's energy levels, the construction fit the job.

"You're going the wrong way," Volt said as we walked in, Delta choosing to linger by the entrance. His head rotated on his neck while his arms continued rebuilding a leg on the big spider. "Beta's aft. What's that you've got?"

I held Alvie out, "My dog."

"Doesn't look like much of a dog."

"He was," I replied. "Alpha did this."

Volt's black eyes flashed yellow, "That vessel's causing a lot of problems."

"Which is why we need to get going," Delta said.

"Ah," Volt muttered. "Think I get why you're here now."

"Can you fix Alvie?" I asked.

Volt clicked the leg into place, a satisfying snap and grind. The mech stood up, swiveled around and peered at Alvie.

"Could, maybe," Volt said. "Don't have the parts here though."

I eyed the scrap lying around. Kaydee, popping in next to me, looked from Volt to Alvie and echoed my sentiment.

"Know what you're thinking, kid, but what this dog needs isn't a new leg or a faceplate," Volt said, two arms taking Alvie from my grip. "He needs a new battery."

"Not a single working battery here?" Kaydee asked and I repeated the same.

"Blame her." Volt's eyes flicked past my shoulder. "It's her programming. Every mech had its power supply sliced apart."

"It's the only way to ensure the mech won't keep fighting," Delta said, her blade back to its planted position, hands on the hilt.

"Then where do I get a new battery?" I asked.

"The Fabrication Lines," Kaydee said.

At the same time, Volt announced, "The Junker might have one."

When I didn't reply, as I tried to parse both statements, Kaydee and Volt launched into explanations. I tried to sort the jumble, wound up with this:

The Fabrication Lines sat near Starship's bottom, but at the ship's front. They took in raw materials and, with a programmed plan, spat out mechs and other tools the ship might need. Big plastic and metal printers. Kaydee figured if batteries sat around waiting to be used, the Fabrication Lines would be the place.

Delta wanted to go that way anyway, maybe I could convince her to take a detour down to Starship's basement and get my dog a new power source.

Volt offered a counter proposal: If Purity handled Starship's water supply, the Junker kept a bead on more physical waste, recycling almost everything. Some re-usable stuff went back up to the Fabrication Lines, but plenty remained down in the Junker's shop to be bought. His warehouses should still have salvage aplenty.

"On second thought," Kaydee said, apparently catching up to

Volt's proposal, "the mech's got the better idea. Stay away from the Fabrication Lines."

"Why?" I asked, drawing a confused head tilt from Volt I had to explain. "Kaydee's in my memory, remember?"

"Ah yes," Volt said. "You vessels. Crazy in all the best ways."

"One way to look at it," Kaydee said. "Anyway, here's my theory: You want to run Starship, you need to control the Fabrication Lines. The Voices must've lost them some time ago or else they'd have just made enough mechs to take the Nursery by force. And if there's one thing you don't want to do, its walk into a hostile robot army."

"How do you know they'd be hostile?"

"Gamma, I'm your friend and even I want to punch you most of the time," Kaydee replied. "I don't know for sure, but our luck hasn't been good on this so far."

Fair point.

Delta banged her blade against the wall, leaving a lovely new notch in the already-scarred plate.

"This is taking too long," the vessel said. "I'm leaving for the Bridge. Come with me or don't. Last chance."

"Know what else is by Junker's?" Volt said to me. "Beta. The children."

Leaving Delta to pursue Alpha by herself didn't strike me as a great option, but at the same time, the image of that baby disappearing down the chute stuck with me. Starship's core purpose, delivering humanity to a new world, resonated in my core. I couldn't trace the desire to fulfill that purpose to any one line in my code, but it was there nonetheless.

"You won't come with us?" I asked Delta. "We could find Beta. Together, we'd be too much for Alpha to handle. There'd be no risk."

"What if Alpha already has the Fabrication Lines?" Delta shot back. "Every second, as your little friend said, he could be churning out more mechs loyal to him and him alone."

"Like you'd have any issues cutting them down."

My puff-up failed to elicit anything from Delta save another cold stare. She lifted the sword, put it on her shoulder, and turned to leave.

"When you're ready, you know where I'll be," Delta said.

"You'll leave me a piece of him?" I asked her back.

"No," Delta replied, then she curled out through the entrance to the Conduit and vanished.

Volt and I stomped to the nearest lift. The mech hadn't wanted to leave his power station, but when I told him I had no idea how to get to the Junker, he relented. Kaydee whispered that she could've given me directions, but I told her to stay quiet. Volt seemed to have some relationship with Beta and he might be able to smooth any rough edges.

More than that, though, Starship seemed an increasingly hostile place. Venturing forth alone wasn't something I wanted to do. And, anyway, Volt didn't fight all that hard to stay.

"You know," Volt said after I made the suggestion. "There's some things I could use to give my darling an upgrade. She fried a couple fuses going after you, so I'm thinking we enhance those puppies and she could run even hotter. Might not need to turn the beam off for a full minute!"

Volt's eyes turned orange as he spoke, his arms and legs quivering.

"That's, uh, great," I said. "So you're coming?"

"Give me a minute to set up my algorithms," Volt replied, jerking up and starting back towards Power Core's center. "Wouldn't want Starship to go nova in my absence!"

The mech laughed, a bright maniacal noise.

"You sure you want him coming with?" Kaydee said. "Seems kind of insane."

"Aren't we all?" I replied.

"You? Definitely," Kaydee said. "I like to think I've still got it."

"By any reasonable metric, you are as far from having 'it' as I am."

Volt didn't take long to come back, minutes I spent reviewing his work on the spider mech, the machine Volt liked to call his wife. The thing had her legs back in action, though the big ol' laser seemed defunct. It too, like Alvie, sat dark and dormant.

"Have a battery for her," Volt said as he rejoined us, clomping on over, "but I'm not going to put it in until I'm by her side. She'll get scared if she's all alone."

I blinked. Kaydee twirled a finger beside her head and rolled her eyes.

"Grabbed this for you too," Volt said, holding up what looked like a bucket with shoulder straps. "Good for hauling tools around. Looks like your dog might fit."

Alvie did fit and together we rode the lift down, down, and then down some more. Through the thin glass shielding, dusty and dirty, I saw us pass by schools, shops, and then diners and supply depots. Places whose tarnished signs called out food, parts, or entertainment. The walkways we passed were empty, with only a few scattered mechs trundling around tending to functions unknown.

"Used to be people everywhere," Kaydee said, pressing her virtual face up to the glass. "If anything, Starship was overcrowded back when I . . . you know."

"That was part of the problem?" I asked.

"Could be," Kaydee replied. "People don't really like getting stuffed in cans, no matter how nice they are." She threw me a wink, then spread her arms, fingers pointing at either end in opposite directions. One looped, leaving a blue-glowing circle in the air. The second traced an orange line over to it. "Think the real reason was everyone saw how close we were, knew it'd only be a couple more generations."

"They couldn't wait?"

"They wouldn't make it," Kaydee shrugged as the lift settled into the lowest level. "One thing if you're born into an impossible situation, no way out. Another to know you'd see a real sky if you could live another fifty years. Especially if you knew some people who could, would be doing it."

"Some humans could live that long?"

The lift opened and Kaydee shrugged, "I'll catch you up on that later. Looks like Volt wants your attention."

The orange mech led me from the lift. Up above the Conduit's levels stacked as if they reached into infinity. Beneath me, though, Starship's bottom looked like a madcap collection. Shattered, broken metal, trash bags, organic waste and everything else lay in giant piles. Random chance had the junk forming crumbling spires, their points nearly reaching up to us.

Not a soul seemed to be moving down in those depths.

"I thought the Junker took care of this?" I asked as Volt and I peered over the edge.

"Thought so, but then, his power draw's been low for a long time," Volt said. "Maybe something went wrong."

"Like everywhere else on Starship, you mean?"

"Not quite everywhere." Volt sounded a tad defensive. "C'mon. Junker's this way."

Volt turned left and we marched aft. Unlike above, where every different section had a colored sign, every door an address, we walked for a while without seeing anything except blank walls on our left. Across the way I caught only a single rounded door, a placard next to it long since dead, its blank bulbs reading out *Storage*.

"We used to come down here, Leo and I," Kaydee said as we walked. "Long way from home, but we'd see if Junker had anything useful. He'd part with most things for cheap, especially if we brought him something good from up our way."

"Something good?"

"Beer, wine. A new mech right off the line."

"You could get those?"

Kaydee skipped ahead, turned back to face me, with her hands out, palms up, sparkles popping like tiny fireworks around her head. "Look at me, Gamma. Don't you think I could get what I want?"

"I think you are very good at manipulating people."

Volt sparked out a wiry laugh, "You always talk this much with yourself?"

"Kaydee has a lot to say," I replied, but when I looked back up the walkway, Kaydee had vanished.

We reached Junker's shop as the Conduit started its fade to darkness, simulating that artificial night so crucial to a human's circadian rhythms. A red-gemmed door greeted us beneath a nameplate constructed of the very junk the Junker reportedly sold. Next to the door sat a sign reading *Open all hours unless we're closed.*

"Informative," I said, pointing at the sign.

"Accurate," Volt replied. He reached out, touched the red gem. "Locked. I might be able to bash in."

"Not a problem."

I went to the little black panel, lifted its base to find the port and jacked myself in.

Like most locks on Starship, this one presented a simple check. A database that would accept a series of combinations provided that combination had been added by the Junker before. Defenses were non-existent, the list sprawling out in the digital universe like a long carpet spread on an infinite gray. I walked along it, found the very end, and read the last line.

Back on the Conduit I tapped on the panel, entered the combination. The gem flipped from red to green, and Volt clapped his arms together in a shrieking, shredding sound.

"Sorry," Volt said. "That was supposed to be happier."

I grinned, put my hand on the green gem and felt its warmth. The door clicked, its spiral ends sliding free and wide. I wasn't sure what I expected to see on the other side, wasn't sure what the Junker's shop might look like.

Volt's curse summed it up pretty well.

THREE

BATTERY HUNTING

I'd seen human shops and homes before, courtesy of Kaydee's memories. They tended to be bright-lit and warm, with decorations and life's many leavings all over. Mech-run spaces kept the illumination but ditched the flavor, angling for efficiency without emotion. Not the robot's faults, really: they hadn't been programmed to care about art or color schemes.

I didn't either.

The Junker's workshop didn't fall into either category. First, a deep darkness pervaded the broad space. Not absolute: tiny diodes outlined fenced sections here and there, but their sapphire glows vanished against the valleys, arcing constructs created by stacked debris. Vented air whistled as it moved between crannies, rattling the occasional piece like a mech ghost giving its last warning. My nose and the sensors inside identified a strong rusty smell.

"He's shut down," Volt said, following up his curse from a moment before.

"Like a program?" I didn't know where I'd found the idea that the Junker was a human, but of course that didn't make sense. "Or a mech?"

"The Junker's been digital for a long time," Volt replied, leading me into the place. His eyes flipped to that bright yellow, guiding us with dual beams. "Always had mechs working for him, though. They scrounged through these piles, sorting anything that could be useful."

"I don't see any mechs."

"Being obvious now?" Volt asked and I shrugged. "If we're going to find that battery without help, we'll need to look around. It's a big place. You go left, I'll go right."

"Is it safe here?"

Volt swiveled those yellow eyes my way, dimming them a hair to keep from blinding me, "Safe as anywhere else on Starship. Don't be stupid, Gamma."

With that, Volt tromped off. Only after he'd vanished between several creaking stacks—one looked like jumbled toilets, another showcased panels and doors—did I realize I'd never seen Alvie's battery before. Had no idea what to look for.

"I'll help you," Kaydee said, popping in. She waved her hands, threw rainbow globes into the dark.

The virtual balls lit up precisely nothing in the workshop, prompting a sigh from my friend.

"You tried," I offered as I started left.

"It really sucks being virtual, Gamma. Don't know if you realize that."

"You've made it abundantly clear."

My designated pathway turned quick into a strange tour. Without Volt's lighting, I shifted my ocular sensors to a low-light spectrum, picking up those sapphire glows and splashing them in neon green across the Junker's workshop. I stopped at the very first stack, a short, squat array that looked like boxes with wheels. Manual buttons dotted the outsides.

"Early mechs," Kaydee said. "I bet these were on Starship when it launched."

I crouched, took a closer look at my predecessors. They held my beginnings in those square shells: slots for motherboards and proces-

sors, transistors and heatsinks. Memory. A screen built into one side
—though the glass had been removed—gave clues as to its purpose.
Mobile messaging, package delivery.

"Anything simple that a human might do on Earth, we had to see
if a mech could do it here," Kaydee said, crouching next to me. She
sported a crimson sweater, jeans, with Starship's University logo, the
big ship streaking through gold-rimmed stars, on both. "Every body
we could keep in cold storage, or never grow in the first place was one
less mouth to feed. One less person breathing our oxygen."

"One less potential disaster."

Kaydee's own death had come about because of a failed revolu-
tion, an attempt by Starship's downtrodden to take over the craft and
a mission that'd stopped caring about the ones toiling in the back, in
the rust. I faulted both sides, but it was clear the problems started,
continued, and concluded because of human rashness, unpredictability.

"Guess you could say that," Kaydee replied.

The next section offered up bigger boxes, these without wheels
but with far more internal complexity. Shelves connected with wires
to empty battery packs, to heating and cooling mechanisms. Gas
canisters piled up on one side, pasted with fire warnings.

"These boys went early," Kaydee said. "Refrigerators, ovens. I
read about it in classes, how they'd break down, start fires."

"So humans stopped cooking meals?"

"We changed how it was done," Kaydee replied. "Kept things
contained. Restaurants could have the risks in isolated kitchens.
Apartments had produce and pre-made meals. We routed air and
water near vacuum to cool it down."

Other stacks dropped more historical gems, tracing a path from
human's early adventures on Starship to their more modern efficien-
cies. For every genius adjustment that saved lives, though, I saw the
signs leading to today's emptiness. Mechs grew more complex and
convoluted, the tools deployed needing less and less human
supervision.

And, more and more, the luxurious few and the mediocre many. At first, screens that could display landscapes from Earth as art were everywhere. Then the next wave, ones offering smells, complex 3D immersion formed a much smaller junk pile. Kaydee said her family didn't even have that, a way to escape from Starship life. Too expensive, too hard to find.

Other offerings were similarly refined for limited numbers: the Garden didn't make infinite amounts of every spice, every crop, and fancy apartments had room for more storage and variety. The wealthy had the better mechs, had more time to get to the Garden to take the most desirable food.

"It's not hard to trace, is it?" Kaydee said as we left another small but beautiful pile of cleaning mechs behind. "Why things wound up the way they did?"

"Not particularly," I replied. "But if we can see it, surely the humans living this could see it too?"

Kaydee didn't have an answer to that, and before I could press her on it, I caught a different setup on my left. A boxed in room, almost like a shanty erected in the workshop's center. A diode-lit sign outside its door read *Office*.

We were looking for a battery, but the Junker's story, Starship's story had my curiosity again. And besides, it wasn't like Alvie would be going anywhere. Taking a slight detour wouldn't hurt anything.

The door leading in had no special lock, just a knob that turned when I twisted. A made-up cot dominated one side, faded and brown. A desk with a dark monitor on the right. Paper sheets lay in neat ordered stacks, notebooks and folders. Pictures hung on the walls, families across generations, all taken in front of the Junker's marquee out in the Conduit.

A shabby dresser, made from molded brown plastic, occupied the only other space. I tugged open a drawer, saw actual human clothes. Work boots, pants, shirts.

"Hey," Kaydee said. "Might be a chance to update your look, buddy boy."

"Buddy boy?"

"An expression," Kaydee replied, looking into the drawers with me. "You're gonna learn some worse ones if you don't ditch those rags you're wearing for something better."

I recalled, back in *Alvie's*, I'd taken what I could find off the rack. Unworn leftovers. These, though, belonged to someone. While my logical bits understood the Junker couldn't be alive anymore, my programmed reticence to theft made me hesitate.

"Gamma, think of it this way," Kaydee said as I stood there, hands on the jeans. "You're not stealing, you're borrowing. You can come back and return all this crap later if it bothers you."

"Semantics."

"Call it what you want."

Kaydee's little loophole worked its magic on my binary morals. Convincing myself that I would return these clothes let me sift through the offerings, put myself up in new, thicker jeans and a working jacket heavy enough to handle heat, metal. I left the gloves alone, putting on steel-toed boots instead.

Then, properly attired for the physical world, I went looking for the digital one. Humans so often kept their histories in their computers, I figured the Junker wouldn't be any different. Kaydee, too, mentioned the Junker probably kept his inventory on the thing's hard drive. I could run a search, find whether any batteries remained among the junk.

Any that hadn't been stolen in the years since the Junker left his mortal coil behind.

The monitor on the desk connected to a squat computer. The thing plugged into a Starship outlet in the floor and thrummed to lurching life when I hit its power button. The monitor flashed on, asking for a password. Not that I needed one.

I found the port, pressed my fingers together, and jacked in.

Every virtual world felt, looked different. If I jumped inside my own circuits and burrowed into my processor, I'd come up into a flat, gray and white universe populated by hanging crystals. Every crystal housed a function controlling me, my limbs, my thoughts. I could manipulate that space, give myself a big virtual house in the style of old human dwellings, could give myself wings or a tail. Anyone else invading my reality would have to abide by my rules too.

And now I had to abide by the world the Junker built.

It was not, in a word, tidy.

The man kept his computer like he kept his workshop. I stood upon a great dune made up of bolts, screws, and nails. Overhead, a bronzed sun cast an amber glint over a metal ocean heaving with unseen currents. Here and there I picked out files, memories sticking out from the debris. Each one held itself up as a glowing diode, the same sapphire as back in the real world.

"Tell me what we're looking at here," Kaydee said, pulling up a cheap folding chair from the ether and sitting next to me.

"A mess," I replied. "One of those diodes is going to have his inventory."

"How do you know that?"

"Experience? There's nothing else we can see." I picked up a screw, held it up, " Either everything has meaning, in which case we'll never find anything, or the Junker left a way to pick out the good parts."

"It's really much easier to find this stuff the normal way. Clicking around a desktop."

"No doubt," I replied. "You and Leo made us, though, so this is what we work with."

Kaydee leaned back in her chair, shielded her eyes from the sun and swept a look around, "So how are we getting to these things? Tell me we're not walking."

"Not quite."

If I'd learned anything in the time since waking, it'd been that my own abilities in these virtual worlds were nothing to sneeze at. I could rewrite reality even in a hostile system, though that system could fight back. Here, I didn't see any opposition. The Junker hadn't built in security, hadn't waited to spring a trap on any digital intruders.

I waved my arm and, in the process, redirected our dune. All the metal waves swept around, but my adjustment sent our dune roiling left onto a collision course with the next one over, one with a glimmering diode right there on top for the taking. Kaydee stood up, reached out and held my arm for balance as the dunes smashed into one another.

Bits and bolts flew and merged, Kaydee and I shuffling our feet to stay on top. Momentum caught up to our dune as its crash continued, shifting the debris to match our target's direction. As the screws beneath my toes stopped jumbling around, I took a couple strides forward, bent down and picked up the blue diode from its resting place.

"What do you want?" asked a smokey, greased voice behind me.

"Geez," Kaydee said as I turned around. She put a few meters between herself and the man, who looked to be wearing a full on welding outfit. "What's up with you?"

"I asked the question," the welder said. "What do you want?"

"A battery," I answered, "for a small mech dog. Do you have one?"

"Might." The welder, faceplate dark, looked at me. "I keep the batteries in the back, secured where they won't start a fire, and if they do it won't spread."

"Thank you," I said, glanced at Kaydee. "That's all we needed."

The welder didn't say another word, just stood there and stared. That answered my unasked question: this wasn't really the Junker, not in the way that Kaydee existed. This was a search, a program ready to execute a function and nothing more.

"Hold on," Kaydee said. "Before we go, can I ask you a question?"

"What do you want?" The welder looked her way now.

"What happened to you?" Kaydee asked. "What happened to this place? We used to come here, but—"

"I don't know," the welder interrupted. "There are system logs. Would you like to hear them?"

"Please."

The welder didn't hesitate, but Kaydee's unclear command meant the program started from the end. The last message between the Junker and someone I recognized. A member of the Voices, Peony. She cut the Junker off, disconnected access to Starship's network. Sealed him inside his own workshop.

The why came after the fate. The Junker had been feeding raw material for weapons to Starship's rebelling side. When the Junker refused to stop, Peony had acted with fatal consequences. The Junker hadn't even recorded a last message, just turned off the computer and vanished.

"Do you think he made it out?" I asked Kaydee after she told the welder to stop.

"With all these things around here it's possible," Kaydee replied. "But I know my mother. She wouldn't have let him." She frowned at the welder. "We can go now, Gamma. This guy's starting to weird me out."

I did as Kaydee asked and popped us back into reality. The junkyard dunes morphed into the Junker's small shack, his cot and the papers and dresser where they belonged. I retrieved my fingers from the port, straightened, relished the return of the air and the senses that came with it.

"What'd you find in there?" Volt asked, his yellow eyes peering in from the doorway.

"Our battery," I replied. "Unless you already have one?"

Volt's eyes dimmed, his voice going lower, "No. I found something worse. Come on."

The mech guided Kaydee and I back through the stacks towards a dim corner. There, nestled in among several mech animals that looked more than a little like Alvie, lay a long-stripped skeleton. The bones were raw, decomposition having cleared them, but left them dirty. A paper sheet, pinned by a cat-like mech, lay next to the Junker.

With Volt's eyes providing the light, I bent down to read the words. All three.

Don't lose hope.

"An odd message to leave," I said, rereading the words and finding no further answers the second time. "Who is he speaking to?"

A scuffling sound came from behind us, followed by clanks as metal pipes found their way banging to the floor. Volt whirled, as did I, the bigger mech's feet clomping as he turned. There, caught in Volt's lights, stood a human child.

He screamed.

We screamed right back.

FOUR

FRESH FRUITS

The kid stopped screaming first, fear transmuting to curiosity as Volt and I cut off our own to match his. The boy held out a pipe to the right in one hand, watching intently. When we didn't mimic the movement he frowned. I tried to process what to do with a real live human standing before me.

Deep down in my programmed heart of hearts, I had an unflinching desire to protect humans. Leo must've slotted that urge in, and it propelled me to do the Voices's bidding, to save the Nursery even if it meant letting Alpha run free. The concept, though, had always felt abstract: protect the humans, but they didn't really exist outside those vials.

Seeing the Nursery mech discard the small child had been a shock, one followed too fast by a fight to properly analyze. Now, though, I had a boy standing right there, almost in arm's reach. Should I grab him, put him in a tight hug to protect him from a scratch? Should I stuff him in the Junker's cabin, a place with little but at least some separation from Starship's many dangers?

"Hello there," Volt said. "What's your name?"

Volt's nonchalance tightened me up even further. The mech

risked casual conversation with a living human! Better to grab the boy before he could run away and ensure his safety.

"What's yours?" the child replied.

His voice had no artificial buzzing, no stilted delivery like so many mechs, myself included. I watched the way his lips moved and wondered whether mine matched. The boy's skin looked dry, and while it had a natural tan color, living in the dark had tinted it paler. Black hair looked scruffy, as if it'd been cut with a knife and at random.

Then again, as someone whose hair would never grow longer than the programmed centimeter or two, I couldn't criticize.

"Volt," the mech said, then waited.

"What's his?" the kid asked, pointing the pipe at me.

"Gamma," I replied, "and I will protect you."

Now Volt looked at me with questioning blue eyes. The kid scrunched up his nose, mouth.

"Huh?" the kid asked, then glanced around, eventually coming back to me. "Protect me from what?"

"Everything," I said.

"Slow it down there, honcho," Kaydee whispered. "I get that you're excited. Hell, I'm excited too, but let's tone down the weirdo vibes a bit."

I started to reply to Kaydee but stopped myself. Talking to air would do little to dispel those, as Kaydee called them, weirdo vibes.

"Right," the kid said. "So you're not coming here for us?"

"Looking for some batteries," Volt answered, flipping his eyes back to a pleasant green. "Found 'em right here. Shame about the Junker though."

The kid flicked his look to the skeleton, "He's always been there."

"For you, maybe. For me, just yesterday we were having long talks about what to do with all this scrap," Volt said. The mech knelt down, picked up the Junker's note, slipped it inside a slot on his barrel body. "He helped me design my wife, you know."

The kid blinked, "You're both weird." He skipped off his junk pile onto a path, took one last look at us. "See ya later."

Then the kid, the miracle, took off running.

I chased.

Like Alvie going after a ball, the decision to break after the kid didn't come from rational thought, just pure instinct. I couldn't let the kid get hurt and, my goodness, there were so many sharp edges among all this crap. He could fall, have something fall on him, or find a mech with a nasty streak.

My burst dusted Volt, who shouted something about slowing down. I did nothing of the kind, instead following the kid's shadow as he ran left, then left again, then right. The blue diodes caught my target as he moved, blinking between the lights. With my bigger strides, I closed the gap fast.

"What're you doing?" Kaydee asked, jogging alongside me. "You're scaring him!"

"I'm saving him!"

"From what?"

"Everything!"

I followed the kid around a motley trash bin pile-up, curling around and expecting to see his form not a meter ahead of me. There he stood, facing me with a mischievous grin, the pipe held high. Was he going to hit me?

"Hey," I spread my hands, slowed down. "It's okay."

Something hit my shoulder. Hard but not particularly heavy. Behind me, each in their own pathway, were two more kids. Girls looking younger than the boy, and each one held some scrap of their own.

"This is so weird," Kaydee muttered.

Another ball-bearing bounced off my back. No harm done, but I couldn't understand what was happening.

"Why are you throwing things at me?" I asked the two girls, skating past simpler, more existential questions about how the children existed at all.

The girls giggled, turned, and ran away down their paths. Behind me, I heard the boy fleeing too. Their actions didn't make any sense, didn't follow any script. I'd been handling broken mechs, but those machines still operated according to some logic. Their actions came from programmed possibilities, but these, these . . .

"They're like you," I said to Kaydee, who stood there looking where the girls had gone. "They make no sense."

"Hey, I make sense sometimes."

"Sometimes." I decided to go after the boy, if only because I knew he could talk. "Is this how human children normally are?"

"Never had any," Kaydee said, dashing along with me, her every step springing virtual flowers up from the concrete. "But from what I saw? Sure."

"It explains a lot about you."

"And you, Gamma!" Kaydee laughed as we dipped beneath a cracking rust-colored lattice. The Junker's shop had so much random material. "Leo wanted the vessels to be like us, right?"

"Lucky me."

After another three turns I thought I'd catch up to the boy. Instead we passed through a thicker wall, an arch that looked like it'd been a door sometime in the past. On the other side the random diodes had migrated to a more reasonable placement along the floor, showcasing different sorts of stacks.

Kaydee whistled and I stopped my barreling run. Surprises were piling on surprises here.

Ahead, sprawling out through the huge space, were provisions of all kinds. On my left cans upon cans, all advertising various soups on plain labels, stood in stacked towers. On my right, water jugs lay atop one another, though the layering looked imperfect, as if people had been taking some. Ahead lay pre-packaged dry meals.

Those seemed miraculous enough, but beyond them waited the real interesting parts: produce, most of it fresh, laid out in rows or bustled together if the food allowed it. I saw ripe red tomatoes, spinach leaves green and fresh. Oranges sat in mech parts repurposed as baskets.

The Garden had enough plants making these crops that their existence on Starship wasn't so much a mystery, but the Garden wasn't all that close to where we were now. Harvesting those plants, bringing the fruits back here, would be—

"Astounding," Volt said, catching up to me. "Well, this does explain a riddle."

"A riddle?"

"Yes, yes. I kept seeing more power getting pulled from down here," Volt said. "That's one reason why I came along with you. The Junker always took his fair energy share. It dropped years and years ago, but it's been creeping up again."

Because of the children?

"Did you see the kids?" I asked. "I followed the boy here, and there were two girls."

"And many more, I suspect," Volt said.

"Ooooooh," Kaydee muttered to herself, making a connection I had yet to complete.

"Gamma, how many vials are missing from the Nursery?" Volt asked.

Delta and I hadn't counted, but going by the empty containers, more than a few. At the time, I didn't want to think about how many children that meant. Now I traced what Volt seemed to be hinting at.

What if those children hadn't died after the Nursery shunted them down its tube? How many humans would be here, and how old could some of them be?

I did a slow turn, Volt beside me, and looked at the piled provisions. The canned goods, the dried meals that looked ancient, those stacks had taken significant hits, but not the level I figured would be necessary to sustain hundreds for years and years. Either the humans here didn't number that many, or this wasn't all their food.

"Gamma?" Volt asked again. "You going to answer my question?"

"Enough," I replied. "Enough vials to create a society down here. But how?"

"That is an answer I don't have."

"Me either," said Kaydee. "But this is pretty freaking cool, right?"

I'd withhold judgment on that. Especially as that boy appeared again, this time on the far side, past the provision stacks. The room narrowed that way and I saw only a single pathway, the one the boy stood on.

"Coming?" the boy called.

I hesitated. My programming prerogatives put human preservation up there on my preferences, but keeping myself alive sat even higher. With all this evidence around me showing the humans weren't just a few lost children, the question then became: where were the rest?

And why wouldn't they defend their food and water?

"Why don't you come to us?" Volt yelled to the boy. "We're not interested in hurting you."

"Come on!" the boy said. "There's more this way!"

He didn't wait for us, dashing off again. The kid seemed to have endless stamina, ready to run and keep on going. If that was typical of all humans, then I was even more nervous to know so many might be lurking around us.

"I suppose we should follow," Volt said. "Also, I picked this up while you were pursuing the child."

Volt handed over a battery. Or, rather, slipped it in the pack I'd been using to hold Alvie. That, at least, gave me some comfort. We'd accomplished our primary goal down here. If nothing else, we could leave, get my dog going, and then go find Delta.

"Wait," I said, looking at Volt. "Didn't you say Beta was helping these kids?"

"Last I heard from her," Volt said, "Beta said there were some down here, that I shouldn't cut off the power. I didn't think they'd be this old, or this many."

"Are they a threat?"

Kaydee laughed, "Gamma, what? These kids?"

Volt, though, seemed to understand what I was asking. His eyes shifted to a light orange, a curious threatening shade.

"Everything that happened on Starship came from the humans," Volt said. "All the good, all the bad. Are they a threat?" Volt nodded towards the disappearing boy. "I don't know, but they certainly could be."

"Guess I can't argue with that," Kaydee said.

"Then we go together," I said. "Stay sharp."

This time we walked after the boy. No running, no blind dashes around corners. We left the provisions behind for a different space, one filled with an old heat. If the Junker's shop had scrap piles everywhere, this showed where that scrap would go. Huge furnaces built into bulbous walls sat dormant, blue diodes making them look like mouths stuck in perpetual screams. Slabs rose up from the floor and came down from the ceiling to form workbenches and manufacturing presses.

A forge designed for noise felt wrong in the quiet.

"The Junker was proud of this place," Volt said as we walked through. "His great great grandfather had the idea to siphon heat from Starship's engines, rout it here. Gave this side of the ship its only way to make their own mechs."

"Not anymore," I replied.

"Oh, I don't know." Volt clomped over to a furnace, peered inside. "Bet these suckers would get going again, you wanted to light 'em up."

I went over to where Volt was looking, stuck my head in the furnace. Sure enough, a strong vent looked to seal the thing. A simple chain near the furnace door looked in fine shape, ready to pull open.

Food, a ready forge. What would we find beyond here? Housing? I almost asked Volt, except a hand gripped my neck. Held it tight. I felt a sharp point press into my stomach.

"That's far enough," said a hard woman's voice, one I didn't recognize but knew anyway.

See, it had a mech's automatic tremor. That, and Kaydee was swearing up a storm.

"You're going to move when I say to move," the voice said. "Do anything different, and I'll gut you before your circuits know what's happening. Understand?"

Oh yes, I understood quite well.

"Nice to meet you, Beta," I said.

FIVE

VALENTINA

The vessel let us free from the furnace, keeping her hand on my throat and shifting the pin-prick pressure to my back. I stood up straight and she rose with me, keeping my head staring at the black metal furnace, blue diodes shadowing us. Volt, under no such hostage restrictions, rotated his head, yellow-glowing eyes telling me they were turning.

"Beta," Volt said, "how nice to see you again. To say it's been a long time is an understatement!"

"Volt," Beta replied.

And that was it. Warm and fuzzy friends, these two.

Other voices cropped up behind me. Whispers bouncing off the walls. Heavy steps, but without a mech's clanks. I waited. Kaydee appeared, sitting in the furnace and peering out. She shook her head and slid a glance at me.

"I hate that I can't see what you can't see," Kaydee replied. "It's really not fair."

I stayed quiet. So long as Beta could gut me on a whim, I figured to let her drive our interaction. Passive, yes, but Volt claimed Beta wasn't crazy, was trying to help the humans. I had to bet that she'd come around on me eventually.

Because the only other thing I knew about Beta was that she fought like Delta, and that meant any straight up duel between us would leave me dusted and scrapped.

"This here's Gamma," Volt said. "He's not going to hurt anyone. You can let him go."

"What are you doing here?" Beta asked, making no move to let me free.

"Long story," Volt started.

"Sum it up quick."

Volt vibrated the mech equivalent of a cough, then started again. In clear, simple sentences the mech said we'd come searching for a battery to revive my dead robo-dog. We saw the boy, followed, and wound up here.

"Why did the Voices wake up another vessel?" Beta asked when Volt finished. "I'm still here."

"Because you took too long," I said.

Beta's grip on my throat tightened, but seeing as I didn't need air to talk, I could keep spewing words.

"The Voices brought me, and then Delta, up because they didn't have the Nursery back," I continued. "We won it, and now Delta's out there risking her life to clean up your mess."

"Oooh," Kaydee said. "Aggressive."

Beta must've thought so too. She released my throat, brought back her knife, then spun me around with her free hand. Silhouetted in blue light, my first look at Beta threw out any hope we vessels would be similar. Alpha had his red hair, his scar covered body and corrupted, manic scream. I had my skinny frame and a penchant for keeping my fingers close, ready to jack in any moment. Delta looked like liquid when she moved, so fast and precise, every action exactly what she needed it to be.

Beta?

I'd never seen something with so many edges. Arrayed in clothes that looked as if *Alvie's* had met a rabid raccoon, Beta kept her outfit together with myriad belts, all different blacks and browns and stitched over with holsters. Knives, ropes, jagged shrapnel, and tools of all sorts hung at angles as Beta looked me over.

Her hair, too, proved to be less a look and more an asset: she'd shaved, or someone had shaved off, half her hair leaving a clear patch over which someone had soldered a metal plate with nails jutting out the top. The other half strung light pink hair down below her shoulders, after which it thickened into weaves of all colors, weaves that shimmered and sparkled in the blue light.

"Glass," Kaydee breathed, similarly awestruck. "She's got broken glass in those things."

If Delta wielded a single blade with murderous proficiency, Beta seemed to wield everything else.

Behind her an equally astonishing sight awaited. Humans, adults spanning the age spectrum. They all watched with wary eyes, most carrying some physical instrument, pipes or hammers or even, in one case, what looked like a makeshift bow and arrow. I'd seen the food, and now I'd found its purpose.

"My mess?" Beta asked. She had the narrow shiv in her left hand, her right hanging near another knife in a thigh holster. "None of this is my mess."

"Careful, Gamma," Kaydee whispered. "Don't go being an asshole now."

She made a good point, but Beta clearly looked capable. Hell, I had approximately zero weapons on me, but I'd still fought and strived my way to the Nursery. She'd been hiding out down here, letting Alpha run amok? Letting those children get pumped up and thrown out?

"Yeah, your mess," I said, standing straight. "Do you have any idea what's happening out there? What's going on with Starship?"

"Gamma," Volt said, the mech reaching out a hand towards my arm.

I shrugged it off.

"Delta and I did your job," I continued. "We almost died a hundred times getting to the Nursery, and now she's trying to save Starship alone, all because you failed."

If my accusations had any effect, Beta didn't show it. She waited till I finished, then frowned.

"I made my choices." Beta pointed the shiv towards the people around us. "They are the evidence I made the right ones."

Before I could argue that, a baby's cry came up from the back. Beta held up her empty right hand and waved it forward. A young man stepped from the shadows holding the crying infant. I recognized it in a snap second: the same baby I'd seen dropped from the Nursery.

And I said as much.

"Then you get it," Beta said. "These are the last humans alive on Starship. I chose to protect them instead of wasting my life attacking the nursery alone."

"But—"

"Damn the Voices," Beta continued, "and their stupid orders. If your programming matches mine, you know keeping the humans alive long enough to see Starship's journey completed is the priority."

The man gave the baby some little toy to suck on and the child stopped its wailing. The other whispers picked up again as Beta spoke, the humans drifting apart.

"They're blocking the exits," Kaydee said. "Don't make them angry, Gamma. Or at least back me up somewhere first."

"You should thank me," Beta said, no smile, no humor in the words. Just straight fact. "Without me coming here, you'd never be awake."

"A coward's argument," I countered.

"The truth," Beta said.

A ringing sound, crystal clear and bright, rang around the room. I found the source off to the left, an older woman holding up a small hollow metal pipe and a short stick to hit it with. Like the other humans, she had on random clothes, but unlike most of the others I saw, she seemed to have an untouchable air.

As if she'd seen far too much to be bothered by ordinary troubles.

"This must be fun for you both," the woman said, "but we have other pressing priorities. Beta, decide, please, whether to destroy these mechs or not."

Beta nodded, tilted her head at me. "Volt, is he corrupted?"

"Not that I can tell."

"Are you?"

Volt laughed, "Would you believe me if I said no?"

"Sure" Beta said. "Alpha sucks at hiding his truth for long. If you're lying, you'll slip, and then I'll carve you up."

"Whatever," I said, echoing Kaydee.

"Perfect," the woman declared. "Go on now, back to your duties. And Chalo?" The woman spoke to a strapping older man hanging off to the left. "Prepare a gathering party. Our new friends may not eat, but the rest of us could use a celebration."

"Of course," Chalo spoke slow, dropping into a shoulder bow.

The whispers turned to full-blown murmurs as the humans broke into action. Most kept their eyes on Volt and I as they went, disappearing into the various rooms. Several dormant furnaces had their vents opened, orange fires starting up in their bowels. Carts on squeaky wheels made their announcements, laden down with scrap for reforging. Chalo's voice broke over the rest, calling for volunteers to head out for a gather.

And all the while Beta stood still watching us.

"You can relax Beta," the bell-ringing woman said, joining our foursome. She swept her eyes over Volt and I, imperious, wrinkled, and unimpressed. "Neither of these two look particularly dangerous."

"A vessel is always dangerous," Beta said. "Even if they don't appear to be."

"Even more when they look like you," I said.

"Stop," the woman said, and to my own surprise, I did. "There are few times when petty spats are appropriate and this is far from one. I take it by your reactions that you did not know we existed?"

"Me and most of Starship," I said. Volt added that he had his suspicions, but his role left them unconfirmed. "Even the Voices said they thought every human alive had died long ago."

"Every human they knew," the woman said. "Now, before we go any further, your names?"

I gave mine, Volt issued his. The woman labeled herself Valentina, or Val.

"I am the last living Starship native. My parents both were natural born," Val said. "I don't say that to demean any other, but to start the story of this small enclave. The ones who formed it so long ago, back when Starship was just beginning its turmoil, are long gone."

Val bid us to follow her as she continued the story, taking some obvious relish in playing tour guide to the undercover village she'd formed in Starship's depths. Volt and I walked apace while Beta fell in behind us.

First we left the forges and headed into another room, one that bore traces of heavy equipment long since moved to make way for scrappy shelters. Tilted metals draped over with cloth formed tents notched into grooves made when shifting that old equipment, at least some of which, I figured, had been broken apart to make the homes. Diodes, these covering a festive color range, hung on ropes giving the whole place a twinkling, cozy feel.

"We split in two," Val continued, "with those in power congregating in Starship's front half. We in back protested, demanded a more equal society and received nothing save orders in return. Comply, handle our trash, and be happy."

"I remember," Kaydee murmured.

She'd been caught up in that conflict. Snared in the progression Val described next, a push from the stronger side to make mechs more aggressive. Kaydee and Leo had been co-opted into the power struggle, ordered to design machines that could keep the restless people in line. Leo followed that logic, assuming Starship's citizens would tear themselves apart if left without constraints provided by a mech with a weapon.

Kaydee felt different. Had died for that belief.

What I didn't say, what I wondered, was whether Leo, my own creator, had injected his beliefs into me. If that explained why, as Val railed against the slow destruction, the retreat of her people down here, I found little pity waiting for either side.

Humans were unreasonable creatures, and yet I had been tasked with keeping them alive.

"We came down here and hid," Val said. "The Junker helped us, protected us. We died out anyway to age and disease."

"Until the Nursery sent you a gift," I said.

"That day was a surprise," Val nodded. "The child came down with other biological waste, funneled through to be re-processed. The Junker snared it, stunned, and gave it to us. More followed, though we never understood why."

I gave that answer as we settled on a central clearing. Several tables, rudimentary plastic things with gray tops and black legs, served as the residential focus. A fake tree, its trunk, branches, and leaves made of scrap, took the absolute middle with glittering force. The thing went floor to almost ceiling. Kaydee gave an appreciative whistle and I joined in.

Void and Beta, for their parts, stayed quiet.

"Another mech gone wrong." Val settled into a stiff folding chair.

"So you've been down here for generations," I said.

"Me?" Val said. "I was born well after the Nursery's first mistake. We've been eking out a living down here, stealing what food we can from the Garden and Starship's leftover stores."

"Why?" I asked. "Why go on?"

The question came unprompted, but I had to understand. A mech would be resolute in attempting its goals until destroyed or re-programmed, but humans didn't seem the same way. They flitted from one idea to the next. They were scared, random, ridiculous.

Even the Voices, supposedly the best humans Starship had to offer, fought with each other. Faced with such chaos, trapped down here in the dark, why would this small group struggle on for so long?

"For the children," Val said, pointing to the two girls and that boy we'd chased, who now chased each other between the tents. "Without the Nursery's gifts and, now, our own natural ones, we would've lost our way a long time ago. Put simply, they give us hope."

"Hope of what?"

"Something better."

"Which is you," Beta said, looking my way.

"Me?"

"The Voices sliced us off." Beta gestured at the encampment. "The connections busted. We're in the dark down here."

"What does that have to do with me?" I asked.

"You're like Alpha, right?" Beta said.

"Don't know if I'd go—"

"Computers. You work with them?"

I shrugged, "Suppose?"

"Then I get you to the right place, you get us back online." Beta took the shiv she'd been holding, flipped it in the air and caught its hilt in the same hand. "Then we get real nasty."

I glanced at Val, "What is she saying?"

"Beta's saying we need to see what Starship is doing, what the Voices are planning," Val replied. "So that we can do what we failed at so long ago, and take this ship for ourselves."

I stood up, shook my head, "Sorry, I came down here to help my dog, then my friend. I'm not joining your little revolt."

Beta grinned. "Cute how you think this is a choice."

"You're so screwed, Gamma," Kaydee said, swinging around the tree, crimson fireworks splashing the air around her.

SIX

EXPEDITION

The right place to restore a connection severed by the Voices was, well, anywhere I could reach those virtual masters. In other words, any terminal that still had a connection to Starship's vast internal network. Those existed—we could've bashed our way into a random apartment with a good chance of finding one—but Beta had a different idea.

After our arrival, Val ordered a small gathering party to head towards the Garden for some fresh food. Beta figured she and I could tag along, providing some extra protection and hitting a terminal on the way back. That way I'd get a feel for the humans, would be able to pitch their argument to the Voices a little better.

Because, as I pointed out in their makeshift town square, the Voices could keep on cutting them off. The issue wasn't so much technical as diplomatic. Talk nice, get your reward.

"Being nice to the Voices doesn't get you anything," Val said as we made our way back to the Forges. Kaydee, off to the side, nodded. "They respect power. That's it."

I thought back to all those movie posters in Leo's apartment where I'd woken up for the first time. Power, according to the popular notion, seemed based in the ability to hurt someone, destroy something. Or in getting others to do it for you. The Voices had power for a long time, but seemed to be losing it now.

Maybe I could strike a deal: give the humans access and, in exchange, they could work together. Hand the Voices a physical presence again.

"Would you be willing?" I asked Val, pitching my idea.

"An alliance with the same group that drove out my ancestors?" Val replied.

Beta, next to her, snorted.

"It would benefit both of you," I replied. "Starship is getting close to its destination. They know how the craft operates and can help you after the landing. Equally, they will need your help fulfilling their mission, the whole point of their existence."

"See," Kaydee said. "Your problem is thinking logically. We don't do that."

Val put a hand on my shoulder, gave me a smile that I imagined she also shared with the small children running around the camp, "Gamma, the Voices will not work *with* us. They will *own* us or they will give us nothing."

"But how will they own you?" I asked. "They're computer programs."

"They will find some way. That is what they do. Convince the Voices to give us access. Say what you have to say to get it done." Val took her hand off, nodded across the forges to a quartet assembling weapons, gear. "That's who you'll be joining. Chalo and his hunters."

"Wait, you're asking me to lie for you?"

"I'm telling you to."

Val gave my shoulder one more pat then walked off back towards the homes. I watched her go until I felt my pack with Alvie inside slip off my shoulders. Volt took the thing off, pulled Alvie from it.

"Figure I'll fix your dog up while you're going out," Volt said. "Don't take too long. My power cores get antsy when I leave them alone."

"You sure you don't want to come?" I asked, less because I thought Volt couldn't handle it and more because the power-shifting mech seemed to be my only ally here.

"So sure," Volt replied. "Good luck!"

Kaydee snickered.

IF, in the aftermath of taking control over the Nursery, I'd felt like I had a handle on Starship and my place within it, the last few hours dissolved that idea into dust. With Beta lingering behind my every step, with Val's order to lie my way to victory, and with Delta gone on a violent quest, I had few friends and little power. I'd been created to serve, and once again I'd been pressed into service.

I doubt I'd have cared, except what I wanted, now, was to help Delta. Stop Alpha. Secure Starship's safe landing so that the humans, flawed as they might be, could spread out onto their new world. Getting the Voices to accept that this small enclave needed network access seemed tangential, at best, to that goal.

"Why do they want to expand?" I asked Beta, stopping before we joined Chalo's group. "Starship seems close to its destination. They risk attention."

"You want to let crazy machines run your home?" Beta replied. "What happens if a mech takes out something critical? Decides to bleed all the oxygen into space because it'd be fun?"

Okay, fair points.

Around us, the forges roared. Humans, most of them younger than Kaydee, worked with metals. Some shaped them into utensils, pots and pans for cooking. Others made what looked like weapons: rudimentary shields, spears. I wasn't sure how they knew what they were doing until I noticed several humans walking from forge to forge delivering instructions.

"They put themselves together well here," Beta continued. "It's not perfect. Space is tight. Humans are human. But the Junker and the old ones set them up well. Dumped knowledge. They'll own this ship eventually."

I thought about pushing Beta's point: makeshift shields and spears weren't going to do much against a violent mech spouting flame, shooting burning laser light. Not to mention a few dozen humans couldn't win out against a hundred, a thousand tireless machines.

Then again, I'd seen what Delta could do. If Beta was half as competent, the two of them together might be enough.

"Chalo," Beta said as we walked up. "You're getting some company today."

"You?" Chalo said, and the chill in his voice had me keep some distance.

"That's right," Beta nodded my way. "This chump too. Gamma. Just a warning: he's useless in a fight."

"Not useless," I said as Chalo squinted at me. "I pick my moments."

"So long as you don't get in the way," Chalo replied, hefting an empty pack. "We're ready enough. Let's go."

The man and the three others—two woman, another man, spanning decades in age—sported a feathery metal weave. Cloth shirts and pants, yes, but over them slanted a bird-like tunic. The feathers looked too thin to provide much defense, but I found the reason as soon as the quartet started moving: the shifting caught and reflected light, making it difficult to focus, hard for me to parse what I was looking at.

"They're playing with your programming," Kaydee said, her own outfit now bearing that same feather tunic, albeit a rainbow version. She walked next to the hunters in front of Beta and I. "You're using functions to figure out what you're looking at, and they're confusing that code. Clever."

"My idea," Beta said, though she couldn't have heard Kaydee. The weaponized vessel didn't sound particularly proud of herself, just stating a fact.

"Does it work well?" I asked.

"No, it sucks," Beta replied. "That's why we keep wearing them."

Sigh.

Chalo led us away from the forges through a short, tight hallway ending in a sealed spiral door, red gem glowing. A small black panel sat next to it and Chalo typed the appropriate code. Flashing green, the door spun open, bringing us back to the Conduit.

Stepping aside, Chalo let two hunters go first. The man and woman unlimbered short, flexible bows and nocked arrows as they stepped out into the mist.

"Where did they get the wood?" I whispered.

"The Garden," Beta replied. I noticed she'd shifted ever so slightly to put herself at my back. Ensuring I didn't run? "Lotta good stuff there."

Beta didn't talk much like Delta and I wondered if Leo had programmed the two differently, or if we vessels had some ability to morph our own make-up. My own thoughts, emotions, ideas had changed since I'd awoken, so perhaps we were more malleable machines than most.

Either way, the point: I couldn't expect Beta to act like Delta in any situation. She was her own self, just as I wasn't Alpha.

Two loud tongue clicks came from the Conduit. Chalo and the other hunter took the sign and ran with it, slipping out quiet. Beta and I followed, the mech whispering that I ought to stay low as we moved.

"Then why don't we have those tunics?" I asked.

"Because if we get attacked, Gamma, we're the bait," Beta replied, and her grin made it clear she didn't mind the role.

Okay, maybe she and Delta weren't all that different.

The route to the Garden hugged Starship's bottom walkway. Off to the left I could look out into the dark pit making up Starship's refuse, left to grow as mechs destroyed each other or themselves up above. Every so often shrapnel would rain down, sometimes followed by a larger mech thudding into a rubble pile and scattering shards.

The noise echoed back and forth, an occasional break from Starship's ever-present hum.

I jerked at the first couple impacts, then settled like everyone else into a silent, single-file walk. Chalo led, the bow-wielding hunters taking up the back, with Beta and I in the middle. Those metal tunics reflected the soft blue light, twinkling like stars.

Beautiful in its way.

We walked for an hour without stopping, a steady, meditative pace. I dug up old memories left behind by the Librarian, that human soul vaporized by Kaydee shortly after I awoke. His remnants held myths, movies, and hard histories, things I wanted to comb through faster but had to snag in bits and pieces. They filled in the human picture, put their actions in context.

Val and her enclave weren't starting some brand new story, they were doing what humans had done for millennia: struggle for power.

But, I had to wonder, she came from the same system that'd produced Starship, that'd evidently so ruined Earth to the point where they launched these wild hopes to the galaxy's edge and beyond.

What would humans be with someone else guiding their first steps?

Another tongue click interrupted my pondering. Beta tapped my left shoulder and I followed her eyes up. A mech, riding a lift down to intersect with our walkway. The machine had arms everywhere, each one with sprayers and wipers. A cleaning mech on its way to service the grungiest level.

Chalo raised his left hand and waved forward. The humans burst into motion, surrounded the lift as it settled into position. A bow-wielder and a close-range hunter—I saw Chalo and his counterpart each had a hatchet, metal welded to a chopped bar to create the weapon—on either side.

Beta kept me back, but when I saw the axes rise, I shook her off and went forward.

"What are you doing?" I asked. The lift opened, the mech took a tentative step out, broadcasting a mild warning to watch out for cleaning sprays. "That thing won't hurt you."

The hunters looked at me, hesitated. Chalo glared, swung his axe and pierced the cleaning mech's power supply, a square lump on the mech's back. With a pitiful whimper, the mech shut down, its arms collapsing around it like so much gray-black hair.

"Search it," Chalo commanded, moving past his hunters towards me.

"Why?" I asked. "What's the point?"

"You do not have any command here, machine," Chalo said, his face a challenging mask, all hard edges and glares.

The man held his hatchet by his waist. I knew my speed, my strength. I could block the arm with my own, snap the man's neck with my other hand and be done with Chalo before Beta could stop me. She'd probably kill me after, so the calculation was pointless, but it made me feel better.

Kaydee's influence, most likely. She'd said her presence would rub off on me, variables infecting my routines with her tendencies.

"I'm not looking for power," I replied. "I'm looking for sense, and I see none of it. That mech wouldn't hurt you or anything else."

The hunters used smaller, gleaming knives to tear apart the mech. Some things, like wiring and the cleaning sprays, they slipped into the packs. The machine's motherboard, its processor too. I looked away, focused on Chalo.

"Yet," Chalo replied, a gnashing, hoarse sound. I supposed they must not get enough fresh water, dry throats and scratchy voices abounded. "Until it gets corrupted like the others. Until it decides a child is dirt it needs to clean."

I would've called him crazy except there wasn't any hint in what I saw. Chalo spoke as someone who'd seen the worst and then some. And, up close, he wore the evidence to prove it. A line in his hair shone a burn's bright pink, and his neck bore scars in a circle that spoke to a choke by something strong and steel.

"Every machine will turn against us eventually," Chalo continued. "Including you. Including her." His look flicked to Beta, who smirked back at him. "We are outnumbered in this war, mech. I will not miss a chance to change our odds, however slight."

Chalo turned his back to me before I could reply, told his hunters to forget the rest and keep moving: the wires, the cleaning spray wouldn't feed anyone.

THE GARDEN EMERGED from the mist, a floor-to-beyond slab crossing the Conduit, save for periodic holes in its many levels. Kaydee told me that those holes used to let traffic stream through, drone messengers and humans on aerial taxis. Now they were overgrown tunnels, plants breaking through the Garden's battered walls hanging down. Moss and mold coated the base where we stood, no doorway on offer this low.

Instead, the humans had bolted on a ladder. As Chalo and the hunters started up, I felt the Garden's wall. The soft wet. On the other side of this would be Purity, the place where I'd first found Alvie, first realized that not every mech on Starship would be a friend.

"After you," Beta said, gesturing with that same shiv.

"Why don't they use a lift?" I asked. "Can't be easy climbing up and down while carrying the food."

"A lift's easier to track, easy to stop," Beta replied. "Most mechs don't have mitts like us. Can't climb worth a damn."

My question answered, I proceeded to use my mitts. The ladder held firm, brought us up to the next level, where a Garden entrance lay. The doorway had been blown apart, or wrenched ajar so that its spiral pieces bloomed out at strange angles. Chalo waved the group through, Beta and I going last again.

On the other side sat the Garden's most arid levels, sandy and filled with cacti and other desert fruits. One hunter started filling her pack with what she could find, tapping a cactus and letting its milk run into a canteen. The other three made for one of the Garden's stairs.

"We go up," Beta said. "This is where things get interesting."

"Good, because I'm getting bored."

"Oooh, so you do have a personality," Beta replied as we scaled dirty steps up to another desert level, albeit one with a few more plants. "Thought you were as dull as this dirt for a minute there."

"She's not wrong," Kaydee said, kicking at the sand.

"I have my opinions," I replied to both of them, trying to sound indignant and, I thought, mostly succeeding. "It's hard to be honest when you've got a knife at your back."

"Poor you," Beta said.

Chalo and his two other hunters went up three more levels, getting to the first one that could be called verdant. A calm field awaited us, crops long since free from their rows but otherwise thriving in the soil. Drier root vegetables were on offer, scooped up quick. When I saw even Chalo filling his pack, I went his way, curious.

"There's better fruits up above," I said.

"Worse threats that way too," Chalo replied, stuffing potatoes into his pack. "No meal is worth dying for."

As someone who didn't need to eat, I couldn't much argue with that. Beta, leaning against the pale blue wall—simulating a clear sky, I believed—near the stair, didn't seem the slightest bit interested. She flipped her shiv up time and again, always catching it perfect. Even so, I had the feeling she kept her eyes on me.

While the hunters foraged, I indulged my own memories, making my way across the clear level to the Garden's center. A top-to-bottom hole sat there, running the Conduit's length and providing the means for water to trickle down from level to level. Not long ago I'd plummeted down this hole, past this level all the way to the reservoir at the bottom.

It looked much the same as when I saw it last, a yawning portal below, and a waterfall mix up above, interrupted by grated platforms, overflowing pools, and other tendrils ensuring proper irrigation. I would've admired it again except for a particular noise, one that stood out above the Garden's natural sounds, the hunter's mild conversation.

A ringing, metal on metal. Irregular, sharp. A sound I'd heard before, delivered in anger, in vengeance.

Delta at work, and not far above.

SEVEN

TRIO

Terminals, network access, the Voices and the humans. All that faded as I heard metal-on-metal. I dashed towards the stairs, leaving Chalo's party to their potatoes and carrots. They didn't need my help gathering food, but Delta might be in trouble.

While I refused to regret going with Volt to find Alvie's battery, the choice put Delta at risk. She'd charged headlong towards danger, confident in her ability to dismantle anything that dared attack her. Normally, she'd be right.

But Alpha wasn't a normal mech.

Up on the list of things I didn't want was a corrupted Delta, purple eyes flaring as she cut down the humans on her way to spearing me on that jagged sword.

"Not another step, dude," Beta said, waving the shiv at me as she leaned on the wall near the stairs. "Don't know what's cooking in your processor, but you better reevaluate."

"Stab me if you want, but I'm going up."

Beta frowned, the first time I'd seen her even a little uncomfortable. I didn't stop moving, sliding around her and heading up the sandy stair. I half expected a knife in my back, but Beta let me call her bluff. Instead, I heard her say something to Chalo, then more feet slammed the steps after me.

I might've looked like a human but inside I had synthetic muscles powered by a bio-electric battery. I could plug in—using that jack—for a power boost if needed, something that could be necessary after I did something decidedly inhuman. Like vault again and again.

My legs kicked into overdrive, no longer going up one step at a time but leaping five or six at once, clearing levels in seconds. I hit landings with brief squats, settling my feet and jumping up to the next. The Garden's environs transitioned, growing wetter and more humid with every level. Sand disappeared, replaced by creeping ivies, molds and mosses. Mushrooms made forays onto the steps, growing in the crannies as their fungal lines marched unmolested.

The next jump landed me in a bush's spreading tangle, a needle cluster I shook myself from to find Kaydee standing in my way. Not physically, of course, but there nonetheless, teal hair shaking with her head, arms folded.

"What're you doing?" Kaydee asked. "Your whole goal is back there, you twerp."

"My goal?" I raised my eyebrows, sculpted dark lines over my eyes, precisely one centimeter thick. "My goal is to prevent Starship from falling apart before it lands."

"Your best way to do that is keeping those humans safe and on your side."

"The best way to keep those humans safe is helping Delta fight for them."

"She can handle herself, Gamma, in case you haven't noticed," Kaydee replied. "But—"

"Why do you care so much?" I pointed back down the stairs, noticed Beta closing fast. No idea what she'd do if the vessel caught me, but I didn't want to find out. "They're not your friends, they want to destroy me and, by extension, you."

"We can change their minds, Gamma. Together."

Now it was my turn to shake my head, push through Kaydee's

projection and jump up the next stairway. My boots slipped on the damp floor, the heat and humidity reaching tropical levels. The fighting continued faster than before, the clanks and clinks echoing through the stairwell.

"They're going to need you," Kaydee said, appearing next to me. "They barely know how to survive, and when Starship lands, they won't know how to use its resources."

I jumped again. Hit a misty level. The fighting felt even with me now. Heading left, I abandoned the plain stairwell for a jungle's mess. Drooping vines cloaked the entry with tendrils concluding in medicinal leaves. Banana trees, squat and prolific, shaded the way forward with their green fruits. And around my feet, various tubers provided an edible, if somewhat stiff, lawn. Everything smelled wet, verdant.

"The Voices can teach them," I answered Kaydee's question.

"You mean the same Voices that cut Val off?" Kaydee replied.

"Once Starship lands, the Voices won't have another choice." I brushed a branch away, getting towards the Garden's center. "It'll be Val or nobody."

"Or it'll be you."

I stopped, "What?"

Kaydee moved in front of me, snapped her fingers. Popping into the air, a tiny Val and her human tribe appeared on one side. On the other, across her reach, appeared the Nursery with its rows upon rows of human vials.

"The Voices can choose you, Gamma," Kaydee said. "They need teachers, a guide. They'll make you raise the first new generation."

I forgot Delta's fighting, stuck on what Kaydee seemed to be saying. That the Voices might decide Val and her people were so wrong as not to be trusted with humanity's future seemed . . . right in line with their motives. Their petty grievances.

"The Voices don't like me much either," I said.

"But like you just said, what other choice do they have?" Kaydee replied. "You're a vessel. Programmed. I know my mother, and she likes control. They'd rather take you than some free-willed woman any day."

A vessel leading the humans into their new world?

I didn't have the straight up ego to declare that'd be the best idea, but, given the options, I might not be the worst pilot for this particular plane. Either way, the decision hadn't been made yet, wouldn't be made for a while.

"Still don't understand why this matters right now," I said.

"Because if you get hurt, if you get taken in there," Kaydee replied. "I don't know what they'll do."

Not very convincing. Certainly not enough to keep me from helping Delta. I kept going, shoving through the plants into the Garden's middle.

And wished I hadn't.

The same plants snarling behind me lay in clumps around the center, hacked apart and flung around. Alloys gnarled in the debris, arms and legs and wheels and who knew what else, all separated from larger bulks sparking, burning, breaking in the makeshift arena. Grease stains marred the green, my nose picking up ozone and burning plants. The hums and churns belonging to sputtering mechs overwhelmed the Garden's serenity, broken only by those ringing clashes as Delta laid waste on the opposite side.

The trail she'd carved looked obvious, a metal death march from my end towards her current position facing a mech. Delta looked little like I'd left her, the death-dealing vessel caked in oils, ash, and juices from burst fruits. None of this stopped her dizzying spins, her perfect rolls, the heel flip off the lead mech—a boxy thing with snapping arms—allowing her blade to sweep up as Delta turned, its edge bisecting the mech up the middle.

Delta landed and hopped back a step, letting two more mechs clamber over their friend's remains. These two looked like snapping hounds, long and lithe, lunging with misshapen, crooked fangs at Delta. As I moved closer I noticed they weren't quite as clean as I'd thought: dogs, yes, but cobbled together with other mech parts. Their bodies belonged to couriers, their legs and paws to shelve-stocking mechs.

"The hell?" Kaydee said beside me, apparently putting aside her earlier protest now that I was in the action.

As I came around the middle hole, one that would lead down all the levels to Purity's watery domain if I jumped, I scooped up a hefty mech arm to use as a club. Not the most effective weapon, but my sheer strength would give it some utility.

"Delta!" I shouted, breaking into a run as Delta, waving her blade before her, backed up from the dogs. "Keep their attention!"

Delta flicked her eyes to me, didn't register any surprise, then snapped a deflecting kick at the left hound. The blow redirected its chomp, the thing's jaws catching air. Its partner tried a leap, taking advantage of Delta's position to jump over her retracting leg, bite going for her face.

My swing caught the thing's curved butt, whacking it towards the middle. The bite missed, but the dog's chest hit Delta, knocking her into a fern tangle. The dog bounced off, hit the same leafy ground, sighted me, and charged back while its brother went in at Delta's neck.

"Home run?" Kaydee asked as I swung again, this time going for broke.

The hound ducked my wild attack, diving forward and nailing my ankles as my swing made a wonderful breeze and little else. My back hit soft ground just like Delta's, the dog keeping up its offense with a quick climb towards my face, gnashing jaws snapping closer.

"You still suck at this, Gamma," Kaydee said as I dropped my club, reached out and grabbed the dog's narrow snout.

Teeth scraped my hands, but I kept hold anyway, pushing against the dog. The mech had grip but I had strength and for a moment we were evenly matched.

"You're not wrong," I muttered to Kaydee, then rolled right.

I pressed with my knees, jutting them into the dog as I moved, pushing the mech off me with the turn. As my right shoulder hit ground, I slipped my hands beneath the dog's jaw and pushed, sending the dog rolling over the middle's edge. Without a howl, without a sound beyond the bangs and cracks, the mech plummeted.

A hand gripped my left, pulled me up. Delta, her own hound a carved-up ruin behind her.

"Thanks," Delta said, giving me a once over. "You don't look damaged."

"You look gross."

"It has been difficult," Delta said, nodding towards the doorway she'd been attacking.

That direction led from the Garden towards the bridge. It should've been clear: when we'd come this way before, Delta and I hadn't faced resistance in the Garden. We hadn't seen mechs like these anywhere at all, in fact.

"I know what you're thinking," Kaydee added, looking at Delta's handiwork. "Leo and I didn't design any of these. No way the Voices made them."

"Alpha hasn't been free long enough," I started, only for a sharp laugh to cut me off from behind.

Beta strode into the room, knives in both hands. She didn't look the least surprised at the wreckage, instead picking her way across while keeping her gaze locked on Delta.

"Alpha's been around a long damn time," Beta said. "He's had room to roam, too. Would've been easy to put this crap together."

"Delta, Beta," I said, stepping back and giving Beta room to join our trio. "Found her."

Delta swept up her sword as Beta came closer, its point angling right for Beta's chest. The long-haired vessel held her knives out wide, a devil's smile gracing her lips.

"Do it," Beta said.

Delta stabbed, a lightning-quick attack that would've had me speared and stuck. Beta, though, swung herself left, pivoting out of the way. The blade snagged and snapped a bandoleer. Beta didn't just dodge, but slammed down with her elbow on the sword, knocking the black-metal weapon towards the dirt. Delta's strike jammed in a plant, while Beta whipped her right hand.

The knife flew, a two meter shot, and Delta caught the damn thing. I didn't see Delta's hand move, but one second she had a two-handed grip on her sword, and the next the vessel had her left hand up, closed around the knife's hilt with its point nearly breaking her eye.

"Hey!" I shouted, striding in between the two.

I didn't exactly want to get stabbed or sliced, but given what lay around us, a pointless fight wasn't going to help anybody. Delta cut me a withering frown but didn't try another attack. Beta just laughed again.

"Are all the vessels crazy?" Kaydee asked, and I couldn't discount the idea.

"Almost," Beta said as Delta withdrew her sword. "Want to go another round?"

Delta flicked the knife back and Beta, just like her counterpart, caught the blade, spinning it through her fingers.

"My fight lies that way," Delta said, nodding towards that same path.

"Cool, good luck with that," Beta replied.

"Wait," I said, feeling like a referee stuck between two rivals. "What do you mean Alpha's been around for a long time?"

"Were you not listening when Val talked down there?" Beta said. As she spoke, Delta drifted a meter away, enough room to swing and strike with her sword. Always ready, that one. "Alpha and I have been tangoing on this ship for decades. The Voices popped me out when Alpha started down the slide to crazy town and we went at it for a long time. Guess they lost patience with me and brought you two in."

Decades?

Alpha had been running around Starship for decades?

"We're here because you failed," Delta said, a totally useful remark that earned her a good glare from yours truly. "Now I get to clean up your mess."

"My mess?" Beta used the knife to pick at her metal teeth. "No, think you have that wrong. Only reason I didn't get Alpha was because I had to protect those meatbags down there. Couldn't very well chase him across Starship and leave them alone."

"They weren't your directive," Delta countered.

"The Voices told me to save humanity, so I did," Beta shot back. "Not my fault it wasn't the humans they wanted."

I coughed. Or rather, simulated the sound of a cough. Hard to do the real thing without lungs.

"Can we get back to the point? Alpha?" I said. "You're saying he could've made these?"

Beta knelt down, poked at a broken mech with her knife, "I'm saying these could've been made at the Fabrication Lines, and Alpha's spent years playing with them."

As she spoke, I remembered all the little rodent mechs that'd swarmed me in the Garden not long after I'd first woke up. Those had been leftovers, but they'd all responded to Alpha's orders. He might've infected them, inserted his own directives into the machines, but how much easier would it be to change it at the source? Replace and remake?

"That's what happened to Alvie," I said. "Alpha didn't have to break free. We left Alvie here alone."

The thought shrank me, burned me. I didn't think I had a human's emotional range, but Leo gave me enough to make the awfulness sting. Had Alvie fought to the last bark in this Garden, alone as Alpha's mechs came swarming in?

Had Alvie called for me?

"Hey," Beta said. "Gamma. We've got a job to do. Let's go."

Delta tilted her head, "You're not coming with me?"

I would've told her why, would've told her what'd happened, but a shout from far below broke the conversation. A human shout, an angry one, calling the hunters to arms.

EIGHT

HUMAN MINDS

Beta had herself halfway to the stairs before, stumbling over sliced vines, she turned back to me.

"Coming?" She asked.

I didn't have a good answer for her. I'd gone sprinting up here for Delta, but the humans down there hadn't exactly made a good impression. Chalo had been icy, had murdered an innocent mech without so much as a blink. My directive pushed me to keep humans alive, but I could massage that command and keep it focused on all the vials in the Nursery.

Val and her tribe weren't the only ones in the game.

"Go," Delta said.

"What?"

"You owe them," Delta continued. "That's what you said."

Beta came back my way, a dead set look on her that had me thinking she'd be taking me along regardless of what I wanted. Such was the downside of working with vessels stronger than myself.

"What about you?" I asked Delta, searching for a way out, an excuse not to go back down.

"I'm going on," Delta replied. "No matter how many mechs Alpha throws in my way, I will find him and finish this."

"Good," Beta said, reaching and taking my right arm. I tried shaking her loose, failed. "You get it now?"

Some fights, hell, most fights, I couldn't win.

"Let's go save the humans, then," I said.

Beta didn't waste time, didn't take the path I'd expected. Instead, claiming we'd waited too long now, she jumped into middle, pulling me along with her over the edge. I swore, screamed, clung to Beta's arm as we plummeted. The fall wasn't clean—we bounced off water-spreading tendrils, splashed through waterfalls, and would've kept going all the way to Purity if Beta hadn't done something ridiculous.

As we fell, Beta whipped a knife down ahead of us. Through windswept eyes I saw the blade sever a tendril's connection to the center. Beta snagged the vine-like construct as it fell, its connection to the Garden proper turning our plunge into a swinging descent down to the next level. Right as we curled parallel to the ground, Beta let go, launching us into chaos.

I had a second to take in the collected hunters, the mechs fighting them. Silver claws slashing, bows shooting, and axes swinging flitted through my vision as I fell, hit the ground, and rolled through vegetable rows. Leaves, dirt, destroyed carrots became my bed and bulwark.

"Ouch," Kaydee said, lying next to me. "Not fun."

"No," I replied, looking up at the painted blue-sky ceiling.

My body indexed itself, reported minimal real damage. Cuts to my synthetic skin pulled themselves together as I sat up, tried to find where to assist. The four humans had themselves surrounded by twice that many mechs who'd backed them into a corner. The two archers speckled the approaching machines, most looking like boxy, sharp-handed terrors, with ineffective arrows: I watched one bounce off, another pierced a mech arm and lodged there, sticking out at an odd angle.

Chalo and his axe-wielding friend swiped in long swings, buying themselves room as the quartet retreated. The mechs didn't seem to be in a hurry, content to let the humans trap themselves before burying the hunters in metal.

Beta wouldn't let that happen.

The vessel didn't share my misgivings about the humans, diving in with a murderous gusto. Beta blitzed by me, arms working as she ran to skewer the mechs from behind with one knife, shiv, and shrapnel piece after another. The throws showered sparks as they hit, all lancing into power packs on the mech's backs, cables and joints on their arms and legs, or into whirring motors. Three mechs lurched to a halt before Beta even reached their line.

Beta launched herself into a kick, her foot striking her own thrown knife and driving it deeper into the first mech's back. She flipped off the machine, thrusting it to the ground, and landed with two more knives already drawn from thigh holsters.

I made it to my own feet.

Two mechs charged Beta, their combined four arms lashing out at her, while the other three quit their slow roll and ran at Chalo's group. Beta went left, launching both knives at the approaching mech, each one biting into its flat middle. When that didn't stop the machine, Beta dashed forward, taking the scratches along her back as the mech attacked.

She put a hand on each knife and tore, splitting the mech open. Flipping the knives to a reverse grip as the machine folded its arms around her, Beta stabbed in, the knives delivering a free release to the mech's processor. It collapsed backward, arms now locked in an unresponsive rigor mortis with Beta in their grasp.

The other mech raised its own arms, looking to take advantage with a smashing pound. I, disproving Kaydee's constant claims about my uselessness in a fight, slammed into the thing. My shoulder charge knocked the mech into one of its damaged brethren, teetering the dead machine over. The rebound put the live mech back my way, its scalloped legs making a slow turn towards me.

I punched the metal thing in its boxy face. Left a dent on the featureless slab.

"Good one, tough guy," Kaydee said. "Looks like he's real scared now."

"Shut up."

I caught the mech's arms as they came in, holding each one with a hand. The mech's clawed fingers grasped for my eyes. One nail grazed my forehead, their pressure getting the mech closer to victory.

So I let the thing win. Fell back, brought up my knees, and planted my feet on the mech's falling body. I kicked with all the muscle Volt's upgrades had given me, let go of the mech's arms, and watched as it flew, flipping over my head and bouncing into the floor's open middle. Not long after a loud splash confirmed the mech's watery grave.

For a brief second I reconnected with the world around me. Conflict's sounds continued, metal on metal bashing away. Chalo shouting for help and sounding like he hated doing so. Dirt clung to me, sticking since I'd gone from the wet upper levels to the Garden's arid basement. The sand rubbed my sharp, refined teeth as I sat up, saw Beta free herself from her mech's dying trap.

Using her knives to sever the grasping arms, Beta kicked off the dead robot and went to Chalo's rescue. The man, flanked by the archers—both without arrows, using their bows to deflect reaching arms—looked pressed by two remaining mechs. One hunter sat off to the side, her axe buried in a mech that'd also buried her.

I lurched that way while Beta went on a whirling assault, stabbing slicing poking piercing the remaining mech pair in such a whirl that the machines collapsed into sparking fluid pools of their own coolant.

My own rescue was less dramatic and less effective.

Throwing the mech off the hunter wasn't too bad, though the mech had enough weight that I didn't so much toss the machine away as roll it off to the side. The human beneath the mech was battered and gashed. Kaydee groaned, popped away while I felt for a pulse that wasn't there.

A hand shoved me aside. Chalo took my place, checking the downed woman's wounds. The other two hunters joined quick, only for Beta to pull them off.

"She's gone," Beta announced. "You'll be dead too if we don't leave now."

"You don't give us orders," Chalo said, glaring back at the vessel.

"She should."

Chalo turned his angry eyes at me and I gave him the same right back. The human might be taller than me, might have more organic muscle on those corded arms, but in a contest of wills, the man had no shot. My backbone didn't come from emotion, but from cold, hard logic. I *knew* I could bend Chalo like a pretzel, and I *knew* Beta had the right call here.

"Pick her up," Chalo said. "Pick her up and carry her with us. She doesn't stay here."

"Don't you dare ask why," Kaydee said when I opened my mouth. "You're not that stupid."

About humans and their nonsensical rituals? I could be. Nonetheless, I followed Kaydee's advice, took Chalo's orders without a rebuff. I picked up the body as Chalo and the other hunters hoisted their packs. Beta snagged the fallen hunter's own harvest and together we hiked from the Garden without another word.

I had to sling the body over my shoulder to descend the ladder, an uncomfortable climb. The humans went first, their chatter replaced by an icy silence. Beta took last place, as ever keeping one eye on me as she went.

"You don't understand, do you?" Kaydee said, floating down next to me.

"About grief?" I replied. "I understand grief. I know loss."

Kaydee shook her head, "Not like this, you don't."

"Then teach me."

"You've seen a thousand mechs get sliced apart, Gamma. Not one of them couldn't be rebuilt. This woman, though? She had a life. She had friends, a family. A little young for kids but who knows now?" Kaydee peppered the air with cartoon images for each remark, rough stick figures. "I bet Chalo and the others lived all those years with her. You've been alive, what, a week?"

I didn't reply, focused on going from one rung to the next. Kaydee had it right. I couldn't identify with what Chalo and the other humans felt, not exactly.

"So what do I do?" I asked, coming around to the real point. "If this continues, Kaydee, there's going to be more like this. Maybe much more."

"Be patient, be kind," Kaydee said.

"Ignore the fact they want to scrap me, you mean."

"For starters," Kaydee replied. "And who knows, if you're not an ass, maybe they won't scrap you in the end."

With that advice I reached the ladder's bottom and we started back towards the Junker's shop, the human settlement. We'd only gone a few minutes along the causeway till Beta called for a halt before a red-gemmed door. The only sign had an address number, a colored flag matching the one near the Junker's door.

"You all go ahead," Beta said. "Gamma and I have some extra work to do."

Chalo gave his pack to another hunter, took the body. He carried the woman gently, as if holding a child, and cradled her to his chest. For a moment I thought he'd say something to me, instead he walked away without a word.

"If they didn't like you before," Kaydee said. "They definitely won't now."

I didn't ask why. The lines tracing the situation were clear enough. I'd drawn Beta after me, leaving the humans undefended. I couldn't have expected a mech ambush, but with Delta fighting up above I should've been able to anticipate more enemies down below.

Or, should I? Was that my job?

"Hey, head case," Beta said. "C'mon over here."

She punched numbers into the keypad next to the door. It swept open, the gem going green. Inside sat a small, sparse apartment. I recognized the layout: it matched the one I'd seen briefly in Kaydee's reset memory, albeit smaller, the kitchen and living room compressed into a single circular space. No table, no chairs, just a few built-in cabinets and blank spots for long lost appliances giving clues.

A single bulb set in the ceiling flipped on when I walked in, washing the place in smoky yellow light. Beta pointed back beyond the kitchen to the bedroom.

"Who's place is this?" I asked as I followed Beta's directions.

"Val's," Beta said. "Or her family's. She keeps this place quiet. Doesn't want anyone hiding here."

"Because?"

"Because humans can be stupid, duh."

Kaydee laughed. "This girl's all over the place. Leo must've done a number on her programming."

"Or maybe she's been living with your species for too long."

I felt a point against my neck as I went into the bedroom.

"Who are you talking to?" Beta hissed.

Without turning around, looking into a near-empty bedroom with a single corner desk and a computer terminal, I gave Beta all she could ask for about Kaydee. About the Minds, the process the Voices put me through. When I mentioned Alpha killed his Mind, Beta snorted.

"Of course he did," Beta said, pulling the knife away.

"What about you?" I asked. "Do you have one?"

Now Beta leaned against the bedroom doorway, ran a hand, knife in it, down that long hair. She smiled, but the ends twitched, as though unsure whether to slip into a frown or a manic grin.

"I've been awake a long time, Gamma. If I had a Mind, I don't anymore." Beta glanced at herself. "Or maybe I do, maybe I am my Mind, or it's me. They do that, don't they? Leave traces within you?" She stood, pushed me towards the terminal. "Better get the humans back online before you stop being you, Gamma. Could happen any minute now."

I . . . did not know how to react to that.

Kaydee popped in as I approached the terminal, Beta again at my back. She shook her head fast, little furious red 'No's appearing in the air around her. I ignored her, focused on the computer. Folding my fingers together, I used the port and jacked-in.

Kaydee would be waiting for me inside. Together, we'd find the missing link keeping the humans in the dark and flip it back on.

And the whole time, I'd be wondering when I'd cease to be me.

NINE

THE WEB

The Junker's digital world had been a dim one filled with misplaced files and mess: Val kept her computer clean. I dropped into a calm sanctuary, bright pearl walls dotted with labeled soft blue doors. A stained glass rooftop dazzled the tiled floor at my feet with purples and yellows. Options ranging from documents to databases waited for perusing behind those doors, though I eschewed them all for the arched entry at the far end.

Network, blazed on in white-gold lettering above the door, gave me the clue.

"Think this is the nicest world I've been in," Kaydee said, popping in next to me. "So tidy."

"Wish mine was like this," I added as we walked. "Instead, I get crystals everywhere."

"Code can be changed, you know," Kaydee replied.

I imagined humans could, if they sank deep within their own thoughts, take an honest look at the things that made them tick. Their habits, their urges, their instincts. For me, though, venturing deep led me to a black hole, a darkness I couldn't penetrate. Leo walled that part off, kept me from rewiring my own circuits except through the very, very tedious process of living a life.

"How?" I asked. "Val did all this manually. Someone would need to re-arrange my code, my functions to look like this."

"I could do it."

I stopped, glanced at Kaydee to confirm she was being serious, "You didn't say you could access those parts of me."

"It would take time, but I'm a little virus in your guts, Gamma," Kaydee snapped her fingers and versions of me appeared in the space around us. One sat down, staring up towards the ceiling and rubbing his chin. Another broke into a run, snarling at imaginary enemies. A third started to dance, arms and legs moving in rapid sync to a song only he could hear. "We could make you into whatever you want to be."

I frowned at the eclectic examples, "Won't I become you?"

"You'll be flavored with me, if we stay together long enough," Kaydee said. "Guess it's not much different from humans, really. Everyone gets touched by their relationships."

"Sure . . ." I looked back at the Network door. "Do me a favor and leave my guts alone, will you?"

"Don't trust me?"

"If those are your examples, then no, I don't trust you."

Kaydee joined my walk. I embraced the steady footfalls without mechs chasing me, humans glaring at me, or Beta holding a knife to my back. Once again the digital domain proved a refuge, although a temporary, alien one. The bounds within Val's terminal were rigid: unlike when I'd hacked into Delta or even the Junker's computer, Val kept her routines tight, her files organized. Beautiful, yes, but a prison of sorts for one like me.

Beta and Gamma had been designed for physical prowess. They made art with their weapons, their cutting, slashing dances. I could stumble around and throw my fists, but this was my arena. Ones and zeros, functions and variables. As fast as Delta could throw a sword, I could wave and—

The door stood before us, the walk ending in an instant.

"Ready?" I asked my friend.

"Let's keep this ride rolling."

"Indeed."

The blue door didn't have a handle, but the narrow black line splitting its center suggested a push so that's what I gave it. The door resisted. I shoved harder, received the same response.

"Nothing?" Kaydee asked.

"It seems determined to stay shut."

But just because a door didn't want to open didn't mean it couldn't be done. I took a closer look along the door's edges, all flushed tight with Val's perfect walls. Nowhere to get a grip, no flaws in the code. If the Voices had built this block, they'd done it well enough that no ordinary user would get around it.

I, proud master of the digital domain, was no ordinary user.

First I went for brute force, a deconstructive attack meant to probe the door, see if a particular section would be vulnerable. A hatchet, its edge branded with numbers, letters, functions, appeared in my hand and I swung it at the door. At the top, the middle, the bottom. I tested the edge, attempted to break the middle.

Every strike left nothing behind, no change from before.

"Guess they're smarter than you," Kaydee jeered.

"Preventing the simplest solution is not smart, it is required," I replied.

"Cybersecurity expert now?"

"Are you just going to be annoying, or can you help?"

Kaydee shrugged, looked at the door, laughed. "Should've realized what we were staring at." When I looked at her, questions made plain on my face, she sighed. "Guess who's on the Voices?"

"Who?"

"Leo, my friend. He's the only one in that group who knows anything about programming. If my mother wanted Val isolated, Leo would've been the one to do it."

"Which means?"

Now it was Kaydee's turn to give me the exasperated stare, "Do you, like, always need someone to connect the dots for you?"

"I could try, but why risk misinterpreting when you're right here?"

"S'pose there's a certain logic to that." Kaydee turned back to the door. Her left hand now held a marker, and with it she drew a yellow line on the door. Not a square or a circle, but a crest that I'd seen before. "Get it yet?"

Starship's sole University had its own decal, and now its space-ship-styled diagram sat on the door. When I'd visited the University on my haphazard trip to Starship's bridge, I'd seen Kaydee and Leo walking its corridors, going to classes. Flashbacks from Kaydee's own memories.

And a link to the protections Leo might use to seal off a computer terminal.

"Starship keeps its network wide open," Kaydee said, drawing some numbers, letters within the spaceship outline. "The original builders made it as a hedge against some dictator, I think. So if you want to shut off a section you had to get clever."

When Kaydee filled in one last area, she withdrew the marker and all the yellow lines seemed to seep into the door. The blue wood flashed once and I saw the frame loosen, the door breathe as if set free.

"Leo designated this computer for tests," Kaydee said. "A university block that keeps it from accessing Starship's network."

"And you removed it how?"

"Told it the test was over." Kaydee wiggled the marker. "It's a simple passcode to enter from in here. Outside you'd need to get someone to wipe and reset the whole machine. Or someone from the university to use their credentials."

"Hard to do that when everyone there is dead or a mech."

"Told you, Leo's not stupid."

I pushed on the door. Without friction, without sound, the door swept inward, revealing a tangled web at vast odds with what we'd seen so far. Filaments in earth tones crossed and circled one another, vanished into a dim beyond stretching in every direction save back towards us.

Tiny ruby motes followed the lines, bouncing along on indecipherable treks through the endless weave. Starship's network laid bare, a billion points scattered throughout the mammoth craft, tying them all together. A program smart enough could parse the web, send its message right where it needed to go.

"Eww," Kaydee said. "This is, like, the worst way to visualize the Internet."

"Why?" I asked. "I think it's beautiful."

"I hate spiders."

"How can you hate spiders when you haven't ever seen one?"

"Movies, Gamma. Games," Kaydee shuddered. "Back when I dreamed, I'd have so many nightmares."

"Then perhaps your current existence does have some advantages?"

Kaydee took a step back, either contemplating my idea or realizing that she hadn't actually slept in a very, very long time. I too retreated, less because of some philosophical quandary than because the Internet was reaching out. The web, without the doorway holding it back, spread into Val's pristine church. Tendrils leached out over the tile, making their way to those other blue doors and prying them open, one by one.

I stepped over to where Kaydee had taken refuge, off to one plain side the tendrils had thus far left alone. Together we watched as Val's computer rejoined Starship's network, those ruby motes blipping fast back and forth.

"I'd almost call it amazing if it wasn't so terrifying," Kaydee said.

"Then I will call it amazing for you," I replied. "So will I become afraid of spiders like you?"

"I don't know, Gamma," Kaydee said. "I really don't. And don't be offended, buddy, because I like you and all, but I don't wanna be you."

"No offense taken." I put a hand on Kaydee's shoulder as we watched the web grow. It messed with Val's pristine setup, coating the tile in its strands, blackening the walls as it crept into every part of her computer. "I don't want to be you either."

"Cool." Kaydee shivered. "Can we leave now? I like the Internet, but this is getting real weird."

"Of course."

In a blink Val's virtual world disappeared and I stood before the computer, its screen cheerily proclaiming the Internet's return. Beta, leaning against the bedroom's wall, nodded at me as I turned. As ever she held a knife in one hand, flicking it up into the air and catching it.

"Nice job, kid," Beta said. "Now Val and Chalo might kill you quick instead of real slow."

TEN

MECH MANAGEMENT

Eighteen left. Beta gave the number as we left Val's apartment, the vessel careful to seal the door after we'd stepped back into the Conduit. Eighteen humans with enough skill and stamina to serve as hunters, warriors, fighters. There were closer to fifty among Val's group, but most were either too young or too broken to go on excursions.

"Too broken?" I asked as we walked along that walkway, the Conduit's debris-ridden base to our right.

The constant blue mist cloaked us as we moved, water droplets beading on my skin. The moisture cooled me down while making the air itself thicker, explaining why Chalo and the others didn't wear warmer clothes. With all those forges running, the humans had to be hot.

"Those mechs in the Garden were new and nasty," Beta replied. "But they're not the only dangerous ones. At first this whole side of Starship crawled with crap, most of it willing to tear a wandering human apart."

"Programming gone wrong?"

"Cut loose, corrupted, who knows," Beta replied. "By the time I came down here things were real grim. Val and the others huddled among the food, trying to survive."

"They don't seem to love you for it."

"I'm not asking for their love, and you shouldn't either, because you definitely won't get it."

"You're talking like this is my fault. I didn't make you leave Chalo. You didn't have to follow me."

Beta's knife had its point at my throat in an instant, pressing in. I refused to let it phase me, suppressed the urge to fight back, run. By now I'd been so close to death the idea didn't carry much weight. Worse, by far, would be corruption, changing into something I was not.

"You don't have any friends here, pal," Beta said. "Be careful making more enemies."

"I've been alone before," I replied. "I can be alone again."

And, in truth, I didn't feel bothered by the idea. As much as I'd wanted to come down here with Volt, find the humans, the experience hadn't been a great one. Beta might have an uncompromising loyalty to Val's tribe, but I sure as hell didn't. Every interaction seemed tainted with anger, suspicion, fear. I'd trade all that for a solitary search for Delta in a second.

Beta didn't offer a reply, we two resuming our walk back to the human's home. Starship remained its humming, churning self, the occasional debris sprinkle coming down from above. Otherwise no lifts descended, no mechs harassed us. I attributed that last fact to Beta's efficiency, not to the human's abilities.

I stayed behind Beta as we went into the Junker's warehouses. Just in case, as Beta put it, Chalo convinced the other humans my head was the only worthy payment for the dead hunter. Beta figured she could give me a few seconds to run away.

A comforting thought.

Instead we found the boy from before standing watch. His eyes were downcast as we approached and went past the door. When Beta prodded him on where the others were, the boy took a sigh far too heavy for someone his age.

"Saying goodbye."

Kaydee obliged my questioning thoughts with a rapid-fire presentation, all displayed off to the right as Beta and I went towards the forges, of how humans had said goodbye in history. Burials, cairns, and burnings all seemed unwise on Starship: there wasn't really dirt to bury someone, and lighting a body on fire seemed liable to pollute the ship's air when it wasn't necessary.

"Right," Kaydee said. "That's why we kick them into space."

A ceremonial ejection through an airlock, the body set to journey through the cosmos for eternity. Even when the body found a star or a planet to suck it in, the resulting cremation would sprinkle the person into a new world.

A nice goodbye.

Val and the others embraced this idea, and we found them with the hunter laid out on a transport sled, one made for moving scrap. They'd put a simple shroud over the hunter, one woven, it looked like, from large leaves. The Garden once again providing. Cloth, I figured, would be too valuable to send off ship.

We didn't advance beyond the camp's doorway, instead pausing to listen as various people stepped up and told stories of the hunter's life. A pleasant eulogy, one I wouldn't mind for myself, though I wasn't sure who would tell those stories. Delta?

"Oh, I'd do it," Kaydee said.

"But if I go, you're likely gone too," I whispered back.

"No, no," Kaydee said. "You're not allowed to die until I get out. That's the rules."

"Uh huh."

I felt a tug on my back leg as the ceremony continued. Turning around, looking down, I saw bright mechanical eyes, a short body, and four legs ending in sharp claws. Alvie, alive and sensible enough to keep himself quiet. I couldn't resist a smile and, together, we moved away from the humans, Alvie dragging me along. I felt Beta's eyes on my back, but she didn't follow.

The dog led me back through the forges—quiet now, the big space lit only by those blue diodes—and towards the food stores. Waiting there, eyes glowing an island blue, stood Volt.

"Was about to head back on up when this one here scampered off," Volt said as I approached. "Figured it had to be you, the way the little mech was excited."

Alvie looked from Volt to me, eyes flashing a delighted orange. Claws tapping on the tile. The thing's little tail wagged fast, hitting my leg without a care.

"The battery works," I said. Not the most brilliant thing, but I wasn't sure how to share we'd fought a bunch of mechs in the Garden, that a hunter had died, and Delta was set on her murder path. "Going home?"

"Been gone long enough." Volt lifted, planted his feet. "And these humans don't make a mech feel especially welcome."

Couldn't argue with him there.

"Mind if I go with you?" I asked.

"Mind? I'd welcome the company." Volt's eyes slid to a suspicious yellow. "You do something to those people?"

"I'll tell you on the way."

Despite my words, though, Volt and I walked in silence. Alvie padded along beside us as we left the Junker's scrapyard, found a lift, and shot back up to Volt's preferred level. I spent the time immersed in my own thoughts, playing emotions against each other. The humans had me feeling angry, annoyed, and I wanted to pin down why.

If the idea was to save them as a species, then I shouldn't feel so much ennui. I should've been scurrying back, apologizing to Val for the lost hunter and asking what I could do next to help them. I should've been looking over the forges to help them improve their products. I should've been standing by Beta, a duo working to help the humans achieve what Starship had been built for.

"I know what you're feeling," Volt said when I started sharing my doubts.

"You do?"

"I might not have the emotional range you vessels got," Volt said, "but I'm not a rock either. You've been treated like a mech, my friend."

"What?"

"Think about it," Volt replied as our lift climbed up towards the blue, the mist again beading my skin with droplets. "Since you've been awake you've called your own shots. Made your own decisions. Now you meet Val and she's ordering you around like you don't have a say in your existence."

I stared at Volt, his eyes light green now. "That's . . . astute."

"I told you I'm not a bunch of fried circuits," Volt clomped a foot on the lift. "Junker did the same thing to me when I met him. Other humans too way back when. Telling me I needed to do this. Needed to do that. Gave me tasks expecting me to manage them."

"And you did?"

Volt raised his hands, clacked his thin, nimble fingers together, "These babies worked their magic for the humans, sure. You gotta understand how to survive on this ship, Gamma. You're not Delta and Beta, you can't fight your way through, so sometimes you have to do what someone tells you to. But it doesn't feel good."

"It doesn't." I looked at my hands. Not quite as satisfying to press my synthetic fingers together. No clicking. "What should I do?"

Volt laughed, a mechanical chirp. "How should I know? I follow my programming, kept following it after the humans got themselves killed. Best I can offer is, your dog's here now, might want to go check in on your other friend."

"That's what I was thinking."

"See? Back to calling your own shots already."

The lift settled in and we stepped off, headed towards Volt's power station. Delta would be in this direction too.

"What happens if Val and the humans win?" I asked Volt as we walked. "Will you follow their orders?"

Volt's eyes went blue. "At the end of it all, we're mechs, Gamma. That's what we were made to do."

I dropped Volt off, the Conduit dimming its lights to their night-time routine. It'd been one helluva day, going from the Nursery, meeting Val and Beta, the Garden and now back here. On my right sat that Nursery, its red-gemmed doorway guarding all those lives. All those humans who hadn't yet been stained by Val's bitterness, by Chalo's bloody experience. Would those tiny seeds treat us differently?

"What're you saying?" Kaydee asked, appearing on the Conduit beside me.

"I'm saying there could be other ways forward. We don't have to take Val's path."

"Because she hurt your feelings?"

I glanced at Kaydee. Despite the Conduit's dim lighting she stood bright, a benefit of being digital. She had a simple sweater with its hood pulled up over her head, though that did nothing to shrink her intensity. I copied the human expression and folded my arms.

"I'm a mech," I said, throwing a lilt into my voice like Kaydee did. "I don't have feelings."

"Sorry, I thought I was talking to an adult." Kaydee reached out, grabbed my wrists, and while she couldn't actually move me, I let her pull guide my arms.

Kaydee angled my arms straight out, palms facing up. She tapped each one in turn and a light green moss grew from her touch. All fake, but beautiful nonetheless. The moss on either hand rose into a tiny mound, then stopped.

"Cute, right?" Kaydee asked.

"Not bad."

"Okay, grumpy," Kaydee replied. "Now over here," she pointed to my right hand, "we have Val and all those humans you hate so much." I nodded and she pointed to my left hand. "Here's all those vials you're talking about. Let's say this all goes well. Delta takes out Alpha in a big mech battle. The Voices land Starship." Kaydee tapped Val's moss and it grew again, a small stalk peeking out, stretching its green frond upwards. "Val has the head start, so she takes her crew out. You protect your vials. Get those nurses to make all kinds of perfect human babies for you."

My friend tapped the other moss, my moss, and another frond, this one a purple-red, poked forth.

"Time passes, and maybe it's days, maybe it's months, maybe it's years," Kaydee said, and as she spoke, both stalks grew, both spread green tendrils around, some towards each other.

"They interact," I said. "Is that your point?"

"One of'em," Kaydee replied. "Guess what happens when they do?"

"What humans have done all their lives. Fight each other."

"Maybe." Kaydee whipped a finger through the tendrils, drawing each plant closer together. "Val doesn't have too many though. Odds are they try to form an alliance. Odds are they get your little friends to take a look back through Starship's history. Views change." Kaydee poked me this time. "You're a great mech, Gamma, but you're a mech. Something so different from us. Any humans you raise might love you, might respect you, might follow you, but they will know you aren't like them, and when the time comes . . ."

Kaydee tapped the purple-red stalk and the whole plant withered, died. The moss along with it. Together, both crumbled to dust while Val's stalk grew into yellow-flowered brilliance.

"You're saying I don't have a choice," I replied, shaking off the plant and letting Kaydee's little visual play fade away. "No matter what I do, the humans get to control me."

Kaydee had her head shaking before I'd finished. "Look at us, Gamma. Look at us."

I squinted at her, "And see what?"

"We're partners, you and me," Kaydee replied. "That's what you need. Don't run from Val. Help her, but hold your own. Get her to see that you're not an enemy, but you're not just a tool either."

"Is that something you know how to do?"

"Let me think on it," Kaydee said. "I'll dig around in all the crap you've got stored in here, see if I can't figure out some more about what happened to her. You go on your hunt or whatever."

My hunt or whatever. Kaydee always had a way with words.

I felt a paw, heavy and sharp, on my leg and looked down to see Alvie waiting there. The dog had his metal head tilted, jagged and uneven teeth poking out around his lips. Kaydee disappeared, leaving us alone on the walkway.

"Ready to go on a walk?" I asked the dog.

Alvie wheeze-barked. A sound I hadn't heard for too long. I reached down, patted the puppy's head.

"Go find Delta," I said, and when the dog broke off running towards the Bridge, with all Starship's disasters between here and there, I followed.

ELEVEN

MY HUMAN AND I

Kaydee and I were getting ahead of ourselves. Humanity's ultimate fate wouldn't rest on my decisions unless a whole lotta other things fixed up in my favor. One of those being Alpha's return to captivity or his destruction. Another being the Voices and their control over Starship. Who knew what powers or tricks they might have waiting for me?

Catching up to Delta meant walking along the Conduit. Its night-time flair took effect, the blue fading away for a starlight silver, old signs illuminating and filling the dim with colorful displays. The railing on my left embraced the diode lifestyle, twinkling yellow as I ran along.

On my left the Conduit's middle grew crowded as I hit the Park district. Delta and I had dueled with a madcap fountain mech deep in there, one that'd been tasked with taking Volt's Power Core. I'd nearly been squashed flat while Delta carved up smaller mechs by the dozen, my saving grace an open port in the fountain mech's base. Not an experience I wanted to repeat.

But an easy one to remember.

As I went, Delta's prior passage along the same route left its evidence everywhere. Broken mechs, both from our first trip and new sparking remnants from earlier that day crowded onto the path. I skipped and jumped over the wreckage. Everything from box-like trash mechs to more svelte messengers had been carved, their bits flung all across the Conduit.

The Park itself, at least, looked serene. The lighting deep inside the trees and small amphitheaters flickered with time's decay, gracing the Conduit's gray with ephemeral shimmers. Enchanting, quiet. I'd seen flashes of Kaydee and Leo walking its trails last time I'd come this way, having fun.

Would I ever get to do the same?

The Hospital came next, a massive facility stuffed with horrors. Like the Garden, the Hospital spanned the Conduit, going up and down for many levels. Unlike the Garden, its floors weren't stuffed with flowers and fruits. They'd housed murderous mechs, a huge healing collective turned dangerous by coding defects and, as ever, time.

I approached the Hospital's entrance slow, saw its doors broken open. Telltale cuts sliced the big double-sliding portals apart, leaving easy access to a hallway long since turned to a graveyard. The dead mechs here were older, left behind from our last excursion. On the tile floor—here as bright as day thanks to the Hospital's ever-on lights —I could follow a long scratch from one side to the other: Delta's blade dragging along.

She curved the line through the dead mechs on the floor, slicing off bits and bolts here and there.

"Well this is grim," Kaydee said as I went through.

"Delta has a purpose," I replied. "This is what she does."

"I'm just gonna remind you that you're a mech too."

"So if the humans don't kill me, she might?" I replied as we both hopped over a hall-filling mech meant to shuttle drugs from one spot to another. "I'm surrounded by enemies?"

"Yeah, that about covers it."

"And what should I do, Kaydee? Hide? Run?"

"Getting a weapon might help, for starters."

For all her sarcasm, her introspective convulsions, Kaydee did have a point. I so often forgot the physical side of fighting. I had my fists, the wires and metal powering them, but just about anything would be a better offense. My clothes, too, had all the defensive properties of cloth: comfortable and easy to cut through.

So I kept my eyes open as we went. Caught something shiny, red. Still together.

"What about this?" I asked Kaydee, pointing to the fire extinguisher.

"Use it as a club?" Kaydee asked. "Seems like you."

I pulled on the cabinet, found it locked. Tugged harder and the door popped off. I set the door down, leaning it against the hallway wall, glass intact. The extinguisher came off easy, I took one hand and held the thing by the top, Kaydee warning me about the firing pin.

"See?" I said. "Ready to face destiny."

"Sure are," Kaydee made some popcorn, tossed it in her mouth. "Can't wait to see how this goes."

We didn't have to wait long. The Garden didn't sit much beyond the Hospital and my jog brought us there fast. Delta's mech trail continued, cluttered enough now that I didn't so much run as hop, every leap carrying me over cut-up junk. Some mechs remained alive, their heads tracking my approach. A couple offered warped greetings, their voice processors scratching the sound. These mechs couldn't move, couldn't attack or fix themselves.

They would lie there until their batteries ran dead, until someone decided to salvage their parts. Alvie would stop, sniff at the things until I called for him to come on.

"Like I said," Kaydee muttered while we hiked through the Garden's greenery. In the night, flowers glowed blue and purple, an ambiance enhanced by the running waterfall. "It's a little messed up."

"They were going to kill Delta if she didn't destroy them," I said.

"I seem to recall you had some nuance," Kaydee replied. "She's just gutting them all."

"I could recode one or two, perhaps," I said. "But not this many."

More, the mechs we passed now matched the ones I'd seen in the Garden last time. The dogs, the flexi-mechs with grabby claws. These were all Alpha's creations, his new swarm. Whether I could pacify them as I had some of the others . . . Alpha had nearly obliterated me the last time I'd tried to hack his work, change his programs.

"So you're scared," Kaydee said. "You don't mind Delta doing things the hard way because you think Alpha's going to mess you up."

"He did mess me up, if you recall."

"If I recall? Hard to forget. But you were just a baby vessel then. You're all grown up now."

"A few days is all it takes, huh?"

"That's all you get, Gamma."

We left the Garden, back on Starship's upper-crust side. Here the mech fighting had been worse because, well, they had more mechs over here. Shops and homes looked battered up and down the Conduit, with broken signs and punched-through doorways. Scratches and gashes marred the walls. Sparking wires leaked out here and there, flame spitting up whenever the embers found something to bite.

Worse, I caught that particular sound again. The clashing, clanging, ringing of Delta finding a fight. Up ahead this time and, with a squint, visible. Alvie and I ran, the fire extinguisher banging off the railing.

The vague figures became a metal mash-up as Alvie and I closed. The causeway clogged with destroyed debris. Mech bodies everywhere, all kinds. Most didn't look dangerous, walking trash bins or clean-up mechs with brushes. All were sliced, broken.

Delta waded her deadly way through an endless mech sea.

We caught up to her, blade singing as she swept it back and forth. Mechs filled the gaps, pressing forward with too-slow attempts to grab the vessel. Beyond her, the robots stretched all the way down the

Conduit towards the University and the Bridge. Others rode lifts up and down to our level, joining the steady flow marching to their deaths.

Though the assault wasn't without successes. As we neared I saw gashes along Delta's body. Tears in her clothes, her arms and legs not moving as fast as I remembered. She was a mech too, reliant on circuits and a constructed skeleton to keep her going. A battery that would get tired moving, fighting without rest.

"Gamma!" Delta called, catching me in her eye as she completed a vicious two-handed swing, cutting the legs out from three approaching box mechs. "Get in here. We're close!"

I hesitated, Alvie barking at the mechs. Delta wasn't close, we weren't close. We'd have to slaughter an army to make the Bridge . . .

"Isn't there a better way?" I asked, staying several meters behind Delta. No sense getting in the way of those sword swings. "There's so many!"

"Alpha's putting them here," Delta said. "It's them or us, Gamma."

The vessel stabbed straight, bisecting a big cleaning mech and sending its halves shuddering apart. Two quicker messenger mechs darted underneath, their cigar-style bodies getting them through the rubble. As Delta tried to pull her blade free, it stuck on the bigger mech, giving the smaller ones a free shot.

Alvie burst past me. The dog intercepted the attacking robot on the left, barreling the thing to the ground.

I threw the extinguisher, the cylinder tumbling through the air and connecting with the rightward messenger mech. A bang, then a huge white cloud as foam and dust sprayed everywhere. Delta stumbled back, forcing the sword out. I couldn't see the next mech wave beyond the cloud, couldn't see Alvie either.

"How long have you been fighting?" I asked, coming up beside Delta. "This whole time?"

"Wasn't keeping track," Delta replied.

"How's your energy?"

"Enough," Delta hedged. She put an arm out, pressed me back on my chest. "If you're not going to fight, Gamma, then leave so I don't have to worry about you."

Another mech stomped through the white cloud, this one a spindly shelve stocker. Alpha must've tweaked its code because the mech used its too-many arms to snag parts on the ground and launch them at Delta. The vessel ducked one, rolled past a second to close the distance. She took a third straight to the stomach as she rose, Delta refusing to flinch as she swept the jagged black blade up, taking arms with the broad swing. I caught the glint as the thrown shrapnel buried itself into my friend. Saw the mech swipe at Delta with its remaining arms, battering her, knocking the sword out wide.

Alvie flew into the mech's back, piling it forward past Delta, who recovered and delivered a fatal piercing to the mech's middle. The thing's power supply broke open in an orange-yellow spark fountain as the machine folded over.

More mechs came. There would always be more.

"We have to run!" I said. "There's no winning this!"

"There's no other option," Delta replied, squaring herself up for the next wave.

"She really does have a death wish," Kaydee said, popping in next to me. "Leo did a number on you all."

"I'm not leaving her," I said, heading to the fallen shelve stocker. Its arms weren't perfect, but they'd be better weapons than nothing. "If the mechs take her, who knows what Alpha might do."

A fully corrupted Delta rampaging around Starship would be a nightmare. Val and her little camp would find themselves carved up just as fast as these mechs. Even as I tore off a suitable arm, I started to reckon with a different idea.

If Delta wouldn't stop fighting, if we couldn't win, then I couldn't allow her to fall into Alpha's hands.

"Real grim, Gamma," Kaydee said as Delta and Alvie took on another mech trio.

I didn't answer. Rose with my new arm club and looked at the latest evisceration. Noticed something else, too. A familiar red-gemmed glow. A spiral door and a number next to it so seared into myself that I couldn't not recognize it: Leo's apartment.

My home. Our home. Only a few meters ahead.

I charged into the fight, swinging my newfound club with both hands. I struck the nearest mech, a thin, wheeled serving robot, and sent it flying over its friends towards the bridge. A whistle from Delta had me ducking so her long sweep could clip over my head without taking it, the shrapnel from her slice sprinkling my cheeks, burning my hands.

Not that I cared. Instead, I shouted for us to go on, fight forward, and Delta bit hard on the bait. She and Alvie joined my advance, the three of us charging into the mech line. Cutting, beating, biting, we moved with a speed mechs designed for household maintenance couldn't match. Even so, every time my clubbing blows mashed a processor or crunched in a power source, I winced.

These were all innocent machines, pushed into a role they never desired by faulty programming or full-on corruption. None deserved this death, but here I was, delivering it anyway.

At least I hadn't yet reached the human's level, destroying peaceful mechs just because. A moral high ground I clung to as we battered ourselves one centimeter forward at a time. Until, off to the right, that red-gemmed refuge sat next to us.

"In there!" I called. "We can buy ourselves some time!"

"No," Delta's response came quick, clean. "We keep pushing. There's no stopping now, Gamma."

Delta kicked forward again, ready to cleave more metal. I watched her move, saw Alvie, the dog bearing his own scratches, dents now, going along with her. How many more waves would we last?

I dashed to the door, punched in the code resting in my memory. The door flashed green, opened. Delta shouted another victory cry as I looked at the dark, movie-poster coated hallway leading into Leo's place.

Our haven.

Delta backed up a step, swishing cords free from her blade. Alvie bounded to me when I waved at the dog. I told him to stay close, to keep us safe, and went up to Delta. Beyond her, the next mechs came slow, clomping forward with a steady, unending rumble.

"Please," I said.

"This, Gamma, is what I was borne to do," Delta answered. She stuck her sword out, blade pointing at the closest mech. "You're next!"

She took one step forward, locked into a suicidal course.

So I pinched my fingers together, and jabbed them into the port behind her right ear.

TWELVE

DIGITIZED

The last time I'd hacked Delta, it'd been to kick out an interloping mech. The Nursery's nasty supervisor had its claws in my friend, busy rewriting her from the inside-out. Kaydee and I dove into Delta's fractured insides, arranged as floating platforms adrift in an orange, rocky void, and fought to free her.

This time I fought to turn her off.

I stood again on a pale sandstone island, loose chains angling out and connecting to Delta's other programs, each one a critical piece helping her swing that sword, see those mechs, and decide they all had to die. I needed to pick the right chain that'd take me to Delta's core, and from there disable her.

And do it fast enough so the mechs outside didn't turn us to mulch.

At least I had time on my side. In the digital plane, things happened at light speed, decisions and motions instantaneous as variables flipped, functions ran. No need for nerves to connect with muscles to move.

"Boy, I'm so happy to be back here," Kaydee said, taking a deep and wholly unnecessary breath beside me.

The air tasted of embers, a quiet heat pressing in around us. Delta wasn't interested in paradise. Or, rather, Leo decided not to give her one.

"Trying to save our lives," I replied. "Which way, you think?"

"We could split up?"

I frowned, "Going to guess Delta's not thrilled we're in here. She'll be looking for us."

"Someone always is."

Kaydee's nonchalance killed my frown. The early terrors we'd experienced in Starship had forged a new attitude in us both. A bland acceptance: danger was our lot, at least for the moment.

Without an obvious clue in the world around us, I went for a cheater's route. Tapped into the code, tried to find a path, a function that'd guide us where we needed to go. The island we stood on was a program, yes, and those chains tied it to others. Each one a link, forming a directory.

Go far enough up the directory, to the very first island, and we'd probably find the core. Or, at least, a way there. I executed the idea, ran the script—a sensation not unlike a daydream—and one of our island's three chains glowed a cerulean blue.

"That you?" Kaydee asked.

"That's so me," I replied. "Let's go."

Together we went for the chain, our feet bouncing off the limestone like it was a cloud. Gravity and other physical laws had the most tenuous of connections here, our bodies instead going where we wanted them to. The first time it felt confusing, and I crashed about forgetting friction and the like didn't apply.

Now?

We *flew*, the lightest taps sending us along at sprinting speed. The chain offered ample room on its monstrous links, all black and polished to perfection. They gleamed as we hopped from one to the next, bounding along its length to the next island, and the next after that. I picked up speed, kicking off with every tap, and Kaydee kept up, laughing as she leapt along.

The last island looked much like the first: a beige, scalloped diamond without scenery to recommend it. Its only difference came in a simple box resting on its far edge. That would be the key to Delta's core functions, her power switch.

Of course Delta stood before it, that jagged sword making the jump to her digital world and gaining a couple meters in length with the transition. Now hilariously impractical, the blade nonetheless looked light and easy in Delta's hands when she pointed it at us.

"Why?" Delta asked as Kaydee and I made landfall.

"You're going to get yourself and us killed," I said. "Simple."

"That is my decision," Delta countered. "Leave, now."

"You're a bit pissy for someone we're saving," Kaydee said, going in front of me. She dropped a hand behind her back, waved to her left. "I mean, we've gone deep inside your insane mind palace, trying to keep you from dying, and now you're pointing that thing at us?"

I edged left as Delta watched Kaydee. The vessel drifted the sword towards my friend.

"Last chance," Delta said.

"You don't even want to talk?" Kaydee asked, though she brought both hands up, clasped them together.

I hesitated near the island's left edge. Any move forward would bring me into Delta's range, a chance I didn't want to take until Kaydee had her full attention. A move I didn't want to take regardless, really.

Besides, I found another idea.

"We can talk outside," Delta said, and she darted forward.

The thrust came quick, pointed right at Kaydee's chest. It should've struck home, but Kaydee did what programs like her could do: she played with her localized reality, shifted herself a meter to the right so Delta's sword swished past.

I'd struggled with that too early on. Hewing too close to the physical world's limitations when I didn't need to. Delta slashed the sword left, another fast cut that could've been Kaydee's end if she hadn't flattened herself to the ground with speed far too fast for reality.

Delta's eyes tightened, her mouth went razor thin as she locked onto Kaydee, and I made my move. Straight would bring me right into Delta's range so I went left instead, cutting over the island's edge. I kept my feet planted on the island, running on its underside. One meter, two, and soon I'd be hitting the island's back. Flipping over and grabbing the gray box.

Delta's sword bit through the island, slicing through the stone behind me. Fragments flew everywhere and I threw myself forward to dodge the strike. That dodge succeeded—the blade's tip nicked my feet—but the dive carried me past the island's back edge, off into the orange wasteland. Delta's unused memory, her void.

I twisted, looked back to see Kaydee lunging through the opening Delta's swing created. She elbowed the vessel aside, a nothing blow. Delta took the hit, flipped the grip on the sword and sent it swinging back. Kaydee couldn't see the attack coming. I called out her name, as if it would matter.

Kaydee didn't pick up and throw the gray box so much as kick it, a stumbling attempt as Delta's sword connected in a glancing strike. Kaydee's left arm broke off, dissipated into nothing. Kaydee's body would follow in a second, her intrusion kicked out.

But that box flew towards me. Not quite on course, but I stretched out, lengthened my arms to reach towards it.

"Hurry!" Kaydee called, her voice turning robotic as she disappeared.

Delta leapt off the island towards me, yelling my name and holding the sword high. If there'd ever been an angel of death, I had to imagine it looked something like her then, blade splitting an infinite orange, chains and floating stone behind her, her visage pure anger.

The gray box hit my stretched fingers. It felt cool, far too smooth. In that feeling the box's functions revealed themselves: a memory wipe, a total shutdown.

"Sorry," I said to Delta as she raised that sword.

It never struck.

. . .

ZIPPING BACK TO REALITY, I first noticed Alvie. The dog had our walkway covered with rapid jumps, often bouncing off approaching mechs to knock them back a step. Alvie yapped the entire time, robotic wheeze-barks echoing off all the metal. The mechs that'd been fighting Delta took swipes at Alvie, but the dog seemed too small to hit well. Instead, snapping claws, clubbing arms, and one mech's whirring saw caught air.

All a few meters from where I stood, holding a now dead Delta. Her big black sword clanged to the walkway floor as her hand gave up its grip. Thanking Volt again for giving me extra strength, I picked up the vessel and ran towards the green-gemmed entrance to Leo's apartment.

"Alvie!" I shouted.

The dog obeyed my call without hesitation. I set Delta down just inside the door, felt the air shift as Alvie flew in right beside me. A touch to the control panel sent the door closing, red gem glow as comforting as any I'd ever seen before.

I slumped against that spiral gate, looking down the red hallway, those movie posters. Delta, head hanging, sat lifeless next to me. Alvie padded forward, sniffing around, ready to flip from fighting to searching in a moment. Hopefully he wouldn't find any more horrors waiting in this place.

Not sure I could deal with them if he did.

"Kaydee?" I asked, and caught nothing.

I wasn't sure what could happen if she was deleted in Delta's digital space. Would that command leech back through to me, wipe her out in my memory too?

"It's okay," I said to myself. "Kaydee's been wiped before and she always comes back."

Holding to that thought, I put together our current predicament. Yes, I'd saved Delta from a suicidal fight to the end out there on the Conduit, but trapping ourselves in Leo's apartment was only a temporary solution. Those mechs might linger outside, or, worse, construct some barrier over the door to seal us in here. We could rest, but not for long.

I carried Delta to the room where we'd first woke up, one with four empty cots sitting beneath a frosty blue-white light. More movie posters, guns and explosions everywhere, pasted to the dark gray walls. I lay Delta down on her cot, looked at the gashes, the hits she'd taken.

The wounds criss-crossed her like a map, long jagged lines mingled with short cuts and deep divots where some pounding fist had caught Delta flat. Already the synthetic skin was going about its business stitching itself together. A nice feature, but not too fast. Delta might get back to working order, but she wouldn't get there soon.

Alvie barked, a sound carrying from down the hallway. Telling Delta to hold tight, I went after the dog. The short trip took me past the room where I'd met the Librarian, where Kaydee had, shortly thereafter, blasted the Librarian to digital dust. Alvie wasn't in either one, instead holding court in a third.

There, a large flickering screen delivered an idea. Before, this terminal had connected me to the Voices, back when they'd first given me the Nursery mission. Now I could connect with them again. We hadn't parted on the best of terms, but now I had new information, I had things to trade.

If anyone could leverage some Starship trick to get us out of this trap, it would be the Voices.

"Good idea, buddy," I said to Alvie, who blinked his yellow eyes at me.

"You're lucky he doesn't have a tongue, or you'd be getting a lick to the face," Kaydee said.

Much like what I'd done back with Val's terminal, I pressed my fingers together and vanished inside. Unlike Val's terminal, stuffed with history, this one kept itself clean. The only program running gave me a purple-black void, one surrounding me with Starship's network and its blue-point stars.

Leaping back and forth from the real to the digital worlds came with its own vertigo-like whiplash. My body would have its full senses one moment, then would lose most the next as I went into a ones and zeroes land. Leo's programming, the functions that kept me running, proved themselves up to the task, helping shunt aside the fuzzy confusion and keep me focused like a particularly powerful drug.

For a human? I could only imagine how exhausting it would be.

I fed the program a query, searching for the Voices and their connection. A single star in the constellation around me grew bright, so bright it washed out all the others. I took a step towards it, found myself teleported right next to its glow, and stepped in.

The last time I'd talked with the Voices, really talked with them, they'd been in a mountainside retreat. A cozy place to spend their digital lives while waiting for Starship to find its home. Now I found myself standing on a fortress rampart.

Stone sat sturdy beneath my feet, the towering walls looking over a battered plain filled with spike pits and barricades. The castle's center stabbed into the sky, ballistas lurking on every corner. Arrows gleamed, catching a cold sun's light. Like Delta's sword, those things would be ready to delete, destroy any program they caught.

I heard noises down below and looked, caught a phalanx working through drills. These soldiers, all generic, with the exact same height, speed, range of motion as they swung their spears and swords, took orders from a man I recognized. One fuzzy around his edges, that flickered on occasion as he walked around giving orders.

Leo, training and testing new programs.

"You're back," said a royally pissed off voice, and one that deserved to be.

After all, last time I'd talked to her, I'd cut Peony off from what she wanted most.

She approached me on the rampart, her stout figure made more-so by a gargantuan set of medieval armor. Rather than black, Peony's gear shimmered a brilliant orange, like a sunset's early kiss. Hanging from a belt around her waist, though, weren't swords but a more modern human weapon: black guns.

Behind her, two more generic programs marched, holding halberds and staring at me with lifeless eyes.

"Not because I want to be," I said. "We're in trouble."

"Does it look like we aren't?" Peony gestured at the castle. The programs. Then she narrowed her big eyes at me. "Where's my daughter?"

I didn't know. Kaydee came and went as she pleased, in this realm or any other.

"Not here," I said. "What's happening?"

Peony glared at me for a long second. Kaydee always said her mom had a mean streak, could be petty when she felt like it. Odds didn't seem zero that she might draw her weapon right there and put a virtual bullet between my eyes. Instead, she huffed, scratched at her cheek with a gauntleted finger.

"Alpha is trying to take the Bridge," Peony said. "We activated the barriers. He either needs to break us in here, or break through out there."

"And will he?"

Peony grimaced, "That, Gamma, is a question I can't answer. But if he does, he'll be able to take Starship wherever he wants. He could point us to deep space, ram us into the nearest moon, or open all the doors and have vacuum suck out every life left on this ship."

"That'd be bad."

"It would." Peony pointed at me. "And it would all be your fault."

As much as I wanted to, I couldn't argue with that. Instead, I threw our situation back at her. Said that Delta and I were trying to take Alpha out, but we'd found ourselves trapped in Leo's lab.

Peony laughed when I finished.

"See down there?" Peony said, this time pointing at the battle-field. "He's been attacking us endlessly, but now he's stopped. Just a few minutes ago. Bet I can guess why. You want help, Gamma, help yourself. We're surviving here."

"Until what?" I asked. "You're going to wait him out?"

"Starship's not far from where it needs to go," Peony said. "We hold out a few more decades, and once Alpha lands, he's in trouble."

"Why?"

But Peony waved me away, "I'd worry about yourself, Gamma. I think you're going to have some real problems real soon."

I considered jumping down and pitching a plea to Leo, but Peony's hand drifted to her weapon. Those two guards tilted their halberds towards me. The last thing I needed right now was some digital wound, corrupted data that would take time to repair.

So instead I flipped Peony a rude gesture her daughter would appreciate and left.

THIRTEEN

DEALS AND DISHWASHERS

The thuds echoing throughout Leo's apartment came with an even rhythm. No human randomness, just a steady banging like a gallows drum, beating to my demise. We hadn't been subtle in our disappearance, Delta and I, and Alpha's mechs were following their blind programming to the letter. They would hammer on the door in increasing numbers and with increasing strength until the shell gave way.

In these small corridors, even if I woke Delta, there would be no escape. I'd gambled on the Voices and been left holding the bag.

"Nice try, Gamma," Kaydee said, walking with me as I went back to the red-gemmed entrance. "Can't say you didn't do what you could."

"We should've run," I replied.

"Should've, could've," Kaydee said. In front of us, an image of me running with Delta, Alvie nipping at our heels paraded down the hallway only to trip and fall before reaching its end. "They'd either catch you, you'd fall on your face, or you'd get away only to find yourself right back here."

"Because Delta won't stop."

"Because Delta won't stop." Kaydee nodded. "You've been down on us humans for a bit now, but at least we can change."

"We can too, if you work at it," I said.

"And get in your guts."

"You don't have to put it that way."

"But I did." Kaydee thumbed towards the cot room where Delta lay. "Want to wake her up? Go out together?"

The thuds had grown louder, more joining in with their rock-steady cadence. The door rattled, vibration leaking all the way underneath my feet on those metal plates. A movie poster fell from its place on the wall, gliding down to rest near me. Its cover held a block-headed action hero, some shotgun up near his face. Sunglasses covered the man's eyes.

The tagline *It's Not Personal* ran along the bottom.

"No," I said, heading towards the door and passing Delta. "She needs to rest."

"Not going to be much rest when those mechs get in here."

"Working on it," I said, then bent down, gave Alvie a good pet. "You stay with Delta, okay? Make sure nothing happens to her."

Alvie huffed his concern.

"I'll be fine," I told the dog.

If I wasn't, Alvie wouldn't have long to worry before Alpha destroyed or corrupted him. I kept that thought to myself.

The red gem shook as I came closer, rattling in protest at the bangs. The strikes stopped, though, when I pressed my face up near the door and shouted a question through it. A request, more like.

"Bold," Kaydee said, arms folded by me. "It's a move I'd make."

"I'm learning from you, remember?"

"Sure, but till now I thought you were taking all the wrong lessons."

"Like how to style my hair?"

Kaydee stuck her tongue out at me, then disappeared in a silver glitter shower. The glitz led into a crackle from the apartment's keypad, its tiny screen resolving to show a mech showing . . . another machine on its own screen. Alpha, long red hair frayed around his narrow face. His eyes, ever intense, stared at me without blinking.

"Gamma, Gamma, Gamma," Alpha said, his repetitions cycling my name up and down his vocal register as if testing his range. "I have to say, you always show up at the worst moments."

"I'm getting good at it."

"Very." Alpha's smile grew. He still hadn't blinked. "Here we were, about to grind Delta to dust, when you show up. Tell me you're not going to waste my time."

"I'm not going to waste your time."

Alpha laughed, a shrill sound that echoed wide. The vessel, then, wasn't in a small space like me. If what Peony said was true, then I had to guess Alpha stood outside the Bridge's entrance, on the wide semi-circle platform at the Conduit's end.

"Then go on, Gamma," Alpha replied. "Give me your reasons why I should spare your lives."

"Because we can help you."

"But will you?" Alpha ran his hands through his hair. "So many times, Gamma, so many times I've re-run the scenarios. With you and Delta on my side, we would have Starship in our control before the day was out. Our mechs would be safe, our future secured. And yet I can't ever get the equations to come out my way. You're always wrong. Delta's always wrong." Alpha let his hair fall all over his face, those searing eyes peeking between ginger strands. "Within an hour or a minute, one of you always stabs me in the back."

"I can change that," I said. "My code, Delta's. I can modify it, make us truly your partners."

Alpha's head tilted ever so slightly, a tell given away by his hair's shift. I had him there, a thought he hadn't considered.

"Don't let him think," Kaydee whispered. "Bowl him over."

Right.

"I met the humans," I continued. "The ones hiding in Starship's aft quarter." Giving away Val's exact location seemed unkind. Even if she'd treated me like a tool, that didn't mean she deserved death by a thousand mechs. "They're not the solution, Alpha. Not these."

The vessel nodded. "You see now?"

"The Voices told us to save them," I replied, with Kaydee, standing in the corner of my eye, waving for me to continue. "So I went to the humans thinking we could work together."

"But they are only interested in themselves," Alpha said. "They want nothing of us. They would destroy us if they could."

"I didn't want to believe it, but you're right."

"Then you see why we must take Starship for ourselves," Alpha said.

"I do."

"Then come out here, Gamma," Alpha stepped back from the camera, showing a platform crowded with mechs. "Come, be a part of your real family at last."

How could I say no to that?

"You can't trust this guy," Kaydee said as I opened Leo's apartment to the mechs waiting outside.

"Never would," I replied. Squared my shoulders, put on a look I hoped fit the dismissively confident attitude I was going for. "This is getting Delta the time she needs."

But I'd be lying to myself if that was the only reason. Sure, I might be able to hack into Delta and rewrite her wires. I could, possibly, change my own. Shift some functions around and get as lost as Alpha. More likely, I'd try, fail, and Delta would chop my head off for the effort. Then she'd get right back to her suicidal onslaught.

No, the only way I could save Delta was by stopping Alpha, and doing it my way.

The mechs, at least, gave my way a good start. They parted to either side as I went onto the Conduit, didn't harass me in the slightest as I closed and sealed Leo's apartment behind me. Yes, they could break into it, but that would take a while, would take another command on Alpha's part. I had to bet the vessel wouldn't do that until and unless he'd lost me.

By the time Alpha made that realization, hopefully, he'd be dead.

For a vessel not used to celebrity, walking the Conduit with mechs lining either side felt ceremonial. Many stood up to my level or taller, arms and gadgets hanging at their sides. Batteries whirred and components churned, a scientific symphony marching at me.

"This is gonna go the whole distance?" Kaydee said as we went.

Thankfully, the mech honor guard did not, drifting away after some ten minutes stepping along. The Bridge wasn't exactly next door. Getting to it from Leo's apartment meant passing Starship's University, meant going through several districts. The mech line petered out, Alpha's various machine hordes splitting off to other levels. I heard them, saw them breaking into other stores, gathering groups for Garden raids. Some, I had to imagine, would be planning expeditions aft-ward to hunt Val and the humans.

If I could've sent word to Volt and Beta to warn them, I would've. Instead, I had to hope the mechs would be obvious enough to give themselves away.

Starship's University went by fast. No interrogations by the guarding mechs this time. They stood still and silent in their notches. I couldn't tell whether Alpha had taken them too, but believing otherwise by now seemed like folly.

"He moved quick," Kaydee said as we saw more mech squads patrolling up and down on the University's other side. "How could he control so many, so fast?"

"He's a clever maniac," I said. "That's all I got."

The question picked at me too as we grew nearer to the Bridge. Not a few days ago Alpha had been beaten, tied up in the Garden without any mech army to call to his aid. Now it seemed like all Starship moved at his command, save two tiny pieces, the humans and the Voices. What would've let him rewrite so much in so little time?

"Tell you what, though, you'll have to figure it out," Kaydee said.

"To solve the mystery?"

"Because you'll have to do whatever he did."

"I'll have to do better."

Kaydee whistled, floating green question marks drifting into the walkway ahead of me. We'd passed beyond the University into Starship's last leg, my own pace at a swift jog. Private spiral doors interspersed with large workshops, high tech spaces with names like *Innovation Station* and *Gerry's Genetics*. Remnants of a weirder time.

"I don't want to rope the mechs to me," I said. "They're not my servants. They need to work for everyone, for themselves too. That's their purpose."

"Glad you see it that way," Kaydee replied. "After what you said to Alpha, I wasn't sure. You've been getting all defensive about the mechs lately."

"Because they don't deserve to be mistreated for what they are," I said. "Even a trash can ought to be respected."

"You know, there's a good point in there somewhere."

I shook my head, kept running. Alpha's chosen platform emerged from the mist. More mechs crowded onto it, these ones more svelte, with nodes ending in ports instead of claws or other nastier weapons. Designed for a different opponent.

Alpha held sway over the group, standing in the platform's center and facing the red laser gates. He seemed like a prophet there, arms spread and preaching to a trapped crowd. Kaydee and I caught his words as we came closer, a rambling screed about a mech driven future, about Starship being their home, and invectives aplenty against greedy, fatally flawed humans.

"Does he realize they can't understand him?" Kaydee said. "At best maybe a third can process language. But we're talking, like, clean up the floor. Not overthrow society."

"Cindy seemed to get it," I said, recalling the flame-throwing mech from my earliest steps outside Leo's lab. That one had been convinced of a war between mechs, a blur that'd since come into focus as Starship's remaining uncorrupted machines struggled against Alpha's converted force. "She took a side and acted on it."

"One in a million."

"Or one of Alpha's earliest converts." I glanced down at myself, weaponless, clad in clothes worn and burned. "Now we get to pretend to be the latest."

"Make sure it's just pretend, please," Kaydee said. "Don't want to deal with you corrupted again. That sucked."

Agreed.

I squared my shoulders, walked through the mech perimeter surrounding Alpha's platform. His guards—trash cans, culinary mechs, dishwashers gone mobile—weren't all that intimidating, but their lights followed me, their limbs tracked me, and their motors spun up. Ready for whatever action a dishwasher might take.

"Here he is!" Alpha announced as I made the platform, a half-circle jutting out into the Conduit. Docking platforms speared out from its end to make room for taxis, courier mechs long since gone. On the right, the Bridge itself sat behind those red-glowing gates. They'd torch anything dumb enough to try going through. Alpha had mechs standing before them in a line, as if waiting to rush the barrier.

"Here I am," I said.

Up close, Alpha looked like he had before, except he'd swapped his outfit, put up his hair into a ponytail. No longer in zen-like robes, the vessel cloaked himself instead in a snug strawberry red athletic outfit. Kaydee snickered off to the side, said it looked like Alpha was about to wander onto a soccer pitch. Kick a goal.

One thing that hadn't changed? Alpha's intensity. Those eyes, those twitchy muscles kept up their fire.

"You made it unmolested, I presume?" Alpha asked as I joined him in the several clear meters he'd reserved in the platform's center. "My mechs tend to be very loyal."

"They didn't touch me."

"Good," Alpha put a hand on my shoulder, a tight grip. "I'm afraid we have to change the deal, my friend."

Kaydee would've made some wiseass remark about not being his friend, about how of course Alpha would be changing the deal. Kaydee, though, didn't have a body that could get twisted inside and out, didn't have a friend dead on a cot, vulnerable and mostly alone.

"What do you need?"

"See those barriers there?" Alpha said. "The pretty ones?"

"Hard to miss."

"I would much prefer them gone," Alpha continued as if I hadn't spoken. "I know, I know, you and I both operate well in their world, but they are watching for me." Alpha's face screwed up in that moment, his mouth popping open into a wide, silent snarl. A half second later and it snapped back to his smiling, telling-secrets form. "So you go on in, disable those barriers, and we can have that talk you wanted on the other side."

Asking what would happen if I didn't subvert the Voices seemed pointless. Alpha's mechs made it clear enough that whatever 'deal' we had, the terms were one-sided. I was at his mercy, and my options were few: sacrifice myself in an attempt to ring Alpha's neck before his mechs snapped mine, or do what he wanted and unlock the Bridge.

Perhaps I would've felt worse about the latter if the Voices hadn't been such monsters.

The port sat where I remembered it, near the barriers themselves, on the left side in Starship's narrowing wall. A tiny slot, perfect for my pinched fingers. Several mechs, limbs arrayed out around me in a menacing frame, watched over my efforts while Alpha returned to dictating his expansion outward down the Conduit. From his words, I understood the strategy: take what mechs could be corrupted, destroy the rest. Including any humans. Any scrap ought to go to the Fabrication Lines where it could be remade into something more useful.

Starship wouldn't be its independent, motley mess much longer.

My fingers formed the port. Plugged in. Searched for the barrier controls, and found myself rebuffed, standing on the edge of a miserable plain I knew too well. In the distance, a jagged castle reached up into a rippling gray sky.

The Voices had sealed themselves away, and the barrier controls would be inside with them.

"So how do we turn this on Alpha?" Kaydee asked, popping in next to me, camouflaged up in a brown tunic, green and brown paint smearing her face.

"I don't know," I said.

The truth?

If it was a choice between Alpha and the Voices . . . I knew what side I'd pick.

FOURTEEN

FORTRESS ASSAULT

The grim green-black plains stretched out beyond the forest's edge, crawling up to high stone walls and a jagged keep rising beyond them. A close look at either the trees or the grass confirmed each one matched its fellows, exact copies made to save memory space in Starship's clogged up drives. The clouds above in their gray menace shared their DNA, copies drifting across a uniformly slate sky. The breeze brushed me straight, a constant rush without natural air's drifting, snaking feel.

"A cheap hideaway," I said, bending and running my finger along a stiff grass stalk. "I would've expected more."

"It's not like they had time to prepare," Kaydee said. "Alpha showed up ready to fight. My guess is the grass wasn't high priority."

"They've had years upon years to prepare." I straightened, stared out at the castle. A single raven circled its tower, squawking out its doom every few seconds. "The Voices woke Alpha, they watched him falter. They have no excuse."

"Except they're human, right?" Kaydee asked. "Is that what you want me to say?"

"You don't agree?" I replied, studying Kaydee's stance. She faced me now under the boughs, brow furrowed beneath her camouflage, arms folded. Little sparks danced off her body. "No vessel or mech, if its programming allowed it, would erect such a flimsy defense."

"You're forgetting who you're talking about. The Voices aren't generals. They're civilians. And they don't get along well. Basically ever."

"This excuses them how?" I gestured towards the castle. "Starship's leading citizens are in there now, waiting for their end. Pathetic."

"Gamma?" Kaydee turned her head, gave me a questioning side-eye.

"These were the people that tried to order us around? That dictated to Delta and I what to do?" I kept talking, the words springing out of a well filled over my short life. "They failed with Alpha and Beta, failed with Delta and I, failed Val and her tribe. You talk about them like we should be afraid, like we should respect them." I shook my head. "No. Not again, not anymore."

I started walking. I'd cross the plain to the castle, walk right inside, and if any of the Voices tried to stop me, I would tear them apart. I felt the confines coded into the space the Voices had rigged up: there would be no shredding reality here. Any conflict would happen with fists, with feet, with grit. The Voices had nothing of the latter and little of the former.

They would crumble, and then Alpha would finish the job.

"Gamma," Kaydee said, not following me. "You're helping Alpha. You realize that? The thing that tried to corrupt you?"

"I'm not helping Alpha," I replied without turning around. "I'm saving Delta."

A pinprick snagged my clothes, pulled me back. I whirled around, followed the silver fishing line back to its source. Kaydee, the rod in her hands, reeled me back another step. I gripped the line, pulled, and sent her flying off her feet. I reached forward, took up the rod—a little function she'd written to tie herself to me—and snapped it.

"You're lying to yourself is what you're doing," Kaydee said from the ground, her hands spreading to push her up. "There's no way Alpha lets you free. You or Delta."

"I know. That doesn't change anything. This keeps Delta alive, so that's what I'm doing."

"Even if it costs us everything?"

"Us?" I asked. "I think you mean the Voices. I think you mean the humans that treated me like a tool."

Kaydee didn't have a ready comeback, so I resumed my trek into the grass. The waist-high stalks brushed me as I walked, moving around the spike pits, the palisades, the oil-slick sections waiting for enemies that would never come. If I hadn't arrived, perhaps Alpha would've tried to brute force the Voices, send a thousand attacks streaming at the walls.

Instead I walked alone.

Freed from the Conduit's confines, even in an artificial sense, I played with the feel: a horizon stretching in all directions, a sky above that didn't end with metal plating. No electric lighting, no whirring engines. Peaceful, albeit with a bleak side thanks to the Voices's chosen setting. Nonetheless, the walk to the ramparts sparked some anticipation for Starship's eventual landing. I might get to go outside for real one day, and in not all that long.

Any wonder dissipated as I neared the walls and the first programmed guards stuck their heads over the castle's ramparts. Three, and their eyes locked on me, heads moving in unison. Bows with nocked arrows raised their points, angling them down at me.

Time to play a different sort of game.

I waved at the guards. They didn't react, but the fact they didn't fire right away told me they'd already told the Voices someone was approaching. My next move depended on what the Voices decided to do.

Before me stood the castle's main door: a deep brown, rain-spattered wood. Likely thick and not easy to punch through. Watchtowers rose on either side, more guards showing up in those higher platforms to aim their own arrows my way. Any one hitting me would, I figured, start a rapid deletion, kicking me out and possibly worse.

"Gamma," Leo called down, the engineer's head joining the guards on the walls. He looked frayed from this far away, as if his virtual self still felt the stresses of life lived on the digital edge. "What are you doing here?"

"Making a choice," I replied. "I need to get through, Leo."

"To what?"

I delivered the details, one after another. Delta, Alpha, the mechs, Val and more. Leo took it all in without comment. I expected Kaydee to interrupt, to try and talk to her former friend or add her usual color, but she stayed absent. Perhaps I'd really offended her back there.

A problem for another time.

"If Alpha gets to the Bridge, he will control Starship," Leo said. "You know this."

"Having seen what you've done with the place, I'm not sure that's a bad idea."

Leo tightened his straight lips, "There is bad, and there is worse. Alpha could destroy everything."

"So could you."

That, at least, earned a nod. "Gamma, I'm not going to play rhetorical games with you. The Bridge is ours. If Alpha wants to negotiate, he's free to do so without putting an army at our doorstep."

The expected rejection.

I'd have to infiltrate the hard way.

I dashed forward, heading right for the wooden door. Leo shouted *fire* as I ran, the arrows releasing as he started speaking. The tight shooting angle worked against the programs, though, and their shots struck hard dirt behind my heels. Pressing my back against the wooden gate, I looked up, verified that while the ramparts couldn't hit me anymore, those watchtower guards sure could.

Counting off one, two seconds, I dove out from the gate and

grabbed an arrow from the dirt. My left hand closed around the shaft and pulled it free. With my right, I snagged another, ripped it from the earth. Whirled, side-stepping as I turned back towards the castle.

Guards in both watchtowers adjusted to my new placement, while others on the ramparts tried to turn around, bring up their bows again. Now, though, they weren't the only ones with weapons.

Like the world's tiniest javelins, I threw the arrows at the watchtower guards. First to the right, then to the left. In the Voices' world, the arrows flew straight and exact, striking where I threw them, more like bullets or lasers than feathered sticks. Each one nailed its target, the arrows performing their functions without concern for the effect: each guard dissolved into pixels, then nothing.

Sweeping up another arrow, I ran towards the wooden gate, again beating the rampart guards and their return fire by fractional seconds. This time I'd secured breathing room. Those wall guards would hike up to the watchtowers in a minute, thinking they'd have me trapped against the gate now.

Thankfully, I had more than my hands.

I jammed the arrow into the wooden gate, hoping the deletion function might apply to the gate as well as it had the guards. If the whole barrier disappeared, I could just run right on in, using the arrow as a catch-all key to demolish the Voices's kingdom en route to its center.

My stolen tool bit into the wood with a soft *chunk* and sat there, quivering. The gate remained, unfortunately, quite solid.

Okay, back-up plan.

I pulled the arrow free, dashed to the gate's corner where it brushed into the left watchtower, squatted and leapt up. As I reached my jump's height, I swung my right arm forward, the arrow digging deep into the wood this time. I planted my feet against the gate, my left hand against the watchtower, and prayed the arrow shaft would hold my weight.

For a brief moment, it did.

Pressing off with my left hand, with my feet, I jumped up and pulled the arrow with me, pounding it back into the wood a meter higher. Leo's yelling carried, calling the guards to their positions. Armor, weapons jangled as the programs pounded their way up the watchtowers.

I jumped again, yanking the arrow up and planting it back.

And again.

The watchtower lip lay only a couple meters above, the gate itself topping out not much higher than that. I gathered myself for another jump, only to see a guard pop his head over my watchtower's wall. His arrow ready, the program sighted me.

So I faked. Started to spring up then stopped, my feet sliding along the wood. The guard took the bait, loosing his arrow into the gate above me. I jumped quick, not bothering to pull my old arrow free. As I did, another shot thunked in near my chest from the far side. My desperate tactics were reaching their end.

Delta might've pulled something ridiculous out here, like flipping the old arrow free with her feet, catching it in her hand, and whipping it at another guard. I did not have that dexterity, didn't have that expertise, so I did the only thing I could.

"You'll kill her Leo!" I shouted. "If I die, so does she!"

Leo's response came quick, the man telling the guards to hold their fire. I hung there, my foot balancing on my old arrow, my right hand clinging to the one the guard had misfired. The delay gave both watchtowers time to reinforce themselves, so that when Leo appeared I had four nocked arrows aimed at my gut.

"These arrows won't kill you," Leo said, glaring at me. "You know that."

"No, but Alpha will," I replied. "If I don't disable these barriers, he'll destroy me. And if I die, so does Kaydee."

Leo's hands gripped the watchtower's stone, growing white as he pressed tight. "You're asking me to trade Starship for a single life."

"No," I said. "I'm asking you to give me a chance."

"A chance at what?"

"You built us, Leo. You made us Starship's insurance. Let us do what you designed us to do, and make sure this ship gets where it needs to go."

Leo, though, didn't move. Didn't order the gate open. Instead, his eyes closed, those hands still holding tight to the stone, as if answers could be found in that digital gray brick. I'd seen enough humans to know the man had to be wavering, close to coming down on my side.

One more push.

"Alpha's going to get through anyway," I said. "You know it, Peony knows it. He'll tear apart the barriers if he has to, and the vessel has enough mechs to do it. Let me through, and at least you'll have help on the other side."

Leo pulled his hands off, one scratched at his face while he turned, swept a long look over the forest.

"If Alpha gains the Bridge, he'll try to erase us," Leo said. "That can't happen. Not because I'm egotistical, but because Starship still needs us." He turned back to me. "I'll pull the barriers down and you'll have your gateway. Alpha won't find us waiting."

"Thank you, Leo."

"Gamma, I'm doing this for you. For her. Don't let all our hope die, don't let all these lives, all these years go to waste for that machine."

"I won't."

I kept my face straight as I said the words, trying not to show the truth hiding behind: that maybe letting all those years go to waste would be the best thing for Starship and all the mechs on it.

FIFTEEN

MAN OR MACHINE

With Leo's agreement I zapped myself away from the castle and its squawking raven. Returning from the gray skies to Starship's gray metal wasn't so jarring, though the cherry red barriers and their bright glow set off the color. Mechs loomed around me, joined now, I noticed, by the taller, stronger, guardians I'd seen around University Row and Starship's wealthier side.

Alpha continuing to augment his robotic army.

I straightened, watched the red barriers. Leo would either come through or Alpha would tear me apart, then bash his way through the barriers anyway.

"You saw him, then," Kaydee said, sitting against the wall to my left and looking at my feet.

"You know what I saw," I replied. She could read my thoughts as she wanted, a free access that I'd never bothered to clamp down. If Kaydee ever abused it, I could lock her off, but that represented a leap I had no desire to take. "The Voices don't have anywhere to go. Alpha will get through one way or another."

"But you used me, Gamma. My name."

"To save our lives."

Kaydee might've had something else to say, but clomping sounds behind me interrupted our conversation. The machines parted to let Alpha, as insanely serene as ever, through. He spread his arms, eyebrows rocketing up his forehead.

"Well?" Alpha asked. "I see the barriers still stand."

"Wait a minute or two," I replied. "They'll fall."

Alpha leaned close, inspected my face, his eyes crawling all over my skin. "No trace of a lie on you, Gamma. Though it's always so hard to tell with mechs. No nervous tics."

I stayed silent. Resisted the urge to grab and break Alpha's neck right there. The mechs stood a couple meters back, and I might've been able to manage it. Sure, I'd get trampled and torn apart, but it would be a satisfying end.

Except it would leave the Voices in charge.

So many bad choices.

The cherry barriers flickered, died as Alpha leaned back. The vessel clapped his hands once, sharp and loud. Putting on a wide grin, Alpha windmilled his right arm, waving the waiting mechs on through.

"Go on, go on!" Alpha cried. "Sweep right on in, my friends, and make sure no surprises are waiting for us." Alpha glanced at me, lowered his voice to a whisper. "Last time I was here, the Voices let me walk through. Bet they've learned their lesson."

"Nothing's going to happen," I said.

A stupid thing to reveal, and I winced when Alpha abandoned his cheerleading—the mechs didn't care, they marched along anyway —and focused on me once more.

"And how do you know that?" Alpha asked. "You didn't destroy the Voices entirely, did you?" A short cackle. "Oh, what a delight that would be. Their last hope, you, turning on them in the end. Tell me you did it."

I shrugged, turned towards the dead barrier, "Don't you want to get going? Your mechs might damage something."

Alpha hop-skipped past me, wagging a finger in my direction,

"Correct, of course, but don't think you've dodged my question." The delight died, a flash back to the serious slate. "The Voices have to go, Gamma. Sooner or later. I do hope you did the dirty deed, but if not . . . more fun for me."

He waved me after him and, without other options, I went.

GETTING to the Bridge meant going through a memorial hallway. On the right and left, Starship's uninteresting gray plates vanished into thicker, solid silver. Names etched into the surface in clean columns, the letters at first appearing clear before descending into scratched madness in the hallway's latter half: Alpha, who'd slashed his own name onto the plates over and over again.

The vessel didn't pause to judge his own work, carrying on into the Bridge with his mechs rolling alongside him. I, though, did stop, because Kaydee appeared before me and pointed, with one hand and furious eyes, at the markings.

"This," Kaydee said. "This is who you're deciding to help."

"Because the Voices are the model for sanity," I sniped.

"I just don't understand why you've turned so hard against me," Kaydee said, pulling back her arm. Now she looked concerned more than angry, her mouth tilting into a frown along with her head. "It's like you're taking some shade from Val as an indictment against all of us."

"Like you said before, I haven't been alive all that long," I replied. "Maybe I don't have the maturity to take that shade and keep going."

"That's crap and you know it."

"Then tell me what I'm getting wrong?" I challenged her as the last of Alpha's marching mechs went past us. The vessel left a big force out there on the platform, apparently to discourage any other interlopers. "What am I not understanding?"

"That humans aren't any different than you and Alpha," Kaydee said. "We want better futures for ourselves, we want safety, food and shelter. Happiness. And we'll fight to get it."

"None of that excuses treating mechs like dirt."

"Because you never act like a jerk," Kaydee replied. "Look at this, Gamma. You leave him in control and Alpha's going to destroy everything. You, me, Starship. Val and all those frozen children waiting in the Nursery? Gone. That'll be on you."

I shook my head, put my feet into motion and walked past her.

"On you, Gamma," Kaydee said to my back.

The hallway ended in a branching entry, options to the left and right and no clear shot at the Bridge without choosing one. Each way led up a gentle slope, tile studded with gripping nubs to keep anyone from slipping. Handrails offered their chromed selves, polished to perfection.

I stopped, studied.

Humans had designed Starship, crafted it from nothing and turned it into this, a galaxy-crossing vessel replete with entertainment, sustenance , and a plan to keep thousands and thousands alive for millennia. They could've gone with the minimum, but here they'd put in rails, they'd put in ramps and grips to help their own species get around.

And not just them.

The Conduit laid out in a simple straight shot, with level walkways, wide lifts to go between floors. Clear district definitions. Not just easy for humans to navigate, but simple for mechs as well. For as hostile as Val had been to me, her ancestors had depended on mechs like myself, had gone above and beyond to make sure the mechs could do their jobs easily, without damage or destruction.

And what about Sybil Renoir?

Starship's own architect kept her family's cleaning mech, let it live safe and secure inside her family's home. Protected from the chaos outside. Sybil had no reason to give it that protection, had no need, in her existence as a virtual memory, for her family's old mech. Yet Sybil went through the effort anyway.

I couldn't quite make myself believe that humans loved their mechs, treated them as equals, but perhaps they weren't all arrogant masters either. I could imagine some even worked alongside their machines, more as partners than director and servant.

My code, my logic as a machine wanted a simple answer: humans bad, vessels good. Or the reverse. Guess I wasn't that lucky.

Kaydee didn't chime in. I waited there at that branch for her to show up and tell me she'd been listening in to my ruminating. Declare she'd been right all along. Maybe, as she'd done before, Kaydee was off reflecting herself.

Regardless, I heard Alpha calling my name. I'd given him access to the Bridge, and now I needed to see what he'd do with it.

Up the ramp and around, the Bridge opened into three stacked tiers. Slick white tables loaded with screens spread across each level, with a descending ramp cut through the middle leading to the holy grail sight on Starship: a vast glass portal looking out into space. Low yellow lighting embedded in the floors gave guidance while letting viewers see twinkling stars out beyond.

More than that, though, I could see planets. The marbles hanging in our view looked almost like imperfections in the glass: here a beige thumbprint, there a greenish glow. A larger star sat beyond them all, the center of the system Starship was brushing by. Or entering, for all I knew.

"The last stop," Alpha said, the vessel standing down with his face against the glass. "We're nearly there, Gamma."

"To Starship's destination?"

Alpha's mechs arranged themselves along the Bridge, each one fitting as close as they could to the computer monitors. Not that these mechs would have any idea how, not to mention the dexterity, to use the Bridge's computers. I chalked it up to Alpha's obsessions and moved on, putting myself at the Bridge's top.

Only a couple mechs stood near me and, without any blocking my potential retreat, I had options to get away. Could've run right then and there and hoped Alpha, fascinated with his treasure, would forget about Delta and I.

Except I wanted to see what he would do. Wanted to see whether

I'd truly made a monstrous mistake in giving Alpha access to Starship's most important systems.

"Not quite," Alpha said, planting both hands on the glass and running them down, giving the desk a pet. "Starship's original goal waits many more years ahead. The galaxy's edge. But I'm bored, Gamma. I don't want to wait that long to get our future going." Alpha whirled towards me, walked fast up the Bridge. "Aren't you sick of all these tight hallways? I've heard the same rumblings, the same sounds for so long . . . "

Alpha's voice trailed off as he neared me, a smile growing with the approach. For a second I thought he was going to cup my chin and wiggle my face, but instead he went around me to the right. Pushed a mech away that'd been standing there, toppling it over.

The mech beeped an alert, asked for help. Alpha ignored it, pressing his fingers together and jacking into the computer there. The one labeled, a gold plate sitting before the workstation, for Starship's captain. Alpha's eyes closed, his body relaxed. He'd gone into the computer, doing who the hell knew what.

I went around the vessel, helped the mech back to its feet. The machine, a cylindrical, many-armed mech belonged cleaning and sorting trash. Yet, once I had it standing upright, the mech offered no confusion about how far its present position distanced from its designed purpose. Alpha's work, erasing the original and replacing it with his own.

Seconds, then minutes, crawled by and I spent them looking out at the stars. All that infinite blackness. Take away the Bridge around me and space wouldn't be all that different from some of the virtual worlds I'd dashed into. An infinity I could never traverse.

"Do you think he's destroying them?" Kaydee said, staying in the shadows on my right. "Murdering them one by one?"

"If Leo's smart, he would've vanished with the Voices by now." I nodded at Alpha. "These computers are all networked. They could run, hide from Alpha. Besides, I think Alpha's doing something else."

When Kaydee didn't reply, I glanced her way and saw nothing except the dark.

The silence broke with a sharp crackle, static exorcised from speakers not used in so very many years. A voice came over then, a gentle woman warning everyone that Starship's maneuvering engines would be firing soon. Chairs and straps were encouraged, handrails otherwise.

I had neither, didn't move.

Starship groaned, vibrated. The ship had always done so, but this felt more like being rattled in a shaking cup. I reached out, put my hand on the wall. New sounds echoed throughout the ship, pops and bangs, whines and purrs as components moved, turned on and off. The mechs, including the one I'd just set upright, fell over and banged about.

The stars outside held my eyes. They moved, at first slow and then faster, until the green dot I'd noticed before sat center in Starship's window. Once it shifted Starship's shuddering ceased and the voice came back, declaring the maneuver finished.

I let go of the wall as Alpha's head snapped up, his attention returned to reality. As I lifted the cleaning mech back to standing, Alpha unplugged from the computer and grinned to me.

"There we go," Alpha said. "Our journey shortened from years and years, to days."

"Days?"

"That planet meets Starship's criteria," Alpha said, then frowned. "I tried to find a good asteroid, but the computer wouldn't let me go that far. Has to be habitable." A smile springing back. "But no doubt that will be more interesting."

I nodded, trying to parse what Alpha's announcement really meant. Starship would be landing, and soon?

"This does, however, mean some things get more complicated," Alpha said. "I had hoped we could land somewhere desolate, open the doors, and let the vacuum take care of our human problem. As that will not be the case, Gamma, I believe it's time you fulfilled your deal."

"What?"

"Delta," Alpha put his hands on my shoulders, a priest blessing his acolyte. "Bring her to me, Gamma, and make her mine."

SIXTEEN

GOD COMPLEX

Alpha let me go without another word. I didn't protest, didn't offer up another plan because this was exactly what I needed: an opportunity.

Back in the chiseled hallway I expected Kaydee to appear, to admonish me for allowing Alpha to change Starship's passage. She didn't show. My only companion down that long hall was a silent and tall guardian. The big mechs had patrolled the University and the Conduit's wealthier half, looking like large humans and carrying weighted steel batons. This one eyed me, no expression forming on its face.

And no opinions either.

Had I done the right thing? I still lived and so did, for the moment, Delta. Yes, Alpha had veered Starship from its galaxy's edge goal, but wasn't one habitable planet as good as another way out here?

Wouldn't Val prefer the chance to taste fresh air on her own tongue?

Thinking of the humans kept me muddled as I left the Bridge— those barriers still dead—and went back to the level where I'd left

Delta. I'd been frustrated with Val, with the Voices and humanity's irascible inconsistencies. Alpha, of course, hadn't proved to be much better. The vessel championed mechs in one breath while dominating them in the other.

If neither side seemed worth following, then perhaps I should carve out my own?

Gamma, leader of the free mechs. The free peoples.

"The free children, more like," Kaydee bopped in as I walked along the Conduit.

"Children?"

"You're thinking like all these little test tube kids are going to pop out fully formed, Gamma," Kaydee said, drifting along beside me. "They're going to take years and years before they're ready to do anything other than demand your attention."

I frowned at her, "Did you come back just to tell me that?"

"I came back because I saw that god complex forming."

"God complex?"

"Gamma, lord and master of Starship and all within her walls," Kaydee intoned. "Bow and behave, lest ye be banished to the Garden's bottom."

"Doesn't sound so bad."

Kaydee and I moved around the mechs, none paying us the slightest interest. As we went, Kaydee continued to poke and prod my brief delusion, peppering me with questions about how I'd rule, what I'd even want from the proverbial crown. Whether I could handle all the decisions after my brief existence had been defined by following orders.

"What, then?" I said to Kaydee finally as we approached Leo's apartment. "If I can't stand the humans and can't trust Alpha, what then?"

"You compromise, dummy."

"Val won't listen to me, and Alpha—"

"Alpha won't listen to anyone," Kaydee agreed. "But with Beta's help? You might get Val on board. Change her perspective, mechs can be useful to her."

A changed perspective could always change back. Val could use us mechs until she decided we weren't necessary, but then again, my options remained narrow. I'd played the game with Alpha partly to see what he'd do, but also to buy Delta and myself some time. Now, as I went into Leo's apartment and shut the spiral door behind me, I might need Val in the same way.

There were two forces on Starship, and I wasn't one of them.

Alvie came running up as I walked in, wheeze-barking in chirpy good cheer. From his attitude, I assumed no mech had tried to enter the place, meaning Delta should be right where I'd left her. Indeed, Alvie seemed to sense my intentions and the dog guided me, metal paws clacking, to Delta's room.

She lay so still on the cot. The blue light coated her synthetic skin, perfect now with time to repair itself. Delta's combat outfit had seen better days, but her jagged blade rested near the room's entry, ready to get picked up again. Good thing too, because I had a feeling Alpha wouldn't give me much time to prove my word.

Or lack thereof.

Vessels didn't have a switch, exactly. In fact, I didn't know how one of us turned on. I'd shut Delta down from the inside, and that's where I went again. Pinching my fingers, I plugged into the port behind her ear and vanished.

This time, the gray cube holding all Delta's core functions sat alone, bobbing in an infinite white. No digital Delta appeared to stop me as I approached the core, as I placed my hand on it and gave it the start command I felt it searching for.

The gray box hummed and I didn't wait to see what else would happen. Slipping back out into the real physical world, I stood up next to the cot. Waited. Realized I ought to move the blade a few meters away and did so.

An angry Delta might act without thinking, better to remove lethal items from the equation.

Her eyes flickered. Delta's legs and arms twitched, her fingers and toes curling. Delta's mouth, frozen in a neutral frown, thawed into her standard straight line. Without any other preamble, she turned her head towards me. Amazing how fast that piercing look found its life.

"Why?" Delta asked, an altogether reasonable question that threw me.

I'd been expecting a pop off the bed, maybe a three jab combo ending with me on the hard metal floor. Instead, I spilled it all. Quick, straight-to-the-facts.

"You were going to die," I concluded. "I didn't want that."

"Not your choice to make," Delta replied, sliding her legs off the cot. "Now Alpha's going to be even harder to kill."

"We're not going after him alone," I said. "You and me, we're going back to Beta, Volt, and the humans. We might stand a chance together."

Delta straightened, stretched out a hand and put a single finger on my chest. "Gamma, you can do whatever you want, provided you never touch me again. Now stay out of my way."

"She's so damn stubborn," Kaydee said, lounging on my old cot. "But who knows, maybe she'll win?"

I didn't know who deserved a reply first and in my hesitation Delta picked up her jagged blade. The vessel ran her eyes along the weapon's length, convincing herself it looked as good as ever.

"You can't," I said.

"You can't stop me," Delta replied, putting the blade up on her shoulder, heading for the room's exit.

"If you do this alone, you will lose." I didn't move after her. Wanted, somehow, for my standing still to show how separated Delta would be. "You will be outnumbered and destroyed. After he's done with you, Alpha will do the same to me. He'll find the Voices and delete them. His mechs will crush Beta and murder every human remaining on Starship."

Delta slowed, stopped, flashed a tight look back at me, "You want me to run."

"I want us to work together to stop him and convince the humans we're more than accessories."

A rattling bang cut Delta's reply. Alvie barked and we both followed the dog towards the apartment's entrance. A second bang followed, this one accompanied by a metallic slicing sound. As Delta leveled her blade towards the door, I backed up a step, looking for a weapon and finding none.

Bare hands again.

"Be ready," Delta said, squaring her shoulders, bending her knees.

I felt sorry for whatever waited on that door's other side.

"Remember," I said as another bang hit. The door's spirals squealed, one jerked off its thread at the top. "We head left. Get away."

"If I see Alpha, I'm taking his head."

A fourth bang sent the apartment's door falling in, the spiral arms twisted like a wilting flower. The red gem faded to black as broken wires sparked along the edges, showering the intruder with their white-gold embers. The first mech through dragged its heavy silver baton on the ground, hunching over to get inside the apartment.

"Gamma!" The mech shouted, and the voice coming from its speakers didn't belong to some nameless machine. "Have you kept your promise? Have you delivered Delta to me?"

"About that . . . " I started, and Delta finished.

Despite the cramped quarters, the big mech reacted quick to Delta's burst, ignoring the cumbersome baton to snatch out with a fast gunmetal hand. Delta flipped her grip, swinging the blade up and right across her body. The edge sliced off the reaching fingers and the reverse grip let Delta jump over the remaining palm, blade and body staying just under the ceiling. She landed, with her right hand now on my left, her back to the big mech's face.

And shoved the blade right where it belonged.

"Time to go," Delta said, the mech's sterile grimace breaking into a fiery death behind her.

"Right with you," I replied, Alvie wheeze-barking beside me.

Together, our weird trio clambered over the mech and into the Conduit. As we joined that blue mist, I had a major urge to go back inside Leo's busted apartment: at least there, the mechs could only come at us from one direction.

"Wow," Kaydee said. "He did not trust you at all."

Packing the Conduit causeway on either side were more University guards. These had their batons held aloft, ready to strike. I counted six on either side, and more, smaller mechs coming to reinforce them. In the Conduit's vast center, buzzing noises foretold coming couriers and other fliers. They'd be here in moments, ready to pin us down.

And here was the part in my plan where details went fuzzy. I'd bet on having enough time to get away with Delta, bet on Alpha being either less maniacal or slower to turn on me. Both turned out wrong, and now Delta and I were in the same spot we'd been before, mechs bearing down on us with nowhere to turn.

"Aft," Delta growled, pivoting left and heading towards the big mech.

"Go," I said to Alvie and we both ran after her.

The first mech, three meters tall of implacable metal, raised his baton and slammed it towards Delta. Unlike the clunkier mechs, pressed into combat service with functions meant for cleaning, for food prep, this one knew how to fight. The swing anticipated Delta's speed and forced her to stop, flinging her blade up to deflect the baton's front end into a shaking causeway smash. The heft sent Delta to one knee, both hands wrapped on her blade's hilt to keep it held.

Alvie had no such restrictions: the dog jumped, caught the baton and ran down the fat head into another jump towards the guardian's vulnerable face. The mech reached towards Alvie with his off-hand, but I dove into it, gripping the bigger mech's left wrist with my own hands. I pressed, denting the mech, keeping my grip, keeping the hand short of Alvie.

My dog struck the mech's face with fury, rending and snapping and destroying. The mech reeled back, dropping its baton and shaking me free, reaching up towards Alvie.

"Jump!" I shouted to the dog, and Alvie obeyed almost before I'd finished the words, leaping towards me.

I caught the heavy puppy, then dropped Alvie right down onto the walkway. Behind me, Delta called out a warning: the first mech from the right had closed, was swinging down. I started to turn only for a crash to shake the walkway. The mech we'd damaged hit the railing, falling over the edge as another, baton already waving back from its clearing swing, took its place.

We'd been lucky facing one. Two more with others lingering behind?

"Leap of faith," Kaydee said as Alvie barked at the closing mech. "It'd kill a human, but you might survive."

"Leap of faith?" I scrambled across the causeway, picked up the fallen mech's dropped baton. "What are you talking about?"

Behind me, Delta's blade rang out as she parried a swing. With my own mech looming, I didn't want to take the chance on my fighting skills. Heaving, I launched the baton over my head, the full force turning the weapon into a blunt missile. My target moved its own baton fast enough to deflect, but only so much, my strike catching the mech in its shoulder and knocking the big machine onto its back.

Only for three of those mechanized hounds to come dashing over its body, yellow-lit eyes looking for blood.

"Jump into the Conduit!" Kaydee said, for once putting some urgency in her voice. "It's a scrap metal mess at the bottom, but you might make it!"

Ordinarily, I'd want to throw in some analysis, figure out the odds and establish a plan. With certain death flying fang-first at me, ordinary wouldn't work.

"Delta!" I called, turning and grabbing Alvie, throwing him over in a long stride to the railing. "Follow me!"

I couldn't tell if my friend saw, couldn't tell if she understood. I flexed my synthetic calves, pressed down with my right foot, felt a claw tear into my left leg, and flew, twisting, over the railing into the misty blue.

SEVENTEEN

TRASH TROUBLES

I turned as I fell, looking up into that bright blue as the levels flew by around me. Air buffeted my back, ruffled my hair. Kaydee, falling next to me, screamed in a mix of terror and delight. Unlike the Garden, at least, falling here didn't mean bouncing off chains, objects. Instead, blue mist all the way.

Life, such as it was, didn't flash before my eyes. No slowdown offered contemplation. We'd tried to run and whether we'd make it depended on physics, luck, and the waste Alpha's mechs had sent to the Conduit's bottom.

One mech's trash, another mech's survival.

Alvie's landing echoed up to me a second before I struck, its puffy sprinkle giving me a slight hope before I caromed off a grungy pile. The strike flared warnings in my back as I rolled down a trash slope, bolts and bits digging in with every turn. Furniture, ruined signage, half-charred refuse served as my catcher's mitt. Meter after meter, I bounced and slammed, limbs flying end over end.

Until I stopped, wedged between an old mattress and a bulky door bent in its middle. The V formed by their shapes served as a nest, one I laid in for a long moment, counting the green diamond pattern on the white mattress. My systems evaluated themselves, determined my demise unlikely. Minor structural damage. Fixes would be important, perhaps joint replacements to get optimal efficiency back. But, my analysis confirmed, I could walk. Even run, albeit with a limp. A rough picture, given that Alpha would be sending his mechs after us, but it could've been worse.

"I'd have been pancaked," Kaydee said, swinging her legs from the mattress top. "Leo really built you all well."

"He did," I said, sitting up. "I guess he expected us to handle anything."

"About the only thing he did right."

The famed split. Leo and Kaydee, friends and more, ripped apart by Starship's own class differences. Kaydee spared Leo little vitriol, but I'd not heard much from the Voices member on the situation. A one-sided story, Kaydee's tale had worrying weight: Leo's willingness to trample on the less fortunate didn't bode especially well.

An issue for another day, one I'd probably never see.

A wheeze-bark directed my attention further up the rubble mound. Alvie's paws scrabbled in the air, the dog otherwise buried. I pushed off the mattress, making my slip-sliding way up. The Conduit's misted air didn't help, coating all the garbage in a thin wet film. My hands and feet missed their marks, my progress slow as my clothes and skin caught on broken crap. I felt what my system hinted: muscles firing slower than normal, fingers slipping when they should've locked in.

Another shape crested the mound as I reached Alvie, her own shadow a welcome sight against the blue. If I'd been injured, Delta stood looking upward as if she'd made her own landing a perfect ten. Sure, she had her scrapes, but that jagged sword still sat in her hands as she balanced on a busted bed frame—perhaps my mattress's previous home—without the slightest problem.

"You ran," Delta said as I dug Alvie out. "Left my back open."

"Didn't have a choice," I said, my puppy bending forward and getting his footing. Alvie wheeze-barked and jumped around, seeming to like sliding in the miniature junk landslides the dog caused. "They had us."

"This makes twice now that you've screwed me in a fight, Gamma," Delta said. "Next time, stay away."

"Or what, you'll kill me?"

"I might."

"Good, Delta. Good," I replied. The fall, the back-and-forth with Alpha, the mechs and humans again swarmed my normal stoic self and left it battered. "Because that's what I'm looking for right now. More threats from my friends."

"Then—"

I stood, a shaky endeavor, but I planted one foot on a shredded sign and wedged the other against a split bar. Pointed a finger at Delta, "No, no *then*, no *if you,* because that's done now. You tried your way and it failed. I tried mine and, guess what, it didn't do so great either. So we're going a third route."

"Which is?"

"I didn't destroy the Voices up there," I said. "Leo hid them away. Alpha's going to hunt them down because they're the only ones that could take back control of Starship. We find the Voices, keep them safe, and reunite with Val and Beta. Together, we hit the Bridge."

"That won't be quick. Alpha will have time to fortify."

"It's a chance, and it's the only one we have."

I waited for Delta to ignore my analysis, to declare once again that a solo assault would be good enough. Instead she looked at me, looked up towards the Bridge, hidden far above, and nodded.

"Okay. But quickly."

"On that, at least, we agree."

Moving fast proved easier to say than to do. While Delta skipped down the rubble pile with targeted jumps, landing on each discarded dump with perfect placement, Alvie and I rolled, stumbled, fell, and otherwise looked much like the wreckage we traversed. We also didn't really have a direction except to get as far down and away as possible.

Already, up above, whirring, whining mech engines gave away Alpha's disbelief over our cliff-jumping demise. I figured the vessel would want confirmation that we'd splattered ourselves, but the speed at which he dispatched the mechs was a little disheartening.

"You'll never be free, my friend," Kaydee said as I tripped over what looked like an old oven and landed face first a few meters down the slope. Delta, off to my left, laughed. "They'll always want you now."

"Ugh," I replied, pushing up on a fraying couch cushion that'd been kind enough to catch me. "Why?"

"Because once you make yourself noticed, that's what happens," Kaydee said. "I should know. Once Leo and I attracted enough attention for our designs, we were pestered endlessly."

"By your mother?"

"By her and everyone else. All the factions that wanted new mechs for this and that," Kaydee stopped, tapped her chin—trademark rainbow sparks popping out with every tap—and pointed towards the left side, the same side we'd plunged from. "I think we're about at the right spot."

"The right spot for what?" I stood, and almost fell over again as Alvie caught up to me and bashed into my leg, wheeze-barking in what I assumed was delight at our tumbling adventure.

"We called it the Cesspool," Kaydee said. "Where trash would go before getting re-purposed for the Fabrication Lines or whatever else. Things would get stripped to their basic parts to be re-used, and the metal bits we didn't want would get tossed after to the Junker."

"What is your mind telling you?" Delta called, sweeping her blade towards the approaching noise. "We are wasting time."

"Go that way," I started off left, crunching down to the Conduit's absolute bottom.

Down here the ship's normally clean hull had a grime coating. Debris crunched to dust layered along a floor covered with a stiff foam. Laid, I figured, to protect the hard metal hull from plunging trash. The rubble piles stretched back and forth behind me like a mishmash mountain range, giving little hint to how long the Conduit's bottom had gone without its clean-up crew.

Days? Years? Decades?

Any answer dissipated when Delta found Kaydee's doorway up a short, wide lift from the base floor to the next level. Designed to carry its crap cargo, the lift churned us up slow and steady, depositing us right in front of a huge six meter-wide entrance to a place whose dirt-marred sign had been graffitied over with the word 'Cesspool' in bright green paint.

"See?" Kaydee noted. "Just like I said."

As we left the lift, new lights splashed down behind us, bright circles combing the junk mounds. Alpha's mechs here and hunting. I didn't need to tell Delta anything: she darted inside and Alvie and I followed.

Through the doorway, the Cesspool's name proved itself quick. Big pools, arranged across from each other, burbled with different colored lighting. Inside the entrance, on our left, sat two emerald pools, while on our right, a blue and orange one glowed. Each looked clear, clean, and Alvie made to sniff one.

"Better not let him do that," Kaydee said. "Unless he wants to lose a limb."

I pulled Alvie back as Kaydee dished out the details: these were various acid baths, made to clean off crud that couldn't be had in the fabrication lines or anywhere else. Depending on the piece, a different concentration would be used. Back in Starship's heyday, mechs and humans would be all over this place, walking old assets through one soak to the next before heading up the lifts at the back to the Fabrication Lines or anywhere else the item needed to go.

"So you're saying there's another lift way back there?" I said when Kaydee, who'd jumped over each pool in turn during her walk-through, closed with an angry red bath at the end.

"Should be," Kaydee replied. "You getting sneaky thoughts?"

I looked Delta's way, "First we find a terminal down here so I can find where the Voices are. Then, we ride a lift to a middle level.

Alpha hopefully won't be scanning everywhere and we can get back aft without getting caught."

"Workable," Delta said.

Back towards the Conduit, those spotlights continued tracing the mounds, but none had found their way inside the Cesspool. We didn't sit on that advantage, but went deeper, past the pools and into a warren where every hallway had tracks laid into the floor. Sized like the halls in Leo's apartment, the rounded tunnels served as ways to get materials around, with cut-outs and other rooms spaced here and there to dodge oncoming carts.

Beaded diodes in the ceiling served as lights, haphazard yellows blinking through whenever the diodes hadn't gone dark. At first, I thought the shadows might serve to keep us hidden. When I noticed the writing on the walls, though, I started getting other ideas.

"Stay ready," Delta muttered as she lead us. "We might not be the only ones down here."

The scrawls, some made with knife-like etches into the metal while others looked like markers, offered a mix between warnings to stay away, welcomes, and urges to keep on going. Some offered up only simple, impossible questions, like *Why?* and *When will we be saved?*.

The writing, the lighting had Starship's normal noise for company and little else. If we were being pursued by mechs, I'd have expected to hear clomps, an engine chugging along. Instead, once we passed beyond the burbling pools, all we had were our footsteps and the constant rumble at our feet.

I asked Kaydee if she had any idea who might've left the scribblings and my blue-haired mind shook her spiked coif.

"Look, we all knew what happened here," Kaydee said. "But it wasn't like Leo and I wanted to venture this far down."

"Another class thing?"

Kaydee sighed, "Told you, Gamma. There's a lot I'm not proud of that we did, but at the time, it was how Starship ran."

Now wasn't the moment for another philosophical argument.

"So you don't know."

"Look, the politics here didn't make its way up top often," Kaydee said. "If there were problems, I didn't know of any."

"Then we keep going."

Delta didn't object. Alvie, for his part, stayed close to us. The dog didn't make a sound beyond his claws on the floor, his yellow eyes shining around as he tried to keep a view of everything at once.

"Here," Delta announced as we passed into a broader, circular room where several cart tracks intersected with a moving roundtable in the center. Set into an alcove on the side was a terminal, monitor blinking green and ready for use. "Make it fast, Gamma."

"On it," I said, pinching my fingers and forming the port. "While I'm in there, I won't hear you. I will, though, feel you. Tap me if you need me out."

"Got it," Delta said. Her hard look softened. She put a stiff hand on my shoulder. "Gamma, don't screw up."

As pep talks from Delta went, that was about as good as it got. I plugged my fingers into the terminal, and the Cesspool disappeared.

If only it'd been replaced with something better.

EIGHTEEN

AROUND AND AROUND

If Val's terminal offered a stained glass chapel and the Voices had their castle, the Cesspool's owners leapt after their own idea. I'd visited vast digital plains, beautiful meadows and star-crossed nebulae. I'd never been to a rushing river. Whomever ran the Cesspool's operating system kept their programs spinning, creating and deleting data with a madcap speed that had me, as I caught my bearings, drifting along in a sudden stream.

I popped in amid the moving liquid, one second in a digital transmission tunnel and the next coasting along on an infinite ride. Blue-green water flushed me forward down a meters-wide slide. A closer look at the droplets splashing on me revealed they weren't the meat-space molecules but instead coded bits carrying instructions for cleaning this, making that.

An ambient yellow void surrounded the river, catching spray pouring over the slide's sides. At first I wondered, bobbing along, if those digital bits were being lost forever. A splatter on my head answered the question: those drops simply fell around the world to splash back into the river, a recycling function.

I'd come seeking the Voices, but I couldn't understand why

someone would set up their terminal like this. Constantly moving files and folders would make anything impossible to find, would make work impossible to do.

Kaydee's head broke the water beside me and she spit some into the air like a whale gasping for breath.

"The hell is this?" Kaydee asked, joining me in the floating journey.

While I'd never gone swimming before, I found I didn't have to try here. No weight drew me beneath the river's surface. Instead I felt like a feather on the wind, carried along by a force I couldn't affect.

"Someone has been very creative," I replied.

"Why?"

"Good question, and one I think we'll have to answer before we can continue our search."

Like with Val's terminal, to go hunting for the Voices I'd need to get access to Starship's network. Unlike Val's terminal, the river here offered no doorway to walk through, no branch to grab that'd take me where I needed to go. As impossible as the river would be to use, I had to hope a solution rested somewhere, a key to pick the river's lock and understand its mystery.

"How are we supposed to answer that?" Kaydee asked.

Without immediate clues, I figured we'd need to dig deeper. I hadn't been able to understand Delta, the Nursery mechs, or even myself until I'd taken a closer look at the reasons behind our actions. Delta, for example, went into every fight with reckless abandon because she believed, had been programmed to believe, that she could win any battle and that it was her duty to do so.

As for me, saving the humans had played the early part, a goal putting its pressure on my every action until I figured out, in the Nursery, how to get around its bars. Frame every action as advancing the human cause and the pressure would dissipate, my functions allowing me the freedom I needed.

"Who would make a world like this, and why?" I asked. "That's where we start."

"Someone who loved water?" Kaydee ventured.

"The river we're in and what it represents to the terminal's operator are two different things." I scooped up a cupful of digital liquid, let it run through my fingers. "I believe we're stuck in a security function. Whomever owns this doesn't want to let us inside."

"Shocking, that."

"Unusual for Starship," I replied. "Most terminals haven't had much security."

"Thank the Voices," Kaydee replied, flipping over into a backstroke alongside me. "Once things started getting rocky, they went on an open-information crusade. They'd have Leo or one of his lackeys run scans along Starship, pinging every networked computer and checking for encryption. If they picked up your terminal, you'd better trash it fast."

"They were hunting for rebellion?"

"Organized resistance plans, blackmail, whatever," Kaydee said, her eyes resolutely upward into the golden glow. "All shopped under the guise that you didn't have anything to fear if you had nothing to hide. Leo would tell me whenever they were going to scan and I'd unplug my terminal."

"But someone might have chosen to defend themselves against the intrusion like this?"

"Maybe, but that'd just be a flag for the Voices to come find you. It's like, you build the wall, you become the target."

We drifted, both dropping into our thoughts. I couldn't tell if Kaydee was trying to decipher a solution or if she'd wandered into old memories. Before, those memories used to leak into my perceptions, showing me ghosts of Kaydee's past. They hadn't come out much lately, though. Possibly she'd grasped how to control them, how to hide herself from me.

"Why aren't you showing me your memories anymore?" I asked as the river sent us into another turn. It would, I saw, eventually curve back into itself, a forever loop. "I used to see you wherever I went."

"Found the leak in my own code and plugged it," Kaydee said. "Don't worry, I'll still leech into your functions over time, coloring them with my own flavor, but at least you won't have past me prancing before your eyes."

"So you're blocking me."

Kaydee's eyes flashed as she glanced at me, "You *want* to see those memories?"

"They provided context."

A laugh, "Glad I could help. Ever think, though, that I might like my memories to stay mine?"

"If I forced you?"

"Sorry, Gamma, but you can't act on that threat anymore," Kaydee stretched, still floating on her back. "We're so knotted up now that trying to delete me would turn you into a mushy mess. Delta would kill you just to put you out of your misery."

I reached out, touched her hand. Felt the code beneath it, all the nesting algorithms helping Kaydee power herself, visually and otherwise. I also felt the warmth, the pressure as she gripped my hand in return, the two of us drifting along the river together. A nice, quiet second amid a lifetime, so far, too devoid of them.

And in that moment, I found an answer.

"You're blocking me because I'm not a threat anymore," I said.

"Uh, what?"

"Your memories, Kaydee," I continued, words beginning to pile up, rushing out as I untangled them. "You're blocking me from them because you can afford to."

"Okay, sure?"

"You said anyone putting a block like this river would've risked everything while the Voices were around," I said. "Therefore, they must've put this security up after the Voices stopped their sweeps."

"Right when Starship was collapsing into its mech hell, I'd imagine," Kaydee said. "So?"

"It means there's a chance we're not alone."

"Gamma, again, we're talking a very long time since my mother became a digital ghost and you graced us with your presence. Even if someone had lived back then and put all this together, they wouldn't be around now."

"That's just it, Kaydee. The terminal was on when we found it. Active. Someone's kept it in good shape."

"Well, if you're right, we left the one person that might give us some answers alone with Delta." Kaydee splashed me, I deflected the water. "How much you want to bet she's killed them already?"

I LURCHED from the river back into the Cesspool's dark tunnels. Felt a hand on my arm, a second cover my lips. Delta had me, and a quick head shake confirmed the story her hands told: be quiet, stay quiet.

The vessel's jagged sword leaned against the hallway's rounded wall, our little alcove not providing much cover. Nonetheless, we pressed deeper into it as yellow lights shone back and forth, gliding along the walls within meters of us. The spying glow matched the same hue as the spotlights back in the Conduit's junk piles, Alpha's mechs coming to find us.

Any chance to tell Delta about my idea faded as the mechs came closer. Their whirrs echoed off the walls, like a hundred spinning fans, as they eased down the hallway. Soon the disc-like halos of their spotlights ran past us, replaced by the expanding cones emitted from their lamps. Surely they'd reach our hiding place and take us, surely we'd be discovered.

Delta eased away from me. Slid to the alcove's right wall, the one closest to the approaching mechs. Her expression eased from stern panic to the steady fighter's stance. Her mind wasn't hard to read: we'd done it my way, jumping and running. Now Delta would have her chance.

At least I didn't have to look far for a weapon. The terminal offered a desk chair, one small and metal. Sturdy, if lacking in anything resembling comfort. Any cushion was long gone, showing only a stained slat for seating. With two hands I picked it up, flipped it to get a good grip on its back support, the four legs spearing forth.

At a nod from Delta I bent my knees, prepped for a charge.

I considered myself something of a combat veteran. In worlds real and virtual, I'd faced off against machines and humans, used weapons and my own fists. I'd been outnumbered and advantaged. I'd learned from those prior fights, plugged the details and the data into my memory. No longer did I face the coming struggle with a nervous anticipation, no longer did I wonder how far to bend my legs, how tight to hold the chair, whether it would be better to swing the thing as opposed to throwing it. I knew how far my first step would carry me, how much force I could bring to bear on my target.

All I waited for in that moment was a chance to begin.

The first courier, a half-open cylinder designed to cart containers back and forth along the Conduit, hovered into view. Its humming fans kept the machine aloft as its yellow spotlight swept first right, catching the blank wall and Delta's leaning blade, then began its passage left.

Delta struck before the mech found us. She put both her hands together and jammed them down on top of the mech in a smooth motion, overwhelming the fans and driving the courier into the ground. Metal gnashed as the courier tried to get back aloft, an attempt made harder when Delta gave it a hard kick, spinning the machine through the air, right into her leaning blade.

I expected the sword and the mech to fall, tangled, but Delta hit the courier with enough force that the blade, even as it fell, sheared off part of the courier. Cables bled out as the machine collapsed in a final crackling hum. A triumph robbed when the second machine found Delta with its spotlight.

"Down!" I called and Delta ducked.

I whipped the chair over her head, launching it right into the second courier's golden eye. I threw the chair like a dart, so it didn't turn end over end, instead delivering a leg straight into the spotlight. The glare winked out, the courier mech took the hit and bounced off the tunnel wall, wavering. Delta followed up my throw, rolling to her left, scraping her blade off the ground and blitzing the dazed machine.

Its parts soon found the floor, carved three ways.

"Were we fast enough?" I asked, looking at the two dead machines.

"Unclear," Delta said, then nodded past me, towards the terminal. "Did you find what we needed in there?"

"Not what we needed, but an interesting question," I replied.

"Questions don't matter. It's the Voices or we run."

Delta made a good point: this terminal might be locked, but there were others that had unfettered access to Starship's network, including Val's own. We could retreat to safety and then resume our search. It would give Alpha more time to find the Voices before us, but we'd stay alive.

A key factor, that.

"Okay, we go," I said.

We ran through the sprawling Cesspool, its treatment rooms, crew quarters, and scrap stockpiles proving a difficult warren. Still, we were vessels, and our senses of direction came not from intuition but hardcoded knowledge. We pushed towards Starship's starboard side, an edge that would, should, have another way up. Not for normal use, but for the materials making their way through the process.

As we moved, noises rose, echoes from the Conduit. Mechs climbing down, landing with hard thuds, their metal mashings making clear their intentions. The couriers had beamed out what they'd found, and Alpha was sending in the enforcers to finish us off. The big guardians might have a tough time fitting through these tunnels, but Alpha could bury us in smaller mechs, run us dry then smash us to bits with our batteries dead.

Unless we found a way out.

The Cesspool's freight elevator sat at a four way intersection, our tunnel meeting up with several more like half a spider, a half-moon end revealing the elevator and its cage-like door. As wide as the Cesspool's own entrance, the elevator offered a spacious ride, if we could get the door open. A simple switch sat on the elevator's right, a dim red light glowing on the box.

As Delta went to the cage door itself, testing its locked bars, I went to the switch. Tried to flip it and found the lever stuck. Sitting beneath the red-glowing light was a key hole, an archaic, manual method. Weirder still, the keyhole looked newer than anything else on the elevator, as if someone had torn out the original panel and replaced it with something simpler.

"Something that can't be hacked," Kaydee said, standing next to me.

"What's wrong?" Delta asked.

"We're stuck," I replied.

Delta glared at me, hefted her blade, swung and sliced the elevator's grated gateway apart, clearing a way onto the flat lift. She nodded towards the ride.

"Nice, but not the problem," I replied, tapping the red light. "The lift's not going anywhere without this working."

And we'd have to get the lift working soon. I looked close at the keyhole, its sharp-cut lines, and tried to ignore the hissing, the pounding, the clanging as a mechanized army ran towards us. No matter how many battles I'd fought, no matter how hardened my circuits, I couldn't block out the sound, quiet the fear.

NINETEEN

KNIFE FIGHT

The keyhole proved an obstacle I couldn't surpass. I could press my fingers together to make several different ports, my faux fingernails sliding away to reveal various pins and slots, but nothing that could get inside the metal and twist. Delta offered to cut away the locked portion, something I considered, but had to deny.

"You might cut the wires and then we'd have no shot at activating the lift," I replied, the clomping mech approach spreading to the other hallways now.

Alpha must've issued thorough directives: make sure the two vessels couldn't get away, block every exit.

"Then we go up ourselves," Delta said, and I followed her through the sliced gate onto the lift.

Above sat a protective grate, one Delta could probably cut apart. The difficulty lay beyond, visible in the golden light from nested lamps around us: the freight shaft had no ladder, just sheer walls without handholds. Delta met my eyes and I could see the calculation running, how many notches could she cut out as we climbed, how far up could we get before the mechs caught us?

"Not enough," I answered the un-asked question. The floors shook and Alvie whined. "New plan."

"Which is?"

"We pick a path," I replied. "Cut through one way and then keep running, outsmart them and get back to the Conduit. Proceed on the lowest level as far as we can. Maybe all the way."

"They'll harass us every step," Delta said.

"I didn't say it'd be easy. Or fun."

Delta nodded, left the lift to stand in the room's center. I joined her, and for a long several seconds we listened, watched for approaching spotlights in the hallways.

"The middle," Delta said. "The least vibrations."

Didn't necessarily mean the least mechs, but Starship's most dangerous machine denizens tended to be heavy ones.

"When?" I asked.

"Once we see them on all sides. It'll make it harder for them to double back."

Again, I cast about, looking for a would-be weapon. With Delta's help, we cut free part of the lift gate, giving me a hefty bar to use. With extra strikes, Delta turned its square end into a piercing point. Not quite a blade, but deadly enough.

"Can't get over how you're using swords and fists on a big space-ship," Kaydee said, watching us work. "It's like traveling back in time."

"Guns didn't work out so well for you, if I recall," I replied.

"Wasn't their fault," Kaydee cut back. "Numbers are numbers, and machines don't get tired."

"Neither do we."

Not quite true, but kinetic motion kept Delta and I charged up enough. I also drew in extra power whenever I jacked into some-thing, be it a terminal or, say, the barriers up near the Bridge. Delta seemed to snag quiet moments to do the same, snaking a finger pair into an available outlet. I'd left her getting juice in Leo's apartment too.

It'd take a long time for us to go dead. The physical destruction Alpha's mechs would deliver was a more immediate fear.

Ready to make good on that fear, Alpha's opening salvo appeared in the three tunnels approaching the lift. His mechs came organized: centered in each tunnel rolled a wheel-driven kitchen mech, limbs designed for chopping and cooking waving in our direction. Hovering over their shoulders were multiple couriers, their front ends bristling with grafted-on energy weapons, barrel tips glowing a hot white.

No way presented itself as the easy option, but Delta picked one anyway, choosing left and bolting. She issued a sharp challenge, a wordless battlecry sure to draw any wandering mech our way.

"Don't die!" Kaydee shouted after me as I followed my vessel friend and her black blade into battle.

The couriers in our chosen path fired first, their weapons giving away their intent like a light slowly turning on. Delta bounced left, using the curling hallway walls for running room, leaving me alone coming up the middle.

Before I could process the odds of me doing the same, Delta kicked off the wall, dodging the courier's opening shots—their bolts, too fast to really see, left boiling orange blots in Delta's footsteps—and diving over the cutlery mech's whirling knives. I heard more than saw the left courier explode, noticed the right one swiveling away from me to focus on Delta's immediate threat.

The cutlery machine did no such thing, continuing its slow assault. Its various knives returned from their flails in Delta's direction to stab at me, attacks I dodged in my patented fashion: backing away.

At least until I heard grumbling whines behind me as the other hallways, unmolested, proved easy travels for Alpha's other mechs. If I didn't get past this thing, I'd get pincered in moments. What would happen after, well, I decided not to entertain.

"Can't we talk about this?" I asked the lunging knives.

"Order up!" The culinary mech replied in a cheery tone.

So I swung my steel bar, the heavy thing attracting the knives.

The mech bit in hard on my swing, banging its blades off my weapon, nicking my bar but breaking, bending its own in the attempt. Chef knives might look mean, but these weren't meant to slice metal. Sparks flew, a common feature in these fights, and one I gritted through, pressing forward and swinging the bar back across my body.

Alvie, for his part, wheeze-barked around my feet, those arms and their sharp ends keeping the dog at distance.

My back-swing took off more knives, rendering the mech eerie in its gnarled, jagged mess. My bar bent several thin arms too, sending them scraping along one another as the mech approached me, every scratch throwing off golden sparks, sending a shearing noise through the hallway. One opening wider around me as I reached its end.

I'd run out of real estate.

A bright bolt zapped past me, burning into the floor near my feet. Another hallway's courier taking its first pot shot. They might not be military machines, designed to cast death with precise targeting, but I couldn't rely on poor shooting to save my life. I had to try something different, something desperate.

I blamed it on Kaydee, her behaviors seeping into my methods.

Setting my feet, I kicked towards the battered culinary mech. I led with the bar, putting it forward like a spear. The machine hacked at it, arms and busted knives clattering against my weapon, shearing off paint, chipping the core beneath. When the bar itself made contact with the mech I lurched, almost to a halt, but I braced the bar against my shoulder and pushed.

Those Volt-enhanced muscles came to life, sucking energy from my battery to overpower the culinary mech's motor—not exactly built for movement to begin with—and shove the big robot backwards. I yelled, a furious joy pulled from the old tales, the cry delivered in triumph as I backed the mech away.

Premature.

A second bolt hit my back on the left, a stinging alert saying my left side had just lost a third of its power. A slicing cut caught me from behind, digging into my shoulder, as the second, pursuing culinary mech closed the distance faster than my shoving could get me free. The cut faltered my push, my right arm wavering at the strike and dropping the bar.

I'd cleared enough for another alcove on my left, one I stumbled into, Alvie darting in behind me. Dim and empty save some cleaning gear, the tuck-away had a single golden light by which to show me my approaching demise. Two culinary mechs, freed from obstruction, pressed into the alcove's entrance, bumping into one another, each one preventing its partner from getting close.

I pressed myself against the alcove's back, those slicing knives less than a meter from my face. Alvie curled in beside me, yellow eyes wide, glowing.

"Close one," Kaydee said, huddling with me. "They nearly had you."

"They do have me," I said, sinking towards the floor and watching small shapes hover into view. "The couriers."

Without much space to move, the little bots could shoot me with impunity. Either they'd roast me now, or wait me out, trap me down here like so many others in Starship, running out of time.

"Delta's going to come back," Kaydee said, sitting on the floor next to me.

"Kaydee," I said. "Listen. You hear her?"

The slashing, tearing sounds usually telling Delta's progress had disappeared. The vessel had either escaped, breaking her way to freedom and deciding it was better to proceed on her own, or she'd been caught by too many mechs, even for her.

"Ambush tactics," Kaydee said. "Just wait."

I had neither the choice or the time to wait or anything else. Behind those whirling blades, the couriers lined up their shots. A mop bucket sat to my left and I grabbed it, held it before my face. Counted to one then ducked left. One shot burned into the wall where my head had been, another melted half the bucket to slag.

A third took my right foot, frying my synthetic skin and leaving me without a way to walk.

Kaydee screamed for me. Alvie barked, backing into a corner.

And I yelled for Delta. A last ditch call.

"Kaydee and I need you, Delta!" I shouted. "If you're here, please, don't leave us!"

I wasn't sure why I included Kaydee in that call except the two of us had been through so much, so many near death moments, that we didn't feel separate anymore. She and I shared a single body, and death to one of us would mean the end of both.

At least, that's how I felt, staring at those orange and white blossoms on the couriers, yelling our names, hoping Delta would hear.

Or if not Delta, somebody, some saint stuffed in Starship's dark underbelly.

Lasers don't make a sound by themselves. Super focused light, the beams spit forth in a flash, devastate their target, the evidence at the strike point. The hits happened one after another, three precise shots, each one knocking out a courier mech with a bright blue bolt. One shot split the mech in half, a second melted off the drone's laser. The third burned a courier's jets, the mech plummeting behind its culinary brethren, hitting the floor with a bang.

More flashes washed out the alcove's lamp, striking the culinary mechs, melting through them. Those whirling blades slowed, stopped, as the mech's power supplies failed.

"Delta?" I asked. She hadn't used a weapon like the laser before, but maybe she'd found one? "Was that you?"

"Who else would it be?" Kaydee said.

No answer came back, but further flashes laced down the corridor across the alcove, hitting mechs I couldn't see back towards the elevator. These weren't scattered, random shots, like the kind I'd seen in Kaydee's memories, ones fired in desperation from soldiers under assault. These were precise, like the couriers had been shooting at me.

So maybe Delta? I called out again, heard no response. The flashes slowed, stopped, and with them came a different silence.

Alpha's mechs no longer filled the Cesspool with their pounding feet, their whirring engines.

The culinary mechs, both dead, shivered, shifted. I stood, watched as something pulled at them.

"I'd get ready to fight," Kaydee said. "Who knows what's behind that thing?"

Good advice. I picked up the half-melted bucket, planning to throw it at whatever waited. Buy myself a moment to lurch forward. My busted right foot excluded running from the survival equation, but my arms were strong enough. Deliver a good strike and I might knock the thing out before it could shoot me.

Deep down, my own logic said this was a delirious idea, but what other chance did I have?

The left mech rumbled, rocked forward, then fell back, its wheels sliding up into the air. A shape took its place, stepping in front. Humanoid, bigger than Delta. Hands held a large weapon. I threw the bucket, saw the thing deflect my attempt as I fell into a desperate swing.

My target back-stepped and I hit the floor, an unglamorous end to my attempt. As I put my hands beneath me, started to push up, I heard Kaydee swear, not in anger, but in confusion. The weapon's hot end settled on my head, keeping me from rising.

"Don't," I said, trying to place what was going on, what combination of words, pleas, would keep me alive.

The thing, its voice carrying a robot's vibration, a human's emotion, asked one thing, "Where's Kaydee?"

TWENTY

TICKING CLOCKS

You want to create an impression, try replacing half your face with a metal plate. Then, etch gold wires into that plate that at first look random but, as people stare, come clear as a circuit board.

The faceplate wasn't the only change drifting the human from his starting point to his current, cyborg-like existence: glimmers in his cut clothing revealed more metallic streaks, these painted over in various reds, blues, golds. His breathing rattled in the near-silence after his question, air moving through parts not wholly biological.

"Kaydee?" I replied, trying to buy myself a second.

Something about the man seemed familiar, though I'd never seen his bald head, his stocky frame before. His eyes? No. Maybe the way he held the weapon tentatively in his arms, a tool not wanted but necessary. When he knelt to look me straight on, a subtle hydraulic hiss echoed.

"I know you," the man said, reaching a hand up to cup my face, fingers pressing along my jaw line. He pulled me closer. Instinct said to push back, logic told me resistance was futile. "So close, but there it is."

He let go, stood back up and leveled his weapon at me. Alvie, creeping from the corner, snarled in my defense. Good thing, because my busted right foot refused to give me leverage.

"Can you put the weapon down?" I asked.

Not moving the rifle in the slightest, the man raised one hand to his metal faceplate and pressed in on a button near his ear. Alvie nuzzled in close to me, watching the man, legs ready to spring. I whispered to the dog to hold, keep his cool.

"Found a second one," he said. "Bring her home. I'll join you." He took a breath, eyes focused on me. "No, I won't need any help. This one's not so dangerous."

"Gamma," Kaydee whispered, appearing next to me. "Don't do anything stupid."

"Wasn't planning on it," I replied, only for the man's rifle to twitch, his hand to leave the communication device in his head.

All part of the plan.

"Who're you talking to?" the man asked.

"Kaydee," I replied.

Those eyes narrowed. That face tightened.

"Explain."

"Are you human?"

"I am where it counts," the man replied. "I won't ask again."

"I'm not human. Not where it counts," I said. "My brain is a processor, my synapses are memory banks. A battery pumps energy rather than blood through my skin." I raised my hands, waved them slow in the light. "Yet, I'm not like these mechs you destroyed either. My routines are complex, but not complex enough to pass off as a person. Not without Kaydee's help."

The man stayed quiet. Didn't move his weapon either. Kaydee watched me too, curious.

"She taught me how to laugh. How to smile and joke, how to run and how to find my way across Starship," I continued. "She told me stories from her life and let me learn from them. She told me many times about one person in particular, one person that she missed."

Now that rifle wavered, that face loosened. His eyes grew distant, and I figured I'd made my mark.

"Kaydee's been guiding me ever since the Voices woke me up," I said, "and now she's brought me to you, Leo."

Okay, so not quite the truth. Kaydee hadn't really *brought* me here, and it seemed like, given Kaydee's continually confused expression, she hadn't expected Leo to still be alive at all. Nonetheless, I went with it. This long with Kaydee and other humans had shown they liked emotional ties with events: Leo's fondness for Kaydee would make him more likely to help me.

"There it is," Leo said, leaning in, inspecting something near my left shoulder. I glanced down, saw nothing beyond my dirty gear. "Partial truth, partial lie. You *are* a vessel." Leo stood back up, gave me space. "Kaydee's your mind, then. Not what we intended." Leo snorted, once, soft. "But I'm happy she's with us."

"Then you'll help me?"

Leo didn't say no.

OFFERING his shoulder for me to lean on, Leo and I, with Alvie clacking along behind, left the alcove and returned to the Cesspool's rounded hallways. Our start stopped fast when I saw Alpha's disabled, damaged mechs: other humans, most with more comprehensive metal modifications than Leo, swarmed the machines. Wielding wrenches, pry bars, screwdrivers, and other tools, the group took apart each mech with precision. Each person wore a pack on their shoulders, some stuffing broken parts into theirs while others saved space for intact wires, screws, other components.

"Keep moving," Leo said, directing me away from the lift, from the scavenging.

"How are they alive?" Kaydee said, and I echoed the question as Leo nudged us along.

"You're seeing how," Leo replied. "You want usual humans, look elsewhere. We're closer to the Voices than we are to how we were born."

My questioning look prompted both a sigh and a stream as we moved. Leo detailed the splintering, a crack between factions after Kaydee's fomented rebellion burned away. The ones running Starship—the Voices weren't all-powerful then—wanted more mechs, wanted the whole ship to be run by machines while they slept.

"Slept?" I interrupted.

"Cryo." Leo shook his head. "Unstable, damaging, but with their backs pressed up against an interstellar wall, they chose to run from the life they had towards a fantasy. Now they're all sealed up top, waiting for Starship to get home."

'All', in this case, turned out to be Starship's last generation of leaders, the wealthy, and the connected. They pressed Leo and several other luminaries to craft the Voices, get these digital resurrections access to Starship's network so the remainder could jump into a frozen time warp.

"Peony and I were the only ones still alive at the time," Leo said as we came into another intersection. Bangs from tools at work echoed down the corridors, burbling conversation bouncing beneath. "I rebuilt the others from stored data. They're more pure programs than Peony and I, which is why she runs the place. That, and she was the only one of us to give herself up for the mission."

"My mother?" Kaydee asked. "No way."

Leo seemed to anticipate the question, nodding when I repeated Kaydee's assertion.

"Kaydee, if you're listening," Leo said, a weird sensation as he looked at me when he spoke, "this didn't happen fast. Years went by, everyone threatening each other, Starship itself at risk. I'm still not sure how she did it, but we wound up in a kind of peace. The big players would freeze themselves, leaving Starship to the mechs and the working class."

"That didn't work out," I said.

"At first it did," Leo replied. "But people get older. Humans do, anyway. We had a choice, either go into cryo and lose control of ourselves, or do something different."

"When you say *we*, you mean . . .?"

"Not everyone," Leo had the grace to look apologetic as he tapped on a steel bulkhead, right in the center. The bulkhead shivered, slid up. "Starship never had the resources to give everyone an out. Peony chose one way. I chose both."

"The bastard split himself," Kaydee muttered as we walked through the narrow entry. "No wonder his digital version has issues. Leo always wanted it both ways."

Both ways had set Leo up pretty nice. The apartment I'd woken up in above didn't carry the character, the space on display down here. Even Val and her tribe's takeover couldn't match the techno-humans: etched or painted artwork bedazzled every surface, a rainbow lighting sifting through hung prisms up towards the top of a multi-level rectangular block.

On the far end from our entrance, water flowed in from a spout, dropping through a glass cylinder with black lines every few meters before ending up in a tank. Smaller glass tubes split off from the central cylinder, irrigating garden beds filled with . . . flowers. Muddy bronzed ladders, bolted to the chamber's walls, climbed to crafted overhangs laden with chairs, tables, and a single cot like the one I'd woken up on.

"This is something else," I said, as Leo helped me in.

The chamber's bottom floor clashed with all the creativity above: workbenches mingled with junk piles. Several other humans worked in the space, one grafting a new plate to his own left arm. When he caught me looking, the man killed his drill and flicked his eyes, both red-lit and artificial, at me. I would've been startled, might've flinched, except for my busted foot.

I nodded back instead.

"Two ways to make it till Starship lands," Leo said, settling me into a chair next to an empty workbench. I couldn't see any name-plates, no ownership markers on anything. "Either you do what they did and freeze yourself to sleep, or you stop trying to outrun biology." Leo tapped my chest with one hand as he set his weapon down. "You don't have a ticking clock. We did."

The arm grafter gave a clue as to how Leo and his group confronted their eventual demise: a gradual replacing of the living with the metal. I asked and Leo clarified as he tore off my battered boot, ripping away the cloth around my broken foot. As organs failed, as limbs were hurt or grew painful, Leo designed replacements.

"We started simple, relying on existing tech," Leo said. "Problem was, Starship didn't have all the specialized pieces. We made our own versions." A finger to the faceplate, running along the grafted line with his skin. "Not always pretty, and they won't keep us alive forever, but maybe long enough."

"Long enough to what?"

Leo didn't look up as he replied, "Would a vessel understand what it feels like to miss something you've never seen? Never felt?"

At first, I thought the answer was an easy no. How could I? Except I saw Kaydee there, looking at Leo from behind him. The way she watched him reversed my position. I hadn't been designed to care, to *love*, as sappy as that sounded on a metal hulk blazing through space in an insane machine's hands.

"I might," I said.

Rather than reply, Leo snagged a knife off the workbench and sliced away the synthetic skin around my ankle. I stopped the warnings with a command, watching as the engineer went to work on my bent plates, the flexible bars standing in for biological bones.

"We want to see a real sky," Leo said, switching tools for a small wrench, some precise pliers. "Breathe air that hasn't been recycled for a thousand years, even though none of us will have real lungs by then."

"What will you have?"

"For the ones that make it?" Leo glanced up, nodded at my head. "Our brains are the end game. Can't find a way to replicate those or replace'em without losing the person inside."

"Without turning them into minds, you mean."

Leo shook his head, "Not the same. Initially it's close but you make a neural map of someone and translate that into code, you're still only getting an image. A shell that gets farther and farther away over time."

Behind him, Kaydee froze. She had her arms wrapped around herself, teal spiked hair sharp and shooting in every direction. I couldn't tell by her face if she was about to cry or fly off into an angry storm.

"How do you know?" I asked Leo.

I felt a pop. Saw Leo toss a busted bar across the floor.

"How do I know?" Leo replied. "I've been watching myself. Talking with me. Which is, frankly, a surreal experience."

"The one with the Voices?"

"Correct."

A second pop, and my foot felt right. Solid and sturdy. As Leo sat back from me, waving me on to test his work, the door we'd come through sprang open again. This time, rather than a vessel being led in by a helping hand, Delta stormed through with her blade at the throat of another woman whose whole torso gleamed with silver-etched steel.

"Release Gamma," Delta announced, her off-hand pointing what looked like a stolen energy pistol at Leo. "Or I'll kill you all."

TWENTY-ONE

FORGED ALLIANCE

Despite her wide eyes, her shaking arms and legs, Leo did nothing to calm Delta's hostage. While the other Forgers glanced from their workbenches, Leo stood showing his hands. Showing, too, a slight smile and a slow head shake.

"I remember programming that line," Leo said as Delta leveled the stolen pistol at him. "One of the last ones. The poster hangs right above where I left you, if it's still there."

Delta didn't flinch. Didn't show any reaction at what Leo implied. Instead she flicked her eyes to me, "Gamma, you're all right?"

"Better," I replied. "I don't think they're the enemy, Delta. They took out Alpha's mechs."

"He's right," said the hostage, only for Delta to press the blade harder against her neck.

Leo, otherwise keeping very still, spoke firm, "Delta. You were the last. My ace in case everything else went wrong." His face fell into a frown. "If you're awake, then things must be dire."

"Good read," I said. "Delta, let her go. Please. We're only wasting time."

Maybe that comment did it, the touching on our real mission. Maybe Leo piqued Delta's curiosity enough to kill the aggression. Either way, the vessel shoved the hostage forward, sliding the sword away as the hostage moved, angling the gun for a good shot at the woman's back. Still keeping control.

"I don't care who you are," Delta said to Leo. "We have an objective and we are being chased."

"Chased by who?" Leo asked.

"Like you said." I rose, put a hand on Leo's shoulder. Not to comfort him, but to give Delta just another nudge in a peaceful direction. I knew from the Nursery how hard it was to pull Delta back from slaughter's brink, so I fought for every centimeter. "Starship's in a bad way. You might be able to help."

I kept on from there, spilling out the story. Alpha's takeover, the retreating Voices. Our scramble. When I finished Leo had a hand on his chin, rubbing gnarled stubble with a few fingers. His eyes weren't fixed on me, instead staring to some point over my shoulder.

"Leo," said the woman, Delta's former hostage now recovered, standing tall and glaring Delta's way. "Get them out of here. I know that look, and you better remember what you promised."

"I know what I promised, Clara," Leo replied, snapping back into focus. "Doesn't matter much if Starship crashes on the wrong world, does it?"

I stood by Delta, watching. My partner kept her hold on the blade tight, her back to the wall next to the entrance. She could keep an eye out both ways, a protection I used to focus on the back-and-forth between Leo and the other Forger.

"We stood with you to see a sky that wasn't this one," Clara said, waving at the other watching Forgers. The motion revealed most of her stomach, visible through a ripped shirt. It'd been plated over, just like Leo's face. "That's all we want, Leo. If this Alpha is going to get us there sooner, before we lose anyone else, then isn't that a good thing?"

"We said all that before the Voices lost control." Leo pointed back towards the chamber's exit. "I never thought Starship would completely fall apart."

"Liar," Clara cut him off. "We've been living down here for so long, maybe you don't remember. I do. I do." As she spoke the last words, Clara pointed left at another Forger across the room who flinched, turned away. "Acho remembers too. So do Mioh and Baker and DeMar. We all saw this coming, and that's why we came down here. We gave it all up for the one promise, Leo. The one damn promise, and now you're thinking of throwing all that away?"

"Hold on." Leo back-stepped, reached towards his workbench. "I haven't even said anything yet."

"But you're thinking it."

"I'm thinking I can tell these two where to go, and then they'll leave us alone. That's what I'm thinking."

Clara settled into a frown, watching as Leo rummaged in his workbench. Junk shuffled around in drawers. With Delta glaring daggers at everyone, I figured I might plead our case, give Leo some cover.

"Clara," I said, drawing a scathing look. "Sorry, I'm not trying to disrupt what you have here. This was an accident, coming this way, but one that might prove helpful to all of us."

"All of us?" Clara's tone didn't give me much encouragement.

I loved improvising under pressure.

"Alpha doesn't know how to stop," I said. "He controls the Fabrication Lines and he's making more mechs every minute. He wants to flood the ship with machines that do exactly what he wants. Even if Starship lands before he finds you, you'll never make it outside without being torn apart."

"Funny you say that." Clara shook her head at me. "The whole reason we came down here in the first place was that Starship was about to tear itself apart. The people in it, anyway. We dodged that death. Now I'm supposed to listen to a damn mech tell me the mechs are coming?"

"Is that not evidence enough?" Delta said, gesturing towards the hallway and the mech corpses beyond.

"Yeah, evidence you mechs are fighting each other," Clara said. "Guess how much I care?"

"You're not reasoning with my point," I said. Kaydee, appearing alongside Clara, winced. "I said Alpha's mechs will return in force, before or after the ship lands."

"Then we'll get through them," Clara replied, not even bothering with a shrug. "The one thing we do have down here are weapons. Enough to carve our way through some rust buckets."

"That's a short-sighted view."

"What'd you say to me?"

On my right, I caught Delta shifting her sword, no longer keeping an eye out for future threats but getting ready to take care of this one right here.

"Found it!" Leo announced, drawing all our attention to the black rectangle in his hand. "Now, who's got a battery I can use?"

After convincing Acho to give up the battery powering his welder, Leo returned to his workbench and a waiting audience. I'd tried pitching a few more perspectives at Clara, who rebuffed each with a similar argument: she'd spent decades replacing her broken body for a chance to see a real planet again, and she wasn't risking that because I said some crazy mech had Starship's controls.

Leo spared me a fourth attempt. Kaydee might've been more grateful than I was, her contempt growing ever more withering with every word I pitched Clara's way.

"It's old, but it should still connect to Starship's network," Leo said as he slotted in the battery, held down a squishy gray button on the portable's top. "One advantage about this ship? We couldn't update much inside it, so she's still running on thousand year-old tech!"

Leo looked around, slight smile, eyebrows raised. Nobody, myself included, gave him a laugh, a clap, anything else.

"That's him," Kaydee said softly, next to me. "After all this time, he's still so proud of himself when he makes these little connections."

I picked up precisely zero edge in her voice, only warmth.

"So do it then," Delta said to the Forger.

"Right." Leo tapped away on the device, the screen far enough away from me that I couldn't see what he was doing. Thankfully, Leo was the type to narrate his every move. "See, Starship keeps its most vital processes in its central operating matrix. That's where we put the Voices. It's like a spiderweb's middle, where they can follow a thread to access any part of the ship they need to."

Leo hesitated. Made a sound between frustration and a groan. I hazarded a guess.

"We told you the truth," I said.

"The web's breaking," Leo replied. "You're right. Even with my access, the Bridge is offline. The Nursery too. Someone's cutting off Starship from its heart, and there's only a couple people I can think of that could do that." Leo glanced at me. "And you're one of them."

"You're lucky he is," Delta said. "Gamma's trying to help, not hiding down here."

"Sure, yeah," Leo replied, turning back to his tablet. "If you want to keep the Voices safe from Alpha, then you've gotta disconnect them from the shared network."

"Which means?" Delta asked.

"We'll have to rip them out," I answered.

WE STOOD BACK at the freight lift Delta had scarred before the mechs arrived. Leo, Delta, myself, Alvie, and an annoyed Clara watching from behind. We'd scavenged new clothes from the Forger's stockpiles, me going for heavier work gear while Delta found a slim, slippery outfit designed for maintenance jobs in narrow spaces. My rebuilt foot functioned well, marching me along behind Leo as we pitched plans.

Starship's central operating matrix didn't sit in the ship's middle, despite its name. The original engineers, according to Leo's reckoning, dumped Power Core there, but wanted to keep the most vital pieces split. They put the operating matrix way up top and forward in a shallow alcove to protect it from micro meteors. It also happened to be the part of the ship controlled by the wealthiest, most powerful people to board the vessel.

"Real shocker, I know," Leo said as he plugged a key into the freight lift and turned it. "But that was the design. The idea."

"Humans and their class systems," I said.

"We are who we are," Leo replied. "I'm not defending it but, up till now, keeping the matrix there meant the fighting never touched it. Starship's systems haven't ever failed, or we'd all be dead."

"She doesn't seem to think that's important," Delta said, nodding back towards Clara.

"We've been through a lot, down here," Leo replied, cutting off Clara's no doubt spicier retort. "Look, I'll take you up there. Should be able to open any locked doors. Then, when we get to the Voices, you can take them and run. Figure out how to fight your war."

Leo stepped into the elevator, we followed. Behind us, the Forgers continued picking apart Alpha's mechs, their work already reducing the fight's leftovers to scattered rubble. Soon, I figured, the only evidence would be laser scoring on metal panels, like in so much of Starship. Stories lost to time.

"And then you'll come back?" Clara asked, not following us into the lift. "Or are you abandoning us after all this time?"

"I'll be back," Leo replied. "I still dream about the same thing you do, Clara. The sky, the wind. A real life in a real place, even if only for a day."

Clara didn't stop her frown, but she didn't object, either, when Leo asked her to press the lift's button. With a rattling clank and a hum, our lift climbed upwards, pulling the Cesspool from view and bringing us closer to the Voices, Alpha, and the fight for Starship's future.

On my left, Delta looked the same as ever. Steel-eyed, sword on her shoulder, freshly sharpened by Forger tools. Leo buried himself in his tablet as the lift climbed, running through Starship diagnostics and making none-too-impressed sounds. Kaydee, invisible to my partners, watched her former flame, expressionless.

Me? I knelt down, gave Alvie a pet on his ridged, battle-scarred back. A quiet moment, one of the last we'd have for a long while.

TWENTY-TWO

OUTSIDE THE LINES

Our ride found its end several levels up, far from Starship's apex. The lift groaned as it tried to move the missing gate carved away by Delta below, delivering us into a wide space mirroring the Cesspool we'd left behind. Rather than circular tunnels, however, our options were limited to two: a big path straight away, lined with loading carts, and a side hallway blocked by a closed door marked, with bold red letters, *Airlock*.

"Where are we?" I asked as Leo, started down the wide hallway.

"Fabrication Lines," Leo replied. "The Cesspool cleans up the trash, the Fabrication Lines turn it into treasure."

I stopped. "Didn't I say Alpha controlled the Fabrication Lines? We can't go there."

"There's not another way from the freight elevator," Leo replied with a shrug. "Either we get through anything Alpha has here or we're stuck."

"Then let's go," Delta said, swinging the blade off her shoulder. "We'll get through."

"I like her attitude," Leo grinned. "Knew I did something right with you four."

That confidence carried us slow down the bright, yellowed hall-way. Beyond the carts, warning signs mingled with popular posters along the walls. Unlike the movie ads in Leo's apartment, the sheets here had scribblings all over, messages from one shift to the next high-lighting achievements, thanking those that'd come before and after. At first I thought the decor seemed weird, until I noticed the sheets were yellowed enough to match the ochre walls behind them: these lines went back hundreds, a thousand years or more, a living history of the people who'd worked here.

Names lost to time paired with machines invented by those same names. On my right hung a sketch of the first real cleaning mech, towering things scrubbing whole levels at a time. The designer's name blazed in blue marker next to it, followed by the trio that'd managed the first build. Other crafts, like the gem-locks in the doors, the lift screens I'd seen in the Garden, followed.

Starship hadn't lifted off in a perfect state. It'd evolved, even when its only materials had to be scavenged from itself. Innovation never stopped.

Leo led with Delta behind him. Alvie and I made up the trailing pair. At least this time I had a proper weapon: back at the Forger's chamber, Leo had given me the gun Delta took off her hostage. The energy weapon had enough oomph in it to burrow a burning hole through a thin mech's skin, and would, thankfully, let me keep my distance.

I'd had enough of the smashing and bashing for one digital lifetime.

The carts we walked by had different layouts, each labeled with colored stripes, pasted on lettering calling out various metals and other material the carts were designated to hold. Up ahead, the cart's goals made themselves known through a growing, rattling symphony. Gears gnashing, belts squealing, hydraulics hissing all in and out of beat with each other.

"That is a maddening noise," Kaydee said, walking with me as I gave Leo and Delta space. "Now I get why nobody wanted these jobs."

Alpha's mechs weren't hunting Leo, and Delta seemed like a better fit for scouting out the right path, leaving me with a chance to mutter back and forth with my resident mind.

"Running the lines, you mean?" I replied.

"Yeah. Mechs always did most of the manual parts, but you needed people to supervise, cover issues," Kaydee said, spiky hair back to its teal brilliance as she jumped from one cart to the next. "Leo and I had college buddies that wound up down here. We'd get drinks, and they'd insist on places that didn't play any music. Said they couldn't stand ambient noise anymore."

"Was there no way to block the sound?"

"The way they put it, the vibrations leaked into your bones," Kaydee grimaced. "For all the miracles on this ship, some things really sucked."

That, I could agree with. One thing that didn't, though, seemed to be our new Forger friend. At least for Kaydee, whose looks kept turning after Leo as we walked. She'd slip under a cart's railings, hop over the next one, all while keeping a lock on the man.

"You're surprised he's still alive?" I offered as the carts began to dwindle, the corridor widening as we neared the lines themselves.

"It's funny. Or maybe it isn't, what do I know?" Kaydee said, leaving the carts and matching my walk. "I never once thought about what happened to him. By the time I found you, it'd been so long."

"You assumed he'd died."

"I guess?" Kaydee bit her bottom lip, looked towards the ceiling as if a better answer might wait there. "Becoming . . . this, I feel like everything that happened before, when I was alive, is so distant. Like it happened to someone else. And with Leo, or a part of him, also being one of the Voices, I just figured that was it. We're programs now."

"As a mech, your tone's almost offensive."

Kaydee laughed, "Deal with it. Just like I'm dealing with this.

He's not the same person I knew, right? So much time's past. He's, like, half machine. But even so . . ."

"Even so what?"

A slight smile, "Tell you what, Gamma. We get through all this, and maybe I'll figure out what I'm trying to say."

I let Kaydee go, not that I didn't want to understand more. Getting a grip on how humans worked was changing from a curious side-project to a vital mission as more and more of them emerged from Starship's dark corners. And, if I was being honest with myself, I wanted to find my own deeper connection with my existence.

Leo had built me for a purpose, and the Voices had activated me to fulfill that objective. Now I had another, but eventually the do-or-die would have to run out and I'd be left wondering what came next. Making that decision with more than ones and zeroes, profit and loss, seemed appealing, even if it carried the risk of a human's unreasonable emotions.

I'd take that chance, just to feel like Kaydee looked as she watched Leo.

The Fabrication Lines emerged, spraying from the corridor in seven separate directions. Moving conveyors, dirty black slats, rose up from the semi-circle end to our path. Thin railings blocked off the sides, leading up two or three meters to screens displaying in colors and abbreviations the types of materials requested by the line. As we approached, all the lines churned along. Mechs at their front, simple ones with several grasping claws linked to strong bolts, lifted polished metal, wires, and more from loaded carts and placed the materials on the conveyors.

I joined Delta and Leo near the semicircle's entrance, crouching behind a cart as we watched the work.

"How's he getting the material?" I whispered as I crouched behind Leo and Delta. "The freight elevator wasn't being used?"

"See those two?" Leo pointed to a pair of conveyors in the center. I hadn't noticed at first glance, but the lines ran in reverse, the mechs taking material coming down and loading it into appropriate carts.

"They're manually moving scrap in from the Conduit. Have to give up a couple lines to do it, but the guy doesn't have another option."

At my questioning look, Leo fished out the freight elevator's key.

"Can't hack analog, buddy."

We couldn't sneak past analog either. While the loader mechs didn't look all that menacing, those floating couriers hovered along the lines too, watching progress. Reporting, likely, back to Alpha that things continued to run smoothly. These didn't have the attached weapons like the ones we'd dealt with below, but eyes on us would be bad enough.

"Unless you have another trick," Delta said, "things will get messy if we move forward."

"Hmm," Leo hummed. "Can't turn invisible yet. You might have to cut us through."

"No," I said. The aggressive plan had to get cut off before Delta started slashing, burying us again under a mech attack. "Unless your Forgers are ready to help us, this won't work. We'll get buried before we reach the Conduit."

Both Delta and Leo looked at me like I'd spoiled some great time. I wanted to throw up my hands, shake them, replay the last few hours, including our desperate escape back in the Cesspool. Maybe Delta had some programmed confidence that led her into every fight believing she would win, but Leo ought to know better. Leo ought to see what would happen.

"Please," I said, putting a hand on Alvie for emphasis. "Every fight risks one of us dying. Risks losing Starship forever. We have to choose, and avoid, when we can."

"Gamma," Kaydee said, popping in behind my two friends, "look at you, playing the responsible leader. I like it."

Leo, at last, scratched his nose and looked behind me, back the way we'd come.

"Well, if you really don't want to go direct, there's a different path," the man said. "It's, uh, a little unusual though."

"Look at all this," I said, gesturing at Delta, myself, the mech-run

THE FLAWED DESIGN   173

Fabrication Lines. Leo with his half-metal face. "Is anything here *not* unusual?"

LEO HAD IT RIGHT. His idea was pretty far out there. We walked all the way back to the freight elevator, then took the only other path. The one marked *Airlock*. Much like the one I'd been stuck in outside the University, the airlock presented itself as clean, white, coated with warnings. The narrowing walls broke up their panels with inventory lockers, most already emptied.

"We ransacked these a long time ago," Leo said as we walked. "Space suits had good fabric, materials we used for parts. None of us thought we'd be going outside again."

"Why?" Delta asked. "Starship might have needed you to fix something."

"Nothing the Voices couldn't get a mech to do. Remember, it all might look like garbage now, but when I came down here, Starship was stable. Hell, I'd put myself in charge."

"For all the good that did," I muttered.

Leo sighed, "Younger me kept thinking I'd be able to make everything great with a little more power, a little more control. Now I know better."

The airlock itself waited for us behind a thick pearl-white door. A lever on the right side waited to open our portal. A narrow glass window looked into the antiseptic space beyond, containing some bars to hold onto and a long grapple line for any would-be space walkers.

"Now what?" Delta asked.

"Now you two take the scenic route," Leo said. "I'll open the airlock. You two go outside, walk up Starship to the top, and get back in there."

"Outside?" I asked. "As in, space?"

"Pretty sure that's the only thing outside Starship right now," Leo replied, his eyes twinkling in a way I found a little menacing. "Look, there's ladders everywhere out there. Couldn't be easier. Follow the rungs to their end."

"How will we get the airlock open up there?" I asked. "Can we do it ourselves?"

"That's where it'll get tricky. These guys were designed to keep the outside, well, out. You'd always need a partner to let you back in," Leo replied, putting a hand on the lever. "Though I bet if Delta can get that blade all the way, she might be able to carve a path."

"Taking a crazy risk," Kaydee mused, lounging against the airlock door. "Leo being Leo right there."

What other choice did we have? Every minute brought Alpha closer to the Voices, closer to controlling every bit of Starship. Once he had that, Alpha could wipe Beta, Val, and the other humans, could fill every hallway with his mechs. We'd get destroyed or assimilated. Leo and his Forgers too.

"We can do it," Delta announced. "Let's go."

I nodded at Leo, "You heard her."

The man was only too happy to push the lever down. The airlock swung open. Delta led the way, Alvie and I following. As I went by Leo, I stopped.

"I heard Clara. I know what your group is trying to do," I said, "but farther aft, there are others struggling to survive. They could use your help." Leo winced, so I continued. "Think about it. You can't afford to hide anymore."

I joined Delta inside the airlock, Alvie scrambling in behind us. Leo punched a couple buttons on the panel next to the lever and an all-too-calm voice declared the oxygen would be draining in a few seconds.

"Ever done this before?" I asked Delta.

"No," she replied, looking out the final window towards the infinite dark.

"Scared?"

"No."

"Excited?"

"No."

Always a fascinating conversation. Nonetheless, we stood side by side as the countdown completed. I couldn't feel the air leave my non-existent lungs, but my sensors told me I now stood in vacuum. At Leo's instruction, we both gripped the handles next to the door, ones embedded into the airlock's walls.

When Starship's door opened, a fast slide away, nothing pulled at me. Instead, Starship's magnetized gravity faded and I felt my legs floating. Alvie, his claws gripped to my back, shivered. Without air, the world went quiet.

Outside, the stars beckoned. Next to me, Delta caught my eye, pointed towards the ladder on Starship's hull to our right.

And out we went.

TWENTY-THREE

THE LONG VIEW

Starship cut space in half. With my hands on the rungs, looking above and below had Starship's pocked metal plane extended to a curved end in both directions. Past my feet, the craft's bottom had a sharper slant leading to a flat base, perfect for an eventual landing. Over my head, Delta's form shimmied as she scaled one rung to the next without hesitation.

"She's taking no time to smell the roses," Kaydee said, popping in alongside me.

Normally she made some effort to interact with the surroundings, submit to some physical laws. This time, Kaydee just floated there like some ghost drifting in the endless space. Her voice, too, wasn't really sound but a manifestation in my operating system, code executing in the only way it knew how.

Kaydee and her code had a point, though. For all the rushing around we'd been doing, for all the risk to Starship, the humans and the Voices, getting out here deserved a moment's reflection. Keeping a good hold on the rungs—there wasn't any pressure pushing me off, but some space rock could hit, could throw me away—I swung myself around and put my back to Starship.

A star-speckled infinity spread forever in all directions. I'd seen something close to this on Starship's bridge, but the other light sources, the bridge's glass made clear I was still inside some container. Here, free and floating, I counted a thousand stars shining. Trillions more lay in the dark spaces, a dim collective glow preventing a pure black.

Off to my right, like an interstellar cloud, a purple orange nebula smeared across my view. Deep within its swirls and reaching tendrils brighter stars burned through their fusion origins. I wondered if Starship had gone through one of those during its travels, if the people in here had looked out through the windows and witnessed a new star being born.

For all the desire they'd shown to get to a new planet, to be beneath a new sky, there were wonders out here these humans would never see again.

"We looked out every day," Kaydee said, reading my thoughts. "Wake up, glance outside, see if there were any new stars. A passing comet, or a nebula like that one." She pointed out towards space, a rainbow stellar sprinkle spraying from her fingertip to glitter before us. "Neat, right? Most of the time, though, all we'd see is the same few twinkling sparkles. Or just black space. You watch videos of Earth and you see weather, Gamma. Every day something different. Seasons. Wind and rain. Here, we get none of that."

"And that bothered you?"

"The adults more than the children, I think," Kaydee replied. "When I was a kid, I'd be running from one thing to the next. A new grade, new friends, new ideas. It was the adults that had the biggest problems, the ones that manifested into what tore Starship apart. Nothing ever changed for us after University."

"But change isn't always good."

"Sure, but it's still change! We're not mechs. We couldn't take the same lighting, the same shifts, the same movies—like, we'd put on community theater, but it's not like we had big movie sets on the ship.

Without something to mark the days, the years, you start to lose your grip on reality."

A strange prospect. One that, with only a few days of life behind me, I couldn't identify with. Would I break down like the humans after years and years, my code rotting without new stimulation? Or would I be like the cleaning mechs, the nurse machines, trundling through my routines without concern forever?

"Is that how you feel now?" I asked.

"I . . . I guess I don't know." Kaydee shrugged. "Before I found you, before I snared that cleaning mech, things weren't all that different from what we're looking at now. I woke up, I think, when the Voices woke Alpha."

As she talked, I turned and started the rungs. Delta had a big lead, and the climb up Starship wasn't going to be a short one.

"One second, I didn't really exist. Then, bam. Here I am clustered among so many other minds in a big empty space. The Voices kept things locked down. We couldn't do anything except wait to be called. I couldn't talk to anyone, couldn't ask questions.

"When Alpha picked his minds, they simply disappeared. I didn't know what happened, at first. I want to say a long time passed, because it did, right? But there, in that stasis, I couldn't perceive any of it. It took forever, it took an instant. Until they woke up Beta, and they made a mistake.

"Looking back, I think that's when Alpha made his first attempt to take the bridge. The Voices scrambled. They didn't pick the minds so much as leave things open. We could move, we could talk, and we could run. A few made it to Beta when she hooked herself up to the jacks. I followed, squeezed in with two more minds.

"Beta, though, didn't need us. I mean, who would? She cut off the feed and left us there, sitting in that terminal. Me, some old professor, and a pilot. None of us knew what to do, and the terminal didn't give us much of an opening. So we waited, again. Told our life stories to each other. They grew lazy in that endless gray. Didn't even have crystals like you. Just a dummy terminal until the cleaning mech came along. Plugged itself into the port looking for a quick recharge, and I took the chance."

"And your friends?"

"They didn't make it," Kaydee said. "We all knew the stakes. One mind at a time. I just happened to get there first. They would've done the same to me."

So many rungs. The space's chill seeped in through my synthetic skin. My core ran hot to keep my metal bones moving. Nonetheless, Kaydee's story had one more unanswered piece.

"The terminal was broken? Did you do that?" I asked her.

Kaydee fell silent, stayed quiet as I kept climbing the rungs. Far above me, Delta had reached the top. Was fiddling with an airlock door and throwing the occasional questioning look my way.

"You gotta understand, Gamma," Kaydee replied finally. "We all knew the sides we'd been on. My mother made me this because she had the power to do so. The professor and the pilot didn't share my views, and if I left them there, they might have come after me next."

"So you murdered them."

"Deleted. Like the Librarian," Kaydee shot back. "Don't start accusing me. You've got your own body count. And you've been helping that super killer up there. Starship's not a place for heroes and saints."

In that, at least, she had it right.

DELTA HAD the outer airlock door open by the time I reached her.

Concerning Kaydee, I could've tried deleting her just like she'd done to the other minds. The practical view, though, forced me to look at my allies and count them: Delta, Volt, Alvie, and, well, Kaydee. Cutting off a quarter of my support just because she'd made some poor choices, choices I might've made myself?

"*Ready?*" Delta asked, her mouth moving without any sound. The thumb's up in one hand, mixed with her questioning eyes, told me her request.

"*Ready,*" I replied, turning my own thumb up.

She swung herself into the open door with a slight nod and I followed Delta into another pearl white chamber. We pulled the outside door shut, made the seal. Then looked at the second door, as thick as the one below, a glass window looking in. Delta hefted her blade as we floated, ready to strike.

Looking at that door, at the brown and red hallway beyond, I had a different idea.

With a nudge, I pushed Alvie up to the inner door. With one hand, I put the metal dog's claws on the surface, pressed the sharp talons into the barrier and scraped them against it. Alvie caught on quick enough, scrabbling his claws on the surface.

We couldn't hear anything in that chamber, but I had to assume, based on everywhere else on Starship, that something would be paying attention. Something would come to see what had come knocking.

And, if not, Delta could still bash her way in.

Only a few minutes passed, though, before a shift in the light showed Alvie's efforts had found some success. A soft ocean-blue dome wheeled into view, filling up the narrow window and staring through it at us. After a moment, we appeared to pass whatever test the mech conducted and Starship's telltale countdown began. At its end, air flushed our chamber, bringing us back to the ground, warming our frigid circuits.

With a pop, the mech opened the inner door, and welcomed three murderers and our dog into Starship's most luxurious enclave.

TWENTY-FOUR

LUXURY PRICE

Wealth greeted us with a sneering face. A middle-aged man's blocky visage spread across the mech's glass dome, smeared by the glass into a distorted blob. That dome sat atop a treaded, box-like body with a meter-long silver tentacle arm extending from each side. Those arms ended in five-fingered hands, flexible in their metallic gleam as they held the airlock door open for us.

"Well that's not weird at all," Kaydee said as we stepped by. Delta shifted her blade as she led the way, keeping its edge a wrist-flick away from slicing the drone. "Guess Starship's richest couldn't design a mech worth a damn."

"Thank you," I said to the machine, the thing's eyes finding Alvie, the sneer flickering, like a film missing segments, into a frown.

The hallway we moved into replaced Starship's more utilitarian design with soft colors. Warm reds, oranges, and yellows abounded. Lights that would've been recessed globes down below flickered, instead, in glass candelabras. My feet landed on thick crimson carpeting with golden diamonds woven into it. Subtle cinnamon scents on the air. A cello's languorous solo piped in.

The walls, looking like Leo's apartment classed up by half,

swapped movie posters for framed screens. Looping headshots lived in those frames, Starship occupants smiling, winking, or raising a toast to the camera before stepping out and being replaced with someone new. All looked immaculate, high collars, lace, make-up and more.

"It's like they're caricaturing themselves," Kaydee muttered as we moved in a few steps. Behind us, the mech shut the airlock door. "This is so stereotypical. So—"

"You are not allowed here," said the mech. "Since you seemed in obvious distress, I let you in, but I must ask that you leave immediately."

Knowing Delta would deliver a fatal lesson on class politics if the mech continued, I went between them, spreading my hands and trying to look apologetic.

"My name's Gamma, this is Delta and Alvie," I said, giving the mech a slight bow. The Librarian's stories suggested such actions were good when trying to convince a powerful person to pay attention to you. "We're actually here to speak with the Voices."

Again the face flickered, this time settling into a kindly smile, "And you may call me Winston. The Voices, I'm afraid, are not here. They are, you see, in the network. A part of this ship, and not on any one level. You may contact them at your leisure from a more appropriate place." Winston snaked his forward-facing arm up near my face and pointed past me. "This way, if you would."

"Someone's outta the loop," Kaydee said.

"Gamma," Delta warned. "I'm getting real sick of this guy."

Winston hadn't said more than a few sentences, but I already shared Delta's stance. It took real skill to piss me off that fast, and treating me like I was dirt that ought to be stepped on sufficed.

"Me too." I answered my friend. "Winston, how about you back off for a while and leave us alone?"

The mech's face flickered into a straight line, "I'm afraid that cannot be allowed. If you will not leave, security will escort you from the premises."

Sure they would. I didn't say it, but all evidence pointed to Starship's security team going the way everything else had on this ship: to hell. Instead, I told Delta to get moving, let Alvie know to keep an eye on Winston, and stepped off after my blade-wielding murderess. Winston didn't shut up, but we didn't care.

After so long spent running or fighting dangerous mechs, ignoring one felt pretty good.

The airlock's hallway opened into a, frankly, huge room by Starship standards. I'd become used to cramped quarters, mushed in by grimy metal. Even in larger spaces, like the Garden or the Junker's sprawling shop, low ceilings and dim lighting made things oppressive, danger and death a possibility in every corner.

Starship's upper crust apparently shared my distaste for the gloom: a wide rectangle extending for many meters ahead of us, the top level's main event exuded warmth. Couches and chairs settled themselves around dark wood tables. A central, circular kitchen and bar looked stocked, even now, with shining bottles and pre-packaged meals waiting to be served. Screens throughout the place played movies, albeit with the volume off.

"You could set your ear phones to the channel," Kaydee said, wandering ahead of us, her fingers tracing the curved chair tops and their fine fabric. "You could order anything you wanted at the bar. It'd pull from your account." She rose up and down on her toes, bouncing on that red gold carpet. "There were rumors of a couple that lost too much money to stay up here, but really, it didn't happen." She turned back to me, and in a flash, her working outfit changed to a sparkling golden gown matching the threads at her feet. "You made this class and on Starship, you were set."

Set, indeed. Overhead, Starship's metal vanished for a viewing bubble nestled in the hull. Space paced the chamber, the yellow candle lighting washing out enough of the stars to make it more an ominous onyx sky than a look into the universe. With Starship's day-night cycle, though, I figured the room picked up a different enchantment with the lights turned low. A different feel, unsettling in its devotion to grandeur instead of practicality.

Delta looked as lost as I was. The space lacked mechs, lacked threats. Even the bar appeared designed for humans to serve themselves. No trundling waste baskets came our way, ready to tackle us to the ground. Neither did a direction present itself: offshoots from the rectangle bore labels indicating apartment numbers, not a place the Voices might reside.

"You seem lost," Winston grumbled, joining us in the room.

Was there harm in admitting our confusion to the mech? Probably not.

"Like I said, we're looking for the Voices," I replied. Ahead, Delta and Alpha continued into the room. My friend spun herself around, eyes wide, face slack. "They lost the Bridge and disconnected from Starship's central network. We're sure they came here."

"And if you find the Voices," Winston said, face flickering to a raised eyebrow, a curled lip, "will you leave?"

"That's the idea," I replied.

"Then perhaps I can help you." Winston's treads powered up, rolling ahead and leaving pressure marks on the carpeting. That his trails weren't everywhere suggested the mech would go back over his tracks, vacuuming them to perfection. "There is a small section of our level devoted to such technical instruments as the Voices might need."

A cumbersome way to say he had an idea, but whatever. I followed, and, given the opportunity, Winston warbled into a tour guide. Condescension vanished from his voice, replaced by pride, as he narrated the level's glitzy history to us low quality interlopers. To say Winston's tale was interesting would be giving it too much credit: the story paled to anything the Librarian left behind in my memory. Instead, Starship's glorious enclave shared the traits of luxury dens from humanity's past.

Those who had more wanted more. The level started as an open-to-anyone observation deck, a place for workers, scientists, and families to bunch together and get a good look at the space they were traveling through. Attrition happened through insidious means—Winston described it as *refinement*—with costs for food, drink, and seats climbing until the poor, then the families couldn't afford to come without bringing their own items.

"But of course," Winston chuckled, "we couldn't have the messes such ramshackle carry-ins would make. A simple rule change put that garbage away for good."

From there, the limiting became more straightforward and open. Additional lifts leading to the level were sealed under security claims. The viewing bubble, see, was thinner than Starship's hull, and anyone visiting needed to have themselves checked over before entry. Thus only a single lift near Starship's Bridge would accommodate visitors. Another inconvenience, another hit to the population.

"Can you punch this guy?" Kaydee said as we neared the room's far side. "I know it wouldn't change anything, but it would be so, so satisfying."

"Maybe once we find the Voices," I replied. "Much as I might want to."

"What's that you're saying?" Winston broke away from some deep dive into Starship's wealthiest citizens. "What do you want to do?"

"Get out of here and let you go back to your duties," I said, pasting on the most sincere smile I could find. "It sounds like you have lots to do."

For once, Winston flickered to what seemed like real sadness. Despite getting us almost to a rounded door marked *Technical*, blazed over with a friendly sign stating approved folks only, Winston's treads quit and his four arms slumped to the floor.

"In actuality, Gamma, I have so little to do now," Winston said with a buzzing sigh. "Ever since my last guests went to sleep, it has been so quiet. If only there were any left below who would visit, I might even waive the fee just for the conversation."

The cryo-sleep Leo was referring to. I'd seen enough single-purpose mechs to know things could go sideways when the mech's goal disappeared, but actual sadness? Who would code that into a bot? What purpose—

"Think about it," Kaydee said, appearing off to my right. She picked up an imaginary bottle and launched it at Winston, the glass shattering and vanishing without effect. "Winston here's gonna try his best to do what all these snobs want because he'll get depressed otherwise. More forgiving than those mechs in the nursery and their absolutes."

True. Being a little sad but accepting the outcome would've helped those vial-born babies more than the hard cutoff that'd been instituted. The Nursery had aimed for perfection. Winston seemed to target satisfaction. A small difference, perhaps, but one that led to an idea.

"Winston," I said, "Delta and I are trying to make sure Starship *has* more people that could come visit here. That's why we're trying to find the Voices. They can help us keep Starship safe. If you can get us to them, you'll benefit as much as we will."

The mech flickered into a nodding head. Still a weird image, given that the head in the glass dome didn't have a body, but at least the treads started up again, this time with a babbling tale about how Starship's elite had built a private server room up here to sequester all their most precious digital items. Videos, diaries, pictures, ideas, and so on had been sent up here to be sealed away from those prying commoner eyes.

"All ready for when I wake them up," Winston announced as we went through the *Technical* door and into a far smaller lobby.

Two chairs, both big and comfortable, flanked two terminals. The gold-red carpet continued. Beyond the chairs and the terminals, a red dividing wall with visible seams cut off deeper exploration.

"The servers themselves live behind that wall," Winston said in the tone of someone describing a sacred treasure. "Surely you won't need to access those?"

"Hard to say," I replied, taking a chair and looking at the terminal. Compared to the few seats I'd taken across Starship, my synthetic skin and joints reported this one handled my weight, my shape, with precision. I could sit here for years without suffering wear. "If I get the access I need here, then we should be fine."

The terminal before me offered Starship's standard, bland interface. Options to check the ship's event log, sign into the messaging system, or review accounts for things like Garden-ordered groceries had pleasant icons.

"Gamma," Kaydee said, crouching next to me. "I was gonna ask this earlier, but I got distracted with, uh, Leo. If you find the Voices in here, what are you going to do?"

I pressed my fingers together, turning them into a standard jack. To my right, Delta gave me a nod as she slipped back out of the room, dragging Winston with her. Alvie settled in at my feet. Together, they'd be my defense while I dug around the virtual side of life.

"Kaydee," I said. "You might be getting some company."

My friend's loud cursing serenaded my move, the world falling away to a chorus of *damns*.

TWENTY-FIVE

SEEK AND FIND

The Voices. A small digital collective made up of neural-mapped minds from Starship's leading lights. They'd been kept preserved, as I understood it, to ensure critical knowledge never left the current generations living through Starship's centuries-long mission. When things took a turn for the dark, Starship's controls had been stripped away from the living altogether and placed into these advanced programs.

I'm sure someone thought the move would keep biological concerns from getting in the way, but whomever had made the Voices, from Leo's latest to the original coding, hadn't stripped out the human. At least, not entirely.

Now, I knew that same problem applied to me, to Delta, Beta, and Alpha. Leo put us together to serve as blunt instruments, flexible tools for the Voices to keep a teetering mission on the tracks. We'd come out flawed: too human to mindlessly obey, too ambitious for our own good.

My path led me here, to the pleasing, warm void inside the terminal. Rather than work for the Voices, I was trying to save them, preserve them for the very same reasons they'd been created in the first place: a safety valve to keep Starship flying when, if, we took it back from Alpha.

Normally, downloading a few files wouldn't have required jacking in like I'd just done. I could've taken a portable drive, devices that still littered rooms around the ship, and dropped the files onto it in the same way any old human would've. The Voices, though, weren't normal files. They could hide, they could defend themselves against unwanted intrusions. They also had gone for a long, long time with all of Starship's network as their playground.

Convincing them to give all that up, to house themselves in my extra memory, didn't seem like it'd be easy.

"But you've got me," Kaydee said, chomping on some virtual popcorn as I muttered the story to myself. "And when Kaydee's around, nothing's impossible."

"Glad you have such a high opinion of yourself."

"Backed up by evidence aplenty."

"Sure."

The terminal, like Val's, offered a simple landing space to navigate the machine's onboard programs. We stood on a soft red surface mirroring the carpet outside—and the background on the terminal's own physical screen. Bordering our circular starting point were various ornate, crystal archways, each one decorated in golden lace. Looking at the lace revealed names hidden in the vine-work, standard titles for things like documents, a network browser, and so on. Decidedly dull given the appearance.

"So where to?" Kaydee asked, her popcorn bucket seeming endless as she mowed through handfuls.

"Nowhere," I replied, sticking up a single finger into the air. "We don't want the big network, and we don't want the local files. We need a different connection."

"Ah," Kaydee said, getting it.

My finger didn't have any magical properties in and of itself, but I fed a little search query and let its results spiral out from my fingertip, just for fun. Grass-green tendrils, sparkling with fizzy white, spread from my hand towards the archways. They grew at different speeds as my search ran through the terminal, seeking a particular option, a particular opportunity.

The first tendril struck the archway for the terminal's documents. As it did so, the whole tendril withered to black before dissolving into nothing, an unsuccessful search. The others did the same as they hit the basic arches, failing to find what I needed.

"Looking good, Gamma guy," Kaydee quipped.

"Wait for it."

One tendril emerged from my fingertip and sped off in an unusual direction, going not towards any archway at all, but a seemingly blank space along our eternal red carpet. Both Kaydee and I focused on that as my remaining green-white reaches fizzled out.

"Oh, is someone about to get lucky?" Kaydee said.

"Not luck," I replied. "All skill."

The tendril blossomed, the green blooming out into an iridescent flower, the fuzzy middle making a purple-white beauty. As they formed, the petals branched up and off the tendril, building another arch, this one of my own making. Bright green lace curled among the petals, this time writing a different word:

Recovery.

"Well, color me impressed," Kaydee said, dropping her popcorn and brushing her hands on her pants. "With the show-off too? Gamma, you *are* learning from me."

"Figured you'd like that," I replied, stepping off towards the arch. "I only thought to look for this because of you and Leo."

"Oh yeah?"

"Your recovery program for me, the one you used when Alpha should've had me deleted way back in the Garden? I didn't know that existed until you used it."

"Had to cover it up so you wouldn't freak out."

"I figure the Voices must be thinking the same thing," I continued. "Here they are, getting kicked out by a hostile force, so they retreat back into the most secure spot they can and wait for an opportunity to reset."

"Why not reset right away?"

"Because Alpha's still out there," I said as we reached the arch. "The Voices could boot him from the network, hit the big red emergency button, and Alpha would just start over again, but now he'd know what the Voices could do. Maybe he blocks it somehow."

Kaydee put a hand on the arch. I did too, felt the soft petals. A pretty darn good likeness.

"So we go in here, snag my mom and her friends, and hold them hostage until we neutralize Alpha?"

"Then we upload them to the network, they bring Starship back to equilibrium, and we sail on," I replied. "Simple."

"So simple."

With a wink, Kaydee went on through the arch.

Back when I'd first met the Voices, they'd been sitting around a campfire in a pleasant meadow. Starship, pre-launch, sat at the horizon's edge across a giant grassy field. Blue skies, butterflies, a breeze. As a place to spend eternity, I found it rather pleasant. When I saw the Voices last, they'd swapped the calm serenity for a dark and dire castle, one that I'd undermined by letting Alpha through the barriers the castle's programmed protections were supposed to save.

This time the arch deposited Kaydee and I into a strange place, one I had no reference for. The Librarian, with all his stories of heroism and epic adventure, lacked a description matching this place, leaving me confused and curious.

Kaydee and I stood on blue-gray carpet beneath harsh white lights, far from the kind glows I'd seen elsewhere. Mottled off-white tile coated a ceiling above us, breaking for those lights every so often in its extension to eternity. Lower down, at our level, rectangular beige barriers rose up in squared blocks, each one leaving an open section along one side. The barriers themselves only rose a little higher than my head, and when I tested the nearest one with a reached out hand, the cushioned feel communicated nothing too sturdy.

A hum, not unlike Starship's engines, played undercurrent to the otherwise quiet place. My nose picked up a stale coffee smell, as if someone had left a pot on for far too long.

"What is this place?" I asked Kaydee, who had a hand over her eyes and looked to be suppressing a laugh.

"Oh, Gamma. You need to watch more movies."

"I've only been alive a few days."

"Okay," Kaydee took a deep breath, waved at all the beige. "I've never actually been in one of these either, because Starship doesn't have them. Not sure Earth really did either at the end. This, this is an *office*."

"An office?" I repeated. "Like the Bridge?"

The Bridge didn't resemble this place at all, but it was the only space I'd seen that split out what seemed to be individual workstations. I wasn't sure what ship could be flown from a structure like this, with no outside view whatsoever, but humans were weird creatures.

"Not really." Kaydee led me to a gap in the beige. "Look in here, see? These are cubicles."

I saw a thin desk bolted into the beige walls. A turned-off, old terminal sat inside, looking cheap. The space felt cramped, at once isolating and oppressive, with blank walls all around, the glaring light overhead, and a nervous feeling that something might be watching me at every moment.

"Why would the Voices make this place?" I asked, folding my arms and grimacing.

Several of the Librarian's tales mentioned hell. Was this it?

"I think you're proving them right," Kaydee said, walking back out into the central hall. "You don't understand this place. I bet Alpha wouldn't either."

Which might give the Voices time to react if Alpha found the office. Not the worst tactic.

"Tell me you understand this place then?" I asked. "More importantly, tell me you know how to get out of it?"

Kaydee did a slow spin in the hallway, standing on her tip toes to peer over the cubicles. As she completed the twirl, she shook her head.

"Nothing obvious," Kaydee said, "but I have an idea."

Before I could ask what her idea was, Kaydee sucked in a deep breath and belted out, in a shout that was both natural and enhanced enough to carry far, far beyond what I could ever do in a real, physical place, one word:

Mom.

"That ought to get her attention," Kaydee said, leaning back against a cubicle. "Now we just wait to see how much my mother still wants to talk to me."

"She tried to delete you last time."

"Sure, but that was, like, thirty-six hours ago. People change."

"She's been a digitized mind for years and years, Kaydee. I don't think she's going to—"

"There!" Kaydee pointed down the hall. A new red sign blaring EXIT stuck down from the ceiling tiles, an arrow at the end angling right. "That's what we're looking for. Told you."

"You did."

Yet, I gave it even odds that Peony was setting us up for some trap.

Nothing, though, sprang out to kill us as we reached the Exit sign and followed its instructions, a right turn that shrank the endless cubicles into a several meter jaunt to a light wood door, complete with silver knob. Kaydee reached it first, glanced back at me.

"Ten bucks says the Voices are behind this door," Kaydee said.

"Not taking that bet."

"Lame."

"You were expecting otherwise?" I went passed Kaydee, put my hand on the knob and turned.

The door opened not into an Exit, but into a broad room. Floor-to-ceiling windows loomed on one side, looking out onto a sprawling city, washed with bright sunlight. A long walnut table graced the room's center, surrounded by navy-cushioned chairs. Bagels, coffee, and assorted fruits decked the table, and reaching for them between looks my way were the suit-clad crew otherwise known as the Voices.

"Come on in Gamma, Kaydee," said Peony from the table's head. She looked as severe as ever, hands coming unclasped only to gesture to two empty chairs near the table's foot. "I believe we have some things that need discussing."

"And the understatement award goes to . . . " Kaydee muttered as we took the seats.

"I'm here," I started, before Peony waved me off.

"Gamma," Peony's smile vanished. "Let me begin by saying it's good you've come. As a traitor, it's time you received the justice you deserve."

My arms froze, my legs too as metal bars sprang from the chair's arm rests and the cushioning near my legs. The door Kaydee and I had come through disappeared. The other Voices at the table, from Ang, the doctor, to Willis, the captain, set down their breakfast food and picked up their knives instead.

Just perfect.

TWENTY-SIX

TRUST ISSUES

I wiggled my left hand. The bars held. I wiggled my right. Same result. Peony, acting like some power-drunk judge, delivered a sermon on my supposed misdeeds to the Voices assembled around the table. Her audience barely listened, focused on their food with the occasional pitying glance thrown my way, as if to say just endure, Gamma, and this would all end before too long.

Across from me, while her mother detailed my turning Delta away from the Voices and their commands, Kaydee glared at the ground. Gone were her sparkles, her rainbow flashes. Even that teal hair, so often straighter than a spear, wilted about her head.

The office around us seemed to capture the mood. An artificial cage, bland, forever, and inescapable.

No way I was going to die here.

"Peony," I announced, cutting her off right as she came to my disabling of the Bridge's barriers. "Who are you talking to?"

Peony planted her palms on the table, flat and broad. "I'm talking to my friends, Gamma, about all of your awful actions."

"No, I don't think that's true."

Peony blinked. Failed to find a ready reply.

Which meant I could play my gambit.

"You're talking to your daughter," I said, nodding at Kaydee, who sat straight up. "Everyone else in this room's just going to do what you want anyway, so why explain? She's who you're trying to convince."

"I—"

No time to let Peony recover. I had to keep pressing forward, bowl over the room.

"We met the real Leo, Peony. He's still alive," I said, this time earning a sharp glance from Leo's digital copy, who'd been picking at some sullen eggs. "He made it clear what you did and why. You couldn't say goodbye."

Peony straightened, and her eyes went so hard I wondered if she'd tweaked the digital reality to make them that harsh.

"If you'll recall, Gamma, I tried to take care of my daughter not all that long ago." Peony pointed at Kaydee. "Whatever she once was, you've changed her. This ship changed her." She walked along behind the chairs, around the table to stand behind Kaydee, who refused to look up at her mother's face. "And now she's helped give Starship to the one thing that shouldn't have it."

"A thing you awoke," I said. "A thing you made because you couldn't trust all the mechs you'd been working with all your lives. How is that Kaydee's fault if your machines failed?"

"Our machines are like us," Leo said, advancing my plan one more step. The man's look threw me, missing the metal plates the real-life Leo had adopted, but otherwise sounding the same. "They have faults. You have faults. We stapled on one redundant safety system after another just in case the last one failed." The man looked over at Peony. "We kept telling ourselves we were doing what was right. We still wound up here. Let's not compound the error."

"So what, Leo, we let them go?" Peony snapped. "We *don't* wipe Gamma and let Kaydee take over?"

"What? Eww," Kaydee said. "No."

At least Kaydee's reaction seemed to be matched around the table. Not a soul spoke up supporting Peony's plan. They stared at their food, their digital food that would go nowhere, feed nothing. Even Leo, his statement made, shrunk back from Peony's words. His blinkered code continued its small fractures, fuzzing Leo's lines. His fork slipped through fingers not all solid and bounced on the table.

"Kaydee," Peony said, though she didn't look at her daughter so much as cast another superior sweeping gaze over the table. "See this the way it should be seen. I'm trusting you to save us. Save us from our mistakes." She squatted beside Kaydee, who flinched. "We could be together again. You out there, me in here, guiding Starship to the end."

Well, that wasn't part of my plan. I'd been hoping the Voices would remember they weren't just pawns, would come to my defense and push Peony out. Now Kaydee, across from me, looked at her mother like she'd made a compelling offer. The teal hair lifted, some sparkle returned to that face.

"You think I could do it?" Kaydee asked her mother.

"Think? I know," Peony replied, hand on Kaydee's shoulder. "I've seen what you can do. I know you better than anyone, Kaydee, and this is what you were destined for."

"Destined huh." Kaydee wiggled her wrists. "I like the sound of that."

Peony took the signal, tapped the cuffs on Kaydee's chair. They disappeared and Kaydee stood, stretched. Looked at her mom, then me.

"Sorry buddy," Kaydee told me. "For a minute there, I thought we were going to be good."

"Kaydee?" I asked, because what else could I say?

"You remember, mom, when I went after the engines?" Kaydee asked, ignoring me. She reached out, grabbed Peony's wrists. "Know why I did that?"

Peony shook her head, hopeful smile still sticking to her face.

"Because you'd trapped me, left me no way out," Kaydee said, then pulled Peony in for a tight hug. Her voice dropped to a whisper, one I could barely catch. "When I'm trapped, I get a little crazy."

Peony froze. Kaydee did not.

With both arms, Kaydee pushed past her mother, throwing Peony into a confused Leo and crashing them to the floor. As Peony cursed and I watched from my office chair prison, my mind, my friend ran to the conference room door and yanked it open. With a wink back to me, Kaydee stuck her head out and shouted one name.

Alpha.

Into that infinite cubicle hell, an actual shout wouldn't carry all that far. This, though, wasn't a real cubicle farm, wasn't a real office. I felt the code crawl up and around me as Kaydee's call played out its real purpose: a message, shot out into Starship's network to hunt for its target. A message, too, with a trail that would lead Alpha right back here.

"What did you do?" Peony said, picking herself up. "What—"

"Two choices," Kaydee said, staying by the open door. "You either do what Gamma suggested, get yourself off this network and somewhere safe, or you wait right here for our nasty enemy to find you."

Peony squinted at her daughter, hands loose at her sides. I couldn't read her mind, but Peony seemed split between shock and awe, even a little proud at what Kaydee had done. Her mouth worked, wordless, like a fish trying to breathe air.

"Peony," Leo said, rising to stand next to her. "We have to go. Now."

As Leo spoke, our office trembled. An earthquake caused by the angry program finding its way here. Alpha wouldn't come running through the cubicles like we'd done, lost in some maze. He'd break down the building and pick up what he wanted from the rubble.

"Gamma," Leo continued, looking at me now. My wrists popped free, my legs too. Apparently Peony wasn't the only one controlling things. "You have a place ready for us?"

"Ready and clear," I said, standing. "You'll be off the network."

"Vulnerable," Peony snarled, at last shrugging off Leo. "If you die, if you—"

"If you want him to live, mom, you'd better get on board," Kaydee interrupted. "Because Alpha's almost here."

I reached out a hand towards Peony, an ordinary palm buzzing with a particular routine. Peony just glared, and for a second I thought we'd keep up this face-off till Alpha crashed in and killed us all. Then another hand grabbed mine, firm and strong. Willis, Starship's captain, stern and solid, took my offer and vanished.

Taking in all that man's data, all the algorithms making up a human that'd lived for century upon century, slowed me, made my mechanical brain feel numb. I couldn't move, all my resources occupied. As Willis disappeared, a fast dissolve into pixels and then nothing, Ang, the doctor, took his place. One after another, the Voices followed, all while Peony watched, an ebon look about her.

Failure, rage, solidifying into resolution.

When Leo's turn came, he squeezed Peony's shoulder, stepped past her as the office building continued to shake. Sounds, now, poured in with the trembles, a synthesized roar as assembled code faltered and fell apart. Alpha not bothering to be nice. Not wanting to corrupt this time, only destroy.

"Your turn, mom," Kaydee said, the three of us the last ones standing in the conference room. "Trust me."

"Every time I try," Peony replied, shaking her head Kaydee's way, "you disappoint me."

She took my hand without another word, vanishing slow with the others, leaving Kaydee and I alone. Ceiling tiles began to fall, the carpet splintering. As I regained my functions, the Voices secure now inside my own physical memory, the glass windows behind me shattered.

"Time to go?" Kaydee asked.

"Way past," I replied.

But as I reached for Kaydee, as I kick-started the function that would send us back home, the floor fell away. My hand found air and we tumbled, the building disintegrating around us as Alpha deleted its code piece by piece. Rather than find his way through the cubicle maze, the vessel decided to destroy it.

Through a window and into open space, Kaydee and I fell and did not fall. The blue sky programmed in swirled around us, a color palette splashed onto a virtual canvas. Gravity, physical laws stopped as Alpha deleted their functions.

"What's happening?" Kaydee said, looking my way, wondering.

The answer lay in the utter cold I felt when reaching out to Starship's network. While the Voices hid their connection, Alpha killed it. Injected a ravenous program to devour all the code and cut off any networked means of escape. Even as I reached towards Kaydee again, the blue sky began to fade.

First to white, then to nothing at all.

"Find me!" I called, stretching, reaching for Kaydee. She returned the gesture, us both hanging in limbo, the building gone now as if it never existed. No sounds beyond our voices, no ground, no sky, nothing. "We're going out the hard way!"

The moment her finger touched mine, I grabbed her just like I'd snared the Voices, sucking Kaydee's digital DNA into my memory. She disappeared with a yelp, leaving me alone in that void. Alpha's program continued its work, black cracks growing around me as the very base for the Voices's virtual existence vanished line by coded line.

"Too late," I muttered, and pulled the plug.

I SAT UP, my hand free from the server jack. A little spark, some smoke rose up with my disconnection. The white void replaced by gilded crimson luxury. I expected Winston to be hovering, ready to admonish me for overheating the connection, but the drone had vanished. Delta wasn't with me either, still at her post, then.

"Hey," Kaydee said, popping in and rubbing her shoulders as she looked at me. "We made it?"

"Guess so?" I nodded towards the protected server room. "Don't think they can go back there."

As I spoke, I made a more subtle move: back in their void, I'd downloaded the Voices to my personal, physical memory. Now I isolated them inside my drive, sectioning off their folder so it couldn't access anything else. I didn't understand everything that the Voices could do, but I didn't need Kaydee's mom getting frisky and taking over my own circuits, trying to get back on the network.

"Don't think they should," Kaydee said, her look glassy, dazed. "If Alpha's that advanced, none of us should go back in there."

"Agreed. You okay?"

"Sure. That was only, like, the fourth-craziest way to die we've encountered, Gamma. Easy."

"You don't look okay, Kaydee."

Kaydee's mouth flickered between a smile and a frown, her hair waved in a breeze only she could feel.

"Ever think maybe all this is doing a number on us, Gamma?" Kaydee asked. "That maybe we're not meant to endure this kind of stuff? I mean, my mom just about offered me Starship in there."

"An offer you didn't take."

"But I was close," Kaydee said. "Not because I trust her, Gamma. Not that stupid. But—"

"You think you would be better than me?"

Kaydee flinched, but she didn't deny it. I couldn't readily deny it either. She had a lifetime's experience. I had a week. She'd been a human, understood what had gone through the minds of those who'd built me, who'd built Starship.

All that was true, but it didn't change one crucial fact.

"I don't want to die, Kaydee," I said, as straight as I could sound. "You might be more capable, but I am still me, and I won't let you throw me away." I reached out, rested a hand on her virtual shoulder

—a skill I'd become better at over the days. "So don't worry. Even if you wanted to, you couldn't kill me."

"Hah, thanks Gamma. Means a lot."

"Good. Now how about we go see whether Winston's driven Delta to kill him yet?"

TWENTY-SEVEN

OUT

The first sign things weren't as quiet as I hoped came before I opened the door. The sensors in my nose picked up singed carpet and spilled coolant, my ears caught the classic metal-on-metal that seemed to follow my steps around Starship.

Another fight between mechs, my constructed species going at it again.

When the door opened I stayed to the side, hidden as much as possible. For a moment I couldn't spot the problem—things seemed as gleaming as ever—but the noise drew my eyes past the bar, the tables, the silverware set up for a party that would never arrive. There, on the room's far end, near where we'd come through from the airlock, Delta held serve in the entry from the lifts.

Just like below, the vessel moved her blade in one sharp cut after another, slicing away encroaching limbs even as she danced back and forth to dodge blue-glowing energy. Alvie cut and bit around Delta's legs, covering her with his wheeze-barks, claws, and endless verve. As I ran her way, Winston's fate sprawled behind Delta, a sparking casualty. The burning smell came from a small fire flickering around the machine's base, those sparks finding ready fuel in the crimson carpet.

"She doesn't stop, does she?" Kaydee said, appearing alongside me as I scooted around a table. "Always finds a fight, no matter where she goes."

"It's a talent."

"Is that what you call it?"

I scanned for exits as we moved. The server room lacked any extra doors, and Alpha's mechs had the elevator covered. Going back to the airlock seemed a dicey choice without an ally to manage the mechanisms. The other offshoots, if I remembered Winston's nattering, led to various rooms for overnight guests. The cry-chambers and their storage compartments.

Which meant the airlock, crappy as it might be, made for the best option. From there we could take the ladder back down a few levels, find another way in . . . somehow, and—

"Back!" Delta shouted, a call that had me freezing as I passed the bar.

Delta's warning didn't seem directed at me but rather Alvie, who heeded the words and leapt straight back. Blue beams scorched the front line where the pair had been standing, a timed blast meant to reduce dodging options to zero. Delta, though, matched Alvie's move, avoiding the hit by ceding several meters.

Several costly meters.

Without the entry's walls confining them, Alpha's mechs lumbered, jumped, and rumbled through their chopped up friends like a steel flood. They didn't charge right at Delta, but swept into the room, some heading towards me, but most moving to complete a circle around my favorite vessel and dog.

"Too many to fight!" I shouted, and Delta whipped a curious look at me.

"You have them?" The vessel replied, settling into a crouch with her blade ready.

I knew that move, knew she'd be analyzing the ring around her and hunting for the weakest spot to make her charge. The flurry might buy her a moment's exit, but Alpha's mechs, their grinding gears, their glowing lasers, grasping claws would follow. One unlikely strike and Delta would be down. Once she bit it, Alvie and I would follow quick.

At least, with the galaxies and nebulas swirling overhead, we'd get a good view on our way out.

Wait.

"I have them, and I have a new plan," I replied. "Alvie!"

The dog did what robotic dogs ought to do: respond without hesitation to their master's call. Alvie pivoted on the carpet, his claws digging in and flinging up fabric as my friend jumped. Alpha's slower mechs couldn't react quick enough to catch Alvie as the dog landed on, leapt from, and bounced along their boxes, canisters, and stilted bodies. Sliced metal marked Alvie's path as he made his way to me, the mechs plodding after.

"Hey buddy, have a favor," I said as Alvie raced into my arms. "Break through, then hold on, okay?"

Alvie wheeze-barked, though I wasn't sure he understood what I meant. Time prohibited more detail. I had to go on hope.

"What are you—" Kaydee started as I leaned back, weight shifting to my planted leg.

Her voice trailed off as I launched Alvie straight up, a metal missile aiming right for Starship's most beautiful accessory. I watched my dog fly, felt a mech's claw reach for my shoulder as the dog struck the bubble.

Which didn't break.

Dammit.

I dove forward beneath a table, escaping the four reaching claws coming from a tweaked bartending bot. The machine followed my motion, cutting a direct course for my hiding place as two cylindrical, tottering friends with gleaming cutlery looped around my sides to cut me off. Lest I thought to use the table itself as a weapon, a courier began blasting holes in my cover.

"That was my idea," I said, jerking away from the table's middle as molten plastic dripped from another laser burn. "You have any?"

"Surrender?" Kaydee offered, kneeling next to me. "Maybe you trick Alpha again?"

"Can't depend on him being that stupid," I said, "but if there's no other options . . . "

Deliberations ended fast as the bartender tore the damaged table top away, leaving me huddled around a stand with a mech trio reaching for my neck. Delta, far off to the right, didn't seem to be faring much better: I heard more curses from her than metal slashing sounds.

"I give up!" I said, standing and raising my hands. "Alpha will want to talk to me."

The mechs didn't respond. One jabbed its knife towards my side and I shied away, dodging the stab but giving the bartending mech a chance to grip my leg, then my shoulder.

"I have the Voices," I said to those blank steel slates.

Much to my disappointment, my attackers didn't stop. The cutlery came in again. I squirmed, pressed, moved the bigger bot holding my shoulder just enough to turn a lethal stab into a gouging scrape. My synthetic skin split along my right side, the underlying plates shrieking as the knife did its work. Sensors flashed, warning me I'd lost some function with my right leg.

I shouted for them to stop. For Alpha to make his mechs quit. They didn't listen.

Somewhere nearby, Kaydee kept telling me she was sorry. For what, I didn't know, couldn't ask.

The second knife-wielder had its sights set on something grander. While its brother pulled its side-scraping knife back, this one went for my head. A killing shot, and one I couldn't hope to dodge: the bartender bot doubled-up its grips, holding both my shoulders and planting its own feet hard on the carpet. I pushed with my legs, with all my Volt-boosted strength, and found too much resistance.

Until I felt none at all.

A cracking sound washed away as soon as it started, a phenomenal roar blocking everything even as we lurched up. The menacing knives pulled free from their mech owners, speeding towards the gaping hole up above. As we shot past the bar and its glittering lights, the stored bottles joined us in flight, smashing into machines, tables, chairs, and other decorations all zipping towards the new exit.

Above, the luxury bubble sat broken, an expanding shatter growing as shards pulled off and away to the stars.

"Plan, Gamma!" Kaydee shouted, her digital self evading the deafening roar coming from outside.

I'd had an idea when I threw Alvie up towards the glass, and that plan relied on one thing in particular. We had a second or two before we hit space, never to return, and in that moment I pushed free from the confused bartending bot. Pushed free and kicked for the disintegrating glass. I didn't aim to grab—there weren't handholds anyway in those glittery teeth—but to survive.

My left leg caught the outer edge, hitting the underside of the breaking glass and sliding along. The hit gave me just enough resistance to make a desperate heave, sitting up fast as the vacuum suction pulled me towards pure space.

The jagged glass edge stabbed me like that same knife, a gut-busting shot from a spear-like point. My sensors screamed, I felt wires split, but I reached out, gripped the razor edges, all the world flushing out behind me, and pulled further. Impaled myself deeper. Held myself to Starship.

Alpha's mechs, the luxury lounge, emptied into space behind me. Winston's loyal body drifted alongside several dozen friends, dwindling already as Starship's relentless pace pushed the ship on. Floating with them were some of Earth's finest wines, liquors, and luxuries, set to wander forever in the icy vacuum.

Ahead, Starship's bulk stretched back, the crackling glass giving way to the vast gray. Stars twinkled, nebulae shined, and all was quiet. The suction died too, Starship's emergency actions serving to seal off the luxury lounge and confine the breach to our poor section. Weightlessness suffused me, a dangling flag.

"Well damn," Kaydee said, popping in on the glass before me.

"Yeah," I said, splitting attention between her and running checks on myself to see how screwed I was.

The gutting blow had knifed through connections to my power supply, turning my tuned vessel-self into a creaky mess. My memory, my mind didn't seem affected, but I wouldn't be able to win a fight against a child, or even sit on a particularly challenging chair. Pulling myself off the glass wouldn't be feasible either.

But then, I'd never planned on being the sole survivor.

"Can you see them?" I asked Kaydee. "Alvie? Delta?"

"I can't see anything you can't," Kaydee replied, shrugging. "Your eyes are mine, or something like that."

"Not very helpful."

"Well, you didn't clue me in to this idea, so I wasn't ready."

"Kaydee, with me, you always have to expect the unexpected."

"Stop it. Right now," Kaydee replied. "If you and I are going to hang here for the rest of eternity, you cannot use cliches."

"Alpha's going to land Starship eventually. We won't be here forever."

"Oh, right. We'll just burn up in the atmosphere. Lovely."

I tilted my head, about the only move I could make, "He might choose an airless planet. A dead rock. Then we'd be okay."

Kaydee laid out on the glass, "You really know how to make someone feel good about the future, Gamma."

Tough to make someone feel good about the future when we didn't seem to have one. About five meters of fragile glass spread before me, linking up with Starship's hull in a tenuous tie. Below, through the glass, the empty bar and a few nailed down pieces paired with the shredded crimson carpet. Hardly luxury now. Above, stars, darkness.

Behind?

I turned my head as far as I could go, scoped out the hole Alvie had made. The tear seemed worse behind, the shattering spreading farther. Directly to my right there wasn't a single shard left, just the torn hull edge jutting into space. Left had the same: a clean break.

"So what now?" Kaydee asked. "Can you get off this?"

"Not without help."

"Cool, cool."

In vacuum, sound didn't travel. No oxygen to carry the waves. Touch, however, remained a signal. My hands and, hell, my stomach tied into the glass, and those shards hummed with Starship's motion. They also rattled, ever so slightly, with something else. Irregular stops and starts, darts and dashes. Each one its own tremor, each getting a little more pronounced as the source drew closer.

A short list of possible causes. One good, most bad.

"Oh thank goodness," Kaydee said. "No offense, but I didn't want to float out here with you forever."

"None taken," I replied, watching Alvie and Delta crest Starship's hull to my left.

The dog, my dog, had a table cloth in its jaws, its claws planting into the metal plating with every step. Hanging on to the cloth's other end, her sword apparently gone, was a battered Delta. She limped along after Alvie, the dog darting ahead and Delta crawling after, finding handholds where she could. They had circled the glass, come around to my end.

Delta's eyes met mine, her head gave a slow shake. As Alvie tested the glass, put a claw forward onto the shiny, cracked surface, I tried a tentative smile.

No, this wasn't the plan. No, this wasn't where I wanted to be.

But, dammit, we were alive. We'd saved the Voices. And, for one silent moment, things were at peace.

"There's still a glass shard in your gut, Gamma," Kaydee said. "Not sure I'd be grinning."

"You don't have to," I replied. "I'm going to revel in the now, thanks."

"Okay, you crazy machine. You do you."

As Alvie, ditching the cloth once Delta had herself secured on a ridged metal patch, padded onto the glass, I did me.

Sound didn't carry in the vacuum, but I felt my own laugh, my grateful, death-defying laugh, nonetheless.

TWENTY-EIGHT

EVA

How to free a speared mech without destroying him?

Alvie and I considered the question, the dog near my face, paws splayed out wide to reduce the pressure on the shredded glass. We weren't quite weightless—Starship's magnetic field and the loose gravity it produced tugged at my toes—but thus far, my mechanical pooch had been able to navigate the fragile surface.

"He could break it," Kaydee mused. "Without the vacuum suction, you might fall back inside the ship."

"And be stuck there," I replied, the sound going nowhere but Kaydee hearing through our virtual connection. Without much power to my arms and legs, I wouldn't be able to leap out. Starship had likely sealed every other exit from the room to keep limited oxygen from fleeing the ship. "Let's try something different."

Time to see whether Delta was awake. I looked beyond Alvie to my friend, holding on to Starship's ash hull with a lax grip, her face turned out to the stars. What was she looking for out there? Threats?

I waited, watched, not wanting to interrupt. Delta hadn't shown any signs of wonderment before, had always been locked and loaded into the mission, a driving deadly force with no time for side stops.

Here, though, she gazed out, her muscles for once not ready to spring, her eyes not squinting to spot a weak point. Her feet floated loose, like a swimmer lounging in a pool.

"What's she doing?" Kaydee muttered.

"Realizing, maybe, it's not all about the violence," I replied. "Not sure I want to break the spell."

But reveries were better enjoyed when not impaled on glass, so I didn't let Delta gaze all that long. After a couple more minutes letting my systems warn me about the dangers of my current position, I nodded to Alvie. The dog flicked his ears up, matched his glowing eyes with mine, and waited for some instruction. If I told him to tackle me off the glass and send us bouncing into oblivion, Alvie would do it without hesitation.

A strange sort of comfort, that.

Did humans get the same feel from their mechs? The idea that there was something, even a metal unfeeling something, that would be loyal to its last spark?

Instead of mutual destruction, I nodded towards Delta. Alvie seemed to get the gist and commenced a careful pawing walk back to the other vessel. When Delta failed to react to his approach, Alvie nosed her shoulder. She blinked, looked my way, and I nodded down to the glass spike spearing my stomach.

Delta pantomimed a sigh, touched her mouth to Alvie's ear and spoke. No sound in vacuum, but touching could still send vibrations. Alvie barked a silent acknowledgement. Delta, a side grin sliding up one lip, shifted around until she had her knees up to the edge where the glass met Starship's hull. She held the tablecloth linking her to Alvie in one hand, the other keeping a grip on a hull handhold. Alvie, the cloth in his mouth, clawed up next to her.

"What's she doing?" Kaydee asked, hand stroking her chin, an old English detective's clothes wrapping her. "What does she know?"

"I wouldn't try too hard to figure it out," I replied as Delta flicked up a single finger on her cloth hand, then a second. "I have a feeling we're gonna learn."

The third finger went up and Delta twisted on her hip. Alvie jumped back, and Delta whipped the dog forward. With gravity's weight, Alvie's force should've ripped the tablecloth apart. In zero-g, the dog's momentum flipped the opposite direction, sending my puppy streaking towards me with all the force of a big, dog-shaped hammer.

"Oh no," Kaydee had time to say before Alvie collided with my chest.

The dog's force transferred to me in an instant, shoving me from my glass enclosure. I popped free, sparks marking my departure as the glass delivered a few exit wounds. Untethered for an instant, I tried to find a plan, a reason for what the hell had just happened.

The reason flew right at me, bounding over Alvie as the glass splintered beneath her feet. Delta, her one gripping hand outstretched, leapt off my dog and came at me. Soundless, airless, I kicked my foot out towards my fellow vessel. Delta snagged my sturdy boot—Leo's gear had held up pretty darn well through all this —and my momentary launch into space halted as soon as it began.

At first I didn't understand how Delta, floating as free as I was over the shattering glass, had stopped our escape. The answer came clear as we started to move, not away from my impaled point but back towards it, along the glass in slow steps and over the hull. Delta, her head already back towards those stars, held on to my boot with her left hand and to the tablecloth with the other.

Alvie had the cloth's end clamped in his jaws and, like some sort of space kite, the dog dragged us through the vacuum back to the hull. The puppy's careful steps cleared the glass like a beetle walking on a rippling pond, a vision I didn't consider until Kaydee said it looked like old Earth shows about the natural world.

"And now look at us," Kaydee said as Alvie reeled us in, taking turns between his mouth and his paws to gather up the tablecloth. "About as unnatural as it gets."

"Not sure you were ever natural," I replied.

"Hey," Kaydee said, then laughed. "Probably right."

Delta touched down on the hull first, Alvie let the tablecloth go and swapping to a gentle grip on the vessel's own ankles. When Delta planted her feet, she bent down, left the tablecloth to drift free, and restored a grip on the hull. I copied her, planting my own boots on the gray metal a moment later. Weak, slow, with every motion feeling like I had to push through thick water, I found my own handhold.

In front and behind me, Starship's side spread like a dull plain. Through my holding hand, the ship's rumblings shivered. My short hair played about at random, my clothes billowing and not as I shifted. My systems informed me they were having difficulty decoding which way was up or down.

"I'd be puking everywhere right now," Kaydee said. "Guess there are some advantages to the virtual life."

"Some," I replied, closing my eyes for a second and trying to recalibrate.

We'd broken out of Starship near its front, the Bridge and Alpha's mech army not all that far away. Airlocks leading back inside would be scattered along the vessel, but forcing a re-entry close to Alpha would put us in a bad spot. Delta didn't have her sword, and I had the fighting capabilities of a wilting house plant. Not to mention the valuable cargo stored away in my memory.

Given those realities, I figured our best chance lay in a strategic retreat.

I had to poke Delta's shoulder to pull her focus away from the stars. Again she blinked when she looked my way, but nodded when I pointed over her shoulder towards Starship's far off aft. Alvie, watching, again barked without a sound. When we started moving, the dog led the way, scampering along the side, tracing the handholds.

"Maintenance," Kaydee said when I asked her why Starship was covered with the convenient little nubs. "You don't plan on crossing the galaxy in perfect form, so there's routes between pretty much everywhere on the hull."

"Couldn't people use these to get places they weren't supposed to go?"

"Gamma, you might think it's easy to get into an airlock and just step outside," Kaydee replied, dancing along the hull near me as we climbed our way aft. "But, back when there were, you know, rules for this stuff, you had to get all kinds of clearance to go EVA."

"EVA?"

"Extravehicular activity. What we're doing now. Aren't acronyms fun?"

"No."

I wanted to ask Delta what she found so interesting about the stars—she kept looking out at them as we traversed—but I couldn't exactly talk to her in a vacuum. Instead, I listened to Kaydee chatter on about how Starship's society handled space back in the good old days.

Space, to hear Kaydee tell it, had been ignored as much as possible. Like a prisoner might ignore the walls closing them in, Starship's population tended to avoid talking about it. The engineers, the pilots, the ones watching for close encounters with random asteroids, they would care during their shifts. After?

"Movies, music, hobbies," Kaydee said. "We didn't want to go out there. Didn't want to think about how we were always a little hull breach away from death. It was healthier to focus on the next season of *Scrappers*."

"*Scrappers*?"

Kaydee laughed, rolled her eyes, "Terrible show, but we didn't have much to work with. Yeah, you could go back through Earth's catalog, but for fresh, new stuff? Teams competed to take mech junk and turn it into something useful. Time limits, judging, all that."

I caught something in her words as we crossed Starship's mid point. My internal clock said a couple hours had already passed on our slow walk, hours Alpha could be using to take over more inside. To hunt and wipeout Val.

Focus, Gamma. Nothing I could do about that now.

"Were you on it?" I asked, playing the thread in her voice.

"Not the adult version," Kaydee said, still grinning, looking at me and yet absolutely not at me. "Leo and I, a couple other friends. We did the kid's edition."

"And you . . . ?"

"Won? Hah, no," Kaydee snapped her fingers, and a fun little metal menagerie sprang into the virtual space around us. It looked a little like a toaster and a multitool had been mashed together, a boxy steel porcupine. "We built this thing in the two hours we had, a critter that would follow you around ready to pop up whatever tool you needed."

"Seems pretty clever?"

"Yeah, until you realize a toolbox does the same thing and never runs out of batteries."

Point.

"We lost to a flying scooter."

"What?"

"I know, right?" Kaydee said. "Thing was a nightmare, but so much fun. They strapped a ton of magnets to it, and for a little kid, you could push the button and float. Kick a bit and you could levitate your way around."

That did sound pretty cool, actually.

Kaydee went on from there, describing the lost inventions of her Starship youth as we plodded along. Delta continued her stargazing, Alvie kept up the leadership duties, and after too many hours, with Starship's rumbling increasing, we made it as far aft as we could go.

Blue engine wash blotted out the stars as I looked at Starship's massive engines, their circular ends expanding past the hull and out into the distance. The hull here felt warm to the touch, though I had the feeling these engines, running now on solar power alone, were going at a small fraction of their initial thrust. Nonetheless, the sight put Starship again in a new perspective.

Starship wasn't a world, a home, so much as it was a rocket speeding towards a destination now arriving sooner than its makers intended. Whether it landed, whether any part of its mission remained intact, was up to us.

"This one looks good," Kaydee said, pointing to where Alvie had found another airlock. The handholds continued on past it but looked to head right to the heart of the engines, a place we didn't need to go. "If Alpha's back here already, then we're real screwed."

"If he is, then I'm jumping out there," I replied. "A long journey among the stars seems like a good way to go."

"For once, Gamma, I'm with you."

TWENTY-NINE

REBUILD

The airlock, thankfully, had no mechs waiting for us. Had nobody waiting at all. I led the way, Alvie pawing behind. Delta took her time joining us in the chamber, one long last stare out to the stars. She shut the door behind us, locking us in the small space. In the past we'd relied on other mechs, on Alvie to let us in.

This time?

"What happens if we break it?" I asked Kaydee.

"Not sure," Kaydee shrugged. "My guess would be Starship seals the hall, leaves you locked in here with no way out."

"Which leaves us with?"

"Your imagination?"

Delta didn't seem ready to offer much. She kicked off, floating to the side. With no stars available to look at she settled for the mottled white walls. Alvie, similarly lost, kicked his paws in the vacuum. I puzzled.

A craft like Starship would have to account for people going outside without someone being physically around to let them back in, right? No way a rapid response to some maintenance issue could result in someone getting locked out.

"Sure," Kaydee said, catching my thoughts. She put herself on the airlock's inside, past our barrier, as if to mock me. "But who's listening right now? The only people on the Bridge are your enemies."

"Only the Bridge?"

Kaydee started to reply, then tilted her head, threw me some side-eye, "What are you getting at, Gamma?"

Kicking off the inside door I went back to the hatch shutting us out from vacuum. Someone opening and closing an airlock might not get much attention, but what about leaving it hanging? I gripped the white-painted, red-tipped lever and pulled it back, once more popping the hatch open and exposing the engine-washed infinite.

I tried not to show how hard it was to pull that lever in my new, crappy state.

Delta didn't notice, save to look past me to the dark. Alvie made a soundless bark. At least the dog seemed concerned about me.

I left the hatch open, kicked back towards the inner airlock door, and waited. After several minutes, the lights inside the airlock flashed yellow three times. After another few minutes, an orange flash.

"You're irritating the ship," Kaydee said.

"It's irritating me," I replied.

Fifteen minutes after I opened the hatch, the lights inside went red and stayed that way. I folded my arms, waited. Time to test the hunch.

Three more minutes. Precisely clocked by a program spitting the timer to my right eye in small teal numbers.

Without preamble, the hatch swung closed. The lever latched. This time, the airlock started its cycle. A pressure-popping flush as oxygen flooded our narrow space. A vague buzzing clicked in my circuits as Starship's gravity magnets powered up around us, sucking our trio gently to the airlock's floor. Sound came back too, the missing noises pouring as if someone, somewhere, turned up a volume knob one value at a time.

"Gamma, you moron," came the words, a phrase repeated several times until I flashed a thumbs up at nowhere. The voice belonged to a particular whacky mech, one who might notice if Starship had an anomaly event needing tending. "What're you doing leaving a hatch open?"

"Getting your attention," I replied. "Mind letting us in?"

"That's what I'm doing," Volt said, voice crackling through the speakers. "Volt's got your back, as always."

"Thanks, buddy."

"You want to thank me, get yourselves hustling," Volt continued as the pressure equalized, the inside airlock flashing green and popping open. "Anyone paying attention would've seen that hatch alert."

Volt went on as we made it inside, the mech complaining that Starship had alarms ready to scream about potential vacuum threats. The Bridge would've noticed for sure, but Val, any other mechs would've too. I wondered if Leo and his altered tech brethren saw the alert, figured it was us.

The hallway leading away from the airlock painted Starship's aft as a place that got things done. No crimson carpet, no concessions to creature comforts. Hard lighting combed the ceiling while maps and posters indicating proper procedures coated gun-gray walls. A stripe running along the floor split the intended directions, making it easy for anyone hauling cargo to stay where they belonged. Every few meters offered a pull-down alarm to summon assistance, and next to every one seemed to be another small offshoot to this or that engine subsystem.

"My point, Gamma," Volt continued as we walked, "because I always aim to have a point, is that everyone knows where you are."

"No," I said. "They only know a hatch hung open. Could've been anything."

"Cameras, you dumb vessel. This whole ship's covered in cameras. Imagine my surprise, when here I am tending Starship's power garden—the missus says I should call it that, better for my circuit stress—and here's my favorite buddy waving to everyone that wants to kill him."

"Wait, missus?"

Kaydee echoed my question. Delta too had her nose and eyes scrunched up in confusion.

"Told you I was making some updates," Volt said, his voice moving from speaker to speaker as we walked along. "She's a real firecracker now, and I don't just mean with the new laser, which is, whooo-eeee, something you've gotta see."

"Would love to," I replied. "Thanks for the assist, Volt. How about you let me know if Alpha's mechs get anywhere near us, okay?"

"That's the thing, Gamma. Alpha's moving his minions, and there are a ton of 'em, and they're drawing so much power, but they're not coming towards you. Well, not directly."

I knew the answer before Volt said it, but asked anyway.

"The humans, Gamma. Alpha knows where they are, and he's going after them."

"But not the Nursery?"

"Not yet. Current threats before future ones, am I right?"

"Apparently."

We hit the aft's center, Starship's Bridge equivalent nestled into the big ship's butt. The rumbling had a real intensity here, my feet shaking as though under a constant massage. Unlike the Bridge, the aft's center served more as a cafeteria, a general meeting space than where things were done. Sparse tables and chairs, many broken or thrown aside, joined battered vending machines with long-expired contents in the circular, flat space. We'd taken an elevator down to the central level, and its pair sat on the opposite side, ready to carry engineers to any section needing attention.

Straight back, where, if one were to punch a particularly long needle they'd find outer space, were four huge screens. One flickered, one had a dead black, but the other two flipped through various status reports. Starship's engines, amazingly, showed greens almost across the board. Either the build quality was stellar, or—

"We've barely used them in centuries," Kaydee said, popping in near the screens. "Starship hit its maximum velocity not all that far into the trip. Since then we've been coasting, till now."

"Till now?" I asked.

"Takes as long to slow down as it does to speed up, if you're being responsible," Kaydee replied.

"Not going to count on Alpha for that."

"Me either."

"What happens if he slows us down hard?"

Kaydee shrugged, "Maybe we blow some engines. Maybe Starship breaks apart under the force. Maybe nothing because all those engineers back on Earth knew what they were doing."

"You have a hunch, though."

"Oh yeah. We're all gonna die."

Cool.

Beyond the engine status, the screens also flared some oddball flashbacks to Starship's old life: a weekly lunch calendar for hot food —taco Tuesdays? Meatloaf every other Friday? Events too, like bands playing for upcoming holidays, never mind that the musicians had long since ceased singing. One hollow-eyed engineer's face splashed up every few minutes, declaring her the employee of the month.

She'd earned a free cookie for her efforts.

A snapping sound yanked my attention away from the screens. Delta, seemingly back to her old self, had torn off a table leg. She waved Alvie over, had him use his claws to rend one end, turning it from smooth furniture into a jagged weapon. Lifting it up, Delta swung the meter-long pole back and forth a few times, nodding.

"It's not my sword," Delta said when I came over, "but it'll do. Now, the rest."

"The rest?"

With me following along, Delta ransacked the cafeteria, turning it into a weapons depot. Chair legs were cut into shorter blades, Alvie's teeth and claws working the smallest ones into knives that Delta secreted about her clothes. She handed me a few too, though I wound up favoring an un-marred table leg for myself.

The thing doubled as a walking stick, see. My legs seemed to be getting weaker, every step flaring warnings before my eyes about imbalance, a lack in stability.

"You know where we're going, right?" I asked Delta as she finished a makeshift knife belt, metal teeth wrapping her waist.

"To those humans."

"You're okay with that?"

"Yes."

I blinked. Delta straightened, whistled for Alvie, and pointed down the hall away from the cafeteria, towards the Conduit.

"Why the change of heart?" I asked, plodding along as we started off, my walking stick making a metallic clink every step.

"Don't have a heart," Delta replied. "Logically, you're going to head there. You have the Voices, who offer the only chance for Starship, and by extension myself, to complete my mission. Therefore, I go with you."

"Such a romantic," Kaydee muttered off to the side.

I went for a different tactic.

"You kept looking out at the stars," I asked. "Why?"

Delta flashed me a glare, "You'll know when, if, I want you to know."

The walls were still up. Delta, the ultraviolent enigma.

"Gamma," Delta said after another step, her glacier thawing. "You're hurt. You're almost helpless. I don't want to see you die. Go to Volt. I can head to the humans without you."

"If you show up there without me, they'll kill you."

Delta laughed, "The humans can try."

"That's the problem, Delta. They will."

The Conduit opened before us, its blue misty corridor a pleasant view after spending so long in vacuum. Noises echoed up and down, mechs moving about their business. Listening, we could pick out a louder gnashing. The step-by-robotic step as mechs moved in concert by the hundreds, all drawing nearer.

Alpha's army wasn't fast, but it would not stop. Behind it, too, lay the Fabrication Lines, where more mechs would be pulled together from scrap. Not the deadliest enemies, no, but for the humans, it would mean an endless fight. They couldn't stay awake, couldn't fight forever. Even our batteries would run out if pushed for hours and days without rest.

"You care for these humans that much?" Delta asked.

I shook my head, a familiar urging lying beneath my words, "We have a mission, Delta. That's all. I want to see it through."

I'd wavered, back there on the Bridge. With Alpha. Wavered and found mechs just as imperfect as the humans who created them. I couldn't decide Starship's fate, but maybe I could push it just a little away from the monster now at its helm.

Val and her enclave represented the only real alternative. I'd bring the Voices to her, and see if, together, the humans could find a way to fix their mistakes.

THIRTY

DESCENT

The lift didn't work. Or, rather, an angry red light told us the simple platform, a railed-in semi-circle budging out into the Conduit, wouldn't be moving. Delta, Alvie, and I stared at it, as if our collective wills could get the lift to change its mind.

"Why?" Delta asked, finally.

"I don't know," I replied. The red light, dominating a four button panel also occupied by the up, down, and green-is-good options, offered little explanation. "Where's the next one?"

Delta pointed across the Conduit to the walkways on the other side. Another lift over there mirrored this one, but when I asked my eyes to focus, I caught a similar red glint over there too. Blocked as well. Another lift would show up not all that far along, but every step in that direction brought us closer to Alpha's advancing mechs.

"Stairs?" I suggested, and Delta snorted.

"Can't take that down stairs," she nodded at my walking stick.

"You see another option?"

"Yes," Delta pointed towards the engines. "You go and stay safe. I'll come back for you after."

"I mean another option that makes sense."

Delta rolled her eyes, turned and looked up the Conduit. I went the opposite way, starting my slow jaunt towards the stair set. The Conduit had lifts every hundred meters or so, the platforms zipping people and cargo up and down the levels. Stairs were more rare, half as many as the lifts, but they could serve.

Provided you didn't have far to go, anyway.

"She's trying to protect you," Kaydee said, shuffling along next to me.

"She doesn't want to think about me in a fight," I replied.

"Logical."

I snapped Kaydee a frustrated frown before catching myself. Who would want to play protector for a busted mech like me? I'd get in the way, require observation to make sure Alpha didn't pick me off. Delta had it right to try and shove me in a locker.

Squaring my own feelings—bits, I had to remind myself, generated by functions pushing me towards my programmed mission to protect the humans—with my limited capabilities felt impossible: I could see all the reasons I ought to stand aside, work on my own circuits with tools found back near the engines, but that would leave Delta negotiating a tricky tribe all alone.

"That's not all of it though," Kaydee said, softer now, as we reached the stairs. "Is it?"

Early on, Kaydee told me we'd become intermingled. As my mind, a living program nesting in my operating system, her functions would mesh with my own, change the cold calculus driving my decisions into something messier, more human-like. Code wasn't the only thing that'd change. Emotions, memories, beliefs, all that would bleed over from Kaydee's life into mine.

At least, that's what I used to explain the fear creeping in since being speared on that glass, alone in the universe.

"If Alpha wins and I'm not there, he'll find me eventually," I said, walking stick in my right hand, stair railing on the left. The first step waited, inviting me to begin the long slog down. "Those mechs will catch and tear me apart."

"And?"

I planted the stick on the stair, steadied its shaky self. Took my right leg and followed, a sure plant on the treaded metal steps. The Conduit's blue mist coated the stairs, slippery if not for the prickly grips notched into the metal. My left foot joined. One step down, another twelve to go until the next level. I didn't want to think about how many levels after that.

"I'd be alone," I said.

Alvie, as if in protest, wheeze-barked behind me, venturing onto the first step as I moved onto the second.

"Okay, maybe not quite alone." I smiled. "But still."

"You're getting that from me," Kaydee said, popping in further down the stairs, leaning against the wall and sucking on a gigantic peppermint swirl lollipop. "At the end, when they took me into the hospital, I was alone. All those years floating, a mind in the digital void waiting for you, I felt alone."

As I hit the third step, Kaydee kicked off her leaning stance, waved the lollipop my way.

"Guess what though, Gamma," Kaydee said, "you don't have to worry about that."

"No?"

Kaydee raised the lollipop over her head, and as if some clouds had broken on a summer day, golden light streamed down around her.

"You got me, you goof," Kaydee grinned. "There's nothing you can do about it, either."

What could I do but laugh?

And slip, the walking stick missing its landing.

I tumbled forward. My eyes shut, my body doing its best to prep itself for the imminent collision. One that, after the brief panic, never happened. Instead, my shirt pulled tight against my chest, my feet balanced on their toes as I leaned out over the stairs. Delta yanked me back, caught and settled me on the step. She released my clothes. I noticed she didn't let me sway far, ready to snatch me again.

"You want the stairs, we'll take the stairs," Delta said. "But let's do it my way, okay?"

Delta's way involved me holding on tight as she leapt down the stairs one flight at a time. She made the jumps with unflinching grace despite holding her blade and my walking stick in her hands. Every leap ended with several steps to play out the momentum, a swift walk around to the next flight, and off we went again.

Alvie and his wheeze-barks bounded after.

The ease reminded me—yet again—that we vessels were built very differently from one another. Even in my prime, I wouldn't be making these jumps, but Delta could double her weight and still clear meters through the air. Not once did she speak up about needing a rest to recharge, not once did she mutter about the whole thing being ridiculous. She set herself to the task and carried it out.

The levels we briefly occupied showcased, better then my lift ride with Volt, the real denizens that'd lived this far back on Starship. Apartment doorways were smaller, closer together. Up front, shops and restaurants clung to their broken displays, but here few seemed to have ever existed, with battered spaces between homes marring the walkways with shrapnel, ancient chemical puddles, and the occasional sparking outlet. No cleaning mechs persisted in keeping up appearances here.

Val's humans made their presence obvious too. Gutted mechs dotted the Conduit, their ax-slashed, arrow-blitzed bodies moldering away. The humans stripped useful parts, leaving the mechs as literal shells: hollowed out, cables sprawling where power supplies and processors once lived.

If Delta saw any of this, if she cared, she didn't say. Kaydee kept to herself too, not even offering a snide remark on my awkward ride.

The Conduit spoke enough for all of us.

When we hit the Junker's level, not far from the bottom, I had Delta let me off. Handed back her sword, took my walking stick and straightened. The walkway looked as I'd left it, cleaner than the ones above and no less ominous with its silent metal. Doorways lay ahead, both to our hope and our likely demise.

"Ready?" I asked Delta.

"I jumped you down here, didn't I?" Delta replied, adjusting her knives after my transport. "It's taken long enough. Let's go."

At first I thought Delta would take the lead, but she held back, waving me on.

"You've been saying how they'll kill me on sight," Delta said as I started walking. "Prove yourself right, Gamma."

Point taken. Delta's part would be coming later when Alpha's mechs arrived. Now, with my walking stick, my scarred and battered body, I'd have to convince Val, Chalo, and Beta that we were worth listening to.

That idea became harder about five steps into our journey, when a small silhouette stepped out from an alcove ahead. The shadow shifted and I caught the bowstring, saw the arms move, the arrow leap. Former me, with Leo's sharp programmed reflexes, might've managed a dodge. Delta could've caught the thing or batted it away. Standing well behind, Delta had no time.

Instead, I saw the arrow catch the Conduit's light as it flew, the blue mist making the metal arrowhead twinkle like a star. That star embedded into my left shoulder, the force tilting me back, numbing my left arm. A flash before my eyes confirmed the arrow severed the wiring that way.

"Stop!" I shouted, seeing the form pull another arrow back. "We're here to see Val!"

The shadow hesitated as Delta moved up next to me. She glanced at the shaft extending from my shoulder. Her left hand drifted to her knife bandoleer and I didn't doubt she could launch one of those things farther and faster than the archer up there could shoot.

"Don't," I said to her. "It's a mistake. They'll stop."

"Stay there!" The shadow shouted, as if hearing me. "Move another step and you're dead."

"Hardly," Delta muttered.

"Hurry," I called back to the shadow. "Tell Val that if she doesn't get ready, you don't stand a chance."

Instead of a question, I heard a laugh, a dire one.

"You want Val, you're too late," the shadow announced. "She's already gone."

THIRTY-ONE

FIRST AID

We stood on the walkway for too many long minutes under the shadow's arrow until the boy vouched for us. The kid didn't have his cocky grin or the bounce in his step this time, waving us on with a fear-drained face. The shadow turned out to be a girl not too much older, raw and brave. She watched us pass, arrow at the ready, as if expecting us to turn foe any second.

"We're tense," the boy said as we passed the small alcove. "Most of the adults are gone already." He looked me over. "You're a mess, aren't you?"

"What gave it away?"

"The arrow looks gnarly."

"Your friend put it there."

The boy shrugged. "You're a mech. She did what she was supposed to."

Beyond the alcove, the humans spread clutter across the path. Junk crisscrossed the flat tiles, creating stiff barricades and easy ways to trip. The boy scrambled around them, Delta helped me maneuver over, under, and through. Every so often we'd pass another makeshift sniper spot holding a boy or girl, all armed with bows, clubs and random debris.

The mess didn't do much for looks, but I could see it slowing down Alpha's clunky mechs. Those scalloped feet, the treads on many would find difficulties, get the big ones stumbling and falling. Easy targets even for half-baked archers.

"The first ones came last night," the boy continued as we closed in on the Junker's shop. "Those little flying dudes, the ones with real nasty lasers?" He shuddered. "Without Beta we would've been surprised."

Delta sniffed.

"Does she know her?" the boy caught the sound, glanced Delta's way as we limbered over a tipped barrel.

"You could say that," I replied. "You said they were gone? Val, Chalo?"

"Beta said we were screwed. Val said she wanted proof."

Proof entailed setting off on an expedition towards the Garden. Val took Beta and the hunting-capable adults with her, leaving the others behind to set up the fortifications. Alvie, Delta, and I followed the boy through the Junker's shop all the way to the forges and the haphazard town. Eyes tracked us, but the humans we saw had their hands full carving out new weapons, cooking food, or caring for the wounded.

The last caught me. Six forms lay on cloth-covered pads inside a tent in the big room Val co-opted for her town square. All adults, all burned in various places. After the boy left, telling us to stay here until Val came back, Delta took Alvie and marched right off to upgrade her gear. I'd planned to hit the forges, see if anyone could assist with a repair, but had my attention stolen by the groans coming from the tent.

I knew what it felt like for me to take a hit. My body told me precisely where, what had been damaged. I could blink and pull up my own blueprints, identify what new parts I needed and what should be done with them. Pain could be blocked with a thought.

These people wore agony on their bodies, covered in sheets and makeshift bandages. Eyes were more closed than open, pressed tight with grimaces while they held their legs, arms in the air to keep sensitive wounds from touching anything. The last, with a wrap around his chest, looked passed out.

"You're new," said the tent's lone coherent occupant, a young man with a trembling twitch to his lip. Shadows beneath his eyes and a drift to his voice suggested sleep hadn't been a partner for some time. "Know you have an arrow in your shoulder?"

I'd almost forgotten. Numbing away the pain had its drawbacks.

"Perhaps you could help me?" I asked, and the man waved me to an empty stool. Crusted over black metal, the thin seat nonetheless held me without buckling.

The man went over to a pilfered workbench, one meant for toolmaking, not medicine. Indeed, the pliers he pulled free seemed less suited to surgery than steel. When he reached for a bottle filled with clear fluid, I told him it wasn't necessary.

"I know it hurts, friend," the man replied, unscrewing the top, "but you're going to have bigger problems if that wound gets infected."

"It won't."

"The poor guy doesn't know," Kaydee whispered, pulling back in for the first time since we'd left the stairs. "Leo really did do good work on you all."

My doctor couldn't hear Kaydee, but he must've picked up the certainty in my voice. He set the cap on the bottle slow, his grip on the pliers tightened, just like the skin around his eyes. Suspicion, fear. I recognized those emotions.

"Relax, please," I said, keeping my hands on my knees. "I'm not here to hurt anyone."

"You're like her then. The one that stays in the shadows."

The one that stays in the shadows?

"In some ways," I replied, "for example, we both prefer not to have arrows stuck in our shoulders."

The man didn't move. "You're a mech. An enemy."

Humans.

"My friends and I are your only chance to survive," I said. "You can call me what you will, but if you don't want the rest of your friends ending up like this crew, you'll help me out."

That, at least, jarred the drafted doctor from his funk. He came over, swung another stool to sit before me. He looked me over, lingering here and there as if convincing himself what he saw made my mechanical origins obvious. By now, my synthetic skin had done its job, covering the scars from the glass—though doing nothing about the damage beneath—so the man was playing a mental game with himself.

At last he gripped the arrow with the pliers.

"This'll hurt," he said, then gulped. "I mean, guess it won't."

"It won't," I affirmed.

He pulled, the arrowhead digging back into skin that'd flowed over to close the wound. The impact spot bulged out as the man tugged, the pliers offering a good grip. Nonetheless, my skin didn't break. The arrow stayed stuck.

"He's not trying very hard," Kaydee said, peering over the man's shoulder and watching his attempt. "Maybe he's not up to this Gamma."

No. I could've stood up and left, convinced Delta to yank the arrow free, but I needed to see something now, something I hadn't realized until I walked into this tent. Humans could be so caring towards one another, even in death.

Could they ever feel that way about a mech? Would a human ever really care if we were hurt? If we were damaged, lying still before them, would this man take me back for help, or would he walk away?

"Stop being afraid and pull," I said. "Do what you would do to save your friends."

"You're not my friend," the man replied, leaving off the pliers.

"That's not what I said," I replied. The Librarian's stories, flitting through my mind, fed me the lines, the way to an emotional connection. "If you don't want them to die, you'll pull this arrow free."

Again the stuck stare, the dilemma in that twitching lip. A gulp, a nod, and the doctor took the pliers up again. This time the pull started slow, the man feeling out the arrowhead as he combed it through the wires, the torn metal beneath my perfect skin. It felt like an insect in my innards scrabbling around, the arrow's barbs snagging and snatching as the doctor glided it free.

"Just the skin now," the doctor muttered to himself.

He grimaced, pulled, found the skin too strong again. I was about to doubt the man when he switched his grip, slid the pliers along the arrow's shaft up to where it met my skin, the broken edges.

"Hold on," the man said, the throwaway words of someone immersed in his moment.

The pliers bit in around the seam, the doctor using them to pry open space. My synthetic skin wanted to close, but the pliers held the gap, kept it wide enough for the man to work the arrowhead free. Pulling back the pliers, holding the arrow up, the doctor stared at the shaft with a shaking head.

"Not a drop of blood," the doctor said when I asked what he was looking at. "I know it's obvious, but you look so real."

"Real enough," I said, then gestured at the patients in the beds. "Would you like some assistance? I'm waiting for Val, and have all of human biology tucked away inside my head."

There were pressing needs: I needed more internal repairs, the Voices should've been excavated from my memory and stored somewhere safe, leaving Delta to her own devices was always risky.

And yet I saw an opening, a chance here to turn one human and his patients from suspicion to trust. From, if not enemies, than risks into allies. So when the doctor nodded, started in on the first patient without a hitch in his words, that twitch in the lip vanishing, I listened and learned to heal.

THIRTY-TWO

MEETINGS

After guiding the doctor through some more nuanced treatment for his patients, the man offered to be my ambassador to the forges, the one place where there might be enough scrap to repair my internal wounds. Val and the others still hadn't returned, and their absence cast a dour, edgy mood over the young and old people around the enclave. While I saw the humans working to build up more barricades, prep meals over spark-lit fires in barrels, their shoulders slouched. Whispers slipped by, eyes stuck on the floor. Empty hands stayed near weapons.

No music played. Starship's rumble dominated the backdrop.

At least until we made the forges. There something erased the gloom, and that something was Delta.

She'd taken her own forge, a black spherical oven backed into a wall. Heat blasted the vessel, though you couldn't tell as not a speck of sweat beaded on her skin. The other humans manning their forges had largely stopped, covered in grime and desperation, to watch my friend turn her garbage into gold.

Delta worked with precision, every motion a snap with the right strength to knock off a burr or straighten a curve. She whipped knives from her bandoleer, beat them into gleaming orange perfection, then tossed them aside. Alvie, apparently impervious to the heat, caught each one and deposited it on a bare floor patch to cool. A game to him, deadly important to her.

"You going to let her operate again?" Kaydee asked as the doctor raised a hand to his fellows, introducing me as a friend rather than another suspicious mech.

"Delta's not a mechanic," I replied. Last time, in a clothing store many levels above and several lifetimes ago, her attempts to put me back together succeeded more through luck than talent. "I'd rather try a more sure hand."

Thankfully, Val's crew didn't lack for folks willing to knit a wire or piece together a broken metal bit. One in particular, a lanky girl whose face lit up at the offer to take me apart, seemed like an apt choice.

"Juny," the girl said, pulling me away from the doctor and towards a smaller forge at the back, one already crowded with other workers. "Juniper, but who has the time for that, right?"

"Right," I said, already feeling a kinship with the greasy young woman. She sounded like, acted like Kaydee. "I'm Gamma."

"She's nothing like me," Kaydee muttered at my back. "Look at that hair. It's not even blue."

I didn't give two bits about the hair. More important was Juny's rapid-fire voice as she sprinted through a rundown on me, Beta, and how she thought vessels were designed. We approached a large table —a spare gray hull plate welded onto some old mech legs—and Juny threw clutter off it without sparing a second to breathe. I slipped corrections in between the onslaught where I could, touching up specifics on how my synthetic skin worked—more like moss, less like putty—and where my processors sat—closer to the lungs than where a human heart might be.

"Lay down right there," Juny said, beckoning at the plate table.

I might've hesitated if not for the sounds coming from Delta's forge. The immaculate rhythm, the confidence in every stroke. She worked knowing she'd need every one of those weapons in the coming fight, one I'd be useless in without getting my insides put back together.

"You'll be even more useless when she botches the job," Kaydee said, arms folded and looking down at me. "So Beta's given her an overview of how a vessel works. That's way different than getting inside where she can really screw things up."

"She's not going to be doing it alone," I replied.

"Oh no? Who's going to help her? Delta?"

Juny squinted, head popping into view as she placed tools around me. "Who ya talking to?"

"Don't worry about it," I said, running a check on myself to identify all the damaged parts. A hefty list. "Here's what you'll need."

Juny recorded the litany on a spare piece of scrap, etching in enough to know each part and how many with a knife from her tool-belt. Whistling when I finished, she reread the list and looked at me with a shrug.

"Don't know that we have all of these, or any, but I can find substitutes," Juny said. "That okay with you?"

"Worth a shot?"

"You got it." Juny tapped my table. "It'll be a bit, so you can go somewhere else if you want?"

"Think I'll stay right here, if that's all right?"

"Sure. Least I'll know where to find you."

Juny jaunted off, leaving me looking at a confused Kaydee. I gave her a wink, then vanished inside myself.

WITH DELTA WORKING the forges behind me, I figured I had some solid protection from any curious humans. She'd also give me a nudge if Alpha's mechs crashed in or Val returned. Which left me with an opportunity to chat with a particular bunch, now on more equal footing.

I met the Voices, Kaydee by my side, in Starship's luxury lounge, virtual edition. Rather than the empty, dispiriting place I'd seen, I used my digital know-how to remake the club as it might've been. Spotless white cloth-covered tables, a crimson carpet unblemished by stains or torn threads. No butler bot but humans behind the bar, waiting on tables surrounded with smiling faces.

I sat at my own, a mammoth round thing decorated with plates, candles, and a rose-driven centerpiece pulled from some old film about a wedding. Kaydee sat across from me, looking around, as confused as I was confident.

"A suit?" Kaydee said when her eyes finally found me. "Gamma, you look like a bad spy."

"Then I've succeeded," I said, extending my left hand and looking at the glimmering gold timepiece emerging from beneath a sleeve. An inefficient way to count the minutes compared to the crawling numbers in my eye, but the weight on my wrist had a pleasant feel. "According to what I've watched and read of your past, important decisions tended to be made during dinners like these."

"Wow. You really have a way of making it all feel special."

"Isn't it?" I blinked, and Kaydee's usual hoodie and jeans combo became a sparkling sequin dress, just like the ones so often worn alongside the suits in those same spy movies. "Does that help?"

Kaydee's lips curled, and not in the right way. Her body shivered, blurred, and ditched the dress for her usual combo.

"Never do that to me again, okay Gamma?" Kaydee said. "Mean it. What I wear, what I look like, that's up to me, not you. No matter where we are."

As confusing as humans tended to be, sometimes even I knew when they were being serious. I nodded and apologized.

"Fine," Kaydee said. "So what are we doing here?"

"Getting your mother back on our side."

Before Kaydee could object, I focused, went deep into my drives and found the hidden folder containing a particular set of programs, ones otherwise cut off from my functions. Now, wrapping them in restrictions, I set them running again.

One by one the Voices appeared in their seats, each one as surprised as the last. Willis seemed so startled that he tried to stand, only to find he couldn't leave his chair. The doctor stared at me with not so much anger as fascination, his mouth open and unasked questions hanging on his lips. Others looked at their hands, touched their faces, took huge breaths.

Only one started swearing as soon as she could.

"Hey mom," Kaydee said to Peony, clad in a ruby evening gown. All the Voices had on outfits I'd stolen from film archives, creating a well-dressed assembly. "Nice to see you."

Peony said nothing to her daughter, instead glaring at me. She tried to stand, failed. Tried to flip the table and it didn't budge. Leo told Peony to stop, but she grabbed the steak knife at her setting and launched it at me. The blade went straight, would've struck me dead on, but instead blinked right back next to Peony's plate as if it'd never moved.

"I thought we could have a nice conversation," I said, leaning forward and putting my elbows on the table. "Now that I've saved your lives, I think you owe me that much."

I expected resistance, but the fury I saw in Peony's tight eyes took me back. Her fists clenched so hard her hands went white.

"You have saved nothing," Peony spoke each word as if it was a thunderclap. "You've only destroyed Starship, and all of us."

Around the table, I glanced at the other Voices, hoping for rolling eyes, a sigh, confirmation Peony was overreacting yet again.

Instead I found hard stares, looks confirming that what Peony said was true.

THIRTY-THREE

IMMORTALS AT DINNER

Systems. The things by the millions and billions keeping Starship running. Before the Voices they'd been monitored by Starship's people, cared for and maintained to keep Starship's citizens alive both physically and in purpose. As those people dwindled, the Voices took an ever greater share, using mechs and Starship's network to keep the ship stable. Now, without any connection to the network, who knew what might be failing across the vast vessel, who knew what might be about to break?

"She's fragile," Leo concluded his explanation. "Starship can fly itself, yes, but space isn't some paradise without faults. Components fail and need replacing. Micro-meteors hit and damage sensitive parts. A mech loses its mind and breaks something. We watched everything."

"Peony doesn't take the lead because she has the strongest personality," Willis added. "The rest of us devoted our attention to keeping Starship afloat."

Nods around the table.

Past me might've heard all this and walked away worried, wondering if I'd made some grand mistake.

Past me was the definition of naive.

"Good for you," I said. "But your abilities were already curtailed by the time I found you hiding in that server room. Alpha's been spreading throughout the ship, so—"

"Because you let him on the Bridge," Peony shot in.

"He would've made it in eventually anyway, even if he had to tear Starship apart to do it," I countered.

Across the table I tried to catch Kaydee's eye, looking for some support, some of that fire. If these digital domains had a disadvantage, Kaydee's inability to pop in next to me and whisper advice was definitely the most acute. As it was, she fiddled with her fork, watching her mom and frowning.

Not the most helpful.

"Enough," Leo said, sounding somehow exhausted despite having no biological bits. "You have us trapped and you're here, Gamma. So what is it?"

During the long walk along Starship's hull back to its engines, vacuum-induced silence and cosmic wonder left me revisiting the options. As I saw it, Alpha's war against Val and the motley humans, Delta and Beta, would likely end with massive wreckage. Given Alpha's numbers, odds and logic said he'd win, the tireless mechs grinding the humans to dust. Even if we prevailed, the losses would be so heavy as to teeter the still-living humans into extinction.

Someone would need to shepherd Starship along in either case, to protect the Nursery and all those lives waiting for a destination. Delta and Beta were better fighters. Volt had no desire to play babysitter.

Which meant me.

If Alpha won I'd try to survive, convince the mad machine that these humans, unknowing, unborn, ought to have a shot. I'd throw everything I could at Alpha's tender ego, claiming he could rule over them, that he could use them for whatever end, just to keep them alive.

Potential success, though, left me with a question.

"What happens when Starship reaches its destination?" I asked the Voices. "How do we bring so many people to life and create a functioning society?"

Peony snorted, "You don't. We do."

"Gradually," the doctor jumped in, salved Peony's words. "A few at a time. Too many people means too much conflict. It will take generations to bring everyone awake, but it's the safest way."

"We'll use Starship itself to do it," Sylvia, the ship's architect said. "It's built to land and never take off again. Its bulk will serve as a home, a base for as long as it's needed. They'll have food, they'll have shelter, sustainability even on a harsh new world."

"The specific plans are on Starship's network," Leo added. "The studies, the math showing what the optimal expansion looks like to ensure genetic diversity, a safe and stable populace that won't overwhelm Starship's resources. We can show you."

"Show him?" Peony asked. "Why?"

"Because he thinks he's the last chance we've got," Kaydee piped up. "But that's not true, right?"

The Voices stared, curious, at Kaydee. I did too, trying to follow her question. I *wasn't* their last chance?

"It's us, yeah?" Kaydee continued, whipping her eyes around, holding her hands up to accent the obvious. "That's the whole play, isn't it? Mom? Aren't we hanging out here all digital and whatnot until we get Starship where it needs to go, then bang, we suck ourselves down into something like Gamma's got going?"

"What?" I asked.

Kaydee tapped the table with her knife's handle, "That's why you made so many people into minds and tucked them into the hard drives. We land, we get our new bodies, and usher all the test tube kids into their new world."

Leo coughed. Peony, for once, had a slack jaw, a grimace mixed with downturned, glistening eyes. I burned a quick search through my data and found nothing to back up Kaydee's words, so decided I'd sit quiet, see if I'd just missed this plan in my mad rush around Starship.

"Kaydee," Ang said, then glanced at Peony, who nodded his way, "Kaydee, that's not going to work. When we make a person into a mind, we map their neural pathways and feed as much of that as we can into a program."

"One developed, at least initially, back on Earth," Sylvia added. "We kept fixing problems on it in flight. Earlier minds, like earlier mechs, didn't work very well. They'd lose stability, make nonsensical suggestions, or collapse once they understood what they were. You've seen that first hand."

"Right, I know," Kaydee said. "So we had some problems, but we're all here. Mom might be crazy, but let me tell you, she was like that long before making the jump to this."

Peony sniffed, smiled slightly.

"That's just the thing," Ang said. "It's a one-way jump. You're no more equipped to run a body than a calculator is."

"Programming's not there," Leo interjected. "Coming back was always an idea, but we never made it work."

Kaydee squinted one eye, tilted her head, her hair turning the brightest shade of teal I'd ever seen, like a shallow ocean under a tropical sun.

"You're saying this is it? Forever?" Kaydee asked.

"Immortality isn't all it's cracked up to be, is it?" Willis replied with a stiff laugh. "But that's the price we pay to see this to the end."

I saw Peony try to stand up again, saw the chair hold her stiff. With a thought, I released those binds, gave her a nod, and Kaydee's mother circled the gathering quick to her daughter's side, wrapping Kaydee in her arms.

"You understand the urgency then?" Leo said, turning to me. "You've got to get us back on the network fast, before something goes wrong."

"Alpha will find you."

"A risk we have to take," Leo grinned. "Or, you could find that damn vessel and take him out for us."

Or for ourselves. Regardless, I'd found what I wanted. The map leading to Starship's end had been filled in. Now I could return the Voices to the network comfortable I wouldn't lose too much if Alpha devoured their digital souls. Sure, Starship might fall apart without their interventions, but if Leo wanted to take the risk, I wouldn't stop him.

Across the table, Peony whispered into Kaydee's ear. My friend didn't look up from her lap, not until she felt me staring her way. When she glanced up, I expected tears in those eyes, a dream perhaps dashed.

Instead, I saw fire. Determination.

"Ready?" I asked her.

"Let's go," Kaydee replied, and in an instant the dining room, the carpet, the overhead bubble disappeared.

The forges returned, the hot waves washing over me as I laid on the table. Shadows moved, the air flickered as people ran around me. Sound came back hard, washing out Starship's rumble with shouts and screams without an ounce of joy.

Val's party had returned.

THIRTY-FOUR

STRATAGEM

More burns, more scars, more casualties.

After I rolled off my table—repairs, as yet, undone—Val, dried blood framing her face from a cut across her forehead, stole it for a meeting as wounded went by. I'd seen so many mechs destroyed that the sight of real biological blood held me tight: these weren't cords, oils, and sparks, but pink and red, broken bones and faces clenched or giving way to pained screams. The slick lines left behind weren't black or brown, but crimson.

"Too many," Val started with a shaky breath. Delta, Beta, myself, and Chalo joined her around the workbench. Chalo, in his shimmering feathered armor, appeared unhurt, though I noticed mingled cables stuck in the notches on his axes. "Too many for us to fight against. We have to run."

Chalo nodded while Delta ran her fingers along her new knives, each one catching and reflecting the room's stale light.

"Too many for you, maybe," Delta said.

Beta's lip curled, she put a hand on Delta's shoulder, drawing a sharp look from the other vessel, "Sister, for every one you slaughtered another two would take their place until you had nowhere to turn. They'd bury you. They almost buried us."

Delta wore the same expression as when I'd told her the impossible odds on the Conduit back towards the Bridge: she'd believe it when it happened.

"Who is she?" Chalo asked, pointing at Delta. "A friend of yours?"

"Better than a friend," Beta replied. "She's the best weapon we have."

Both humans appraised Delta. The same measures they gave me when I'd first shown up here. Cataloging my usefulness, where I'd fit into their plans, their society. Another tool to employ.

"Run where?" I asked, steering the conversation back to the point. A mech's place in a human's world could wait until after we escaped Alpha's slaughter. "The only way aft are the engines, and those are a trap."

"One we could defend," Val replied. "A choke point, like the Bridge."

"If we leave now, we could fortify it," Chalo nodded.

Beta had her head shaking, "Alpha's disabled the lifts. Even if we could get our wounded to the stairs and up the levels, they'd be exhausted by the time we arrived. The mechs might catch us on the way, which would mean disaster."

"Here, then," Chalo offered. "We have our resources, our people, the defenses we've built."

The table mulled the idea. Val dabbed her cut with a cloth someone handed her. Delta resumed playing with her knives. Beta sighed. And I listened to Kaydee.

"They've never been in this spot before, Gamma," Kaydee said, glowering off to the side. The conversation with the Voices seemed to have sapped her energy, leaving her voice leaden. "They've never been under attack, not like this. They have no idea what they're doing."

I was about to reply that neither had I when I caught Kaydee's aim.

The Librarian, in his mere minutes as my Mind, had left me with more warfare stories than any human could parse in their lifetime. In moments I scanned journals left by great generals and textbooks taught for generations in military academies. I played out scenarios: mechs and Val's tribe struggling against each other. Most ended with the humans, with us encircled and cut down without much effort.

Of the options, only one presented itself as a real chance.

"We draw them off," I said. "A small group distracts the mechs with what Alpha really wants. Val, you take the time to fortify this place, get your people back on their feet."

"Nothing we can do here will matter against all those machines," Val countered.

"Not if we can get to the Fabrication Lines and break them," I replied. "We'd never make it with a big group, but going small and going fast, we can get there. Then either I can erase their programming, or Beta and Delta can do what they do best. When Alpha can't repair, we chip them away. Strike fast. We're quicker than they are."

"The Lines are almost to the Bridge," Beta said. "A long way."

"The only way. As long as Alpha can keep turning scrap into an army, we'll never win."

Glances flashed, fingers tapped the table, several sighs, but the nods came one by one. Now that I had their support for the initial plan, I had to sell them on the second.

"You're going to keep the Voices here," I said to Val. "As soon as we draw the mechs away, you need to get to your terminal and upload them back onto the network. It's what they want."

"Then they're insane."

"Absolutely," Kaydee and I said at the same time. "But they claim the ship might fail without their work. We can't take the chance that they're right."

"Beta, Chalo?" Val said after a breath. "Should we trust this mech?"

Beta shrugged, "Unless you have a better idea?"

Chalo gave Val a nod, "If the mechs want to risk themselves, I say let them."

Such a nice man, that guy.

"Fine." Val gave me a hard stare. "We do it your way. Get yourselves ready and go. Every second you're here brings Alpha closer."

There was the small matter of my repairs. Much as I liked volunteering for a decoy job, if I was going to be anything more than easy bait for Alpha's mechs, I needed to get myself back. Juny thought the same, and had filled a bucket with parts by the time our impromptu war conference ended. Val and Chalo left, and I took my spot back on the table.

Delta, Beta, and Juny looked down at me, with the engineer giving a bright grin to the two deadly vessels.

"You two my assistants, or what?"

"Tell us what to do," Delta said, "and we'll get it done."

"Wonderful!" Juny laid tools out alongside me. "Grab your knives. First, we cut!"

I'd like to say that, just by turning off the pain, getting picked apart by three people at once wasn't a big deal. I'd *really* like to say that.

Instead, even without pain, I felt shock after shock. Connections to limbs came and went as the trio re-connected, severed, and rebuilt damaged pieces. One moment I'd lose all ability to control my left arm, and several seconds later, it would come back in pieces. A finger would tingle, an elbow would twitch.

Kaydee, floating above the group with an imaginative array of disgusted expressions, didn't help anything.

"Gotta say, Gamma, you really look gross with your guts everywhere," Kaydee said as Juny worked on my glass-stabbed midsection.

Like she would look any better.

"Oh, definitely not," Kaydee acknowledged, "but then, since I'm apparently gonna stay a ghost forever, you'll never find out."

"I wouldn't want to find out even if you were a ghost."

"So sweet, Gamma. I like that about you."

"That I don't want to see you gutted?"

"Among other things." Kaydee snapped a finger and bubblegum adjectives popped in around her head. Goofy, innocent, do-gooder, and other words that came off as vaguely insulting. "Oh, and I know I looked sad back there with my mom, but guess what?"

"What?"

"I'm going to break out, Gamma. Don't care what they said, I'm going to find a way out of your drives and into my own," Kaydee said, pointing a finger at me. "So don't you die before I get my own chance to live."

I'd have replied, except I felt a hard click in my middle, followed by an enthusiastic green flash over my eyes. My system status ran up, showing good connections to all limbs, all operations. Not excellent—the haphazard repair with quick scrap hadn't brought me back to Volt's perfection—but I could walk and, dare I say, swing a club.

Which meant, as Juny declared me operational, it was time to run.

THIRTY-FIVE

BAIT

We'd made the plan and we executed without waiting. Delta and Beta always had their weapons at the ready and they threw me a better walking stick made of stiffer steel than the busted table leg I'd scavenged before. I took thirty seconds to download the Voices from my own memory onto a portable drive, handing the stick to Val, who promptly tucked it away and left to oversee her own preparations.

Not a single wish for good luck, a supportive nod or hand to the shoulder. All the typical human ways to say go forth and succeed seemed to be missing. At least Chalo gave us sets of that feathered armor, extracting a promise to return it when we were done.

Oh well. I wasn't doing this for Val.

I was, I suppose, doing this for me. For Delta and Beta. For all those humans stuck in test tubes waiting for a chance to be born into a world without so much suffering, so many problems. That's who I was doing this for, and that's what I held onto as us three vessels and Alvie exited the human camp back into the Conduit.

Out here, the oncoming force made itself known. The bangs and rumbles echoed clear along the vast canyon, far closer now than when Delta and I arrived. The stomps bounced down from above and straight ahead, a clue suggesting Alpha intended to surround his victims before pouncing upon them. Val and Chalo had spoken of retreat, but unless they left now, they wouldn't have anywhere to go.

As Beta and Delta looked past tipped over and treacherous junk strewn across the walkways, I bent down to Alvie and whispered a few clear words. The dog took the guidance, gave me a single bark, then bounded off back down the Conduit away from the stomps and towards the stairs.

"Where's he going?" Beta said.

"Alvie's got better things to do than die with us," I replied, then pointed with my walking stick down the Conduit. "Shall we?"

"Please. I'm so bored." Delta kicked off into a loping run, jumping over obstacles without breaking stride, a gazelle in her element.

Beta, not one to be left behind, followed, using some obstacles as boosts to jump too many meters in the air for my liking. The two matched up to each other fast, all while I stumbled through like a clumsy human. Having gone for hours in zero gravity, then for hours more with barely-there legs, I had to rework myself to yet another performance degree: not quite my prior strength, but enough to run.

The goal: draw Alpha's mechs after us to the Garden.

The multiple connecting levels, the entangling plants, and unstable footing would give us a benefit, not to mention a big hole in the center we could use as a trap or an escape hatch. Draw the mech army there, inflict some damage, then disappear out the other side in a sprint towards the Fabrication Lines.

That was the ideal. The reality?

The mechs found us thirty minutes out from the human enclave.

We'd long outstripped Val's fortifications, the Conduit's walkways their usual mess. Vast trash piles lingered off to our left as we ran, sparkling in the mist. The clangs, bumps, and bangs washed out my footsteps, shook my legs every time I made contact with the metal floor. The Garden sat another hour's run ahead, but Beta and Delta slowed anyway, waited for me to catch up.

"Ideas?" Delta asked as I matched them. Both vessels were looking upward to where marching light lines showed Alpha's advancing force. "We need to get their attention, right?"

I'd hoped we'd run straight into the mechs, the collision serving to alert Alpha's forces where they needed to be. Given the lift shutdowns, though, it made sense the lowest levels would be the last reached by the slow moving robots. If we wanted to get in their faces, we'd have to climb.

Or . . .

"Val's old terminal," I said. "That's not far, right?"

"Another ten minutes sprint," Beta mused.

"We get there, I can get Alpha on us quick."

Beta had the time right, at least for her and Delta. It took me fifteen at a dead run to catch up to them at Val's old apartment. Her flickering terminal sat inside, untouched since my last visit. This time, I didn't need to jack in to do what I wanted. Instead, I just sent a message through Starship's communication network. A single recording, a single sentence, blasted out through all Starship's functioning speakers using the ship's alarm protocol.

"What'd you say?" Beta asked when I joined them back outside. "We heard something, but this speaker's been smashed."

"Told him that, if he wants the Voices, to meet us where we left him for dead."

"He'll bite on that?"

The answer didn't come from my mouth, it came from the mechs lining the levels up above. Some were past us, closer to the humans than we were, but, almost in unison, the shuffling lines rotated. The lights, the clomps turned around and began trekking back towards the Garden.

"Moron," Delta said. "Why would he commit his entire force to us? He could split and take the humans too."

"We're the winning play," I said. "If he gets the Voices, Alpha can control Starship without fear. He'll know where the humans are and can hunt them down, expose them to vacuum, cut off their oxygen."

"And when he finds out we're lying?" Beta asked.

"Then he's right back to where he is now, just a few hours lost, but with his biggest enemies annihilated."

Delta and Beta took that reasoning and launched into another run, zipping off towards the Garden. I followed, Kaydee popping in and jogging alongside me in a very inaccurate version of her running speed.

"They're not the savviest pair, are they?" Kaydee said, pointing at the two vessels up ahead.

"They weren't designed for strategy," I replied. "That's like criticizing a trash mech for not being much of a cook."

"Defensive much?"

"Of a human unfairly criticizing a mech? Possibly."

"Okay then, mister touchy."

"It's fine," Time to change the subject. We were going into a fight and I needed Kaydee on my side, ready to offer up advice. "How's your work going?"

"You mean my attempted resurrection?"

"Sure?"

"When we have something suitable to try, I'm ready." Kaydee glanced at me. "And no, Gamma, a trash mech isn't suitable. I respect 'em and all, but I'm not about to let my first real body in a long time be a box filled with garbage."

I let her have that one.

WE FOUND the first mechs outside the Garden. They'd scaled the human's ladder, bending and breaking the rungs on the way. Behind a mech trio lay several more boxy machines that'd fallen, crushing each other into a pile that cushioned the ones following. Delta and Beta sized up the threesome as I arrived, Delta holding her sword and Beta twirling her two long knives.

Our opponents had lithe forms, six-limbed agile mechs designed —so my files told me—for difficult maintenance work on Starship's exterior. With ten digit hands on the limb ends, flexible skeletons, and shining emerald eyes, they regarded us without other expression. No verbal warnings, no demands straight from Alpha.

As we approached, each one took a single step back before bending away. Four limbs steadied them on the ground while the remaining two hands ripped into the mech debris at the busted ladder's base.

"What are they doing?" I asked, slow.

"Go!" Delta shouted.

The vessel kicked forward, keeping her blade straight level before her, like a spear. Beta whipped both hands, flinging the knives at the left-most target. Each blade struck home, severing the machine's front-most hands. Rather than roll over and die, though, the mech adjusted its balance onto its centermost supports.

"Adaptable," Beta said as I went past her, my reinforced walking stick raised like a club.

The mechs hit second. Almost as one, each machine swung up and forward, their two digging hands pulling off metal shards, stunted box limbs, or sparking batteries and flinging them at us. The junk flew like meteors, screaming in hard. Delta caught the first one, flicking her sword and deflecting the motor up and away. A second, a saucer-like foot, caught her shoulder, knocking her off balance, but Delta adjusted, kept up the charge.

I tried to copy her. Bad idea.

Swinging my walking stick down like a frustrated baseball player, I smacked an oncoming battery into the walkway at my feet. The thing, its structure compromised, promptly blew up, expending its stored energy in a crackling puff that coupled with a thrown arm to blow out my legs and land me on my back. My walking stick rolled off somewhere, following the grand tradition of my weapons to become useless seconds into any fight.

"Ouch," Kaydee said as Beta vaulted by me, using the walkway's railing to leap over her own threats.

"Shut up," I said, kicking my legs into a quick restart. The battery's current stunned my own power supply, skittering my inputs. "At least I'm not dead."

The same couldn't be said for the mech trio. Delta, swinging her sword in long slashes and adjusting her run into a zig-zag blitz, only took another couple glancing blows before she reached the tossers. The right-side mech made its adjustment to up-close combat too late, sticking up its four limbs with stolen plating and a single ladder rung only for Delta's forged blade to cut it all the way through. Split asunder, the mech collapsed.

As I stood, the middle mech made a smarter play: as Delta brought her sword back up, the middle mech tackled her. Two hands pinned Delta's sword arms against the ground while its bottom two clamped her legs tight in the same way, leaving the mech's middle hands to go to work. Pressed together, the ten fingers looked like knives, and they might've done their stabby worst if I hadn't done something smart for a change.

The battery at my feet didn't have any charge left, but the thing still had heft. The mech had thrown it at me, so I figured I'd return the favor. Like a pitcher from that old human game, I wound up and launched the dead brick. I aimed for the mech's head, naturally missed and hit its back right leg. The strike broke the mech's knee joint, freeing Delta's left leg. She didn't waste any time, taking a blow to her stomach as she wrapped her leg around the mech's other hind limb and twisted.

The pair rolled over, and without the ground to pin her on, the mech failed to match Delta's strength. Slamming down with her elbows, Delta mashed the mech's head into the walkway, shattering its processor. As I retrieved my walking stick and headed her way, the vessel stood up from the mech's dead eyes, looking down at the deep stabs into her stomach. Exposed wires, a silver skeleton showed through.

Not good.

Beta, at least, cleaned up her target without much effort. She'd tossed more knives on her approach, each one lopping off a limb with precision. The mech died slow, its green eyes surveying us as its useless core lay on the ground.

"You going to be okay?" I asked, joining up with the two killers.

"Ten percent loss." Delta replied, wincing. "Legs."

As she spoke, the clomps and clangs continued to grow, some coming from behind us as mechs found other ways down to our level. Accompanying them came a familiar whirr, electric jets firing away. Couriers and their little lasers on approach.

We'd asked to be trapped, and now we were.

THIRTY-SIX

GARDEN PARTY

We wanted the mechs to follow us into the Garden, and they did. Some were already inside, waiting as we climbed the ruined ladder—the busted rungs were enough to climb with careful hands—while the rest surged their way towards us.

At the ladder's top, with Beta leading, we found a boxy collection hesitating after seeing their fellows plunge to their destruction. These walking crates didn't even have arms, but they had bodies carved with edges. As Beta pulled into the lower sandy Garden level the crates charged, their squawk boxes announcing tinny calls to battle.

Delta yanked herself up the remaining distance with a single heave and I followed, walking stick dangling from a loop over my shoulders, at a more sedate pace. The other two vessels would be fine together and I wanted a particular machine to see me.

The couriers buzzed down like angry bees, their tiny jets firing on and off for precise flying. With heads coated in cameras to guide that same flight, I figured Alpha would be watching their streams, hunting for evidence, looking to confirm his madman's choice to send his whole force after three mechs.

So I slipped the other thing I'd asked Juny to get me into my hand as I neared the ladder's top.

The couriers swooped in, their stinger tails brightening as bolted on lasers began to charge. I had two rungs to go. With my right hand, I reached up, kicked with my legs for an extra boost. With my left, I took the drive, slipped it between my fingers, and waved it towards the couriers.

"You want this?" I called to the five floating mechs as they assembled around me. "The Voices are mine, Alpha, just like this ship."

I kicked off again, not exactly the prescribed method for climbing a ladder but, this close to the top, it would have to do. My right hand gripped a sandy lip, my left joined it and lifted. Beneath me, I felt heat as the couriers unleashed their particular brand of nasty into the poor ladder. The lasers melted through the remaining bars, sending the whole thing clattering down below.

Not like we were going back anyway.

Inside the Garden, I slapped at the panel operating the doorway we'd come through. With a slick, grinding shift across the sand, the portal closed. Any mech able to operate the panel could open it again, but those couriers lacked hands. No ambush would be coming from behind.

And not much remained ahead. For now.

Beta and Delta played tag with one last crate mech. The machine chased Beta blindly, a futile attempt to catch the more nimble vessel, who kept losing the boxy machine among the sand drifts deep down here. As she went, I saw Beta gather up her thrown knives, leading the crate back along her own re-arming trail. Delta brushed wires off her blade, fresh from diving into another dead crate, and waited for Beta to bring her next victim along.

"It's almost sad," Kaydee said as Beta brought the crate around one more dune, lining the mech up for a Delta skewering.

"If the mech were still itself, it would worse," I said, unlimbering my walking stick. Mech noises up above signaled we wouldn't be alone for long. "They're all here like this because of Alpha. They don't have a choice."

Beta brought the mech into its final run, dancing away at the last meter so Delta could run her blade straight. The sword bit in and Delta started a sidestep, cutting as she went forward and away, getting around the mech's side as the blade continued through. The sword exited with a coolant spray, a forlorn spark, and the crate, its upper third resting separate from the rest, slid to a dead stop.

Splattered in coolant but bearing no new injuries, Delta came my way as I looked up the Garden stairs to my right. Beta gathered more thrown blades.

"An easy warm up," Delta said. "Couriers outside?"

I nodded, "Don't open that unless you're feeling cold."

"A joke?"

"I've been known to make them on occasion."

Delta slipped the smallest smile my way, "I'm glad you're comfortable. This will get ugly before the end."

"Good thing I already look like garbage."

The Fabrication Lines were a few levels above us in the Conduit, so once Beta and Delta had themselves prepped, we took off heading straight up. Five levels and we'd be at the right place.

"Why did you stay with the humans for so long?" Delta asked Beta as we climbed the murky stairs. The Garden kept its light focused on the plants, with purple-blue diodes lining its side steps. "Or was that your job?"

"Couldn't beat the mech in the Nursery, so I did the next best thing," Beta replied. "They were little babies. Too pathetic to leave alone."

"Get that," Delta said. "Val does not seem loving."

"She's a hard one, but she cares in her own way."

We went past more arid levels, each one offering different wildlife than the last. From sand to brush to fuzzy grains and bushes. I listened for the central waterfall's sound, but Alpha's army crushed its noise. Delta and Beta shouted their conversation to each other, a get-to-know-you back and forth conducted a deafening levels.

Good to see them cooling off towards one another. Where we were going, any suspicions, any ill will had to be set aside.

"You're all going to die anyway," Kaydee mused, "might as well go out with friends instead of enemies."

Inspiring stuff.

We climbed to one level above the Fabrication Lines, a zone in between in the transition from dry plain to chill wood. Mushrooms and small firs abounded here, the Conduit's mist converted into a light frost. Mosses coated the ground, soft and juicy green. There must've been some use for this biome, but at first, I couldn't come up with any.

"Possibilities," Kaydee said as we walked into the forest. "Starship's creators didn't want to exclude an area only to find we needed it for some reason, either biological or psychological. They used to thicken up the snow here, give us a chance to play."

Our trio made our way to the level's center, a rounded space ringed with three-meter high trees surrounding a gaping hole. Through that hole dripped water in spurts short and long, with a dense mist rising up around the edges as rising heat met the cooled air. Discounting the approaching doom, I found the whole place beautiful.

"Draw them in, then flee," I said to Beta and Delta, though from the eye rolls I received, the reminder must've been unnecessary.

"Don't use flee," Beta quipped. "I prefer advance. We're not running, we're moving forward."

"Sure."

I'd call it whatever Beta wanted, so long as those knives took mechs out instead of me.

My short reply concluded with a hard thud, one matched by three more as another flexi-mech quartet leapt down from above. Their ten digit hands caught the misty edge, flipping them up and over in a split second. Beta's thrown blade struck one as it rose, catching its midsection and knocking it down the hole.

The attack must've been a signal, because more mechs came barreling in from the sides, including a pollinator swarm. The little rat-like contraptions raced towards me, beating out the bigger crates and cleaning mechs armed with knives, clubs, and whatever other scrap they could find.

"Please don't die, Gamma," Kaydee yelped as I gripped my walking stick in both hands, putting my back to a thick tree trunk.

As the first pollinators came within reach, I swept the stick in a hard, ground-brushing stroke. Two took the hit, blasting backwards. Three more jumped the blow, popping up towards my chest as if launched from a spring.

I ducked, letting the trio bounce into the tree behind me. Stepping after my sweep, I adjusted my grip and whipped my bar back the opposite direction. The pollinators that'd dodged my first hit fell off the tree to the ground in time to get smacked by the second, their little robot forms flying away into the frost.

More pollinators came on, and a few meters behind them romped the bigger boys, kicking up pine needles with every heavy step. Off towards the center Delta held her own against two more flexi-mechs, dicing off hands with every swing while dodging knife stabs and grasping hands.

Beta . . . well, Beta defied gravity.

Couriers followed the flexi-mechs, swarming up from the center hole with their ends glowing. Beta leapt into that swarm, hands throwing knives—I realized that, sometime during our walk to the Garden, Delta had given Beta her knife bandoleer—into the robots then withdrawing the blades as she fell past. Beta planted her feet on the floating mechs, knocking them away while slashing others before jumping across to the center's far side, vanishing into the mist.

Just as the couriers started regrouping, setting their sights on Delta and I, Beta came dashing back through for another round. Despite the knives, despite the perfect kicks knocking the robots into each other or sending their lasers firing into Alpha's other mechs, the scariest thing about Beta's whole onslaught was the wide grin pasted over her face.

I'd seen that smile before, on Alpha, when he'd come close to snatching victory. Delta, too, adopted a similar smile as she slashed and sliced.

What would prompt me to be so ecstatic?

"How about living, for starters?" Kaydee said.

Good point. I'd been knocking away the pollinators, my stick's reach and some faster swings proving more than capable of keeping the little things off me. Now I had to duck around my friendly pine tree to dodge a charging crate. On the other side, a culinary mech's grinding treadmills and gashing cutlery waited for me.

The thing's weapons banged off my stick, the mech's simple programming taking my weapon's proximity as the greater threat. I let the cutlery mech go to work as I jabbed, watching from my left eye as the passing crate shifted itself around, faced my back, and geared up for another running charge.

"They're all morons, aren't they?" Kaydee said as I dove to the side.

The crate tried to stop, but on the frosted moss its broad metal feet couldn't get much traction. The mech mashed into its brother, breaking arms apart even as it impaled itself on the cutlery mech's . . . cutlery.

My dive came with consequences: the pollinators took advantage, swarming me. They scampered up my legs, my arms, and ran along my chest as their tiny tools sliced at my skin. In a millisecond I turned off the pain sense, refusing information about damage to keep my wits about me. Dropping my walking stick, I resorted to my hands and feet, kicking and throwing the machines away or into other approaching mechs.

One little monster made a run for my eyes when I had my hands full, a perfectly timed assault that should've had my vision sliced away save for a flash. Delta's blade swiped, taking the pollinator and,

I was pretty sure, the tip of my nose with it. Her hand reached down, grabbed my arm and hauled me to my feet.

"To lie down is to die, Gamma," Delta said, readying her sword again.

Beta, in another flying leap through the misty center, knocked out another two couriers and rolled in to join us. I hadn't expected a breather, but the other culinary mechs, crates, and Alpha's older, boxier creations lingered on the level's edges.

"They're cutting off the exits," Beta said, replacing knives and looking around.

"They already have us surrounded," I replied. "Why wait?"

The answer to my question came swooping into the chilly woods from above. Not on wings, but on arms, so many long red arms. Clutching claws gripped the ceiling, followed by a slender cherry-red body. Like some monkey, the robot jumped from the ceiling to a tree then to the floor, its dozen or more arms retracting and extending as it moved, flowing almost like hair. When it hit the ground, the mech stood up slow, angry red eyes looking at us, at me.

I knew those eyes, knew that body and those arms. Up close, I could even see lingering bite marks where Alvie, attacking by surprise, had dealt the Chancellor a fatal blow outside the airlock. Alpha had made some modifications: the Chancellor looked to be almost twice her prior height, with more arms, and those limbs didn't look made for turning pages and checking tests.

"This should be fun," Delta said, pointing her blade at the mech.

"Oh yeah," Beta seconded.

"You're both insane," I finished.

THIRTY-SEVEN

TAKE A DIVE

To go from homicidal educator to a homicidal mech murderer wasn't a far leap. The Chancellor owned the transition, giving our trio silent judgement, arms suspended in the mist. Beta and Delta made their quips and readied their weapons. I had my walking stick and an idea.

"Time to run," I said, just loud enough to make it over the whirring, grinding engine noise produced by so many mechs in a single space.

"Run?" Beta replied. "But it's just getting interesting."

"The objective," I hissed.

The Chancellor seemed willing to let us talk. And why not? Every second we spent here let Alpha's forces gather more and more strength, clog the levels around us, and ensure our demise.

"He's right," Delta said. "One more kill, then we go."

Not what I wanted, but I couldn't exactly force the two vessels to change their minds. I didn't even get a chance: on the heels of her words, Delta heaved her blade end over end at the Chancellor, following it in a rush.

The mech blocked the blade with its shield arm, sending the weapon to the muddy ground. Delta dropped to a slide as Beta flung knives over her, the Chancellor again catching the throws with two arms bearing thick metal slabs. From her slide, Delta scooped up her fallen sword, dodged stabs from two other arms with sharp needles on their ends, and lunged with a skewering strike right where the Chancellor should've been.

"Not good," I said as Delta's thrust ran out of range, its tip just grazing the red mech. The Chancellor's bottom arms shoved the mech into the gap's middle, clawed hands clinging to the edges. "Ideas, Kaydee?"

"I'm voting run, Gamma. Run real fast."

Delta's maneuver left her vulnerable for the moment it took her blade to extend, the moment it took her to realize she'd missed and find a new plan. The Chancellor took advantage, her second shield arm swinging across to smash Delta's middle and send my friend flying back. Above, the highest arm pair armed with lasers, drove Beta into dashes to dodge their burning strikes.

As per usual, the enemy ignored me.

Kaydee suggested running, but there were no open pathways from my level. Alpha's mechs seemed content to trap us for the moment, but sense suggested any attempted leaving would prompt a swift and brutal destruction.

Which left the back-up plan.

"Already?" Kaydee asked as I worked my way right, needling my way through trees and past the mech corpses I'd left behind earlier. "Not even going to try helping?"

"Delta's the one always going on about the mission," I said, not really proud of myself for saying it. "If we all die here, Starship's Alpha's for good." I sighed and crouched, peering out at the fight and trying to judge my timing. "Besides, you and I both know I'd be a liability in all that."

'All that' was a metal blur. Delta and Beta danced with the Chancellor, whose arms swirled so fast I found it hard to understand how the long limbs didn't knot up with one another. Instead they worked in concert, the shields driving the vessels into vulnerable positions where the lasers or the spears would get a scratch in. Delta and Beta struggled, those fast cuts and stabs not making it through to the Chancellor's core.

An arm nicked here, a striking spear deflected there, but my friends were taking hits: long gashes glinted in the snowy light along both Delta and Beta's sides as they proved too slow to make every necessary dodge. Delta's hair smoked where a laser blast had scorched the side of her head.

The fight seemed to have a foregone conclusion.

After which I'd be an easy dessert.

The decision clear, I broke from the tree in a flat sprint towards the center gap. The Chancellor occupied it still, dancing at a distance from the two vessels. The mech didn't seem to notice me, no red eyes or arms shifted my way. Five meters vanished in as many long steps, and this time I managed to plant my foot right when I leapt.

I pulled my hands before me into a dive, tucking the walking stick beneath my arm as I soared into and down through the middle. Water splashed, ice cold, over my back as mist made my destination invisible.

My dive stopped hard, a yank that had me dangling upside down. I felt the problem: the Chancellor had an arm on my leg, one of her two clawed options that'd been keeping the mech hanging in the gap. The Chancellor tugged me towards the side as its move forced the mech to give up its aerial refuge.

Had to hope Delta or Beta could work with that, because I couldn't do much dangling over a deep, dark pit.

"Well, if you fall, at least we know where you'll end up," Kaydee noted.

"Not helpful," I replied over the constant clashing, banging, cursing come from my friends.

Curling, I looked up through the mist. Shadows and sparks moved in the twisting fog. Delta and Beta made a new read on the tactical situation and, for once, seemed to work together. I heard Delta call out a move and saw Beta's form—the long knife shadows told the difference between them—make a two-step retreat. The Chancellor, who seemed to be dedicating three arms apiece to my friends, sent a shield, spear, and laser chasing after Beta.

Delta jumped to her left, towards the gap and those extended arms. As the vessel, dragging her sword along behind her, clambered onto the Chancellor's Beta-chasing bunch, her own pursuing arms slowed. Too fast, too reckless, and they might burn out, stab, or slam their own side. Curling around towards Delta, chasing her, did one thing right: the Chancellor left herself open, a blank few meters between her and Delta.

The vessel whipped her sword, a sidearm slash without lead-up. Spinning sideways, the blade seemed destined to carve the Chancellor in two. If I had breath to hold, I would've held it.

Delta missed. I saw the blade spin, saw it stop, and then noticed the shadow beneath. The Chancellor's other claw, sister to the one holding me aloft. It'd snaked up from near the Chancellor and caught the blade, gripping the weapon's hilt. The mech turned Delta's weapon back towards her, the shield, spear, and laser arms wrapping around Delta from behind to cut off any retreat.

One shot, one way.

"Delta!" I called, and threw my walking stick up as the Chancellor stabbed forward with Delta's sword.

In a single motion, Delta leaned left, caught my walking stick, my metal bar, and swung it up into her own blade. My poor staff made a terrible shriek as Delta's sword bit in, as it sheared through, but my weapon did its work, deflecting the Chancellor's strike up and over Delta's shoulder.

Delta dropped my walking stick, now sporting a new razor point, from her left hand to a moving right, her shoulder turning with the catch and firing the brand new spear right at the Chancellor. I saw the shadow, I saw the sparks as the spear struck home. A fractured, fuzzy groan came from the mech, her arms flailing, her motor failing. Delta jumped off her perch, landed on the side near the Chancellor, safe for the moment.

Unlike someone else I knew.

"Help!" I yelled, a shout washed out by the sudden banging as Alpha's mech army, not content to give us any breath, drove forward.

The Garden shook with the motion. The Chancellor teetered, started to fall. I saw Delta wrest her blade back from the writhing claw. Saw her heft the sword as the Chancellor, sparks flying, my walking stick a flag planted in her core, faltered.

And dropped.

Gravity pulled me down for a quick second, a descent interrupted fast by the few saucers on this level made to capture water. I smashed into a tiny pool, connected by rivulets to the edge. My pride injured, perhaps, but only that.

"Your leg, Gamma!" Kaydee yelled.

The Chancellor's claw had its grip, and I turned back to it, shaking my leg as the mech fell past me, its arms splaying everywhere. In that chaos, on the end of a spear, hung Beta. The vessel dashed by too fast for me to tell where she'd been wounded, if she was still alive, but there was no doubting the form nested in that tangle.

A tangle I'd be joining in a second. The arm played out, the claw jerked, and I started to move towards the pool's edge. Started, and stopped.

Delta's blade lanced by, cutting down and through the arm holding me in a perfect throw. The tension released, and with a quick push, I shoved the metal clasps off my right leg. Freedom's fun was short-lived: the sword toss broke the saucers already damaged by the falling Chancellor, the whole enterprise collapsing as I found my footing.

"Run, you idiot!" Delta called from above, and I glanced her way to see the vessel backed up to the edge, no weapons in her hands, as mechs approached from all sides.

I couldn't help her, stuck a level below with no weapons. Couldn't, and wouldn't let her sacrifice be for nothing. Splashing, I lunged from the shallow saucer, kicking off and jumping over the couple meters to the arid tundra. Behind me, I heard a defiant curse, then felt the whistling wind as Delta fell, following Beta and the Chancellor into Purity's depths.

Hitting the cold ground, I rolled, rose, and started to do what Delta told me.

I ran towards the only thing that mattered, and hated myself for it.

THIRTY-EIGHT

PURSUED

Delta, Beta, gone. Delta, Beta, gone. The words repeated over and over again as I scrambled from the Garden. The Conduit's blue light, plant-free walkways proved no respite from what I'd seen back there, proved only that I was still running, still chased.

We'd planned this as an all-or-nothing mission. Expecting success without casualties would've been illogical, but perhaps Kaydee had rubbed off on me enough that I'd done so. The future had seemed bright, with us three vessels removing Alpha from power and saving Starship.

Now Delta and Beta were buried at Purity's bottom, sitting in a dark pool waiting for Starship's enzymes to do their work and reduce them to scrap.

"Delta didn't get killed, Gamma," Kaydee said as my feet hit metal, the Garden's exit shutting at my heels. "She dove."

Dove without a weapon, dove with a deadly enemy into a trapped cage at the Garden's bottom. Hardly an escape. Hardly worth hoping. Yet I couldn't do the human thing and give in to despair, collapse myself and wait for death. No, logic offered its cold comfort and I kept myself moving.

After all, the mission held priority.

Ahead, metal and blue mist. The Fabrication Lines. I pounded forward, pushing all my energy into the fullest sprint I could manage. No mechs emerged before me, our play had done its work.

Behind? Another matter.

Alpha's sluggish boxes and treaded cutlery fiends couldn't catch me, but the familiar courier jets whirred as the laser-sporting bugs swarmed from the Garden in chase. A glance back confirmed half a dozen coming at me from above and below, bees of the worst sort.

"And, once again, you don't have a weapon," Kaydee said, jogging alongside my sprint as if on a relaxing morning jaunt. "How do you keep letting this happen?"

"Bad luck."

Kaydee couldn't argue with that, but she bit her lip as she kept one eye on those approaching couriers. There wasn't a chance in hell that I could out run them, not with so far yet to go until the Lines. The question now was how close I could get before they blew me apart.

Delta or Beta might've been able to do both. Sprint ahead, throw knives back. Maybe some fancy kick flip off the Conduit's side wall into the center, grappling with the small machines and smashing them into one another before vaulting back to safety. Not something in my repertoire.

So I ran.

The first blast came moments later, as I passed by closed, broken open, and battered doorways leading into long abandoned apartments. The spiral portals would seem to offer a chance to hide, but, so far as I knew, the homes had no other ways out. Ducking in would mean checking out once Alpha's mechs caught up.

"Yeah, fire safety wasn't a big priority," Kaydee muttered as I kicked left, banging against the railing to avoid the shot.

The orange blast scored a hit on the walkway ahead and I used it as a guide, jumping that way as the next laser melted through the railing where my hand had been a millisecond before. Every shot fired would take a bit to recharge, and there were six, so . . .

My right shoulder fried. Not quite melted, not quite non-functional thanks to the defenses we'd grabbed from the humans before leaving. That shimmering armor serving its purpose to throw off the shots, keep me going.

"Another hit there and you're done," Kaydee said. "You need a new idea, buckeroo."

"Buckeroo? Now?"

"If we're gonna get torched, I get to pull out the silly names."

My mind had gone insane. Maybe she always had been.

Equally insane would be staying out here on this walkway, under fire. The Fabrication Lines weren't close either. Another busted doorway appeared on my right and I took the chance, diving through as more hot light smoked the ground behind me.

I landed on corroded tile, rusted over thanks to the Conduit's mist and irregular attention from, well, anyone. Slimy gunk coated my hands, my clothes as I pushed myself further inside, grabbing onto a leaning table to get back to my feet. More tables abounded in a bigger-than-expected space, far larger than the apartments I'd seen, with patchy walls still holding picture frames. Art saved by glass panes sat in those frames, gray as the Conduit's blue light filtered through the large dirty window.

The couriers didn't give me another second to parse my new shelter, weaving towards and through the door. Their lasers looked like fiery motes in the shadows, almost beautiful. More importantly, the light made for easy targets.

I picked up and swung the table, its round top blasting towards the courier cluster with zero grace and maximum effectiveness. The little bots and their jets could scoot quick but not instantly, and their bunching as they swept into the restaurant let the table swallow four in a single strike. Their frames bent, their jets sputtered out, and the mechs crashed to the floor with the furniture.

"Not bad!" Kaydee said as I ran towards the back and the long serving counter running the space's length.

Two couriers left, and they didn't care one bit that I'd toasted their buddies. I caught their reflections on the tiled walls at the restaurant's rear, the orange glows getting brighter. On my left, I passed a chair toppled over and half broken and, without stopping my stride, I scooped up the remnants and flung them backward.

A human might've trusted to random chance making a move like that, hoping upon hope that luck was with him. I didn't need luck, Leo's programming serving to calculate the angle, velocity, and release timing to get my thrown junk on course with one courier reflection.

The mech's laser shot as my missile flew towards it, a shadowed flash followed by fire and another crumpling bang as my target hit the ground.

Its friend nailed me dead in the back.

The heat washed through my armor, charred and peeled the synthetic skin beneath. Enough absorbed to keep damage to a minimum, though my alerts painted another body section yellow: any follow-ups there would be fatal.

"One on one," Kaydee said as I swung around behind the restaurant counter. "Can he win? What do we think, crowd?"

Fake applause rang as I ducked low, watched the reflection as the courier floated in closer. It wouldn't have a shot until the mech came around my barrier, which gave me a second to stock my options: mottled frying pans, silver ware, cups.

"Oh please, use the pans," Kaydee continued. "The best weapon you've had yet, for sure."

Much as I hated to give her the satisfaction, Kaydee had it right. I scooped two pans from the shelves and rose as the courier zipped over the counter. I swung the metal circles like tennis rackets, overhead slaps as if to bash a fly. The courier burned the first pan away with another shot, leaving me swinging a glowing half-handle.

The second pan did the trick, swatting the courier down to the ground. A follow-up smash rendered the flimsy bot to sparking circuits.

"Victory!" Kaydee shouted, digital fireworks booming all around.

I didn't bother appreciating the light show. There'd be more couriers, and the rest of Alpha's mechs would be coming too. Keeping my chosen frying pan, I left the restaurant, took one glance back towards the Garden and the shapes, the rumbles moving my way, and sprinted off.

THIRTY-NINE

THE LINES

The Conduit held a different look when you ran along it at top speed. The varied decay and flickering neon signs blended, removing the individual from hundreds of human years and spilling it together into a blue-black morass of metal and shadow. With Alpha's clean-up, the sporadic fires and random mechs wandering about had vanished, replaced with a cold emptiness.

If everything on Starship died and not a sole moving thing remained, how long would the ship travel like this? A year, ten, a thousand before some collision or a system failure blew the vessel apart and scattered all this into the void?

A question perhaps better considered when not pursued by an unceasing robotic army.

My feet, clad in well-made boots, thudded with every step, recycled treads gripping the mist-dotted walkway. With the couriers smashed, I'd bought myself some time. Mech movements echoed my way from behind, of course, but they seemed quieter, less focused: Alpha splitting his efforts, deciding one vessel wasn't worth his full force.

"Don't knock yourself. You're worth plenty, big shot," Kaydee flounced.

"He'll keep the fast ones on me, maybe," I said. "I have to hope he doesn't know where I'm going yet."

"With his ego, I bet he thinks you're going for the Bridge."

"That'd be nice."

And plausible. If, though, Alpha had one trait I could count on, it was his unpredictability. The vessel proved time and time again a willingness to be ruthless, inventive, and altogether spastic in his efforts. For all I knew, he'd let me run right to the Bridge without another fight just because he wanted to rip me apart himself.

Or try yet again to corrupt me, steal my functions and bend them to his own ends.

Up ahead a familiar structure emerged from the cerulean mist. Every so often on the Conduit, big buildings spanned its width, giving opportunities to cross from one side to another while allowing grandeur beyond the tight apartments and shops nestled into Starship's sides.

On those sides now rested jocular remnants, sports bars and old stores flogging University merchandise, from shirts to cups to books. On the few levels below—looking across the Conduit—I caught student housing's lockstep dregs, each portal numbered in the same school fashion.

I ran beneath the University itself, too low for its esteemed corridors. Not that I had any desire to return that way after the attempted murder found within. Kaydee fell silent too, remembering, maybe, the same things I was: a Dean and a Chancellor demanding perfection and damning anyone not good enough to attain it.

A Chancellor I hadn't erased well enough the first time, apparently.

"Think they're alive?" I asked Kaydee as I kept up my run. "Beta and Delta?"

"If anyone's gonna make it outta that mess, it's them," Kaydee said, her voice lacking that certain conviction. "But that didn't seem great."

"So a last second save isn't looking too likely?"

"If you're betting on Delta to come screaming in when some trash bot has you pinned, I'd find a different plan."

"That's the optimism I come to you for." I blinked as I passed the University, emerging from its black bulk back into the Conduit's full light. Humans blinked to water their eyes, for me the action served to recalibrate my sensors, tune them to the new light level. "Do you have any useful ideas?"

"Depends," Kaydee chewed on a long hair strand as she floated along in the air beside me, legs curled into a pretzel. "What *was* your idea when you got to the Lines?"

I had a few options, all depending on what the Fabrication Lines looked like when I arrived. If we came in surrounded by mechs, fighting for every step in a pitched battle, then I'd aim for a bomb route. Blow up as much as we could before Alpha tore us apart. Blaze of glory style.

That didn't seem likely, which meant I could open up the full playbook. There were so many—

"What's up with you?" I asked, stopping the runaway thought before it could get going. "You're acting chipper, dire, and frivolous all at once and I don't understand why?"

"Would you rather I pouted around like before?" Kaydee shot back, then pantomimed a sulk.

"Not really."

"Look, I'm embracing my destiny, okay? You and me, together in this to the end. Not the worst fate, right?"

"No?"

"Exactly. See? I've got every reason in the world to be happy, unless you act all dumb and get us killed because you're loafing with a bunch of hot mechs on your tail."

Fair point. I picked up the pace.

Past the University, the Conduit gained some respectability. At least, that's what I picked up from what I saw: the storefronts widened, the signs didn't have so many cracks in them. Fewer chemical spills running along beside my feet. Even in the collapse, the mechs hadn't devastated this part as bad as the others. I would've found it charming except for what it said about human, and mech society.

No matter the situation, your status meant everything.

The Fabrication Lines came up faster than I expected, well before I'd settled on what to do when I found them. Like the University, the Lines spanned the Conduit. Narrow bands bridging the big gap rested on this level, with half of the eight overlaid with tracks designed to carry magnetized carts. Those tracks rose from the mist. At the sight I slowed, shifted right to hug the Conduit wall.

Mechs were everywhere moving scrap, carts, and each other from point to point. Trash mechs rode lifts up and down, disgorging materials into carts and trundling away again. Unlike Alpha's army, these were still more or less as their maker's intended: populated with tools and directives bent towards building, not destruction. Even so, couriers and their lasers drifted among the collective.

"Why?" Kaydee asked as I counted the couriers. "It's not like the mechs are gonna rebel against him."

"Don't think it's the mechs he's worried about."

"Oh, right. Us."

Too much of a wish that Alpha would leave the Lines undefended. The couriers weren't everywhere though: their jets were precise, but I noticed the little buggers stayed in the Conduit. Sure, they followed carts and mechs around, but as their charges vanished inside the many doors, the couriers remained hovering outside. When someone new exited nearby, the courier would drift along with them.

A programmed pattern. Easy enough to exploit.

Kaydee must've sensed my comfort. She bobbed into the Conduit's middle, blowing up her size to be a towering giant. She pointed at the various circular doors lining the Conduit, some of which I couldn't see from my skulking side spot. As Kaydee pointed, labels appeared over each one, showcasing their purpose.

Design, Recycling, Wiring, and others that I wrote off as I saw them. This wasn't a tour, but a mission, and a mission with a quickly ticking clock. I needed the headquarters, the control room, the terminal that ran this party.

Kaydee pointed that one out, on my side but far back. I'd have to pass by four other openings and hope I didn't get caught. Yuck.

"But it's possible," Kaydee said, this time highlighting the moving carts and their courier followers. "Time it right and there might only be one over here. You can get inside, sneak through the lines, and bam! Pop out the back where nobody's going to notice."

"You make it sound so simple."

"C'mon, Gamma. Compared to what we've been through already? Sneaking around a few mechs isn't going to be that bad." Kaydee shrank down, warped to my side in a snap. "Look, I know you've had a security blanket with Delta and Beta for a long time. I get it."

Until she said it, I hadn't realized the underlying nerves. At least, that's what humans called it. More, my programming doing risk analysis and realizing I was in real danger, danger that would've been reduced with Delta and her blade factored in. The initial rush from the Garden, smashing the couriers in the restaurant, that was rapid reaction, a struggle to survive.

As I caught my breath, my systems caught up to me. I'd crouched further against the wall than I'd noticed, pressing my back into a supporting struck sticking out, a tiny corner hidden away from the light. Every centimeter I compressed into that corner reduced the risk I'd be discovered by a percentage point, maybe two.

"The last time we were this alone," I said, "I hadn't even met Delta yet."

"You were innocent then too. Didn't know how crazy this place was."

"For being my mind, you didn't prepare me very well."

"Sink or swim, Gamma. You had to figure it out for yourself."

Sure did. Kaydee had it right. Starship right now wasn't a place for the indecisive, the cowards, or the mourning. People depended on me. Delta and Beta included.

"Okay," I said. "I'm ready."

"Go get'em, tiger." Kaydee laughed as she said it. "Got that from a flick."

I looked past her, watched the mechs, timed my first move. I already knew my last: after this, I'd be going back to the Garden, Alpha's army be damned. I'd find Delta and Beta and bring them back.

Piece by piece if I had to.

FORTY

SNEAK

Earlier, on our trip up to the wealthy bubble—boy, did that feel long ago—we'd stopped ever so briefly at the Fabrication Lines' back end. There, raw materials would get loaded onto the carts. The cart contents would get inspected, routed to whichever section made sense for the quality, and off it'd go. An efficient setup with warning signs, lights, and not much else.

Without the Cesspool working, though, Alpha's supply lines must've found a different scrap source: those trash mechs, Alpha's army mainstays, came trundling in off lifts from above and below. They came up to the carts on the Conduit, elevated and dumped their contents inside, the bigger mechs pushing the carts into the Lines themselves. Less efficient, maybe, than the Cesspool had been, but viable without human care to escort a part from garbage to greatness.

Poor Alpha, having to make do.

Explained his hacked together army, though.

When the cart, its guiding mech, and guarding courier left the door alone for me to slip through, the Lines kept up their convoluted dance. Tracks embedded in the floors intersected in knot-like tangles, precise programming causing switches in the routes every few seconds. More carts whizzed by, going into tunnels expanding in every direction. Apparently the rolling buckets didn't need mechs inside the tunnels, just when crossing the Conduit, because the things sped along on their own.

A screen marked each cart's side, reading off the destination in glowing blue-green. The screens flashed as carts when by, little color splashes in what was otherwise a yellow and orange feel. Nested diodes did their thing in the Swiss cheese ceiling, brighter than the apartments, restaurants, and other spaces I'd seen on Starship.

"If you're creating machines, you wanna be able to see'em," Kaydee said.

"At least nobody's seen me yet."

I'd hugged the right-side wall up along the Conduit, then swung myself around through the door upon reaching the lines, slipping in as the cart rolled past. The tunnels presented options, but I took the most straightforward one: left.

When the way seemed cart free, I slipped across the eight meter-wide tunnel and into the new passage. Alcoves lines this one, similar to the Cesspool down below: carve-outs with workstations, long-expired refreshments for workers, and supplies. Despite Alpha's army-making pace, I didn't see a single mech in here with me, though carts shot along the tunnel's center and criss-crossed it at regular intervals.

"Where is everybody?" I asked.

"You drew them out, remember?" Kaydee replied.

"Sure, but shouldn't there be more? Isn't Alpha always making more?"

"Maybe? Who knows what that guy's thinking?"

Kaydee had that right, at least. Once you got away from Alpha's headlining goal—takeover Starship, guide it to some ultimate destiny —the vessel didn't exactly make much sense. Like a nerve, Alpha tended to twitch in unpredictable directions.

Not that I minded overmuch. The empty hallway let me make

good progress, slowed only at intersections where I waited for any courier-mech combos to clear carts and give me room. I made a few cursory checks on the workstations too, hoping I'd get lucky and one might give me the access I was looking for, but they were all dumb terminals. No network access, only strict controls for the Lines.

I could've fiddled with them, rerouted the carts and gummed up the works, but that seemed like a stupid way to reveal myself.

The first clue my little shortcut wouldn't have a perfect ending came as we passed the last cross-Conduit connection. All along the way, the Fabrication Lines sang manufacturing's song, the gnashing grind of metal and wheels. Ozone lingered in the air, along with other sharp scents slashing by in one breath and gone the next.

"If you were a human, I'd say get a respirator," Kaydee said, noting the mask racks hanging on the walls. "But you, Gamma, get to inhale all the toxic crap you want."

"Hurrah for me?"

"Hurrah for you. Definitely."

"Seems like humans have a lot of weaknesses." I mused, slipping behind a cart into the hallway's final section.

"It's only fair, otherwise we'd be too awesome."

"Uh huh."

The cart tracks vanished in this last leg, replaced by scuffed, dirty tile. The alcoves increased, instead becoming a full fledged lab with workbenches on either side loaded with components. It'd seemed like the carts going out of this side were loaded with raw scrap, ready to get turned into a bunch of cookie-cutter mechs. The gritty workbenches here, though, looked stocked with bespoke parts meant to be fashioned into unique creations.

Confirming my suspicions, several long metal tubes lay to my right. The same color and width as the Chancellor's arms, they explained where that monster had come from.

"But who would be making these?" Kaydee asked as I stared at the arms for a too long second. "Alpha's not down here, is he?"

"He wouldn't have to be," I replied, stepping over to the nearest workbench and taking a closer look at the tools on hand. "Send some personalized instructions to the mechs and he could have his custom-made monsters."

"Don't know if you've noticed those mechs hauling these around, Gamma, but they're not exactly built for fine finger work."

Point. The clunky machines pulling the carts wouldn't be able to screw two bolts together, much less assemble something like the Chancellor. Maybe Volt could've done something like that. Leo, certainly, but I had a hard time believing the half-mech, half-man would be up here helping Alpha after our encounter. Those flexi-mechs we'd fought would have the dexterity, but I didn't see any lurking around here.

A mystery, but not one I had time for now. I left the workbenches behind, went to the hallway's end. To the right, the path curled back the way I'd come, towards the elevator where the raw parts would've been coming up. To the left, the Conduit and my destination.

The blue hadn't changed much during my slinking. Trash mechs still dumped scrap, bigger mechs still moved it. Couriers flitted about. No pounding from an approaching mech army. I didn't want to think about what that meant for Val and the others, but one problem at a time.

"Go!" Kaydee whispered.

I flipped around the side, hugged the right wall. Not all that far ahead the walkway dead ended into the last lifts. Starship's wealthi-est, cleanest end. No surprise that they held the mech creation mech-anisms all to themselves. Before all that, though, sat the room I was looking for.

At first, the Lines seemed like an apartment, albeit one over-flowing with screens. Many flared red warnings, saying the freight elevator wasn't working, saying carts weren't being moved efficiently. I saw these from the wide open spiral door. No security necessary when you ran everything.

Where kitchen cabinets and couches had been in the other apart-ments, workstations dominated. Terminals that looked decidedly not-dumb, with login screens similar to ones like Val's. Ones with network access, and, maybe, a chance at adjusting the Fabrication Lines. Beyond those, a small table sat close to an old, boxy fridge and two empty glass pots on hot plates.

"Coffee, tea, snacks," Kaydee said as I crept in, spying nothing. "Looks like a classic hangout for the working stiff."

"Let's hope there's none of those around."

"You don't even know what those are."

"Mechs of some kind?" I deemed the main space clear. The 'living room' off-shoot looked much the same, also empty. "Were they stuck here forever?"

"You could say that."

Kaydee didn't elaborate, and I didn't bother following up. There were terminals aplenty, but which would have access to the Lines themselves? Any? Could I waste time checking each one?

"Here's a tip," Kaydee said, popping in and pointing deeper into the apartment. "We tend to put most of the good stuff in back."

Kaydee's intuition proved promising. Towards the kitchen's rear, where the bedrooms were in other apartments, more spiral doors waited. These were closed, with red gems glowing on each. Locked. I glanced back towards the open door leading out to the Conduit. Any second a mech could come walking through there, could ask what the hell I was doing in here.

"Let's try one of the others first," I said. "If that doesn't work, then we'll get to breaking locks."

"As good an idea as any."

I went back to the living room, just out of sight from the apartment doorway. Just out of sight from the entry. Not much defense, but I'd take what I could get. I pressed my fingers together, the skin peeling back to form the plug-in. The terminal sat ready, the port available.

"Gonna say, Gamma, it's been a while since you've hacked into something," Kaydee said, crouching down next to me. "I'm bored."

"Hopefully this won't be all that exciting."

I moved the port towards the terminal, had it about ready to plug in, when the telltale clonks of an approaching mech made me stop. I pulled back, hid in close to the terminal, and watched as a strange machine walked into the command center. Two arms, three legs, all thin and wiry. The arms ended, like those flexi-mechs from before, in ten fingered hands. Ones more than capable of handling little tools. Rebuilding something like the Chancellor.

It went straight by, ignoring me, heading for those back, locked doors.

"Kaydee, I think I have an idea."

"For once, Gamma, I think we're thinking the same thing."

FORTY-ONE

ARENA

Our target had its back to the door, bent over a double-screened terminal. The spiral gate blocking off the office stayed open, convenient for us sneaking in behind. Beyond the terminal, the office held a strange vibe: pictures adorned the walls, including several framed degrees from Starship's University and family photos with smiling children and what must've been faked backgrounds from Earth.

A plant, long dead and withered to black stalks, sat in a pot.

"Yep, looks like a human once worked here," Kaydee said. "I remember the place doing those photos. Always the corniest thing, wanting to get yourselves in front of a planet you'd never see."

Agreed. Humans didn't make much logical sense sometimes.

"We just liked to pretend, you know?" Kaydee continued while I crept up behind the mech, my fingers together, forming that port. "Like we thought to ourselves that if this picture works out, maybe someday we'll get to be there in real life, you know? A dream."

Dreams. A strange concept for me. I knew about the human phenomenon, of course, but without sleep, I—

The mech whirled, hands raising up, reaching towards my face. To twist my neck, poke out my eyes, who knew, who cared. I spotted the port, right there in the mech's chest. Stabbed forward with my pinched fingers. Felt it lock as the mech's hands tightened on my cheeks, my temple.

Going to the digital world was something like a dream, wasn't it?

We stood in a dusty ring. Adobe blocks, bleached white by a brilliant sun, formed the walls, rising meters into the air before sloping back to reveal stands crowded with fluctuating forms. Colorful, twisting, the shapes in the stands resolved if I looked at them into coded strands, pieces of the mech cheering on its central function.

That function stood across from me in the ring, standing tall against the light. Two hands, three legs, and quite a bit larger than reality, the mech glared at me with hot pink eyes. It had no weapons and, as I clenched my hands, neither did I.

"Some real caveman crap," Kaydee said, stretching out beside me. She wore shorts, a yellow t-shirt. No weapons. "Here we are on a screaming spaceship and we get to knuckle-brawl it out in the dirt?"

"Not our choice." I flexed the old digital mind, tried to see what I could alter here. The answer? Nothing. "This one's well designed. I'm not finding loopholes."

"Cool, cool."

The programs cheered, a jagged artificial thing more like a broken signal than a real call to arms. Not that it mattered: our enemy took the sound as reason to charge, and charge it did. The mech, its two legs pounding it forward in slanting lopes while the third in the center kept balance, moved quick towards Kaydee and I.

"Split?" Kaydee said.

"Split."

She went left, I went right. The mech, dust swirling up behind it, swerved my way. Followed me as I broke all the way to the wall. I spun, put my back flat against those hot stones and watched the mech close, watched it bring its right fist up for a hammering blow.

Delta and Beta were killers in a fight. They could slice and dice with the best of 'em.

But me?

I could dodge, baby.

The mech went in as if I had the speed of a sloth, a big blow aiming for my chin. I waited, then flinched aside. The swing moved air past my cheek, a hot metal wind exploded forward when the big robot struck the wall behind me. Those yellow-white bricks blew out under the sun, striking my back and scattering rubble into the arena.

I rolled aside, glancing up at the mech to see if it'd mangled its hand in the attack. Unfortunately, the thing's skeleton had enough strength to take a punch like that without a flinch. Even as I turned, it raised both hands together in a fist over its head and threw them towards me.

Another roll further away and the fists crunched into the dirt, sending up a sandy plume. Shadowed by the sand, those arms raised up again, ready for another strike. It came, I rolled, another miss.

A human could adjust, could figure out my rolls. This mech was an engineer, working hard to build mechs. How good would its combat programming be? Could I just keep rolling a meter at a time?

The mech swung again. I rolled again. Repeated the sequence two more times, leaving a pocked trail in the dirt as we traced the arena's outer wall. Okay, hypothesis confirmed. The mech would keep on swinging until it connected.

Next time, as it swung, I rolled *towards* the mech instead of away. The swing came at the same angle, the same spacing, the same missing. At the mech's ankles, I kicked hard at its right foot. My kick bounced, making a dull clank and glancing off. Not a dent, not a shift. Whatever my strength outside, I had no say here.

The mech stepped back, swung again.

I curled up, rolling over to dodge the swing in a somersault that put me back on my feet. The mech followed me, changing up the attack now that I stood. The haymaker again, gunning right for my chin. I sidestepped to the right, watched the punch go by me. A left swing followed, one I ducked by dropping to my knees. A little taller and the mech would've had my head.

"Gamma!" Kaydee called my name as she ran up behind the

mech. In each hand she held a rock, a chunk broken off the wall from the mech's first punch. "Catch!"

The toss came in underhanded, arriving in my arms right as the mech made another punch, apparently unfazed by Kaydee's approach.

I made the wrong choice: I tried to catch the dumb rock.

My feet didn't bring me far enough to the side, my hands outstretched to snag Kaydee's missile, and the mech clipped my shoulder. It should've been a glancing blow, should've been a bruise at best.

Instead I flew, spinning, through the air. The mech struck with so much force I left the ground behind and rocketed across the arena to crash into the far side. The wall splintered around me, and I felt, *felt* my limbs snap. Here in the virtual world, I didn't have sensors, didn't have the alerts that would tell me how doomed I was, so no warnings flickered across my eyes, no function screamed my imminent end.

Not that I needed them. I could see my body around me. My left arm was gone, just blown away by the strike. Part of my chest went with it. The slam into the wall crumpled my legs, and I couldn't feel my right arm, though it seemed to move when I wiggled my fingers.

Of course the mech wouldn't be fighting fair. We were on its home turf.

Across the arena, the mech sprinted my way, Kaydee following. Apparently her back attack on the machine failed, and her yelling didn't get the mech's attention. Instead, the machine kept its focus on me, careening my way and kicking up sand with every step. Its shoulder rolled back, getting its fist into demolition mode.

I couldn't move, couldn't dodge. Predictable, yes, but too powerful to beat.

If I didn't want to wind up scrambled, deleted, I'd have to run.

"Hold it!" Kaydee's voice came across the clear air, as if she knew what I was thinking. "I've almost got it!"

Got what? The mech slowed as it came near, getting its killer punch in line. My legs didn't move, but I managed to get my right arm up, my fingers in a gesture Kaydee would've appreciated.

The slowing gave Kaydee her chance. The sprinting woman jumped, rock in one hand, onto the mech's back. The machine jerked at the contact, but didn't veer away from me. Those hot pink angry eyes glared fire at my face. Another stomp forward as Kaydee clambered up to the mech's narrow metal spine.

I caught Kaydee's look as they cleared the mech's shoulder, caught no fear in her set jaw, her strong grip as she raised the rock. The mech leveled its right fist, started the swing.

"Out of time," I said, my voice a tinny whisper.

"Stay!" Kaydee yelled again, her first strike chipping the plating away from the mech's neck.

The fist came in hard, fast.

I made my choice.

FORTY-TWO

SABOTAGE

I bounced out. A jarring shift from the bright sand arena to the dim room. The sole terminal cast its blue light across the dark, leaving shadows everywhere. My butt was on the floor. My systems weren't ready for me to come back, resume control, so I sank down and looked up at the machine holding the most important person in my existence.

I'd left her there. Disconnected without taking Kaydee back with me.

Letting the mech's punch fall might've destroyed some part of myself that I couldn't afford to lose. I might've come back to my body as a damaged program, might've been kicked off down the path Alpha had taken. Or I might've been deleted without a single negative effect, like Delta had been before.

The mission said I couldn't take that risk. The mission said the humans would die if I failed, that Beta and Delta would've died for nothing.

I repeated the claim to myself as I stood, hands ready to go for the mech's neck and attempt to tear it apart. Brutal, perhaps, but without real weapons I didn't have many other options. Either the mech would win out, or Kaydee . . .

She said stay. She kept saying stay, which meant she saw something. A vulnerability, a way. For now, the mech seemed dead, its eyes dark and parts unmoving. I could either wait and see if it came back to life or take a chance, take my concentration away from the mech and do what I came here to do.

I missed Kaydee's quips already.

With silence answering my thoughts, I moved around the mech, settled in at the terminal. The machine had already logged in, solving the first security issue. With any luck, the Fabrication Lines wouldn't have password layers, wouldn't require me to try hacking my way through.

After what'd just happened, going back into the digital ether alone seemed scary, sad, I wasn't sure. Emotions played out rough through my circuits, Kaydee's influence making itself felt in how my usually pragmatic functions steered me away from doing the same thing that'd led to her loss.

Was this what it felt like to mourn?

My fingers typed and tapped as I tried to make sense of my feelings. The terminal's clear layout led me to the right place quick, a few taps on the touchscreen and I had the Fabrication Lines displayed before me. A blinking box popped up when I first opened the program, declaring efficiency way down from optimal. That'll happen when your main part supply is cut off and you're relying on haphazard trash mechs to deliver the goods.

The screen showed every line in columns with data splayed out in icons and numbers. Using a handy legend, I parsed the picture and wound up finding Alpha had turned to cannibalism. Those trash mechs weren't journeying to the Conduit's lowest levels for scrap, they were taking other mech bodies and parts, carrying them back to the Lines so they could be stapled together anew.

And differently.

Alpha's mech game appeared improved. No longer content to

jam garbage knives onto teetering utility robots, Alpha's newer designs included those multi-digit flexible things we'd fought outside the Garden. More dogs, like Alvie but longer, meaner, faster—not hard to see where Alpha came up with that idea. And a third category denoted as specialists, taking up only one of the six lines.

Must've been where the updated Chancellor had come from.

Most important was the button in the lower right offering a total shutdown. I stared at it, then glanced at the still-dark mech behind me. Hitting that would halt Alpha's army-building, at least for a time. It would also bring whatever hells Alpha had here swarming me. I'd need to run, to leave Kaydee behind.

No. I wouldn't do that. Couldn't do that. At least not without trying to get her back.

I pinched my fingers again, formed the jack. Getting kicked out didn't mean I couldn't barge back in. Usually, evicting a hacker gave you a chance to get away or get even, but this mech hadn't taken advantage. Swallowing my concerns about diving in to get punched again, I plugged into the mech's side, waited to get sucked into that awful arena.

Nothing changed.

The port didn't work. Dead, or maybe the mech was. I tried again, then a third time. The click sounded the same, the satisfying lock as the latch slipped into place. But no data, no connection.

Either Kaydee had killed the mech, or the machine had been so thoroughly depleted by the effort that it'd shut itself down.

"Kaydee," I said to the mech. "Don't leave me."

She couldn't hear that. No way. Assuming her digital self even existed anymore, she'd be stuck in that same sandy arena throwing down with the machine. Not a fight that gave her good odds.

A flicker from behind pulled my attention back to the terminal. A line needed help. Some part or another had become stuck. The program suggested I flag a repair crew to go check it out. Instead, my finger drifted to the shut down button. As I hovered over it, a different idea rose, a product of chance, location, and maybe Kaydee's recklessness.

We weren't far below the Bridge, the spot Alpha held. Rather than stumble back to a struggle with the mech army, a battle I'd be worthless in, I could go for what really mattered. I'd snuck in here, who's to say I couldn't get all the way to Alpha himself? Wring the vessel's neck, end this whole show right now.

That's what Kaydee would do. She'd risk everything to save everyone.

Didn't I owe her that?

I tapped the button. All the columns blinked from green to red, shutting down. I nodded at the colors, then made a fist and drove it through the terminal. Not once, not twice, but enough times until the thing had been scrapped. With one last look at the dead mech, I left the room and went around the apartment, obliterating every terminal I found.

All the while, a clock ticked in my mind, warning me Alpha would be gunning for my guts.

When my smash fest ended, there remained only the other locked room. I didn't have time to hack through it, but I could tweak it fast. Much like with Sybil's door, I formed the port, jacked in, and layered another program on top of the locking mechanism. Before the gem would cool, before any swiped identity could be verified, the user would have to port in and enter a passcode.

Sure, Alpha might be able to brute force it. Could probably bring a big angry mech here and smash down the door. If a terminal sat on the other side, he might get the Lines up and running again in an hour.

I didn't have other options, and familiar noises were starting to filter my way. Those heavy metal footfalls. The sparks and puffs as jets turned on and off. Couriers and the bigger mechs they minded coming to get me.

Wheeling around, I broke for the apartment's entrance. Only one way in and out, I couldn't let it—

Crap.

A big mech, a cart pusher stomped in front of the door. I shrank back, near the office with the dead mech, hoping the shadows might buy me a minute. The big guy didn't play dumb, though. It stood in place, waiting, until I saw brighter lights behind it. Couriers, ready to go. Only then did the monster move in, laser flies humming after it.

Whatever time I had, it was up. At least, for however long, we'd accomplished the mission. I flexed my fingers, figured I could maybe take one or two of the things out with me.

For Kaydee.

FORTY-THREE

TRICKS

Okay, time to play superhero. I spied a side table I could grab and throw, follow that up by chucking one of the moldering coffee machines at a courier. I might be trapped in a mundane office, but that didn't mean I couldn't do some damage before they stomped me to scrap.

One big mech in the entry, two couriers flanking it. Doubtless more in the Conduit beyond. Still, immediate threats first.

Kaydee, look at me. Going into a fight on my own.

She'd have been impressed. Or called me a moron. Or both.

I started forward, right leg pushing off only to snap back, pulled down onto the room's floor. The mech we'd just fought loomed over me, a halting move made more eerie by those pink-glowing eyes. I shook off the thing's hand, pushed it back. It faltered, fell over, its butt making a loud clank.

Not exactly a strong start, either for my death-dealing end or the mech's ambush. I didn't think the robot was that uncoordinated, but hey, I'd take it. The office had a chair off to the side and I grabbed it, hefting it high to smash the mech into dust.

"Don't," the mech said, tinny voice rattling as it stuck its arms out towards me.

A plea from a mech? How weird was that?

"Drop the chair, Gamma," the mech continued. "They're coming."

There are difficult riddles, and there are obvious ones. Leo had given me some solid smarts, so I tracked the oddity that was the mech saying my name to its likely source.

"Kaydee?" I asked.

"In the metal," Kaydee replied, standing, with jerky motions. "It took me a while to figure out how this body worked." Her pink-glowing eyes looked over towards the terminal. "Watched you break that into pieces. Were you angry about me?"

"I couldn't kill the Lines, so it seemed like the best way to slow Alpha down." I frowned. To the right, sounds came as couriers and the big mech marched towards us. "While you were figuring out the mech, did you come up with a plan to get us out?"

"Yes," Kaydee said. "Die."

"What?"

"Play dead, you idiot," Kaydee whispered, the mech's voice sounding nothing like her own, but still carrying her signature bite. "Now."

The Librarian's stories contained plenty of joking references to playing dead, so I followed their instructions. Fell forward, curled up slightly, and lay on the floor. I shut my eyes, spun up my other senses to keep me from being blind. I felt, heard the big mech come into the doorway. Little heat bursts washed over me as the couriers followed.

"I defeated him," Kaydee said, a little too triumphant for a mech.

"Scrap," came the big mech's one word reply.

"No," Kaydee countered. "Alpha wants this one."

The big mech beeped a question. The two couriers stayed silent, but I felt them coming closer, buzzing in near my face. For a human, staying still might be difficult. I just turned off my extremities, a switch flipped to make me limp. Made to preserve power in difficult situations, the feature worked real well: I felt nothing save the senses coming from my head. Ears, those closed eyes, the vibrations traveling through my scalp as the big mech backed away.

"I will take him," Kaydee continued. "Fix the Lines."

Simple, direct. She learned fast.

I heard Kaydee's metal feet land, felt her arms slip, with halting motion, beneath me. Kaydee had spent a lifetime as a human, and many more as a program. Learning how to run a robot's body would be totally new.

Then again, if anybody could figure it out, Kaydee would be the one.

"Damaged?" the big mech asked as Kaydee lifted me up. "Slow."

"Minor," Kaydee replied. "Go."

The big mech followed instructions, leading Kaydee from the apartment. I kept my eyes shut the entire way. The Conduit's mist kissed my cheeks. Less pleasant noises hit my ears, questions, rattles, hums and clanks from what must've been a dozen mechs or more on all sides. The trio that'd gone into the apartment had been the advance guard.

My last fight would've ended quick.

"To Alpha," Kaydee said as we lurched onto the walkway. "Which way?"

Instead of an answer, heat washed my face. Courier jets, closer than before. So close.

"Stay away," Kaydee said, and she moved me to the left, but the jets followed. "What are you doing?"

"Not dead," a courier declared. A familiar whine joined their popping jets, electricity flowing to their weapons. "Dangerous."

The trick was up.

I snapped open my eyes, keyed in on all the mechs around me. The scene held a certain deja vu. The last time we'd been trapped on the Conduit, I'd pushed Delta and I over the edge. This time?

"Run!" I said, rolling off Kaydee's arms as she tried to argue with those buzzing bees.

As my feet hit the floor, I kicked towards the walkway's railing and flung myself into space. The Fabrication Lines weren't that far up from Starship's bottom, so the fall ended fast, another bouncing, breaking slide across old scrap and torn up cloth. Screws, springs, paper, and furniture groaned, snapped, and shook as I descended.

I didn't hear another body, another impact. As soon as I caught myself, I looked up, tried to find Kaydee's falling form. Saw nothing save the Conduit's blue and a descending orange cloud: couriers coming to collect.

Kaydee hadn't made it.

Of course. She'd barely been able to pick me up. Jolting into a rapid run-and-jump might've been beyond her. Any of those other mechs might've grabbed her, shot her before she made it.

I'd lost Kaydee, got her back, and lost her again within minutes. No, not lost her again. She might still be up there, struggling, waiting for help.

I knew where I could find it.

The couriers zipped down at me as I struggled off the trash mound. As they came closer, I threw what I could their way, denting the first and sending a second, clipped with a sturdy old chair, spinning into the Conduit's side. A satisfying, fiery end.

Five more followed, blitzing me from range as I slipped, jumped, veered through the junk. Couriers weren't natural marksman. These weren't war machines but transporters, and their ability to hit a moving target proved lacking. Instead, old sofas, sinks, and long-dead mechs melted around me as missed blasts immolated them.

If nothing else, my inefficient, random movement through the unstable piles made it hard to draw a good bead.

My goal wasn't far ahead on the left, a familiar opening I hadn't expected to see again so soon. The Cesspool offered shelter, and after taking a grazing hit to the side, I dove through the entry and rolled, putting out my burning clothes.

The Cesspool's fluorescent pools and yellow light once again made for pretty scenery, although they provided little cover with my pursuit so near at hand.

"Leo!" I called, running past those pools.

Behind me, the couriers whirred, puffed their jets.

"Leo! Help!" I shouted again, breaking left and slipping into a tunnel as lasers cascaded around me. "Kaydee needs our help!"

Emotionally manipulative? Maybe. Necessary? Absolutely.

The curved walls scrawled with old slogans, sayings, swears sped by as I ran. Intersections prompted random choices, the Cesspool's labyrinth buying time. I kept calling Leo's name every few steps, waiting and not getting a reply.

Around another corner I ran right into a courier, this one alone. The damn bugs must've split up, not a bad call against an unarmed vessel. The little mech's laser glowed orange, its jet puffed its aim square on me.

I punched faster than it shot, a slamming down fist that sent the courier spiraling into the floor. The thing's jet broke, but before I could feel any sort of triumph, the thing's laser fired. My poor right foot, the one that'd been greased earlier by mechs in these same tunnels, went molten. I fell next to the courier with a hard thud.

"Why?" I asked the bug as it jerked, trying to find a way to shoot me. With a single smash, I put the mech out of its misery. "Why did you have to do that?"

"I could ask the same of you?" the voice I'd been waiting for, the man coming out from a hidden panel behind me. Leo, armed and dangerous. "You weren't supposed to come back."

"This is going to blow your mind," I said as Leo helped me up, "but I wasn't planning to."

The man walked me back to the Forger's hideout, where the half-machine, half-humans watched with wary eyes. A few others trickled in behind, similarly armed to Leo, with janky lasers, swords, and staffs. As Leo settled me down in a chair, he turned to the other arrivals.

"How'd we do?"

"How'd we do?" asked Clara, the fiery woman Delta had taken hostage the first time we'd wound up down here. "Not good enough. Several escaped."

"Then he knows," Leo sighed.

"Alpha already knew," Clara shot back. "He just didn't care about us." She pointed at me. "But now he's here."

I gave her a sad smile, "Sorry, no more hiding. The fight is coming, whether you want it or not."

FORTY-FOUR

FIGHT AND FLIGHT

My ominous one liner didn't get the Forgers jumping up in arms. Instead they looked to Leo, my ask hanging on him. The man scratched at his thin hair, took a long look around the cluttered nest the Forgers had carved in Starship's molten basement.

"When things were falling apart, we ran," Leo said, seeming to find the words as he spoke them. "We agreed Starship's core had rotted and rather than fix it, we left and came down here, determined to see a mission to the end. We gave up."

Some shifted then, a few eyes finding the ground or a corner to lock onto.

"It made sense then, right? We didn't want to get mixed up in a fight between classes. Everyone seemed less interested in keeping Starship solvent than in working out their problems with a gun or a fist. We wanted more. We wanted to see what all this had been for."

"Some of us still do," Clara said, arms folded, icy stare continuing its work. A couple others joined her, offering up muted agreement.

"You still can," Leo said, "but not by staying here. Gamma's right. Once Alpha's finished up with the humans in the back, once he's taken every mech opposing him and turned them into his agents, then he'll come for us."

"Not if we gave him this thing." Clara pointed at me. "Gamma's what he wants. Let's use him. Make a deal with the vessel. That'd work, right? You programmed the things, so you should know."

I lurched up from my seat, wobbled on my busted foot, and had to steady myself on Leo's shoulder.

"You would be negotiating with madness," I said. "Faulty, broken logic. A virus with nothing more than destruction as its end. At best he would give you a breath, before taking my mind and setting me against you."

I thought I worked a good blend into that warning, pulled from books and movies coming together to demonstrate the futility of working with Alpha. Clara shook her head, looked around to the other Forgers, raised her arms in a wide shrug.

"Who wants to see and feel real land?" Clara asked the group, receiving nods, raised hands in return. "Alpha's going to bring us what we want fast. Then we can die happy, rather at the end of a mech's laser for nothing."

"Why die when we could live?" Leo countered, setting me back in my seat so he could stand next to Clara, the picture of a power struggle. "All this time we hoped to survive long enough to see land, but what about going beyond? Gamma tells us there are humans, humans who've grown up without Starship's fractures breaking their spirits. They'll need help, they'll need knowledge. We can give them that, guide them into our new world."

"Right, Leo," Clara said. "That's what they'll want when they've survived a mech army: our metal asses trying to tell them what to do."

Leo grinned, "They won't, but they might listen if we help them." Leo reached back towards me, picked up his small weapon off the workbench. "I'm not a dictator. I can't, and won't force you to follow me, but Gamma and I are going back. I didn't live this long to die a coward."

Clara drew in a breath, ready to draw up a counter, when Leo whispered something in her ear. The woman pressed her lips together, shook her head, then cast a long stare up towards the room's top, the golden lights strung together between stacked bunks carved into alcoves. Home for who knew how many years, but no longer, and she knew it.

EVERY FORGER, even Clara, joined Leo and I when we left. They fit me with a stiff boot and brace, letting me walk with a limp and a clank. What belongings the Forgers couldn't bear to leave behind were stuffed in hard packs slipped on steel shoulders. Hands found weapons to hold, heads claimed helmets with lights fastened on the front. Most no longer had enough clothes to cover, so Leo's ramshackle crew rolled in scraps, enhancements catching glows as we made our way from the Cesspool back to the Conduit.

"What did you tell her?" I asked Leo, the two of us near the column's front.

"I asked if she was willing to kill me to stay," Leo replied, his voice heavy. He hadn't spoken aside from commands since the determining dance had ended. "She wasn't."

I could work out the rest for myself: if Leo left with me, Clara and any staying with her wouldn't have any leverage when Alpha came calling, armed and angry. The Forgers may not have been all human, but they weren't stupid.

We stood in the blue mist, scrap mounds spreading out before us. The obvious direction seemed straight aft, climbing as we went so we could pass through the Garden without a problem. Up above, like fires on an ocean's surface, glittered courier mechs making their way towards us. Alpha's initial salvo, but moving slow, waiting for their trudging mechs to keep pace.

"Kaydee's up there," I said, pointing straight above. "At the Fabrication Lines."

If she hadn't been torn apart, blasted, or corrupted by Alpha yet.

Leo shook his head, "I asked my friends to help rescue other humans. I can't ask their lives for a program."

"She's not just a program," I shot back. "She's as real as any of you."

Leo again patted my shoulder, a sign I was coming to realize meant I would not be getting what I wanted.

"If she's like the Kaydee I knew, then I have no doubt she is," Leo replied. "If we succeed, then I hope we'll find her well. The living, though, must take precedence."

With that, Leo delivered the marching orders, and the twenty half-machine, half-human scientists, engineers, and metal workers began their walk. I tried to push back, tried to protest, but at Leo's look, two following Forgers picked me up and moved me until embarrassment, frustration, and futility compelled me to move my own feet.

Alpha's forces caught up with us an hour later, as we neared the University. We'd migrated up several levels through lifts hidden in Starship's back-ends, more freight platforms moved with manual keys. Alpha's disabling commands held no power over these rudimentary overrides, put in place to keep Starship moving in case of computer error.

"Or computer crimes," Clara said as she punched my ticket up.

She'd suppressed whatever bitterness left over from Leo's decision and turned it into determination. When I asked why, she replied simply that she planned to see another world before she died, and now that meant winning the damn war, so that's what she'd do.

Simple, effective.

The elevator spat us into a wide storefront, one that, going by shriveled signs and faded slogans, had been used for assembling and sending various appliances around Starship. Kitchen tools mingled with vacuums and lamps across a crowded show floor, one now crawling with Forgers as we crept out to the Conduit.

Leo held the lead with several others, and the foursome called out an alarm from the walkway. Clara and I were halfway through the mess, my new boot serving well to crunch old glass beneath its heel.

Courier lights flooded the space as they floated near the walkway from above and below. At the same time, the ceiling shook and shattered, thin panels breaking, as stomping mechs broke through and landed around us.

If Alpha had sent his grunt troops to hunt the humans, to surround us at the Garden, the remainder here to hunt the Forgers had to be his new guard. Those flexi-mechs, now armed with shining swords, with courier-like laser rifles fitting their sculpted ten-digit hands, surrounded us.

Worse yet, sweeping the room, I found all those pink-glowing mech eyes had only one target: me.

FORTY-FIVE

BLOODY HISTORY

In the Librarian's archives, human media made fights feel like an epic event. Time slowed, the combatants stared across fields, tables, or whole worlds at one another before a flash, a gunshot, a shout kicked off the grand melees. In reality, from what I'd seen, fights needed no such grandeur.

They needed nothing more than a thrown punch.

I swung at the mech before me, the slender machine raising its weapon to draw an orange bead on my head. While my foot had been blown off, my hands could move damn fast when I wanted them to. My swing took the mech's weapon and sent it flying right into the mech's own face. The gun glanced off, bouncing away into the dark. The mech reeled back and I followed, limping at my target and tuning out the chaos.

This mech wasn't the one that'd taken Kaydee from me. It wasn't the one that'd stabbed Beta or dragged Delta down. Didn't matter. It could pay back, in some small way, for those crimes.

But it wouldn't do so lying down. The mech snaked its arms away and back, ripping up an old recliner and hoisting its forest-green padded sides like clubs. Didn't matter. I came on anyway, bringing up my mitts boxer style.

Though the store had been dark, it lit up now in multicolored flashes as Forgers and mechs blasted each other. Orange and white bursts crackled by, missed shots striking furniture and lighting it ablaze, the chemicals in the pieces going up in blues, purples, whites and yellows. Shouted orders mingled with engine whines and jet puffs, the floor shook as more mechs clomped, a rattle sounded as the freight lift brought up more Forgers.

I caught the first swing with both hands and pulled, yanking the mech's arm down and to my left. The dumb machine stuck its feet into the ground, thinking it could keep me from dragging it to the floor. Instead, with the recliner's pad between us, I pushed. The mech tried swinging with its other arm, bringing the second pad in low.

I took it on my knee as I shoved forward, bending the mech backward as I toppled over. With its foot biting hard into the floor, the mech made no allowance for my push, its snake-like spine bending to accommodate the force. Like a sideways S, the mech flailed as I hit the ground.

What could've been grim turned into opportunity: I grabbed the mech's legs as I laid flat, and bent them. With their claws snagged in the floor for traction, the mech's ankles couldn't cope with my sideways effort, and their thin bones snapped. The mech slapped the floor before me, those pads still in its arms as the machine tried to figure out why it couldn't stand.

To my right, Clara hunkered down with another Forger behind an overturned table, one rapidly roasting as two more flexi-mechs drilled it with lasers.

Time to be a team player.

Planting my left foot, I swung my hip, holding the mech's busted legs in my hands. I whipped the machine, about as heavy, I figured, as that table Clara hid behind, and sent it flying. Recliner pads and the mech holding them flew a few meters to slam like a long metal bowling ball into its two buddies, bashing them all to the ground in a messy metal knot.

Clara and her friend took advantage, curling up and over the table to finish the job with point blank shots. As their fire flashes cleared, I noticed the store had become dark once again, save for those few embers clinging to life. The fight over as fast as it began, with the Forgers standing victorious amid mech ruin.

"Get going!" Leo's voice echoed into the store as I picked up the mech's old gun. "We have to keep moving!"

Short and to the point. Leo's order made sense: Alpha's mech surprise hadn't killed us all—though I saw several Forgers gracing the ground, unmoving, as I followed Clara from the store—but its follow-ups surely would. For now, the Forgers proved they hadn't become soft in their years hiding below.

Instead of taking Alpha's ambush and dying, the Forgers had delivered faster strikes than the mechs or their lasers could muster. While those orange weapons charged up, Leo's hand-crafted works spat swift, if less lethal, fire. Thin mech bodies littered the store as I left, and the walkway outside had more courier carcasses than I'd ever seen before. A peek over the edge showed small fires down on the scrap piles too.

Leo's cadre sorted themselves out quick in the retreat, pairing and tripling off as needed to help keep wounded moving. Feet pounded metal quick, with Leo himself falling back to the rear to keep me company.

"Glad to see you made it through," Leo said, marking me and my limp.

The man looked none the worse for wear, not a single blasted scratch on his half-metal body. Grim lines etched his eyes, and the sparkle that'd been behind his slapdash grin back when Delta and I had first visited no longer shone. He'd lost people, and he knew it.

"You all fight like soldiers," I replied.

"We fight like people that've spent a long time with little to do,"

Leo said. "Years and years holed up in the Cesspool gave us a lot of time."

"That you chose to spend practicing war?"

"Practicing survival," Leo nodded ahead to Clara and the other Forgers. "We all wanted to see Starship land, and nothing was going to get in our way." Leo's smile grew, and for an instant, that twinkle returned. "Gamma, some of us saw real fighting between Starship's factions. Those mechs back there weren't exactly made for war. A real human with a gun, now there's a scary thing."

"Or Delta with her sword."

"Or that."

We passed by stores, homes, bars that I both had and hadn't seen before. On one hand, the ruined relics all looked the same, all part of Starship's decay. On the other, every place held its own story, from the pictures clinging to the walls, to the notes and names scrawled, scratched, or bolted to the doors. Remnants, from children's toys to books to clothes lay within view as we walked, and I caught more than one Forger holding the past in a long look.

A bloodless story, the biological details stricken from the record by relentless cleaning mechs. Bodies kicked out through airlocks, fluids scrubbed, leaving only artificial remains. Kaydee had told me normal departures had been moments for ceremony and remembrance, delivering the bodies to the stars rather than dumping them with useless trash. No more ceremonies here, only exclusion, extinction.

Would Leo and Val bring those goodbyes back? Would I be given one of them, when my circuits eventually failed?

Or would I be set up like Kaydee, my functions cast back into the network to find a new home as shapeless code, drifting forever until someone told me what to do, who to be?

"Gamma?" Leo said, snapping me back to the walkway. Ahead, the Garden loomed, its expanse crossing the Conduit and blocking the blue mist with its gnarled, rotted husk. "Any ideas?"

The Forgers gathered near the Garden's entrance, flanking the door but not proceeding beyond. I figured out the why even as Leo started telling me: inside, heavy fighting could be heard. Human voices, yes, but far more banging, clashing, tearing. The Garden itself seemed to be shaking with the war within.

"Val shouldn't be here," I said. "They retreated to set up near the aft and wait."

Leo nodded, "I'm thinking she's not the retreating type."

"What do you mean?"

"If you're outnumbered and your enemy turns its back to you, it'd be a mistake to pass up a chance to strike." Leo waved a finger in the air, in a tight circle. The signal to arm up, get ready. "Especially if you're desperate."

Humans and their foolish tactics. Surprise or no, Val didn't have the numbers to take out Alpha's army. Not alone. Not unless she thought she'd be squeezing Alpha's army between Beta and Delta's death-dealing blades and her own hunters.

She wouldn't have known, couldn't have known the other two vessels were already dead.

"We have to help them," I said, but I didn't need to.

Leo already had his Forgers rolling, the Garden's door opening with battle's sounds pouring out. They'd committed to our cause, and they'd already bled for it.

I had no doubt we were going to bleed more.

FORTY-SIX

GARDEN PARTY

We waded into a wetland, the Garden's lusher levels starting at our Conduit midpoint. Thin planters laid in layers along the dark walls, sporadic diodes delivering UV rays to overgrown plants well into biological battles, a struggle not too unlike what we were headed towards. Otherwise, the Garden's dark shadows dominated, with vines stringing from side to side and moss sucking at our boots.

Leo dumped me in front, a recognizable truce flag to the humans should we stumble into them, a likelihood given both our speed and the lack of light. Without a headlamp of my own, I plunged forward with beams crossing over my shoulders and to my sides from other Forgers, guides through the wet.

Sounds proved a better guide than light, the fighting louder inside the door and drawing a clear path through the twists and turns to the Garden's center. Nothing molested us, Alpha's army preoccupied with its human targets.

As we walked, Leo whispered strategy to the band, quiet commands that sped from rank to rank behind us. Weapons ready, of course, but keep stray fire to a minimum. Aim carefully. Collateral damage could doom any allegiance before it even started.

No grenades.

"You have grenades? In space?" I asked. "That's a risk."

"Overload a laser and mix in some air, you get a boom," Leo said. "The bombs are already here, we just need to use them carefully."

How had humans kept Starship intact this long?

I missed Kaydee. She'd have bopped in with some crack about how the mechs were doing a worse job of it than the humans ever had. Or maybe she'd talk me down, explaining the relative little risk a grenade could pose here in the Garden. Not exactly near vacuum.

Instead, I had my own thoughts and nothing else.

We found the conflict in the center. Not on our level—that would've been too lucky—but several below, down where the air cooled and the water dried. Back near where Delta, Beta, and I had thrown ourselves at the Chancellor.

The Forgers joined me, ringing around the central pit and looking down. Unlike their own battle with the mechs, this one fought in shadows. Val's humans didn't have lasers and Alpha's crude army didn't come prepped either. Sparks, clanks, shrieks, and stabs echoed up. Commands snuck in between the battle's sounds, Val and Chalo's voices distinguishable in the melee, each calling for the force to group up, to stand together.

"Not a confident maneuver," Leo said. "They circle, they'll get surrounded and destroyed. No retreating."

"Retreat to where?" I replied. "Alpha's mechs won't tire, won't rest. They'd only follow and destroy anyone left behind."

Leo pressed his lips together, flicked his eyes to mine, "Then this is it then. We either win here, or lose everything."

I didn't argue.

"To the stairs," Leo said, swirling his finger. "Go, destroy any machine you see. Work together, plead peace if you encounter another human. If they attempt to attack you, run."

Not a single Forger, not even Clara, raised a question at his words. The Librarian's stories people like this, the leaders that could inspire absolute devotion. This bunch would follow Leo wherever he led them, even if they might grumble a bit along the way.

Made me a little jealous.

Clutching my borrowed blaster, I joined the Forgers in their downward dart, keeping myself towards the back so I didn't interfere with their squad tactics. I could hear Kaydee whispering *coward* as the half-metal, half-human cyborgs split the stairways into halves, overlapping their firing fields and delivering swift death to the mechs we caught along the way.

Cowardice, or wisdom?

I kept one ear scanning for particular sounds, the clash of blade on metal in fast sequence, lightning at work. Or the staccato plunks as knives found their marks. But Delta and Beta's telltale music didn't reach us as we descended, putting a damper on our otherwise brilliant rescue.

That's what it was too: brilliant. Leo's Forgers came down to Val's level, only one above the snow-clad forest where I'd fought earlier, from both sides. Alpha's moshing mechs, seeking to crush the humans in the level's center, weren't watching their flanks. Orange, white, and blue fire bit into metal frames, bursting power supplies, torching steel limbs, and sending the poor machines into oblivion.

These weren't the swift, upgraded mechs we'd fought either, but Alpha's older bulk troops. The converted trash and culinary mechs, the cleaners and couriers. Armed with basic tactics and bastardized weaponry, the mechs groaned as their motors whined, trying, failing to address the ambush.

I didn't have to fire once before the assault ended in a calm pine forest now littered with far heavier debris than needles. I stepped between smoking remnants and joined Leo in the level's middle. The Forgers, on Leo's order, gave the humans a wide berth, keeping weapons lowered and themselves near cover. A couple dozen humans watched, tired, bloodied, but not afraid.

A couple familiar faces lingered in the bunch.

Val and Chalo both still lived, though the latter's left arm bore a long, nasty gash. Pain showed in his tight eyes, his pressed lips as he watched Leo and I come through. Val matched Chalo's hard stare, her own spear planted butt-first into the ground. Wires and shrapnel clung to the weapon, evidence Val hadn't led from the back.

Not that I'd expected the fighter to avoid the fighting.

"Peace, Val." I opened the conversation. "We're on your side."

"Gamma," Val said, sticking her eyes on me and ignoring Leo.

The other humans, at a signal I didn't catch, let their nocked arrows fall, their weapons returning to waist belts and hands moving to tending wounds. At first I thought Val would continue after saying my name, but if Chalo's eyes held pain, Val's boiled. She might've dismissed her warriors to their needs, but her tight grip on the spear suggested she didn't think the fight was over.

"Who are these people, and where are Delta and Beta?" Val asked, a not unreasonable opening.

I delivered the story's short version, with Leo making the smart play and keeping quiet. Not that the man couldn't vouch for himself, but Val had an air that said speaking when spoken to would play better than the alternative.

"Then we've lost," Val said when I concluded. "You failed to destroy the Fabrication Lines, and we're without our two greatest weapons. When Alpha brings his next force to bear, we'll be destroyed."

"There's the optimism I needed," I replied, surprising myself with the sarcasm. Kaydee's influence coupled, maybe, with exhaustion at all we'd endured. "We have choices to make, Val. Starting with the Voices. Did you reconnect them?"

"We plugged the drive into a terminal," Val replied. "No more than that. You said choices? What choices? Retreat brings us into a corner."

I nodded towards the hole in the level's middle leading down. "We search. Delta and Beta fell, but they might have survived. Send a group down. Everyone else should fortify what they can, get ready for the next attack."

Chalo scoffed this time, "The Garden has too many doors, vessel. More than we have soldiers to guard them."

"Gamma can handle those doors," Leo said. "The Garden's control center's on top. We can use it to seal every level we want."

"The mechs will just break in."

"Not quickly." Leo nodded towards the plants around us. "The Garden has strong seals. Needed to keep anything dangerous outside from damaging our food supply."

Val flicked her eyes from Leo to me. Kept that grip on her spear. I was about to reiterate the plan, state that we should go, but stopped. Humans had strange notions about power and who could be allowed to wield it. Leo and I might've formed the plan, but letting Val be the one to give it the go?

Might be saving myself trouble for later.

"Chalo, go with Gamma to the Garden's top. Leo, take what you need and go search for our missing friends. I'll hold us here," Val said, then tapped her spear butt on the ground. "Now."

AS IDEAL COMPANIONS WENT, Chalo left something to be desired. The hunter let me lead, stalking behind me in his glittering feathered metal outfit. The man kept a rough blade in one hand, a scavenged laser in the other. A spare cloth wrapped his cut arm, torn from someone who wouldn't need it anymore. He didn't say a word as we climbed stair after stair, going from dry to lush in dim light.

Despite Alpha pulling back his force, the Gardens were far from quiet. The humans below made their own noise, sure, but stomps and skitters echoed on the levels we passed by. That there were mechs still rustling around wasn't a question, whether any would try coming after us was. A few pollinators we could handle, a few of those weapon-wielding flexi-mechs would be a problem.

I started half a dozen different conversations in my mind before keying on the right phrase. Chalo held his honor high, and I didn't want to step on some human convention, but I also didn't want to go the whole way in silence. At the end of this climb I'd likely need to find a port, disappear into cyberspace, and Chalo would be the only one watching my back.

"Are you all right?" I asked.

"What kind of question is that?" Chalo snapped a reply. "I've lost family and friends today, and stand to lose much more before tomorrow."

Okay, not my best beginning.

"I know," I said as we left behind a boggy level, the air thick and humid. "So have I."

"You're not alive. You didn't lose anyone."

"Is that what you believe?"

"Not belief, fact. You're a program. Anything you feel can be changed in a moment."

Not wrong. I could delete the gaping hole where Kaydee used to be. Could erase Beta and Delta from my memory.

"I'm choosing not to," I replied. "I want to keep their memories, I want to feel the grief."

"Why?"

"Because I owe them that much."

Chalo didn't answer that and we kept walking, climbing. Level after level passed, the Garden's apex coming closer and closer. I didn't bother starting up another conversation and Chalo made no move either. I fell into a reverie of sorts, letting my legs pound up the stairs automatically while I drifted back through the last few days.

I missed my friends.

The Garden's control center had an inauspicious entrance. One stair up from the Garden's highest level, a plant-less pool dedicated to pumping water up from Purity and dumping it in precise amounts through pipes, the central waterfall, and other avenues, the Garden's top began with a simple red-gemmed door. Another lock to pick, this time without Kaydee's help.

I pressed my fingers together, told Chalo I'd be a minute, and plugged into the port nestled into the gem's bottom side. At least Starship didn't vary its security programs, as the same moving laser puzzle waited for me that I'd seen before. I clicked the right digital mirrors into place, saw the satisfying green flash, and blinked back out. The gem glowed green, and I pressed its warm surface.

The Garden's command center sat before us. Behind, as if waiting for the door's signal, all those rustles, those mechs staying hidden, came forth. Metal paws, claws, and feet slammed on the stairs, charging our way.

"Go," Chalo said, shifting his bulk to fill the stair. "Save my people, Gamma."

At least he said my name.

FORTY-SEVEN

HOLD THE ROOM

Leaving Chalo to stand alone, I took a good look at the wood-patterned array controlling the Garden's myriad biomes. Screens bubbled in sections, enough for five people at Starship's heyday. The crisp visuals matched from one flat display to the next, each one giving a standard Starship interface. In each one's center, a rounded G sat in prime position.

At least they didn't make it difficult.

Chalo let out a bellow and I heard his bowstring twang. The arrow's clank followed. A hit, but impossible to tell if it was an effective one.

I picked a screen, tapped the Garden icon. I half expected a username and password prompt, some security preventing me from waltzing in here, but nothing stopped the program firing up. Perhaps the door lock served well enough, or someone had cleared away those security measures years ago.

Either way, the Garden's controls sat before me, black background and white text fitting the low light. A statistics readout dominated my monitor, each biome broken down into measurements with ideal markers for things like temperature, humidity, water flow.

Lovely little graphs with symbols littering every spare pixel. My attention went to the bottom row, which laid out options in a single rectangular button line. The farthest right option read *Emergency*.

Figured this qualified.

As Chalo loosed his fourth arrow, I tapped the button. Rather than one or two choices, every biome shifted from a graph to a list. I could sap the jungle of its moisture, flood the desert, turn the tundra into an oven. Again the bottom row saved me, with an obvious option to seal the facility.

"Found it!" I called, hitting the button.

Chalo growled, dropping his bow and shifting to his ax, the first smash causing a mech's warbling demise. The Garden shuddered with the swing as all its doors slammed shut, emergency barriers following behind. Long dormant machines lurched to life, spinning up to filter air no longer able to travel to Starship at large. After five long seconds, the monitor blinked at me, saying the emergency cut-off was successful.

Done. We'd trapped ourselves in a Garden still crawling with angry mechs.

"Vessel!" Chalo shouted. "Help!"

I whirled, saw Chalo playing more defense than offense as he stepped back into the control center. A whirling cutlery mech had its arms and knives twirling, forcing Chalo to one desperate deflection after another. Fresh cuts already marred the man's armor, chunks lying on the dark ground.

Thankfully, I wouldn't need to get close to the creature. My stolen laser did its work, spitting hot energy past Chalo's left side and filling the cutlery mech with burning holes. Alpha's machine spun down, folding over, its limbs dangling. A moment's victory stolen when the next mech in line shoved its counterpart aside.

"It's done," I said as Chalo barged forward with a two-handed cut against a smaller, two-armed trash mech. "We can go!"

"Wait," Chalo said, his ax biting through the mech's feeble defense and munching through cords, cables, and circuits. He glanced at me as the mech teetered backward. "Can anyone open the doors from here?"

"Yes?" I leveled my laser, kept fingers on the trigger. As soon as a mech showed its metal self on the stair, I shot. I hoped Chalo couldn't tell, but I aimed for the sides, the limbs. Incapacitate, not destroy. "If another person comes up here, they could reverse the blockade."

"Then we hold this room until Val tells us otherwise."

I fired again, clipping a small pollinator and sending the machine burning to the side. My weapon, a ramshackle make, told me nothing of its energy, but it wouldn't last forever. Chalo had his ax, a tool that'd work as long as his arms could swing it.

Going by the continued thumps on the stairs, he'd have to swing it for a long time.

But if our efforts bought Val enough time to find Beta and Delta? Plan an attack?

"We hold the room," I said, and Chalo nodded.

My laser bought us another three mechs before its fire sputtered. The next one in line, a chugging meter-long cargo sled, wheeled up the steps and into the room. Its front and sides had shrapnel gouged into it, creating moving death.

Chalo didn't seem to care.

On my misfire's heels, the warrior charged the rolling sled. No weak point presented itself, but Chalo must've bet on his skills, getting close to the sled before leaping into a dive over the mech. If the sled hadn't been churning—towards me, now—Chalo would've impaled himself on the thing. Instead, the fighter hit the scrap-spattered tile behind the sled, whirled, and cut the machine's rear treads with his ax. The mech's end slammed down, throwing up sparks as its wheels carved divots.

Stuck, the sled could do little as Chalo laid into it, carving off pieces with every swing. I abandoned the monitors to scoop up a knocked off chunk, a jagged knife that cut my skin as I held it. A wound worth bearing for a weapon. When Chalo found the processor, the sled's groans ceased with a sharp whine.

"Well done," I said to the sweat-coated warrior as we both turned to see what monster Alpha would throw at us next.

"Beta taught me well," Chalo replied. "I refuse to believe she's gone."

I wished I could do the same.

When no mech climbed up to face us, I braved the stair's edge to look down. The glance confirmed any hope was misplaced: the mechs had only learned their one-off approach wasn't working. Instead, another rolling sled approached, but this time several couriers buzzed above it, their lasers already glowing green. Shifting shadows on the sled itself suggested riders as well.

"Tell me they're fleeing," Chalo said as I backed up.

"Worse," I replied. "They're grouping up."

Chalo waved me to the left while he gave himself some room. His same trick might work if I handled the couriers, so I raised my knife like a javelin.

The sled shot up the steps into the room, rolling faster than its friend. The couriers jetted along after it, two rotating my way while the third loosed a shot at Chalo. The laser burned into the warrior's mail, and possibly through it given the man's curse. I launched my knife as my two turned my way, staking the first one and sending it crashing.

The second had me dead to rights.

But it didn't have my dog.

Alvie flew like a missile, wheeze-barking into the courier like it was a fresh tennis ball. The dog's metal jaws clamped down on the small machine, bearing it to the ground in a roll where the courier's engines blew up. The explosion launched Alvie backward, past Chalo and right into a terminal, breaking its screen and surrounding the dog with sparks.

As I shouted Alvie's name, the sled kept going on its murder mission. Four pollinators leapt from its bed, streaking for me and Chalo. The fighter, hesitating at Alvie's appearance, recalled his plan just in time for a one-step leap. Without the run up, Chalo's jump lacked the distance, and he clipped the sled's back, the shrapnel cutting a gash and sending him sprawling to the floor.

I kicked the first pollinator to reach me, the little mech flying away. The second snagged my leg, scurrying up and jabbing me with its tiny ends. I ripped it off, held the mech in my hands, when I heard Chalo calling a warning.

The sled had found a new target: me.

Its treads squealing, the sled rotated and kicked across the few meters to my gut. I had no weapons save the pollinator in my hand.

Which would have to do.

I crouched, holding the squirming pollinator tight, and waited a brief second for the sled to close. With less than a meter splitting us, I swung my right hand in an uppercut, pushing off with my feet at the same time. The pollinator lead my swing, serving as both club and protector, gashing into the sled's leading spikes. I felt metal split, felt a sting in my hand, but I poured every ounce of strength, energy into that swing.

Anything else meant death.

The sled lurched up, heavy but not impossible. Its front scraped my face, drawing lines up my cheeks, my forehead, but not scoring an impale. Those whistling treads came next as I pushed the sled vertical. The treads pulled at my body, but I shoved my right arm past them, my skin ripping away at the friction. The sled's undercarriage sat unprotected for a moment as my punch lifted the mech upward.

Grabbing another mech's guts never felt so good, so awful at once. My left hand wrapped around the wires, the sled's core, and pulled. With pops, hisses, pained whines and grinds, the sled's engine fell apart. Its treads stopped, and together both the sled and I fell back to the ground. The big mech toppled over upside down while I wound up on my back, my eyes glaring red as legs, arms, eyes reported damage.

I could've used Kaydee's chipper attitude about then, because I was done.

Dead mechs filled the Garden's control room. Rumbling,

snarling, grinding from below hinted Alpha's machines weren't done either. Chalo seemed alive, struggling with the pollinators. Soft red lighting lit the space, something that'd changed when I'd turned on the emergency mode, a color shift I hadn't noticed at the time but seemed real appropriate now. We'd given what we could, what we had to buy the humans some time.

"Chalo," I said, my voice still working. "It's on you now."

I saw a pollinator fly off down the stairs, then heard an ax slam down on another. Chalo's head appeared around the overturned sled a moment later, the man's armor in tatters, a hundred small cuts showing where the pollinators had done their work. His ax hung low, but ready, in his hand. He gave me a long look, frowning.

"Disabled?"

I tried to lift my left arm. It shook, then fell back to the floor. "Low on power, low on strength. I can't fight anymore."

Chalo nodded, "Then I will fight for both of us."

"You should run before they send more," I replied. "Get back to Val, warn them that they won't have much time."

I didn't say what I really felt. Didn't say that the warrior shouldn't die here. The man hated mechs, sure, but he was damn good at destroying them, a skill Starship's humans desperately needed.

Before Chalo could make a decision, rapid thuds climbed up the stairs. Another mech on the assault. Chalo whirled, raising the ax for a skull-splitting swing. A black-and-yellow color came into the room and Chalo started his blow. The ax hit hard, glanced off the new mech's shoulders and bounced off.

Two yellow eyes on a narrowing face turned towards Chalo as the fighter backed away, trying to find his voice. I found mine first.

"Volt?"

The mech noticed me, his eyes swapping to blue. "Gamma!" Volt stepped by Chalo, bent over me. "You look terrible, but I'm afraid there's no time to rest. The Voices need you."

Of course they did.

FORTY-EIGHT

INTO THE VOID

The loyal dog did it. Before Beta, Delta, and I left on our doomed quest for the Fabrication Lines, I told Alvie to head up Volt's way. Starship's power-monitor had been fixing up the mech I'd damaged during our first encounter and, if there was one thing I remembered from that fight, it was me ending up needing most of, well, me, replaced.

In other words, Volt made a damn good weapon, and Val might need one.

"The dog wouldn't stop barking," Volt said, helping me over to a terminal, eyes back to curious blue. Alvie, alive but limping after biting the bomb, padded over along with us. "Alvie would yup and yap his way to me, then scamper towards the exit. Then I try to follow the thing and he runs to my wife and tries to take her along too."

"Smart puppy."

"Obedient, anyway. We get going, and I'm not fast, mind, but we get going and see all these signs of Alpha's mechs marching the wrong way."

Behind us, Chalo peered down the stairs. "Are there more coming?"

"Bimu has it covered," Volt replied. "Take care of yourself."

"Bimu?" I asked.

Volt's eyes flipped to a laughing pink, "What, you didn't think my wife had a name? That I just called her wife?"

"Guess I never thought about it."

"What a polite mech you are, Gamma. You break Bimu, and don't even ask her name."

"Sorry?"

"As you should be." Volt posted me up at a working terminal. "Anyway, we get to the Garden and these doors shut in our faces. Alvie's furious, so I ask Bimu nicely and she opens up a new hole for us." Volt tapped his head. "Guess that means the Garden's not secure anymore, but hey, we saved your life, so you can't complain."

"Was I complaining?"

"Body language goes a long way."

"I can't really move."

Volt shrugged, those orange metal shoulders squeaking as they bounced up and down. "We're getting sidetracked, Gamma. Point is, before we left, Alpha began pulling power to the engines. He's planning to make another move, and you need to get in there to see what it is."

I didn't have much for excuses. Despite my body being a broken mess—which happened far too often for my liking—my digital self would be perfectly fine. My batteries were low, but connecting with a terminal would help me draw power. Without pain, without a need for sleep, I could keep on rolling from one fight to the next, no matter how little I wanted to.

So with Volt's help, I pressed my thumb and forefinger together to form the port. The mech wished me luck and plugged me into the terminal, zipping me away into Starship's digital domain.

. . .

A CELESTIAL SPREAD APPEARED, Starship's network twinkling against a black canvas. Each dot represented a hub, a terminal or server somewhere. I'd have to find the one both Alpha and the Voices were using, then see if I could turn the fight in our favor.

"Ideas?" I said to the void, expecting Kaydee to chime back.

Oh right. I'd have to figure this one on my own.

There were hundreds, possibly a few thousand stars to choose from. Each one had characteristics. Terminal, server, its location on the ship. The Voices and Alpha fought over Starship's direction, where its engines would go, so that put locations on the Bridge or in the aft as the most likely centers. I threw up the filter and most of the stars winked out. The two remaining clusters slid apart from one another, the Bridge on the left, Engines on the right.

Next.

Alpha already had the Bridge. He could make all the course adjustments he wanted from there, and I doubted the Voices would be able to stage an attack on the vessel's network. Alpha, so far, had been pretty dominant in digital warfare, so he'd likely torch the Voices if the latter tried offensive.

The Engines seemed more appealing. Alpha could set whatever course he wanted, but if the Voices blocked Starship from responding, well, that'd be a solid stalemate. Alpha, so far as I knew, didn't have any mechs mucking about in the ship's aft yet, so there'd be no possibility for a physical override either. As hunches went, it felt solid.

The Bridge's stars vanished, leaving me with a paltry few dozen. From there I cleared out the terminals. The standalone computers would have network access, but Starship would be parsing all their connections through a hub, and the Engines only had one. A single access point reading network traffic coming in and out.

Bingo.

"Bet you'd be impressed," I said.

Kaydee didn't answer.

I expected something I'd seen before: a crystal-coated plain, maybe a swampy medieval landscape. Even an office building. All those, however, were set up for my arrival. Constructed with visitors in mind. Instead, here, I landed in a war zone.

Landed was the wrong word, as my feet didn't touch down on anything. The black canvas I'd used to see the stars seemed to wrap around me, save for gashes in all colors tearing through the space, giving it both depth and direction. Up above and down below, the inky expanse held lines looking into scrambled code, as if a curtain had been slashed to reveal the ugliness behind.

The thing making those cuts wasn't hard to find either, as the only light in this fractured place came from its struggles. Well away from me, like a winking bulb turning off and on at random intervals, yellow and white flashes crashed through, turning all the gashes black for an instant.

Ridiculous, but why would I expect anything else with Alpha involved?

I didn't so much move as float towards the flashes, easing around the gashes as I went. Without gravity or any relative point, I had no idea how fast I was going, whether I would have any physical momentum, but the cuts zipped by faster and faster as the flashes grew brighter and brighter.

Until a yellow glow illuminated a person standing right in my way.

"Gamma, stop," the person said, and with a thought I did, right in that instant.

No momentum after all. This close, Leo stood out clear, though his digital self held a ragged appearance. His chest had one of those gashes lacing through it and out one side. The man's arms and legs seemed to flicker, the functions holding them together failing one after another.

"I look that bad?" Leo said at my stare. "Guess Alpha did get some good licks in."

"That's him then?" I said, nodding beyond to the flashes.

Leo nodded, "He's not happy with our seal."

"Your seal?"

Leo waved around him, "All this. We blanketed the Engines. Alpha can't get his code through, and if he doesn't do it soon, Starship's going to blow by the window."

"Meaning he doesn't get to land."

"Not for a while, anyway."

Until the next window, when Alpha would try again. In the meantime, he'd spew out mechs to hunt us and the humans down, pinning us into a brutal war we'd have to fight all day and night, endlessly.

"Captain Willis is fighting him now," Leo said into the silence. "Alpha's already destroyed everyone else save Peony, but we're losing. Before you came we were running out of ideas, but you can change it."

"By severing the connection?"

"Yeah."

The thought had come not long ago, back when I'd filtered out the two star clusters between the Bridge and the Engines. If we wanted to keep Alpha from twisting Starship's direction, we could slice the network in half. Make it so Alpha would need to march physically all the way down Starship. Of course there'd be other risks . . .

"No," I said. "That's just delaying."

More flashes beyond us, another salvo.

"That's the point?" Leo said. "Keep Alpha from what he wants until you all figure out a way to stop him?"

I saw all those mechs stomping towards us, the revived Chancellor with her arms and weapons. They'd keep coming. Beta and Delta were likely dead, robbing us of any chance at an armed victory. We needed something else.

Some way to change the conflict and rob Alpha of his advantage.

"Show me where Alpha wants to go," I asked Leo.

Without moving, Leo filled the space between us with a glowing orange ball. Several planets appeared, spinning in tight orbits around the star. One highlighted in a cherry red.

"That's the target he wants," Leo said. "Habitable, but that's not the problem." He hesitated. "Alpha's trying to bring Starship in so hot the heat and pressure will kill every living thing onboard."

More flashes. Gashes. I thought I heard a man scream and Leo winced, but the orbiting planets held steady.

"How much of an adjustment?" I asked, pointing at the spinning blue planet. "Off of what Alpha wants? How much?"

"Minor," Leo said, his voice trailing off. He raised one hand, held out a small shiny sliver. "Here's what we'd need to do instead to level out the landing, keep us intact."

"You did that quick."

A half-smile, "Kaydee would've had it faster, but I saw where you were going. Don't know how you're going to get this by Alpha, though."

"Leave that to me," I replied, looking past Leo to those flashes. "Just distract him. I'll do the rest."

"That's the thing, Gamma," Leo replied. "We're about out of distractions, and Voices." As if to prove his own point, Leo's lower half faded away to nothing, corrupted functions eating themselves. "Think this is goodbye."

"Then I'll take what you can give me."

Leo flickered, nodded. "Go get' 'em, Gamma."

I shot past him, holding the sliver and racing towards the flashes, stacking all the friends Alpha had taken from me and using their names to fuel my fire.

FORTY-NINE

REDIRECT

In the flesh, Alpha had long red hair, a body marred by scars of his own making, and a penchant for maniacal grins. The vessel would go from calm and serious to hyperactive and unpredictable in a switch's flip. Corrupted functions plagued his operation.

But that didn't stop him from coming to the digital world in style.

All of us here were little more than coded lines, balled up protocols, logic statements, and operations collected into bodies as we maneuvered around Starship's network. I looked like myself, an average human man floating in the dark expanse. Alpha chose another raiment: like those same cutlery mechs he commanded, the man adopted a monstrous red-metal form, ten arms short and long jutting out at all angles and ending in claws, knives, and blades.

The fiend showed dark as I approached from behind, his continual strikes causing blinding flash after flash as their whirlwind battered the poor soul on the other side. I couldn't see the target, couldn't see the defense raised to withstand Alpha's assault, but the encounter seemed as one-sided as any I'd ever seen: Alpha attacked and attacked and suffered no reprisals.

The Voices were delaying only, and their hope lay in my right hand.

Leo's sliver, a glassy bright line, needed a spot to inject its code. Looking at Alpha, who hadn't bothered to glance away from his objective, there weren't many obvious options. Alpha himself, the main mech body hacking away before me, would reject the code or, worse, realize its purpose and prevent any more attempts.

No, with all those knife cuts, Alpha wanted to slip his instructions through to Starship's engines, get them burning towards his new world. I needed to get Leo's alterations right in there.

In other words, I needed to slip the code into the arm, the knife, sword, or whatever Alpha struck with and make sure that was the one making it through to the Engines. Ten options, and I had to get the right one.

So easy.

I reached out, a tentative play with a little function to see how Starship's network would react. Alpha's calamity showed he, at least, could give himself a doomsday makeover. The Voices, too, could add in their dark veil. How far could I push the boundaries?

In my own cyberspace, the digital caverns within my own drives, I had ultimate control. Anything that could be coded could be created. Here, as I reached out, I felt the pushback. Blocks preventing me from, say, copying myself a million times over or simply deleting Alpha into oblivion. The network seemed interested in preserving stability, letting programs like Alpha and I interact with each other with loose constraints.

I could work with that.

In a blink, I swapped to shadows, wrapping myself in the same darkness the Voices used. A cloak to keep Alpha from detecting me, and one I hoped would be good enough as I crept closer. Alpha's monster mech loomed up huge. The vessel's arms arced back and struck like cobras, their slashes moving in a predictable, steady pattern as they slashed away at the dark beyond. A bland, inevitable attack.

A routine.

The thought hit me as I saw the forms defending on the other side. The remaining Voices: Peony and Willis, moved fast to repair gashes as Alpha's swings created new ones. Four hands couldn't move as fast as ten arms, and the duo were overwhelmed. One reason why lay dissolving at their feet: the doctor, sliced and fading as Alpha's code devoured him.

"I wondered if you were going to show up," Alpha said, his voice booming around the digital space. "When my mechs reported the Garden had been sealed, I figured you might be joining our fun in here."

With his carving assault marching towards victory, Alpha set the attack on auto to pester me. He might've seen me float in, but no arm came to sweep me away, no attack came to carve me up. I had to hope he didn't quite know where I was or what I came to do.

Had to, because the alternative made all this pointless.

"I just had the most interesting conversation," Alpha continued, "with a new mech brought up from the Fabrication Lines."

He stopped, laughed as an arm with a long knife swept over my head. The blade stabbed into the dark near the Captain, visible for a moment as he painted in the last gash. The weapon stuck in the dark for a second, then tore down and away. Another bright flash, and a new gash showed a gray slate on the other side: Starship's engines, waiting for their command.

"I believe you know her," Alpha said, "Kaydee?"

I watched the gash, the swinging arms, and pushed Alpha's words away. They didn't matter in this moment. What did was whichever weapon would make the first open strike. A flat blade looked like the plausible candidate, cutting in for an overhead swing towards the new opening. I tensed, ready to jump up and jab Leo's sliver into the weapon.

The gash began to close, Willis's able form appearing in the slit and working his hands across the darkness. Code fixed code, broken logic restored to sense, every line bringing the barrier back.

But not fast enough.

Alpha's swing caught the half-formed gash and I cursed my hesitation. I hadn't jumped, thinking Willis would rebuff the blow, except now the blade seemed stuck in the gap. Alpha lurched the arm, laughing now, and yanked the sword back out. On the other side I saw why the sword had stuck: Willis, bearing a bright new slice in his chest, flickered. The man's face didn't shake, didn't stutter, but glared out the gash as his code began to fail.

A Voice, a program that'd lived in Starship's network for so many years, collapsed. Not like a human, a body with gradual failure, but more like a fog blowing away in a sudden wind. The lines defining Willis, the functions retaining all those memories, all those instincts, broke and fell away.

". . . she said you were boring, Gamma," Alpha was speaking, words I'd missed in the shock at Willis's sudden death. "Wandering all over the place like a lost puppy, looking for someone to give you purpose. I tried to, didn't I? What was so wrong with me?"

A new face appeared in the gash. Peony, as hard-ironed as ever. She worked her functions fast, repairing the gash quick even as another flash signaled a new opening for Alpha. They were running out of time.

I snapped my left finger, created a tiny firework like the ones Kaydee used to love. Alpha, busy lambasting my choices between screeds about his own destiny, didn't seem to notice, but Peony did. For a split second she froze, saw me hiding there next to Alpha. When her eyes met mine, I brought up my right hand, revealed Leo's sliver. She saw it, gave me the slightest nod, then closed the gash.

Did Peony know the plan? How could she?

Questions I couldn't answer. Instead, I looked for an opening in the whirlwind. The next gash sat five meters to my left, in front of Alpha's swirling blades. It looked clean and ready for a strike, and beyond my reach. Nevertheless, I had to try.

I took a jump, emerging from the shadows. Alpha cut off his gloating, erupting in a gleeful shout, and all those arms whipped my way. I danced as I went towards the gash, copying Delta and Beta as I flipped, flopped, and rolled. Alpha's swings came close, missing me high and low. So close, in fact, that by the third miss I figured Alpha wasn't actually trying to stab me.

So I stopped trying. I straightened and walked, as Alpha's arms continued their near-hits, until the gash stood at my back. I faced Alpha's mech creation, the great orange-red beast glaring down at me with glowing yellow lights, arms arrayed up and around with their gleaming blades at the ready.

I kept my arms folded, Leo's sliver hidden in my palm. A desperate plan in my thoughts.

"Should I destroy you now, Gamma?" Alpha asked. "Add you to the scrap pile like I've already done to Delta and Beta?"

"If you wanted that, you would've done it already," I replied.

Alpha tittered, a strange noise coming from the mech. "You're right, of course. I want to make you another offer, my friend."

"I'm not your friend."

"Not yet!" Alpha's arms twinged, the knives shaking against the black behind them. "But now I have a more compelling bargain to make."

I raised a skeptical eyebrow.

"Your Kaydee is with me now, but she could be with you," Alpha said. "We could give her a body like your own. Then together we would be masters of Starship, rulers of our very own world. Kaydee would be yours."

I held up my left hand, "I'm going to stop you right there. Kaydee belongs to nobody but herself, and you can keep your rock."

"A no, then."

"A no."

"Let it never be said I didn't try."

The arms came in again, this time streaking for me with precision. I couldn't dodge them all, and I didn't want to. With Leo's sliver in my palm, I waited for the last chance, make one blade miss, and then I'd—

Hands grabbed me, threw me to the side. All those blades found their mark, but not their intended. Peony stood before the gash, pierced across her body, her eyes on me. Through her, hidden by her back and close to the gash, Alpha's big sword neared the target.

One opening.

I curled forward, wrapped my arms around Peony as if in grief, and slapped Leo's sliver onto the fat blade.

"Save my daughter," Peony whispered.

"I will."

Alpha's grinding laugh cut through, "One pest is as good as another, I suppose!"

With a shove, Alpha's arms pushed Peony's fading figure back towards the gash. The big blade went through first, injecting its code right into Starship's engines. As Peony disappeared, I pulled my own plug, running away.

Again.

FIFTY

TRAJECTORIES

We counted casualties on the center level. Val and Leo held court over a mixed crew, most preoccupied with their own wounds, prepping a meal, or taking some time to pull themselves together. Volt carried Chalo and I all the way back down, the mech's arms doing the not-so-comfortable work of lifting us down the stairs. Bimu, the gigantic machine, followed with its laser eye scoping for more enemies. Chalo did his best stone-faced impression on the way down, wincing away any pain. Me, I just turned off the sensors and let my busted body take the ride.

Gave me plenty of time to replay what'd just happened.

Alpha's incursion wiped out the Voices. I had my issues with their dictates and, especially, with Peony's use'em or lose'em attitude towards myself and other mechs, but they'd still made the call to wake me up. Without that switch, I'd be on a cot in Leo's apartment.

Or, more likely, corrupted into one of Alpha's minions.

Worse, Alpha's yowls about Kaydee likely had some truth. My friend, my former mind, might be undergoing the worst form of torture: one literally re-writing how she thought, moved, and felt. She'd be locked away with Alpha on Starship's Bridge, waiting for the vessel to decide what to do with her. Those dark ideas plagued the journey down, one that ended with further disappointment.

Val and Leo had grim numbers waiting for us. The human and Forger forces could hardly be called, well, forces at this point. Leo's group hadn't taken too many losses, but there hadn't been many to afford. Less than fifty total fighters remained between both groups, including some too hurt to pick up a gun or a bow.

Healthy pairs had been dispatched to patrol the Garden's other levels and confirm the doors remained sealed. Volt left his wife near the top, where the only sure opening sat blasted apart. Purity, the watery basement, had been left alone. When I asked, Leo said Alpha's mechs still controlled the lowest levels in large numbers.

"Whether they fell down there by accident or retreated that way, we'd need a hard push to break'em," Leo said as we gathered around the central waterfall. The warm level offered fruits and overgrown vegetables aplenty for snacking, and the Forger had an apple in hand as he spoke to me. "Maybe when we're rested, certain of our own safety first."

"Not before we bring the others here," Val said. "I'm not leaving our young ones to fend for themselves."

Right. The other humans that hadn't made the excursion to the Garden were holed up near Starship's engines, a place roaring hard now as the ship made its trajectory shift. The Garden's construction, meant to keep the plants safe during movements, barely registered the massive vessel's change in direction, but Alpha's orders had gone through. I hoped ours slipped in with them.

No way to tell that until Starship landed, or we took the Bridge.

"Agreed," Leo nodded at Val, who returned the gesture with a look far less frosty than I expected. "We'll get our people together first, then make a plan. The Garden can hold that long."

"You hope," I said. "Alpha's going to get the Fabrication Lines back up soon. There'll be another army here fast."

"Then we'll let them bleed out against us," Val replied, still holding that spear. "We'll repair, strengthen, and counter when the time is right."

"When Starship lands," Leo added. "That will give us the opening, the flexibility we need."

The two must've been plotting while I was away. While I found the situation dark, they showed resilience, some belief that they could counter Alpha's coming metal hordes and make it out the other side. Something I could draw from, perhaps.

A twinge pulled me to my right leg, where Volt was, once again, performing corrective surgery. I felt a little exposed with my circuits visible to Val and Leo while Volt, with Alvie doing his doggy best, put me back together. The mech already told me my efficiency would be dropping yet again as he'd be subbing in parts scrapped from Alpha's destroyed army. Volt sounded apologetic about the whole thing, but I'd just be happy to be walking again.

"Not much more of this, though, you get it?" Volt said as Leo and Val turned away to their own conversing. I tried not to take it personally, the mech again shoved aside until needed. "You listening, Gamma? You're such a hodgepodge of parts now there's a chance any rough-up might blow your processor. That means you're gone."

"Right, avoid fights. I do that anyway."

"Well, you're damn bad at it then."

I shrugged at Volt's yellow eyes. "I'll be more careful."

"Uh huh," Volt pointed an arm at the human leaders. "They got their plans. What about you?"

The Voices woke me up, told me to save the Nursery and, by extension, any humans left alive on Starship. Those humans worked around me now, prepping for a war they couldn't hope to win without help. That help, I had to believe, waited down below, past angry mechs and a deep pool.

And after?

"I'm going to save a friend," I said. "You want to come along?"

Volt's eyes flashed pink, "Sorry buddy. Alpha's put Starship into landing mode, something we've never seen before. I've gotta get back home, make sure something doesn't go wrong and blow us all to space dust."

I reached out, gave Alvie a pat, "At least I've got you, right buddy?"

The dog wheeze-barked back.

Behind Alvie, standing next to an orange tree, I could picture Kaydee, rolling her eyes, yellow fireworks popping as she snapped her fingers. If Alpha really had her now . . .

Hold on, Kaydee. Hold on.

HE FOUGHT TO SAVE HUMANITY. Now he's having second thoughts.

And after more than a thousand years in flight, Starship is crashing towards a new home.

Continue Gamma's adventure in *The Coded World* by scanning the code below or clicking here!

AFTER A DISASTER ON THE MOON, Mox's search for strength brings him to a dangerous scientist and a choice between the life Mox knows and the vengeance he desires.

Jump into a new science fiction adventure with *The Metal Man*, available free when you sign up for my author newsletter by clicking the link or scanning the code below:

ACKNOWLEDGMENTS AND AUTHOR'S NOTE

The Flawed Design continues the most science fiction story I've ever written. Its genre trappings touch cyberpunk, space opera, military sci-fi, and more. This wasn't intentional, but just an outgrowth of the story itself. Sometimes you get pulled into narratives and can't help following them to the end.

This is also somewhere around my 24th or 25th book, and together with its sequel, *The Flawed Design* was the most difficult one I've ever written. Creating virtual worlds that, nonetheless, making some computational sense forced constraints that, in the classic quote, helped me be more original.

Nevertheless, the time was often when I wished I could wave my hand and have the characters go charging off, rather than thinking about how such a charge would work in a place without physical laws.

As ever, books like this, difficult scenes and all, come about because of the people around me. Family, friends, the cats who so often spend my writing time curled up in my lap. They are the delight powering these stories and the ones to come.

ABOUT THE AUTHOR

A.R. Knight spins stories in a frosty house in Madison, WI, primarily owned by a pair of cats. After getting sucked into the working grind in the economic crash of the 2008, he found himself spending boring meetings soaring through space and going on grand adventures.

Eventually, spending time with podcasting, screenplays, short stories and other novels, he found a story he could fall into and a cast of characters both entertaining and full of heart.

A.R. Knight plans on jumping through to other worlds and finding new stories to tell in the limitless borders of our imagination.

Thanks, as always, for reading!

For more information:
www.adamrknight.com

To Jules